A worried expression crossed Cathy's face as she adjusted her seat belt. "Maybe there really is something wrong." She touched his arm as he slid in behind the steering wheel. "Maybe you'd better go back and—"

He didn't hear what else she said. Her words were swallowed up in a deafening roar, the shock wave of an explosion hitting them like a massive hammer, hard enough to rock the car sideways on its suspension.

Sikes shielded her with his body, a rush of flame heat rolling over his back. With one forearm he gathered Cathy tight to his chest. He could just hear her gasp of shock as he looked back over his shoulder toward the clinic.

Or where the clinic had been.

As the first blackened fragments began to rain down upon the car, a tower of fire, churning with coils of smoke, rose into the sky.

Alien Nation Titles

Published by POCKET BOOKS

#8

ALIEN NATION™

CROSS OF BLOOD

K. W. JETER

POCKET BOOKS
New York   London   Toronto   Sydney   Tokyo   Singapore

An *Original* Publication of POCKET BOOKS

POCKET BOOKS, a division of Simon & Schuster Inc.
1230 Avenue of the Americas, New York, NY 10020

ISBN: 0-671-87184-6

First Pocket Books printing July 1995

10 9 8 7 6 5 4 3 2 1

POCKET and colophon are registered trademarks of
Simon & Schuster Inc.

Printed in the U.S.A.

To Bob Stephens

CROSS OF BLOOD

CHAPTER 1

THE DEAD SPOKE.

It didn't matter that he was dreaming, that he was safe in bed, his wife Susan beside him; George Francisco could feel the blankets across his chest, and still his hearts labored against the soft weight. Not fright, but dread, the wordless, deep perception of the sacred's approach, tensed his pulse. He squeezed his eyes shut tighter, but the vision behind them remained.

The dead spread wide its arms, the light of a world without form or substance streaming through the folds of a tattered robe, outlining the corpse that stood revealed before him.

He could feel the sheet sweating in his clenched fists, but still there was no waking, no escape. He wanted to cry out to Susan, to rescue him—a touch of her hand, he knew, would be enough. She could still be asleep, and he would turn and wrap his own arms around her, and he would be safe . . . at least for another night. Until the next night's dreaming.

1

The dead spoke his name.

That had never happened before, in all the chain of nights and dreams that had enwrapped him. Though he had known it was coming. It was inevitable. Every time that he had managed to fall asleep, the figure had stepped closer toward him. When he had first seen it—how many nights ago?—the robed figure had seemed hardly more than a distant speck, the light surrounding it a tunnel into an infinitely remote darkness. And now it stood so close to him, he could have reached out in his dreaming and touched it . . . if he had dared.

Again, his name, in a whisper that was softer than his own forced breath. Not the name that had been given him on this world, the new home that his people had found, but his old one, in the gently curved and twined syllables that his people had spoken before. The name that the other dead, his mother and father, had given him.

Stangya . . .

He shook his head, feeling the back of his skull roll against the pillow. "No . . ." His murmured denial brushed across his lips. "That's not my name. Not any more . . ."

The figure's pitying gaze—sensed, but not seen by him—pierced his breast. *Your true name. The name of your blood.*

No reply was possible. He wanted to shout aloud, cry that his name, in the world outside his dreaming, was George and nothing more—it had to be. He was glad that the past was as dead as the figure who stood before him. But his voice stayed locked in his throat.

Not dead. One of the outstretched arms turned, the shadowed hand reaching toward him. *Nothing ever dies. You know that, don't you?*

A stone broke inside, as though he had managed to strike it into shards with his fist. "No! You're dead . . . it's impossible . . . ." His shouting rang inside his ear canals. "No—"

2

"George?" Another voice, living but not his, spoke the name. "Honey, are you all right?"

His eyes flew open, to the smaller, comforting darkness of the bedroom. Awake, not dreaming; his wife beside him; his panicked breath began to slow. Through the eyeletted curtains that Susan had mail-ordered from Lands' End, the first smoldering red traces of dawn could be seen, cutting at a horizontal angle through L.A.'s dense air. He was grateful for that sight; it would only be a little while longer before the alarm clock on the bedside table went off in its usual trilling bomblike way. Even though he felt exhausted from the rigors of fitful sleep, it would be easier facing the daylight world than more of a night like this. Though they had all become like this lately, he noted glumly.

"It's nothing." Propped up on one elbow, George leaned over and kissed his wife's brow. "Don't worry. I think perhaps I shouldn't have eaten that squirrel pancreas just before coming to bed." He thumped his breastbone with the side of his fist. "A bit too rich."

"Mm." Susan sleepily regarded him. Eyes closing, she nuzzled her face against the pillow. "There was that infomercial . . . on the TV . . ." Her voice sank to a drowsy mumble. "Time lock for the refrigerator . . . maybe we should get that . . ."

He didn't have to say anything; she was already asleep. He lay back down, gazing at the ceiling's faintly discernible outlines.

Stangya . . .

The dead's voice, his name; it whispered in memory. He squeezed his eyes shut, not to sleep, but to make all that go away for a little while.

It looked like Jesus had climbed down from the wall of Sister Mary Torquemada's fourth grade classroom, presumably with the same heavy, brass-edged ruler in His hand that the parochial school nuns employed with such painful effectiveness. Inside Matt Sikes's

3

head, a nine-year-old boy was already crying out that he hadn't done it. *I mighta done it last time, but I didn't do it this time. It was somebody else, honest to God . . .*

"Oh, man . . ." He could hear himself groaning aloud. He rolled his tongue around his dry mouth. The taste indicated that some small animal had camped there, sneaking in during the couple of hours in which he had actually managed to catch some sleep.

One eye peeled open, enough to glance over at the figure beside him in the rumpled bedcovers. Cathy lay on one side, her back toward him; his thrashing around and mumbling didn't seem to have woken her the way it had a couple of times before. His other eye opened, the better to study the tapering line of spots that ran down her spine. The other evening, he and Cathy had gone out fancy for dinner, celebrating the six-month 'anniversary' of her moving in with him. She had worn one of those slinky Newcomer fashion numbers that exposed her back right down to where the swell of her rounded butt started—it'd clicked right into boyhood memories of seeing Marilyn Monroe in *Some Like It Hot,* wearing a pretty similar item. When they'd gotten back home, he had kissed Cathy between the shoulder blades, and had discovered she'd put on something that both smelled and tasted kind of like cinnamon, the net effect of which had been like hooking his 110-volt libido up to a 220-volt wire.

Simmer down, boy. Cathy's spots were a lot more pleasant to contemplate than these Goddamn stupid dreams. Matt pushed his hair away from his sweat-dampened brow.

The outstretched arms, with that spooky ghost light streaming from behind like the cheap special effects in some imitation Spielberg movie, was what made him think of Christ. Though there was no way the figure in the recurring dreams could be the Big Guy; the nuns' bloodiest, stigmata-laden crucifixes had never inspired in him the same heart-pounding apprehension and shouting nerves that this nightly vision was capable of. The dreams were altogether creepier than whatever Catholic damage he might still be lugging around with him. How long had they been going on now? It seemed like months, maybe even years, though he knew rationally that it was only a matter of a few weeks. Though every single night, he reminded himself; no wonder he'd been traipsing into the station the last few mornings with dark raccoon circles under his eyes and generally feeling like the wrath of God. The other police detectives' jokes, concerning the effect that stepping up to live-in status with Cathy was having on him, were getting pretty old.

He sat up, swinging his legs out from under the covers and getting a cold shock from the floor on his bare feet. Glancing over his shoulder, he saw that Cathy was still asleep, each small breath just barely visible in the blue streetlight that tinged the room. Quietly as possible, he stepped toward the bathroom.

Sitting on the lowered lid of the john, an edge of cold porcelain against his back, Matt considered that there had been a time when he would have headed to the fridge for a beer after getting uprooted from sleep like that. Bad dreams and flashbacks were occupational hazards for cops—they came with the territory. Which meant alcohol was a hazard, too. But he'd cut way back on that dismal action, even before Cathy had moved in with him. One, to clean up his act for her sake, and two, just because it no longer seemed necessary. A six-pack of Rolling Rock lasted a month in the refrigerator these days. Why bother, when he could just as well wrap his arms around the woman he loved and lay his head in that angle of shoulder and neck that seemed like home—the one that nature on both Earth and Tencton had made for weary men.

That was what worried him about these dreams. He knew he had a good thing going with Cathy; he didn't want to screw it up. After the flaming wreckage of his long-ago first marriage, and the desperate fun of his born-again bachelor days, this was heaven on a bun. *Nice time to start losing your mind,* he thought glumly.

He didn't even know what the damn things meant. Only that the figure in the tattered robes, face shadowed in darkness, had gotten closer with each successive night's dreaming; it had been the night before last when the figure had spread its arms in that Christ-like pose. And then this night . . .

This night it had spoken to him.

A shiver brushed across Sikes's bare shoulders. Spooked to the max, even here in the little room's bright mirrored light. Memory touched his heart with a fingertip of ice. First, the dream figure had spoken his name . . . Matthew . . . and that had been bad enough. How come nightmares always seemed to have your name and address in their Rolodexes? What came after that, though, had been worse. Something about a stream of blood—no, two streams of blood— that was what the creepy dream figure had whispered about. There had been more, but Sikes couldn't remember it now; by that point, he had been scrambling up from the depths of sleep, like an out-of-air diver heading for the surface with aching lungs.

That sure didn't sound good. He slowly shook his head. Whatever the dream wanted to tell him, it didn't seem like anything he wanted a piece of.

He stood up, rubbing his stiff face. Through the window across from the sink, he looked out to the street three stories below. The streetlights flickered off as he watched; enough dawn light had seeped between the surrounding building to trigger the lamps' photocells. Thank God it's morning—he could shower, get dressed, and get out without any pretense about going back to bed for a couple more sleepless hours.

In the apartment's thin silvery light, he stood beside the bed, gazing down at Cathy. She was taking the day off from her job, something about a doctor's appointment—nothing serious, just the results of her last checkup. But a good excuse to sleep late; he knew the kind of drowsy smile he'd get from her when he bent down and kissed her goodbye.

Gathering up his trousers and a fresh shirt from the closet, he headed back to the bathroom. These dreams could go stuff themselves, as far as he was concerned. He'd come far enough awake to start feeling irritated about them.

In the shower, he stood with the water stinging straight into his face, as though that would be enough to wash the dream shadows from his vision.

He sat and watched her sleep. Sitting at the end of the bed, the lumpy contraption that folded out of the wall with a squeak of rusting metal—he'd tried oiling the ancient hinges and connections but it had done no good; she'd laughed and hugged him, and told him it didn't matter. But somehow it still did matter to him, though he hadn't told her so. Now, in the first light of morning, he sat holding his breath, keeping so still that he wouldn't cause the slightest noise from the metal frame beneath them, so he wouldn't wake her up.

Albert knew it was time to get going, to get down the building's unlit flights of stairs (sometimes the old elevator worked and sometimes it didn't; he'd learned not to trust it) and out to the bus stop at the corner. The daily journey to the station required two transfers and over an hour each way; by the time he got to work, he was so exhausted from standing up, jammed tight with everybody else who was so poor they had to ride the RTD, that he could barely fumble the mop closet open.

All these little spaces, the packed, grumbling bus and this tiny studio apartment—the kitchen was so small that for him and May to be in there at the same time required maneuvers like that Earth dance called a "waltz"—they all had some unpleasant memory hooked to them. He even knew what it was. To be so

7

cramped up, feeling other people's elbows in your ribs, their breath right in your face—that was the way it had been aboard the slave ships, the big silver-metal pods floating their way among the stars. Narrow bunks stacked on top of each other, dark corridors filled with the stink of unwashed sweat, the sounds of whispers and muffled, fearful sobbing . . . Albert's spine contracted just thinking about those bad things.

On the Day of Descent, the Tenctonese had been freed . . . of the Masters and the Overseers, and those little tiny spaces. Or at least some of them had; Albert looked around the apartment, such as it was, and felt a familiar glumness weigh down his soul. From slaves to Newcomers; it must have been worth it. Sometimes he couldn't help wondering about that.

You'd better go, he told himself; the hands on the plastic clock on top of the TV had inched farther around, just while he had been sitting here, watching May sleep. He'd come to dread the bus ride; sometimes there were tough tert kids aboard, Purist wannabes in their cheap green nylon jackets and high-laced ass-kicking boots. They always gave him a hard time, because they could tell he was a *zabeet;* he hated being called a retard and all the other nasty words they had in their mouths. He was sure that the only thing that kept them from beating him up was that they knew he worked at the police station, and that he had friends like Detective Sikes, who wasn't averse to dispensing what he called "shoe-leather therapy." Still, the glowering punks worried him. Some day, he knew, there'd be trouble.

His shoulders lifted in a sigh. Wouldn't it be nice, he thought, to crawl back into bed and fall back asleep, all nestled up against May? The way he could on Saturday and Sunday mornings, spending the whole day there with Mrs. Einstein—she liked to call herself that, she had ever since the day they'd gotten married, right in their friends George and Susan's front room.

This room here didn't seem so small on mornings like that; it seemed like a little world all to itself.

The notion of bed was so enticing that he just barely caught himself, toppling sideways toward her. Albert shook himself awake, through sheer will power. The bus ride, and the janitor job at the end of it—that was all for her; that was why he did it. He just wished . . . he could feel his hearts swelling, as though they might burst inside his chest . . . he just wished that what he did got more for her. More than this crummy little apartment; more of what she deserved. She was so pretty, sleeping like that . . .

From the back of one of the kitchen chairs, he took his jacket and slipped it on. Zipping it up, the thought came to him about how wishes could come true. There must have been a lot of wishes aboard the slave ship to have brought everybody here to their new home. So it did work that way; it had to.

He thought those things because he could feel the envelope inside the jacket's pocket, the letter that had come for him yesterday. Even without opening it, he had felt the power radiating out of it, the power to make wishes and dreams come true. Somehow he just knew, as though the words on the folded piece of paper inside were as heavy as magic gold pieces in an old Earthly fairy tale.

He hadn't gotten a blink of sleep all last night, just from thinking about it all. May didn't know; he hadn't told her yet. But soon he'd have to. He'd have to open the envelope and read the letter inside, and then he'd have to tell her. That everything was going to change; nothing would be the same from then on . . .

And that was what scared him. He touched the envelope through the fabric of the jacket. That was what had kept him from reading it right away: the thought that one whole world would be turned into another, like climbing out from the slave ship onto the surface of this planet. It made him feel dizzy; the desire to enfold May in his arms and hang on tight to her was almost overwhelming.

A glance at the clock told him that now he'd have to run to catch the bus. He reached down and pulled the blanket over May's shoulder, then headed for the door.

Outside, as Albert trotted down the cracked sidewalk, the cement glittering with bits of broken glass, it looked like the whole city was waking up. He could see lights coming on in the windows above, shadows moving against the drawn curtains. All those bleary-eyed people trudging up from sleep—for a moment, he wondered what their night dreams had been.

He spotted the bus coming less than a block away, and sprinted for the corner.

CHAPTER 2

"MAN, I HATE going out in the field first thing in the morning." Sikes held his arms straight out to the steering wheel, peering at the road ahead with heavy-lidded eyes; he knew that always made his partner nervous. "I haven't even had any coffee yet."

Beside him, George Francisco sat stiff as though a steel girder had been welded to his Newcomer spine—as stiff as when he'd first started working with Sikes. "Do you think, Matt, that, uh, I could drive instead?"

"Naw, I wouldn't hear of it—you look worse than I do." That much was true. For the last several days—actually, the last couple of weeks, come to think of it—George had been shambling into the station looking like warmed-over hell, as though he were going through sympathy pains for Sikes's cumulative lack of sleep. "Whassamatter, Susan on your case again?"

"What?" George's eyes flicked toward the leather briefcase, stuffed full of departmental paperwork, that he'd laid on the car's back seat. Then he nodded. "On my case—yes, of course. Actually . . ." He locked his gaze straight ahead through the windshield. "Actually, things are going fine for Susan and me. Couldn't be better."

Yeah, right. Sikes one-handed the car around a corner, getting a satisfying squeal from the fishtailing rear tires. *God save me from married partners—* though now, he realized, he was practically one of those himself. Cathy's live-in status with him was an open secret all over the station; the payroll office had even dropped onto his desk a form for adding her to his health insurance benefits.

Above the car, an obnoxious Purple Haze billboard's sensors had registered their approach. HEY, GENTS—the giant LCD display started rolling through its program, showing both a human and a Newcomer female seductively smiling from behind astonishing cleavage. WANT TO GIT . . . WET? Right now, the invitation didn't make Sikes feel any better.

"Though of course," mulled George aloud, "there's always . . . tension in even the most successful marriages. You know, small, inconsequential problems." He turned and smiled thinly. "As I'm sure you'll find out."

"Give me a break," Sikes muttered under his breath. *I've been there already.* He could feel his own irritation rising. George and Susan had shown a lot of smug satisfaction about the change in his living arrangements—the two of them had been playing Yenta the Matchmaker for him and Cathy for quite a while now. "What was that address again?"

"It's just off Wilshire." George glanced at the dispatcher slip in his hand, then pointed. "The victim said it would be easy to spot. It's the only house with . . . with one of *those* out front."

He caught the note of revulsion and anger in his partner's voice, but made no comment. Sikes's own feelings about this kind of incident were a close match.

They had already passed the art museum, with its

designer coils of razor wire ringing the buildings on all sides. A left turn brought them into the old Hancock Park district, or what was left of it. His soul settled lower inside him, like a leaking balloon. When he'd been a kid, this had been el primo upscale real estate, old-money mansions that seemed to have been around as long as the tar pits just to the west. Whatever childhood Gatsby-style ambitions he might have once had, now he wouldn't live here on a bet. The mansions had all been divvied up into flop apartments, with plasterboard walls you could practically read a newspaper through. The encroaching tide of the Little Tencton slums, that had already submerged K-Town and the Guatemalan barrios, was already lapping at the graffiti-stained walls here.

"This must be it."

Sikes pulled the car over to the curb. A Newcomer, looking like a downtown businessman in suit and tie, was waiting for them on the sidewalk. His face held the aggrieved expression of an early Christian martyr who had finally reached his limit and was now seriously pissed.

Groups of gawking kids, human and Newcomer, scattered a few meters back as the two police detectives got out of the car. At a carefully judged safe distance, the kids watched and whispered among themselves.

George went right up to the man. "Are you Mister Tartan?" He flipped open his notepad. "Stewart Tartan?"

The man nodded. "That's right."

"We tried to get here as soon as we could. Now, what time was it when . . ."

The voices faded to a murmur behind Sikes as he walked over to the scene of the crime. Dead center in the Tartan front lawn, Sikes set his hands on his hips as he gazed at the object before him.

Sprouting up in the midst of the closely cut grass, like some nightmare weed, was a seven-foot-high cross, scrap lumber nailed together, then wrapped with rags, the whole thing soaked in blood.

The morning sun had already turned the grisly assemblage rank; Sikes had been able to smell it as soon as the car had turned the corner. Flies buzzed the cross's still-dripping arms and the dark pool that had soaked into the ground at its base.

"What's the scoop?" Sikes glanced over his shoulder as his partner approached.

"Basically similar to the other incidents we've seen." George still had the open notepad in his hand, but didn't bother looking at it. "Neither Mr. Tartan or his wife saw or heard anything unusual during the night; they have a four-year-old boy who says he saw 'shadows' outside his bedroom window. Naturally, the child can't give any indication of what time that might have been. Tartan stepped outside his front door about seven AM, to take the boy to his preschool, and that's when he found . . . this." George pointed to the cross with his thumb.

"What a great way to start your morning." One of the flies looped close to Sikes's face; he swatted it away. "How long's the family been living here?" He glanced toward the house—from the corner of his eye, he had seen a child's face peering around the drapes pulled across the front window. An anxious-looking Newcomer woman, presumably Mrs. Tartan, had drawn the kid back.

"Approximately three months."

"Well, what d'ya think?" He turned, surveying the neighborhood. The Tartan house was a tiny fortress of order and middle-class values surrounded by ragged urban entropy. He figured they must've gotten a good deal on the place and had thought they could turn the neighborhood around with the sheer force of their staunch personalities. "Outsiders, or just the lovely neighbors, dinking with the new folks?"

"Perhaps," said George drily, "you should ask them."

14

His partner wasn't referring to the Tartans. Sikes looked past him and saw that a gleaming white van with dark-tinted windows had pulled up at the curb, right behind their car. The circular emblem of the Human Defense League, that always reminded him of a swastika if he squinted at it, was neatly painted on the van's side.

"Oh, great—" Sikes shook his head in disgust. "Now I really am pissed off."

"Now, Matt, let's just keep cold . . ."

"You keep cool. I'm not in the mood." He pushed past George's restraining arm.

Two members of the HDL's elite—*what a laugh*, thought Sikes—Sturm troops, the Marc Guerin Commandos, had emerged from the van. One of them had a professional-looking Hi-8 video camera. He lifted it to his shoulder and began taping the scene, sweeping the lens from the corner of the block and across the Tartan front lawn.

"All right, what're you clowns doing here?" Sikes planted himself in front of the leader of the pair. He'd had dealings with this jerk before, going back to collaring him for shoplifting out of Little Tencton convenience stores. Now the kid had traded his green nylon jacket for a spiff white uniform with a black Sam Browne belt and spit-shined boots. "Admiring your handiwork?"

The HDL punk turned a smug expression toward Sikes. "We had nothing to do with this."

"Yeah? So why show up now?"

A shrug. "We're here to document the natural aversion that this beleaguered human community has shown to the introduction of this alien filth in their midst. The debate as to the final solution of this so-called Newcomer problem is, unfortunately, ongoing; we're merely gathering evidence as to the instinctual human response to these creatures."

Sikes could feel the muscles of his face tightening. He knew that the other was choosing his words for maximum offensiveness—and succeeding. "I oughta final solution your ass, creep." His right hand had already balled into a fist at his side.

"Matt . . . perhaps right now's not a good time for that." George had grabbed his partner's arm. "We have company, I'm afraid."

Another van had shown up across the increasingly crowded street. On its side was the emblem of a local news station; the top bristled with remote-broadcast antennae. Another, bigger camera was already pushing its way through the onlookers.

"What's going on, officer?" The lens was stuck right in Sikes's face; he could see his distorted reflection in its glass. "Kind of a heavy response for a simple act of vandalism, isn't it?"

Next to the cameraman was another familiar face; Sikes had seen him before, both on the TV screen and in encounters like this. Mike Bolander or Wolander or something like that—he had built up an audience by first editorializing that Purists like the Human Defense League might have a worthwhile point, then coming right out later and saying they did.

"No comment." Sikes pushed the newsman's microphone away. "Why don't you talk to my partner? Maybe he can stomach you." He turned and walked a few steps away.

"All right." The camera and mike swung toward George. "How about it? What's the deal?"

George kept his face carefully expressionless. "The Los Angeles Police Department takes seriously all such incidents of this nature. It's not just vandalism; technically, it comes under municipal, state, and even federal hate-crimes statutes—"

"Come on." Bolander/Wolander/whatever had a face like a fox terrier that had been dropped on its muzzle as a pup, giving him a crooked, knowing smile. "Some people might say that was an example of obvious favoritism toward your own kind."

"Hardly." The Newcomer police detective stayed

cool. "This is a routine crime-scene investigation. If anyone is treating it with more attention than it deserves, it's you." He pointed toward the camera.

A younger, more excitable clone of Bolander, complete with tape machine on a shoulder strap, trotted after Sikes. "Any chance this is human blood? Or Newcomer?" He used his mike to point toward the cross.

"Don't be an idiot." Sikes rolled his gaze up to the sky. "They get this stuff from some butcher shop. 'Human blood'—jeez."

He gazed over the twerp's head. *Not looking good,* thought Sikes. The crowd had swelled exponentially since the arrival of the news van. The mass of people was reaching the jostling density that usually spelled trouble. The two uniformed HDL members had retreated to alongside their own van, and were watching —and videotaping—developments with evident satisfaction.

"Hey! The guy's right!" The shout that Sikes had dreaded rang out from the crowd. He spotted a gangly, unshaven human—male, early twenties—gesturing angrily over the heads surrounding him. "Goddamn slags think they own the place!"

"Yeah?" A burly Newcomer in an Adidas tracksuit drew himself to full height. "At least we can pay for it, tert."

"Call for backup," said George in a low voice. A roiling, seismic motion passed through the crowd, accompanied by more shouts and curses.

Sikes was already pushing his way toward the car. As he dived inside and punched the radio's call button, he could see George shoving Mr. Tartan back into the safety of the house.

Knots of fighting bodies had already formed by the time the sirens could be heard coming down Wilshire Boulevard. The news camera caught all the action.

"Should we go help them?" George had made his way back to the car; he watched the blue-uniformed officers slapping on plastic wrist-restraints. A row of Newcomers and humans lay facedown on the sidewalk, hands trussed behind their backs.

"Naw, let the grunts handle it." Sikes turned the key in the ignition. Everything was over—except for the paperwork. Both the news van and the HDL vehicle were long gone. "Keeps 'em in shape."

George shook his head as his partner made a U-turn in the now vacated street. "That certainly could have gone better."

"Yeah, well . . ." Sikes slumped down, driving one-handed. He fished out his shades and slipped them on against the daylight glare. "I knew I should've had my coffee first."

She looked up and saw the love of her life in the thick of a mob that looked as if they were about to kill him.

Oh, great, thought Cathy. It wasn't even noon yet, and Matt was out in the city somewhere, getting his butt into a jam. She could've almost laughed—it was so typical of him—if she hadn't also been concerned about his safety. The crowd surrounding Matt and George's car appeared to be mixed human and Newcomer, and had, even on the TV screen up in the corner of the clinic's waiting room, the churning, chaotic look of imminent violence. The volume was turned down too low for her to tell exactly what was going on; she only relaxed when the video camera turned toward the flashing lights of the back-up units arriving on the scene. There was a brief glimpse of Matt safely ensconced in the car, radio mike still in his hand and a disgusted look on his face. *My man*—she shook her head. *It figures.*

Nobody else in the waiting room showed any surprise or even interest in the events on the morning news. They all kept leafing through old issues of *The New Yorker* and *National Geographic,* barely even glancing up at the screen. Stuff like this, Cathy supposed, was pretty much dog-bites-man here in Los Angeles.

That was a gloomy thought. She felt a small, familiar weight settle upon her soul. The news show had gone to a commercial—a trio of evening-gowned Newcomer women draped themselves across a grand piano, smiling at the enormous animated White Gold bottle working the keys. Cathy looked away, to a framed picture on the wall, the snowy Cascade Mountains, the trees' shadows interlacing across the perfect whiteness. *What a pretty world,* she thought. *Even now . . .*

She felt tired. She hadn't been sleeping at all well lately. Perhaps when she had come in to see the doctor before, when he had run all the regular tests on her, she should have mentioned the weird dreams she had been having. They seemed to have been going on for weeks or even months now, which put her even more in sympathy with poor Matt. She had known him long enough to be familiar with how much job pressure a police detective carried around inside him. And now that he was revving up to take the Detective Two exams again, it was no wonder that he was popping awake at all hours of the night and prowling around the apartment with the lights off. So far she had managed to keep him from discovering that she had usually been lying there awake as well.

She had done that, keeping her back to him in the bed, her breathing low and still, even though it would have been so nice to have turned to him for comfort, letting him wrap his arms around her, soothing away with a kiss on her brow the disquieting image of the silhouetted figure, arms outstretched before streaming light. Every night's dreaming had brought the figure closer, the faceless shadow falling across her vision, its voice whispering her name. And then saying more . . . but what? Nothing that made any sense, at least nothing that she could remember in the daylight hours. Something about blood . . .

Cathy shook her head, closing her eyes to the magazine page on her lap. She knew she had done the right thing by not telling Matt about the dreams; he had enough piled on his shoulders right now.

"Ms. Frankel?" A voice broke into her thoughts. From the counter's little window of frosted glass, one of the doctor's office staff smiled and called to her. "Could you come on back? Dr. Takata's ready for you now."

The white-coated doctor came into the small consulting office a couple of minutes after she had taken a seat. "Cathy—how's it going?" Under his arm, he had a manila folder stuffed with computer printouts and X-ray transparencies.

"I thought you were supposed to tell me."

"Sure thing." Dr. Takata sat down behind the desk, flipped open the folder, and spread out the papers before himself. "I think I've got some pretty good news for you here—it'll explain a lot of these minor symptoms you've been experiencing." He spoke a few words, then looked up at her and smiled.

Cathy didn't smile back at him. A few seconds passed before she spoke. "What did you say?" She couldn't have heard that right.

Dr. Takata leaned back in his chair, spreading his hands like a magician who had pulled off a small but deft bit of legerdemain. "Pregnant," he repeated. "In the family way, as they used to put it here on Earth. So, congratulations."

I knew I should have gone to a Newcomer doctor. She meant, in her unspoken thoughts, a Newcomer who was a doctor. There were only a few of those, and they were usually outside of the health insurance loop. Most doctors who specialized in Newcomer medicine were humans, just like Takata sitting across from her now.

"I don't think you understand," said Cathy, slowly

20

and distinctly. "It's impossible for me to be pregnant."

"Well . . ." Dr. Takata shrugged. "I don't know how long you and your partner have been trying, but—"

"We haven't been trying. We can't even try. The only person I've had sex with—for about the last year—is a human male. So like I said . . . it's not possible."

The doctor gazed at her in silence, then drummed his fingers on the manila folder before him. "Cathy . . . Ms. Frankel . . . your personal living arrangements are not really a concern of mine—except to the degree that they affect your health, of course. It's not my place to make judgments about these things. But let's face it—getting pregnant is quite a bit more of a, shall we say, deliberative process for Newcomers than it is for humans. Just the matter of the couple having to arrange for the services of a *binnaum* makes it that way—though I suppose a female who wasn't being completely forthright with her male partner could, with some difficulty, manage it without his knowledge." He smiled gently. "I don't think, Cathy, that would really be your style. So if we're done kidding around—"

"I'm not joking." She leaned across the desk toward him, her hands pressed flat against its surface. "I haven't had sex with anybody except Matt Sikes. And he's human; I'm quite sure of that. You must've made some mistake."

Takata shook his head. "I hardly think so. The only factor that can account for the elevated level of the bardok enzyme in your blood workup would be pregnancy; nothing else in a Tenctonese female does it. That alone is an infallible indicator." He shrugged. "There were a couple of minor anomalous readings along with it, so I ran all the analyses twice, just to be sure. Believe me, there's no mistake about this."

"Then there's some other screwup." Cathy jabbed her finger at the computer printouts. "Those are

somebody else's test results—you must've misla-
belled the blood samples or something."

A shake of the head. "Every sample is bar-coded
right on the container at the time it's drawn from the
patient. Plus, there's the DNA pattern from the blood;
that's unique to every Newcomer individual, and this
one—" He tapped the printout. "This one is yours.
All right? No lab screwup, no mistake in the paperwork; nothing. Just pregnancy."

"No . . ." She shook her head, eyes closed. "It's
not . . ."

"Cathy. As I said before, I'm not being judgmental
about your personal affairs. If you choose to have a
sexual relationship with a human male, that's your
business. And what you choose to tell that person
about any other sexual activity in which you might be
engaged—that's your business, too. But I'm sure
you're aware that a Tenctonese pregnancy is, relatively
speaking, not a simple matter. There are critical
arrangements to be made; the biological father needs
to be notified that fertilization has taken place, so he
can begin preparing himself to receive the embryo and
carry it to term . . ."

She squeezed her eyes shut tighter. In the brightly lit
office, the world outside her dizzied head, the doctor's
voice kept hammering softly at her. She could feel her
nails digging into the palms as her hands balled into
fists.

"No!" Cathy heard a voice shouting and knew that
it was her own. "I didn't . . . there isn't anyone else.
There's just been Matt . . ."

When she opened her eyes, she saw Dr. Takata
peering intently at her. After a moment, he glanced
down at the numbers and notations on the papers in
front of him.

"Interesting . . ." The doctor's voice lowered to a
murmur. "Then of course, it would be impossible—
wouldn't it?" His gaze swung back up to her face.

"Tell you what, Cathy, I need to talk to . . . a couple of my colleagues. I'll get back to you on this . . ."

She nodded, feeling miserable. And even more exhausted than she had before. It didn't matter to her what the doctor was going to do. She would have wished herself safely back home and in bed. And asleep—if she weren't so afraid of her dreams.

CHAPTER 3

"WAY TO GO, gentlemen." Captain Grazer leaned back in his chair, a thick cigar in his hand. "What're you going to do if you catch a jaywalker? Draw down on him while he's still in the middle of the street?"

That didn't sound good—Albert could tell when the station's captain was indulging in his trademark heavy sarcasm. He busied himself with cleaning up the office, while Grazer went on grilling George and his partner, Sikes.

"Come on. Give us a break." That was Sikes's irritated voice. "We got jumped, all right? First by those HDL jerks, then those news vultures showed up. They were all looking for trouble—that's what they live for."

"So you had to give it to them?" Captain Grazer peeled one finger away from the cigar and used it to jab at the controls of the VCR beside his desk. "That's real accommodating of you."

Albert emptied the captain's ashtray into the wheeled rubbish bin, swabbed out the square of cut glass with a rag, and set it back down on the desk just in time for it to catch the next flick of gray ash. He caught a glimpse—actually, he had been sneaking looks the whole time he had been in the office—of the images on the video monitor. A streetful of angry, shouting faces, with poor George and poor Sikes stuck in the midst of them. And before that, a shot of something even sadder and grimmer, something infuriating—Albert felt his chest tightening, his own anger rising as high as it ever could.

On the screen had been a cross made of wood and rags, soaked in a butchered animal's blood, the red mess soaking into the grass and dirt in front of some Newcomer's home. No *binnaum* was so dumb as to be ignorant of what that meant. Albert dumped out the wastebasket, then slammed it back down behind the desk, hard enough to catch the captain by surprise —right now, he didn't care about the scowl Grazer sent his way. The grisly cross was a Purist symbol, something that bad and mean humans did to show how much they hated the Newcomers. And what the Purists intended to do to them someday. Blood on the ground, a thick red pool of it . . .

"With all due respect, Captain—" George spoke now, smoother and more mollifying than his partner. "I think a review of the radio log and our incident report will indicate that there was no deviation from standard procedure." He pointed to the frozen image on the monitor screen, the VCR below set in Pause mode. "Even what's gone out on the news is fairly mild, at least by recent standards. No hospitalizations, no major property damage—it's my opinion that it would have to be a remarkably slow news day for this footage to turn up on the evening broadcasts."

Albert started in on the office's window blinds. Even though Captain Grazer had installed—at his own expense—elaborate air filtration units, so he could go on smoking his Coronas and Churchills without getting into trouble with the county work-place regulations, a yellow guck still collected on the thin aluminum slats. As Albert spritzed them with an ammonia solution, it struck him—not for the first time—that getting on TV was not always a good thing. Even though he himself had enjoyed the five times he had been on the screen in the last year, first the little segments on a local personality show, then the bits on *A Current Affair* and even *Good Morning America,* his favorite. He had to admit that had all been pretty exciting; some of the detectives and beat cops had teased him by asking for his autograph, but even that had been fun once he'd gotten over his shy embarrassment.

"Jesus, Albert—" The smell of ammonia had drifted over to the desk; Captain Grazer waved his hand in front of his face. "What the hell are you doing? You want to run a gas chamber, we'll send you up to San Quentin, for Christ's sake."

"Sorry, I'm just about done here." Albert wiped a fresh rag across the blinds.

"Hey—take it easy on the celebrity," said Sikes. "He makes you look good, remember?"

"Yeah, well, he's still the station's janitor." The ember at the tip of Grazer's cigar glowed an angry red. "Maybe if he spent more time being a janitor, and less on all that other stuff, he wouldn't have to come in here while I'm trying to get some real work accomplished."

"All done, Captain." Albert stowed his spray bottle and rag back into the tray on the rubbish bin. "I'm sorry I, uh, got in your way . . ."

"Never mind." Behind the cigar pointing toward the door, Grazer's expression looked sourer than Albert could remember it ever having been before. "Just go."

"You know, it's not the ammonia that makes for such a lovely atmosphere around here—" Sikes's voice filtered through the door as Albert pulled it shut behind himself. "It's not even that damn cigar. It's you . . ."

Everybody seemed to be having a bad day. Deep in thought, Albert pushed the rubbish bin toward the maintenance area at the back of the station. Even without all that business on the TV, the cross soaked in blood and the people all upset in different ways about it, he still would have been able to look at George and his partner, and catch some silent radiation that spoke of heavy troubles. Both the detectives looked so tired, and their heads were so jumbled up with the thoughts inside—the words and images were almost pushing out through their skulls.

He tilted the bin's contents into the Dumpster behind the station, then came back inside. Most mornings, he worked straight through without taking a break, at least until it was time for the lunch that May always packed him the night before. But today his own fatigue and big thoughts weighed him down too much. He pulled out the little stool he kept inside the supply closet and sat down, his shoulders rounding with a sigh.

The closet, with its constant nose-wrinkling odor of cleansers and bulk papers goods and drying floor mops, was Albert's private territory. On the inside of the door, his collection of press clippings and magazine articles, even a photo of him with Joan Lunden on the GMA interview set, had been carefully arrayed into a personal Hall of Fame. His buddy, Officer Zepeda, had sealed everything into flat plastic evidence bags for him, to make sure that every scrap of paper was kept safe and untorn; she had even gone out and gotten the *People* magazine framed. His own smiling face gazed out from under the glass, right beside the big words "Sherlock With a Push Broom." The photographer had taken his picture with the broom in question, shoving a small mound of trash down one of the station's hallways, with him in his janitor uniform even though he'd offered to go home and put on his good suit or one of the really nice traditional Tenctonese outfits that May had sewn for him.

"They want the contrast," Zepeda had explained to him. She had tapped her fingertip against his forehead. "Between that quirky brain of yours and your everyday schlub getup."

She must have been right about that; she was generally right about everything she told him. Unfortunately, that included her prediction that Captain Grazer was going to become increasingly grumpy about all the attention that Albert was getting. "Grazer thinks there's room for only one genius around here—so it better be him. *Comprende?*" It took a while, because he didn't want to, but he supposed he finally understood. That made him sad, sitting there and looking up at the clippings; all he'd ever wanted to do was help.

And that was what the people who had written to him said they wanted. To help them. He had finally gotten up the nerve to tear open the letter he had been carrying around and read the letter inside. A corner of the white paper stuck out of the pocket of his jacket, hanging on a nail farther inside the closet. They'd made it sound as if they really needed him—so it couldn't be a bad thing, could it? If he did what they wanted.

Albert felt his brow creasing, as his thoughts became deeper and darker and harder to pick apart. He had to consider what he wanted as well. What he wanted to do for May. *That's the important thing,* he told himself. He had to remember that . . .

"Hey, whatcha doin', Albert? Cracking another case?"

He looked up and saw Lieutenant Dobbs's wide mahogany face smiling around the edge of the closet door. "No—" Albert shook his head. "Just . . . resting. That's all."

"Good idea. You don't want to burn out the ol' cerebral circuits." Dobbs pointed a thumb over his shoulder. "There's a phone call for you. Why don't you take it at my desk? I'm just heading out."

"Oh." A twitch, neither of fear or even surprise, pulled at Albert's spine. Somehow he had known this also had been coming his way. "Thanks."

Standing beside Dobbs's desk, with the rows of detectives and other department officers around him, Albert punched the flashing button on the telephone. "Hello?" He kept his voice low; he didn't want to disturb the others.

"Mr. Einstein?" The voice on the line had a pumped up enthusiastic quality to it. "Hi, this is Bob Dierdorf over at Precognosis Consulting. How are ya today?"

"Uh . . . I'm fine." Albert glanced over his shoulder, wondering if anyone else had been able to hear the words that had come booming at his ear. The man's name was the same as the signature at the bottom of the letter tucked in Albert's jacket.

"Great, great, glad to hear it. Say, I was wondering if you received the little communication I sent you."

He nodded, then remembered to speak aloud. "Yes . . . I think I did."

"'Think you did'—that's pretty cagey, Mr. Einstein, I'll have to say." Dierdorf emitted a short, sincere-sounding laugh. "You know, there's a bunch of us over here who'd really like to get together with you for a chat. There's some things we need to talk about. Lots of things."

"Well . . ."

Dierdorf jumped back in. "Now, if the dollar amount I mentioned in my letter wasn't quite enough to whet your appetite, then that's something we can discuss as well. I just wanted to get some figures out on the table, get things rolling, so to speak."

"Well, actually . . ."

"So I can assume that the basic amount was at least in the ballpark, Mr. Einstein?"

He had wanted to say that the number with the dollar sign in front and all the zeroes for a tail was more money than he had ever dreamed of, more money than he could even imagine; maybe this Bob Dierdorf had made a mistake or something. Albert knew how hard arithmetic could be. He wanted to say all that, but his mouth was too slow; he didn't have a chance against the other's onslaught of words.

"I'll send a car around this evening, then. We've already reserved a table at l'Orangerie; the other vice presidents and I are pretty much regulars there."

"Gee . . . I don't know if I could afford going to a place like that . . ." Albert had never heard of it, but just from the name it sounded expensive.

Dierdorf's hearty laugh went off like a cannon. "That's pretty good. But don't worry—this one's on us." The laugh shifted into a chuckle. "Though considering what we're planning on paying you, pretty soon you'll be able to buy the restaurant. See you tonight, okay? Looking forward to it."

"Sure . . ." Before Albert could say anything more, the connection was broken. He set the phone back down on the desk. That was sure strange, he thought.

As he turned around in a slow daze, he saw the door to Captain Grazer's office opening. George and Sikes came out, the human detective rolling his eyes upward and shaking his head in annoyed disgust; George's expression was more carefully maintained.

From beind the two, Grazer spotted Albert. "Hey!" The captain pointed at him. "Albert—were you making a personal call?"

It took a moment for Albert to reply. "Somebody called me," he said.

"No personal calls during your shift; I've told you before." The captain's scowl deepened. "How about making an effort to remember that?"

George and Sikes had drifted over to the table with the coffee urn on it. Leaning over to fill his cup, the one with the Dodgers emblem on it, Sikes watched the scene with eyes drawn down to little simmering slits.

"Yes, sir." Albert nodded. "I'll try—"

Grazer had already stomped back into his office and slammed the door shut. The detectives and other officers shook their heads and went back to their work.

"Mister Charm," said Officer Zepeda, from over by the case files.

"It's okay." Albert looked over toward her. "It doesn't bother me."

Actually . . . it did. Sometimes, when the captain yelled at him for no good reason, a little spark of resentment flared inside him. This time, it was accompanied by a new thought.

If somebody could get so rich that they could buy a whole restaurant . . . how much, he wondered, would it take to buy a police station?

"What the hell's this?"

George Francisco looked up. His partner, at the desk across from his own, was holding up a small rectangular object. Sikes was regarding the thing with the mingled repulsion and fascination that a particularly large and hairy insect might evoke.

"It appears," said George, "to be an audiocassette in its standard, small plastic container." He set down the inter-station memo that he had begun to read. "Surely, Matt, you've seen one of those before."

"Yeah, my glove compartment's full of 'em. I've just never seen one with Ol' Laughing Boy's picture on it." Sikes turned the case around to show the color photograph of Captain Grazer.

"How . . . interesting." George poked further through the papers in his In box. "There seems to be one here for me as well." He held up an identical cassette, the image of the captain smiling confidently from inside the clear plastic.

"We all got them," said the detective across the aisle. "Check it out—you're gonna love this."

George had already opened the case and extracted the folded leaflet inside. "I believe I detect signs of a commercial venture . . ."

"Yeah, right." Sikes slumped down in his chair. "If 'commercial venture' is Tenctonese for 'scam' that is." He pried open his cassette's leaflet. "God save us from Grazer's get-rich-quick schemes."

He made no reply. Above several paragraphs of dense type, the leaflet was headed *Get GIT!*

"'GIT?' What the hell's 'GIT?'" demanded Sikes.

"Man, I told you it was gonna be good." The detective who had spoken up before turned a heavy-lidded gaze toward them. "It stands for Grazer Intellinomics Training." He tapped the side of his head. "It's like a mind thing."

"'The new science of cerebro-perceptual control,'" George read aloud. "'Truths as ancient as the pyramids, yet also the next step in humanoid evolution . . .'"

Sikes groaned, pitching forward until his brow hit the top of his desk with a thump.

"'A revolution in the management of interpersonal relationships—'"

"Please . . . no . . ." With his head still down, Sikes feebly raised a hand as if drowning. "I can't take it . . ."

There was a certain mild sadistic pleasure to be gotten here, noted George. Or perhaps masochistic. "'Transform and achieve new levels of mastery in any individual's sexual endeavors—'"

"Huh?" Sikes raised his head and picked up the cassette lying in front of him. "All that's in here?"

"Hell, no," said the detective across the aisle. "The man's not gonna give away all his see-crets for nothing. That's just a taste of his eternal wisdom. You sign up for the whole twenty-tape course and extra additional seminar sessions conveniently located at a hotel in your neighborhood, then you wind up in the same exalted state as His Enlightedness. Like, Stud City."

"Oh, sure." Officer Zepeda stood in the aisle between the desks. "As if Grazer's pipe laying has gotten him in the Guinness Book of World Records. In his dreams, maybe." She walked on with an armful of file folders.

"Hey." The detective spread his hands wide. "Would the man charge for something if it wasn't for real?"

"In a second." Sikes flopped back in his chair. "Come on, George, let's get out of here. I think there's a beer bottle somewhere with an important clue on the bottom."

George frowned. "It's a little early for that sort of thing, don't you think?"

"I just want to sit in a dark place and *look* at a bottle of beer. And reminisce about when I was younger and stupider and didn't have so many worries." Sikes stood up and rooted through his pockets for his keys. "Come on, be a pal."

He hesitated for a moment, then picked up the stack of memos and dropped them back into his In box.

Six blocks from the station, they found a windowless establishment that was like a cavern fitted with torn red Naugahyde. Or it found them; the car, with Sikes behind the wheel, had been drawn to the place as if it were some dingy black hole in space.

"Used to come here a lot." True to his word, Sikes had taken one hit from the long-neck Bud that the bartender had set in front of him, then he had pushed it aside. "Cheaper'n therapy, and you don't have to worry about the department shrink dropping a loony code in your personnel file."

For the sake of appearances, George had ordered a White Gold; some off-brand, even lumpier and more clotted, filled the glass. It tasted oddly good, even at this hour; the temptation to drink it all was hard to resist.

"I understood that humans believed friends were best suited for that purpose." He took another sip of the sour milk. "To talk over one's troubles with."

"Naw, they just get in the way." Sikes prodded a row of peanuts into line on the bartop. "When you're absolutely bent on feeling sorry for yourself, the last thing you want is somebody trying to cheer you out of it. Or somebody who's got troubles even worse than your own."

"Matt—what do you have to feel sorry about?" The gloomy tone in his partner's voice worried him. "You do an important job that you're good at and that you even sometimes enjoy; your promotion chances are excellent—you're a clinch to pass the Detective Two exams this time—"

"Cinch," interjected Sikes. "The word is 'cinch.' And I'm glad you're so confident about those exams."

"Whatever." George pressed on. "You're surrounded by friends who hold you in esteem; and you're in a warm, supportive relationship with a female of considerable personal and intellectual attainment—and one, I might add, with a high degree of physical attractiveness."

"Yeah . . ." Sikes nodded. "Cathy's not chopped liver, that's for sure."

"Is that supposed to be good or bad?" The human phrase had always puzzled George. A whole vocabulary of endearments and compliments existed in the Tenctonese language, based upon the attractiveness of organ meats, similar to the humans' use of 'honey' and 'peach.'

Sikes didn't hear the question; he had sunk lower in his brooding thoughts. "Yeah, you're right—what've I got to complain about?" He rubbed his eyes. "Maybe I'm just tired . . ."

"That could be." George felt a twinge of sympathy, based on the load of fatigue that he was carrying around himself. The bar was so dark and warm in a humid, spilled-beer way; it would have been easy for him to have laid his head down and gone to sleep, sitting right here on the wobbling chrome stool. He pulled himself fully awake with an effort. "I take it you've been studying hard? For the exams?"

His partner shrugged. "Off and on. I've got most of that stuff down so cold . . ." Sikes watched his own fingernail tapping against the side of the beer bottle. "Hell, it's not the Detective Two exams. It's not Cathy, it's not anything. I've just been . . . having trouble sleeping lately. Don't know why."

Trouble sleeping . . . His partner's words echoed inside George's head, as though the bar's dim interior had been transported there. He sipped at his glass. The sour milk now tasted flat and unexalting; he could barely swallow it.

"That's odd . . . you should say that . . ." Brows creased, George studied the glass in front of him.

Sikes glanced round at him. "What do you mean?"

He was on the verge of telling Sikes; the words were on his tongue, ready to come out. A confession, a plea for sympathy, an acknowledgement of some bond between himself and his human partner; he didn't know. Perhaps just a simple statement of fact. That his sleep had been troubled as well. He could see, even without closing his eyes, the shadowed image from his dreaming, the arms outstretched against the light of another world; he could hear his name being spoken, like the pronouncement of a fate from which even his waking couldn't save him. . . .

He stopped himself from speaking. He swallowed the words into the clot that had already formed at the base of his throat.

"Nothing." George managed to shake his head. "Nothing . . . I just . . . never mind."

Still looking at the glass on the wet-ringed bar, he could feel Sikes's gaze upon him growing sharper. Sikes would be trying, he knew, to tune in on that silent telepathic wavelength that grew between partners. Right now, that frequency was jammed, but it

35

didn't stop Sikes from attempting to figure out what was walking around inside George's skull, the word that he had almost shouted aloud from the depths of sleep, the name that could be put to the hidden face that had whispered his.

"Ah, screw it." Sikes pushed his barely touched glass of beer farther away. He dug a couple of bills from his wallet and laid them down on the damp imitation-woodgrain surface. "I knew I wasn't thirsty. Come on, let's blow this Popsicle stand."

They emerged from the bar into hammering sunlight, both of them squinting and blinded until they could fumble their shades on.

Sikes didn't say anything more all the way back to the station. Sitting at his own desk again, George felt an obscure guilt knotting in his gut. As though, helpless himself, he had let his partner down somehow.

CHAPTER 4

"YOU'RE WHAT?"

Cathy didn't bring her gaze up to meet his. She sat at the table in their apartment's kitchen area, her hands laid out flat, as though to stop them from trembling.

He didn't wait for her to reply. "Is this some kind of joke?" If it were, it didn't seem very funny to Sikes. It was just stupid.

"That's what the doctor said." Cathy spoke to her hands, as though she were having this conversation with them. "That I was pregnant."

"Yeah, right." He turned away from the table, took the two steps necessary to reach the refrigerator, pulled it open and glared inside. Unseeing for a few seconds, it took him that long to decipher the visual clutter of bottles and plastic containers. He finally recognized the six-pack of Rolling Rock, right next to an opened and resealed packet of raw ox spleen tidbits. As he elbowed the fridge door shut and twisted the cap off the cold green bottle, through a sheer act of will he forced himself to lighten up. "Christ, sweetheart, you really had me going there." He leaned against the sink's edge and tilted the bottle to his mouth. "Must've been a harder day than I thought—I usually don't fall for these gags quite so easy."

She turned her damp face toward him. "I'm not joking, Matt. It's true; the doctor did tell me I'm pregnant. And he showed me the test results and things. And . . ." On the table, her hands grasped each other, twisting and squeezing, the knuckles turning white. "And . . . I know it's true. I can feel it."

"Okay . . ." Sikes slowly nodded. He had taken another hit of beer. The effect inside him was little more than a hiss of steam, as though he had poured the beer onto a black stone cooking in the desert sun. "So exactly what is it you're trying to tell me?" He felt vastly unamused now. "Because, you know, pregnant isn't something you get out of a catalogue. You can't sit in front of the TV and order it off the Home Merchandise Network." As though from a distance, he could hear his own voice, and it sounded like another person, the one he'd been the last year with his ex-wife, the two of them piling into each other like tanker trucks full of sulphuric acid.

Cathy at least wasn't playing that game. "Matt . . . please," she said miserably. "Don't . . ."

There was no stopping himself now. "Because if you're pregnant, you didn't get pregnant by me. Because that's impossible." The beer bottle was about to break into green splinters in his fist. "You're a Newcomer, remember—"

"Matt . . ."

Just as it used to with the other person, the one he'd thought was safely dead and would never come back, a black roaring noise welled up inside his head. "—and I'm a human. All right?" The last few months with his ex-wife, it had always been like this, blind shouting and feeling as though his blood pressure would pop his chest open like a paper bag. "And a Newcomer female can't get herself knocked up by sleeping with a human male. There's just no way. Jeez!" He slammed the bottle down on the counter; the beer foamed up the neck and sizzled over his hand.

Cathy laid her head down on her arms and began weeping, great ache-filled sobs that wrenched her shoulder blades together.

Sikes stood watching her, a dark tide pulling back from his heart, leaving mute and broken debris behind. He had been a couple seconds away from the final question, the last one he'd shouted at his ex-wife—*So who is he? Who's the guy?*—in the bad days of his past.

The roaring noise had died away, letting him hear Cathy crying. That was one thing, at least, that Newcomers and humans had in common, especially the women; you hurt them, they cry. Way to go, he told himself bleakly. He felt like the proverbial ten pounds of mandrill shit.

He wiped his beer-soaked hand on his trousers leg. For a moment, the urge swept through him, to go and lean over Cathy, to kiss her on top of her head as he had done so many times before, to grab her shoulders and pull her up from the chair, to turn her and hold her tight against himself, kissing her tears and trying to stop any more from coming . . .

He couldn't. The dead and never-dead past, and all the bad memories that went with it (his ex-wife hadn't cried when he'd asked her that last, fatal question; she'd laughed) held him back. Sikes pushed himself away from the counter and headed for the apartment door, a long way distant.

Every step rang on the bare floor like a nail driven into his heart. When he pulled the door shut behind him, he could still hear her crying.

Looking at his father was like looking in a mirror. One that showed him something that he didn't particularly want to see.

The argument between Buck Francisco and his dad

had reached that point, like a temporary lull in a driving storm, where both sides seemed to have run out of words. They had reached that stage quickly, within ten minutes of the first verbal shots being fired. There had been nothing to hold the two of them back, to keep the row from reaching maximum velocity and destructive capability. Buck's mom had taken his sister Emily and the baby out to the nearest shopping mall; he and his father had the big empty house all to themselves. And their tempers.

Here we go again. Buck slumped down against the sofa cushions, gazing at the dead big-screen TV on the other side of the room as his father came back from the kitchen.

"All I'm trying to say is—" His father was keeping his voice carefully controlled, much lower in volume than it had been just a minute ago. He had a popped-open can of MelloWhite lo-cal sour milk dangling in his hand. "—That this is our home. It's our world now, Buck. It's the only one we have." His voice strained with a pleading tone. "What's the point of not trying to fit in?"

Buck glanced over at his father. Right now, George Francisco didn't look like the shining Tenctonese success story that everyone else thought he was, the tough, bright Newcomer vaulting his way through the ranks of the L.A. police bureaucracy. Right now, the knot of his plain rep-stripe necktie was tugged loose at his collar, the rest of his inevitable white shirt wrinkled and pulled from his trousers' waistband. He must have had a hell of a day. His suit jacket was tossed across the back of one of the dining room chairs, like a discarded gray rag. For a moment, Buck felt a twinge of pity as he looked at his dad, with his perpetual load-of-troubles expression and tired eyes, more tired now than he had ever seen them before.

At the same time, a spark of anger bounced off the steeled hearts in Buck's chest. His father being this worn-out was the whole problem, the reason behind the shouting match, or at least this latest installment of it. His father was grinding himself down to dust by trying to be something he wasn't. Something that no Tenctonese could ever be.

Human . . .

Buck felt his own eyes narrowing in hatred, as though it wasn't his burnt-out old man standing there, but one of those smug, self-satisfied terts that his father, with his suit and tie and his head aching from being used as a hammer against every wall, so desperately emulated.

"Yeah?" Buck spat out his words, like gristle found in raw meat. "And just what exactly is it you get when you 'fit in'?"

A baffled look crossed his dad's face. "What do you get?" He raised his arms, the can of sour milk in one hand, in a gesture that took in the living room, all the rest of the house surrounding it, and the streets and city beyond the walls. "That's how we've gotten . . . everything."

"Great," said Buck in disgust. He folded his own arms across his chest. "You've sold out your Tenctonese heritage—your *chavez*—for an extra-wide fridge in the kitchen and a cable TV hookup with all the premium channels. What a deal."

"The refrigerator . . ." His father's puzzlement flipped right back over to anger, bursting through whatever resolutions he'd just made to keep his temper in check. "You listen to me, Buck. I've got some news for you. The refrigerator, the TV, the house, everything here—those are all nothing."

"Is that right? Why do you have 'em, then?"

"Don't get smart with me, young man. Your mother and your sister—even the baby—seem to have more appreciation of all I've done to make life pleasant for this family. And I recall plenty of times seeing you with your head stuck inside that refrigerator, rooting around for something to eat. But that's not the point." He brought his voice level again, tightly controlled.

41

"What's important isn't the number and variety of things this world gave us. What's important is that this world gave us freedom."

Buck rolled his eyes, gazing up to the ceiling. He'd heard this song before.

"You can be as cynical as you like about that, Buck; it's still the truth." His father set the MelloWhite can down on the dining table; he must have realized that it made an incongruous prop for a lecture of this type. "I thought you were old enough to remember. But perhaps you've forgotten."

"Remember what?"

"What it was like before . . . before the Day of Descent." His father's voice softened. "What it was like on the slave ships, Buck. For us . . . for all of us. Your people." He turned his gaze away, toward the sliding window that opened onto the house's patio. In the dimming shades of twilight, the landscaping around the pool could still be seen, the split-leaf philodendrons dark and shiny, the blooms of the passion flower vine that was Susan's favorite, drooping in on themselves as though wilted from the long day's heat. In the sky of amethyst and smoke, a distant passenger jet banked toward LAX and the ocean. "It wasn't like this, Buck. I'm surprised . . . you don't remember." His father's voice was almost a whisper. "It was so dark, and crowded there . . . with all of us on top of one another. And we possessed nothing, not even our own lives." A bitter smile tugged at one corner of his mouth. "You talk about all the things we have now, as if to have them were a sin in the eyes of Celine and Andarko. But you don't seem to remember what it was like to have nothing." He held out his hands before him, regarding them as if they were no longer part of his body. "To be nothing. Don't you understand, Buck? That's what this world gave us. It gave us our lives."

He'd heard it all before, and even now, hearing it again, Buck had to resist the tug of the passion in his father's voice. That hope, that light, the sun spilling across the mountains that ringed the desert where the ship had landed . . . a new world. His father was wrong about one thing: he did remember what it had been like before the Day of Descent. As a child, in that dark hell, he'd lost the ability to cry. There had been no point to it; misery had been endless, the salt upon their tongues, the stifling breath inside their throats. But he'd been granted the eyes of a child again, and the tears, when he'd first looked out across that vast, empty landscape, to a horizon edged with a fiery brightness. He'd turned away from his family, to hide those tears from them.

That had been a long time ago. But even now, it would be so easy for him to be carried away by his father's words, to believe in that bright promise once again . . .

To be fooled.

Buck looked up at his father. Inside his chest, he could feel his hearts clenching like doubled fists. "Sure," said Buck. "They gave us our lives. Just so they could take them away from us again." He flicked a hand toward the television. The gesture said enough: every day, the TV's blank screen had seemed to become even more of a window onto another world, a darker one, filled with hate-contorted faces, uniformed Purists, fists waving in the air . . . and crosses soaked in bloody rags, propped up in front of Newcomer homes just like this one. "You just . . . don't . . . get it. The terts don't want us here. They never did; they were lying to us. And now they're getting set to do something about us slags. The humans have probably got their final solution to the Newcomer problem just about ready."

His father wearily shook his head. "Buck, that is just paranoid nonsense. I'll grant you there are problems between the humans and our people; there are bound to be. Do you think I don't know that? I have to deal with groups like the Human Defense League

43

every day. But what about our friends? What about humans like my partner Matt? Your sister Emily calls him 'Uncle Matt'—do you really think that someone like him wants to rid this world of our people? You can't be serious."

"Sikes is your friend." Buck spat out his next words. "I don't have humans for friends. You don't understand—if they can't kill us one way, they'll do it another. The humans will act like they're our friends, they'll do all sorts of nice and cozy and wonderful things for us . . . and then one day we'll be gone. Because there won't be any more Tenctonese left. We'll all be just like them, the humans. Or we'll have died trying."

For a moment, Buck's father closed his eyes, trying to compose himself. "I have devoted my life—this life that's been given to me by this world—to building peace between the humans and our people." As he looked at his son, his expression was both stern and grieving. "I don't know if there's room in this house— in this family—for someone with so much hatred in his hearts."

The shouting and the fury had come to an end. The only words that could be spoken now were hollow things, like the rustling of dry leaves after a storm had passed.

"Fine by me." Buck grabbed his jacket from the end of the couch and stood up. "Nobody has to make room for me."

He pulled the front door shut with an echoing slam behind himself.

Outside, the family station wagon had just pulled up in the driveway. Emily had already scrambled out, arms full of bags from The Gap and Mervyn's; behind her, Buck's mother was busy unstrapping the baby's car seat. She looked up as he stalked past.

"Buck—where are you going?" She sounded alarmed, as though she had caught the expression on his face.

He made no reply, but went on striding down the sidewalk, past all the well-groomed lawns and sprawling houses.

"Hey!" his sister cried after him. "Buck . . ."

Past the lawns and houses, and into the soft blue islands of the streetlights. Toward the distant, hard-edged outline of the city. He kept walking, the night air already cold on his face.

"Mr. Einstein—glad you could make it."

His hand was caught like a startled bird and pumped vigorously up and down. The napkin slid from Albert's lap and floated to the restaurant's intricate gold-threaded carpet.

The man who had come striding up to the table now pulled back the last empty chair and sat down. One of the pretty waitresses from the bar section immediately placed a scotch and soda, clinking with ice cubes, in front of him, then retreated.

"Albert, this is Mr. Vogel." Sitting on the table's other side, the human named Dierdorf smiled even more broadly than before. "He's the president of Precognosis."

"Um . . ." Albert could feel his feet beneath the table beginning to swell, in the usual Tenctonese sign of nervousness. He resisted the impulse to reach down and loosen his shoelaces. "I'm . . . pleased to meet you, Mr. Boggle."

"Vogel. And call me Harve." He waved off the menu that another waiter had extended toward him. "Just the usual, André."

The waiter nodded in a way that seemed more intimidating than servile to Albert, then turned haughtily away. Albert wondered if they were going to get anything to eat here.

"Okay if I call you Albert?" Broad-shouldered and with styled silver hair that looked like a movie star's, Vogel leaned toward him. "Or do you prefer Al?"

The notion of choosing between one name or another triggered a small panic attack. His mind went blank, or even more so; a few seconds passed before he realized he was still staring wide-eyed at Vogel. "Al . . ." He struggled to take a deep breath. "Albert's fine." He pointed toward the other immaculately dressed human. "That's what . . . Mr. Dierdorf's been calling me."

"No, no; you mean Bob." Vogel winked at him. "I really want us all to be on a first-name basis, Albert, because Precognosis isn't like an ordinary company; it's more like a family. We work very closely together. And that's how we want to work with you."

Both the humans were looking at him with the same sparkling, smiling, oppressive force; Albert felt as though he were in a TV wildlife documentary, the one he and May had watched, where a deer had been caught frozen and unable to move in the glare of a poacher's spotlight. He wished May were with him right now; she was smarter than him, even if she might not be quite as smart as this Vogel and Dierdorf. She might have been able to figure out what he was supposed to do next.

"I . . ." Making his mouth work took an effort of sheer will. "I don't even know what it is you want me to do."

An unsmiling glance passed between the two humans, communicating something that Albert wasn't able to discern. Then Vogel turned back to him, laying the manicured fingertips of one hand on his.

"Mr. Einstein—Albert—there's nothing you have to worry about." Vogel's words were resonant with sincerity. "There's nothing on which we're going to ask you to trust us, that we're not immediately willing to prove to you. Look." Vogel reached inside his suit jacket and pulled out a checkbook; he flipped it open and scrawled quickly with the fountain pen that Dierdorf handed to him. "This is for you." He pushed the check across the white tablecloth. "That's just for the privilege of meeting you; of meeting somebody with your tremendous God-given talents. Go on, take it. You keep that whether we wind up doing business together or not."

Albert bent over the check, afraid to touch it. He could see that there were several zeroes written on it, along with a big fat number one at the front. He felt a little dizzy; he couldn't make out quite how much money the check represented, but he was sure it was more than he'd ever made pushing a broom at the police station.

"But . . . but why?" He looked up at Vogel. "Why would you give me something like . . . like that?" He poked a finger toward the check lying between himself and the human.

"We have some real good reasons, Albert." Dierdorf leaned into the conversation, as Vogel sat back in his chair. "Right now, I imagine you're a little confused, because you don't really know what it is our company does. Let me fill in the picture." The polished smile flashed again. "Basically, Precognosis is the leading provider—in the world, Albert—of what we like to call enhanced market research. Do you know what market research is, Albert?"

"Um. You . . . you tell people where to go. To the market, to buy stuff."

Dierdorf's smile gentled. "Not quite. We tell the other people—the people who make 'stuff'—what to put in the markets. And in the stores, and on television and in the movie theaters. So that people like you—and us—can go into the stores, or turn on the TV, or go to the movies, and we'll be sure to find exactly what we really want to buy."

"Albert, do you know how much it costs to put a new product on the shelves of your local supermarket?" Vogel's expression had turned into a serious, deliberative frown. "Say, something like a new line of fruit-flavored sour milks? Or a dehydrated raw liver snack chip?"

He thought hard for an answer. "A lot?"

"A lot, Albert." Vogel nodded. "Millions of dollars. It can be billions of dollars, for a total design shift and reorienting of market position. You've got your design costs, your acquisition or retooling of production facilities, the setting up of your distribution networks . . . it's very expensive, Albert. Same thing with making a movie or producing a new TV show; there's always a lot of money at stake, and it's all riding on being right about what people want, and more importantly, what they want to buy."

"That's where people like us—market research firms—come in," said Dierdorf. "It's our job to go and find out what people want. We find out whether some new snack chip that a company is thinking of making is even something that people would want to put in their mouths. Now, there's a lot of traditional ways of doing that kind of research: you talk to people, you give them questionnaires, you do focus groups, you wire them up for galvanic skin responses, muscle twitches, eye pupil dilation indices, you do prototype taste tests, limited regional marketing . . . there's a whole raft of things that researchers have usually done, to try to figure out what people want. But you know what the problem is with those methods, Albert?"

He shook his head. Dierdorf's list had frightened him; he'd had a vision from an old black-and-white movie that he and May had watched late at night, of a mad scientist's laboratory, with crackling electric bolts arcing over a hapless figure strapped to a table.

"Two things, Albert. One, they're expensive; a company can wind up spending millions just on its market research. And two, even if you spend all that money, you could still be wrong. The results just aren't accurate enough. And all that money, millions and billions of dollars, goes down the drain."

"Gosh." He hoped that Dierdorf and Vogel didn't think it was all his fault.

"Now, Albert—" Vogel's tone became even more

kind and fatherly. "Do you remember that afternoon you came to our offices? The ones downtown? You remember what we had you do then?"

"Sure." It had been a whole day, not just an afternoon. Everybody had been really nice to him. They'd fed him lunch, not at a restaurant, but right there in one of the conference rooms; it'd been a buffet, a big spread of all kinds of food, that twenty people couldn't have put away. He'd been told to fill his plate with whatever looked good to him. The only weird thing had been the human woman in a white lab coat, who had followed him around the table, watching him and marking things down on the clipboard she'd carried with her. It had only been later, at home with May, that he'd realized the big lunch might have also been part of their tests, along with the quick little videos they'd shown him and the rows of empty boxes, stuff he'd never seen at the supermarket, that they'd asked him to pick and choose from. Sitting here with Dierdorf and Vogel, he remembered and slowly nodded. "Yeah, that was kind of fun."

"Do you know what those tests were all about? What we were looking for?"

Albert considered for a moment, then shook his head. "No. I sure don't."

"We were looking—" Dierdorf leaned across the table, his voice serious and confidential. "For a picker."

"Oh." He felt a sense of disappointment bob up inside him. He knew what a picker was; and that it was just about the only job on this planet worse than being a janitor. What that had to do with the tests he'd taken, he hadn't the slightest idea. He'd already figured out that these two humans were going to offer him a job of some kind—and that he wouldn't take it. There'd be no way he could leave all his friends at the station. Still, it would've been nice if it'd been something a little better than that. So he could tell May about it. "I don't know . . ." Albert shook his head.

"Thanks, but . . . I don't think I'd be very good at climbing those ladders all day long, and picking apples and stuff off the trees. And strawberries would be even worse—don't they grow kinda low to the ground? I'd probably throw my back out or something."

Dierdorf and Vogel exchanged puzzled glances, then both men smiled and rolled their heads back as if they'd just figured out the punch line of a joke. "No, no, Albert; that's not the kind of picker I meant." Dierdorf, still smiling, had turned back to him. "Not a fruit picker. You're too important a person for that sort of work. I mean a . . . well, a *future* picker. It takes a very rare talent to do the kind of work we're talking about. We're looking for someone who just *knows* what's going to happen with a product or a service that one of our client companies is thinking of putting out in the marketplace. The kind of person that, if you put products X, Y, and Z in front of him, can just tell by pure instinct which is the one that's going to be the big hit, that everybody is going to rush to buy. That takes a magical kind of talent, Albert. Your kind of talent."

"I'm not sure . . . I understand . . ."

Before Albert had recovered from Dierdorf's rush of words—he felt like he was trying to come up for air from a swiftly tumbling river—he was hit with more from Vogel. "That's what the tests were all about," said the other human. "They were a long series of choices, Albert, one after another. Just so we could see what things you liked, what things you didn't like. And you know what?"

Terrified, he shook his head.

"A ninety-nine point nine correspondence with our previously established database of consumer preferences." Dierdorf's earnest face pressed toward Albert. "Nobody—and I mean nobody—has ever hit that level before."

Leaning back in his chair, Vogel rubbed his chin.

"There was what's-his-name . . . Peter Hoaglund; he got up around ninety-six, maybe ninety-seven."

"Yeah, when he was sober." A scowl clouded Dierdorf's face. "Don't talk to me about that Hoaglund maniac. Jesus." With a visible effort, Dierdorf pumped up the smile he displayed to Albert. "Trust me; it's a rare talent. And yours is the finest example anyone's ever come across. We had a pretty good idea that you'd be a top candidate when we read those newspaper and magazine articles about your little detective work down at the police station—"

"Those weren't any big deal," said Albert. "I just made some lucky guesses is all."

"'Lucky guesses'—that's good. But they weren't just luck, Albert. That's the kind of thing that a natural-born picker is always doing. Guessing . . . and being right. And being right about the future—about what people, Newcomers and humans alike, are going to want to eat and drink and wear and see, and buy . . . that's our business, Albert. And the more often we're right about those things, the more money we make. But it's not just about money." Dierdorf's expression took on the heavy, brow-knitted quality that Albert had only seen before with the preachers on late-night television. "The more often we're right, the happier we make people. Because we help them get what they want . . . before they even know what it is they want. You'd like to help make people happy, wouldn't you, Albert?"

He shrugged nervously. "Yeah . . . I suppose . . ."

"Everybody does, Albert. It's a natural instinct on the part of all sentient creatures—to create and share happiness."

The sincerity that Dierdorf radiated was so intense, Albert almost burst into tears. "But . . . but what would you want me to do?"

"Just like those tests," said Vogel, as the other human nodded in agreement. "Like that day you spent with us. We put some products in front of you, and you pick out the one you like best. Or we show you a little video, the rough cut of a commercial or a new TV show, and you tell us what you think about it. That's all. We're just interested in knowing what you like. Because that's what everybody will like. Or at least ninety-nine point nine percent."

"What if . . . what if I don't like any of the things?"

"No problem. We just tell our clients to take 'em all away, and come back with something better."

Albert's feet pressed uncomfortably against the inside of his shoes. He was very nervous. Everything was so confusing—the flood of words, the way the two humans looked straight into his eyes without blinking, as if their combined gaze could pin his trembling brain to the back of his skull—he felt adrift on a great ocean, swept by dark and dangerous currents. He didn't know what to do right now; that was why he was afraid.

Dierdorf must have been some kind of mind reader; he nodded in perfect understanding, as though Albert had blurted out his inner fears. "You don't have to decide right now. We know that it's a big decision . . . no, a big responsibility. You could become one of the most important people in the world, Albert. That's why we want you to take your time to think about all this."

He nodded in mute gratefulness. For a moment, he'd had the uncanny feeling that everybody in the restaurant, the people at the other tables and all the waiters, had been watching him, wanting to know what his answer would be.

"I . . . I will. I mean . . . I'll think about it."

Dierdorf raised a hand. "That's all we're asking. No, actually, there is something else. Here, give me that back." He reached over and snatched away the check that had still been lying in front of Albert.

He watched the human tear the check in half. He knew it had been too good to be true.

"I want you to be abso-*lute*-ly certain about our interest in acquiring your services." Vogel once again extracted his checkbook from inside his jacket. He flipped it open and scribbled rapidly with the same glittering fountain pen. "There. Try this one on for size." He held the filled-out check across the table.

Without daring to touch it, Albert regarded the blue rectangle of paper. "What . . . what is it?" He knew it was a check; he just wanted to be sure what it was for.

"Well, Albert, let's think of it as payment for an option on your talents. Our company isn't the only one in the business of predicting consumer responses . . . though of course, we like to think we're the best. But we just want to make sure that even if you don't come to work for Precognosis, you won't act as a picker for any of our competitors. Fair enough?"

He wasn't exactly sure what the human meant, but he couldn't resist any longer. Curiosity drove his hand forward, to take the new check from Vogel's hand. He turned it around, so he could read the number written out beneath his own name . . .

He found himself looking up at the restaurant's ceiling, the intricately worked carpet beneath the back of his head. The faces of Dierdorf and Vogel and one of the waiters floated above him. What was he doing on the floor?

"Are you all right?" Dierdorf gripped his forearm and helped him up. The waiter took his other arm. Now there really were people glancing over from the tables nearby.

"I'm . . . I'm fine." Albert nodded slowly. "I must have . . . slipped off the chair. That's all."

A little gap opened inside his memory, covering the second or two from when he had looked at the check Vogel had written, to finding himself flat on the restaurant floor.

And in that gap, he hadn't been in the restaurant at all, but far away. Floating above the dark ocean that had once frightened him. Something had come sailing

53

across the white-laced waves, and he had recognized it as the *karabla,* the sacred boat of the Tenctonese faith. But strangely, the gentle deities of Celine and Andarko hadn't been aboard the small shining craft; instead, it had been the human figure of Santa Claus, laughing deep behind his beard, and opening up the sack slung from his shoulder, reaching in and tossing out handfuls of round golden shapes . . .

That had been all he had seen, in that quick non-moment. But it was enough. Sitting back down, Albert picked up the check that had fluttered to the tablecloth, held it up, and looked at the row of elegant zeroes marching across the upper right corner, even more than there had been on the first one.

"Now remember, that's just an option payment." Dierdorf's voice came from both near and far away. "Your salary and profit shares and stock options would be considerably higher . . ."

He didn't bother to listen. Suddenly, he wasn't afraid anymore. He couldn't wait to take the check home and show it to May.

CHAPTER 5

"YOU TOLD HIM *WHAT?*" Susan turned away from the
kitchen counter, where she had just deposited the
dishes brought in from the dining room table. The
water rushing into the sink sounded an odd counterpoint to the amazed note in her voice.

George felt equally taken aback; he hadn't expected
the look his wife gave him now. In his hands were the
two glasses, his and Susan's, the insides coated with a
film of sour milk; he had returned home as his family
had been finishing supper without him. He hadn't
been hungry; his stomach roiled unhappily from the
ghastly snack bits, little scraps of irradiated lung and
spleen sealed in plastic, that he'd eaten—against his
better judgment—while he'd been at the bar with his
partner Sikes.

"It was simply the best advice I could give him." He
reached past Susan to set the glasses down. "I'm sure
it's a hard situation for Matt to face, but he has to do
it."

"Do what?" Their daughter Emily looked up from

55

the open dishwasher, where she had been carefully placing the knives and forks in their designated bin. "What're you talking about?"

They had completely forgotten about the girl's presence, and that she might be listening to what they were saying. "Emily, honey—" Susan took her by the shoulders and pointed her toward the doorway. "Why don't you go upstairs and do your homework? We'll take care of the dishes."

"I don't have any homework." Emily dug in her heels. "I did it already."

"Then why don't you go up to your room and think about tomorrow's homework?"

George flinched inside, hearing the tone in his wife's voice: seemingly mild and calm, but with the words actually strung along a taut steel wire.

"Oh, all right." Emily knew what that tone meant as well. She lifted and dropped her shoulders dramatically, and headed for the door. There she turned around and studied her parents. "Is this something to do with Uncle Matt?"

His daughter's narrow-eyed gaze seemed to pierce right through George. "Why would you think that, sweethearts?"

"Because—" Emily wrinkled her nose. "You smell like an ashtray."

He raised a hand and sniffed the cuff of his jacket. She was right.

"You always smell like an ashtray after you've been out drinking with Uncle Matt."

"That's quite enough, young lady." Susan pointed sternly toward the stairs beyond the doorway. "Scoot."

George felt subtly chastened, as though his older daughter and his wife had somehow conspired to expose some failure of his. The smell of stale tobacco smoke—which of course meant a bar—there were no other public places left where smoking was allowed—marked him like some Earth-style Biblical curse. He couldn't remember which of the human progenitors it was supposed to have been, Cain or Abel, with the mark of ashes on the brow. No, that's wrong, he told himself. That's the other, some Jewish thing. Maybe; he couldn't be sure right now. The glass of sour milk he'd had at the dining room table, on top of the ones he'd downed while he'd been sitting beside Matt on the wobbling bar stools, had muddled his thought processes.

Of course, it had all seemed like a good idea before. When Matt had called him from the pay phone next to the bar's restrooms, there had been little choice but to go out and have this steer session with his partner.

"Bull," Matt had corrected him when he got there. "It's a bull session. Bulls're bigger'n steers." Matt had already been drinking; his words had started to blur together. "Bulls're for big problems. Like I got."

It had been the same bar they had both been at earlier that day; George had felt trapped in a time loop, something from one of those old *Twilight Zone* episodes that Emily had developed a craze for watching on the cable's Sci-Fi Channel. He had felt the same claustrophobic twinge, the sense of the walls with their faux-neon beer and sour milk signs closing in on him. Out of loyalty to his partner, he had climbed up onto the bar stool beside Matt and ordered a round. Then, as both he and Matt sat hunched over their glasses, he had listened, according to the ancient traditions of Earthly male-bonding ritual, to Matt's problems.

Or the one problem, really. Cathy's pregnancy.

Standing now in the kitchen with his wife, George watched as Susan looked up toward the ceiling. They both could hear Emily's bedroom door opening, then closing. Which meant that they were effectively alone, except for the gurgling and cooing of their other daughter Vessna, still in her expensive, genuine wicker Moses basket out in the dining room. Those baby noises were the only sounds that came to them from the vast, empty reaches of the house.

Susan turned her steeliest glare toward him. The gloves are off, thought George. Whatever that Earth expression was supposed to mean.

"So let me get this straight." Susan folded her arms across her breasts. "Matt told you that Cathy is pregnant."

"Well . . . yes." George nodded. "And it's apparently true. That's what the doctor had told Cathy."

"And then you told Matt . . . that he should leave Cathy."

He could see that they were approaching, as the marriage counselors on the afternoon talks shows would put it, the core issue of their disagreement. He could also feel—weirdly—the bright-lit walls of the kitchen closing in on him, the way the darker ones in the bar had done.

"Of course I told him that." He kept his voice carefully modulated, so that it embodied the spirit of sweet reason. That way, he hoped—and with good cause; it had worked in the past—Susan would be pulled, as though by celestial mechanics, into the same rhetorical orbit, and the spat between them would be avoided. "That was the most rational position to take."

It wasn't working this time; he could see two little simmering sparks right at the centers of Susan's eyes. Or he had seen them for a moment; his wife's eyes had narrowed to slits as she looked at him.

"Would you care to tell me," Susan said icily, "just where you got this bright notion about interfering in Matt and Cathy's lives?"

"Now, I'd hardly call it interfering. Matt asked me for my help; that's why I went to talk with him. What else could I do?"

"And this is your idea of helping? To split the two of them up?"

"There is a certain moral issue involved here." He heard the anger rising in his own voice, and took a deep breath in an attempt to throttle the emotion back down. "Cathy is pregnant; that is the undeniable fact of the matter. The doctor went back over his records and his test procedures, to make sure there was no mistake. So now we all have to reconcile ourselves to the implications of that fact."

"Implications? What implications?" Susan set her hands on her hips. "She's pregnant. Big deal."

"'Big deal?'" He stared at her in amazement. "I can't believe I just heard you say that. It *is* a big deal. For better or worse, Matt and Cathy have had an interspecies sexual relationship—"

"Oh, that's very nicely put. How romantic. I had thought that perhaps the two of them just happened to love each other."

George sighed. This wasn't going to be easy; he felt as if he had wandered into a mine pasture. Or something like that. "Nevertheless, Susan; there is simply no biological way that Cathy could have gotten pregnant by Matt. So the first implication is that she has been having a sexual relationship with someone else."

"People . . . make . . . mistakes." Each of Susan's words was like the rap of a hammer against his forehead. "That may not be biology, but it's also a fact. These things happen."

"Perhaps so. But becoming pregnant didn't just 'happen' for Cathy. She is a Tenctonese female, the same as you. Susan, you're the mother of our three children; you know it's different for us. We may live on Earth now, but something like this will never be as simple for us as it is for humans. It's not a matter of a mistake, or a little indiscretion on Cathy's part. Besides the other sexual partner, whoever the Tenctonese male might have been, there's the *binnaum* that's necessary to complete the fertilization of the ovum—so presumably Cathy must have deliberately made the arrangements for one." George fell silent for a moment, wondering who the *binnaum* could have been. For his and Susan's last pregnancy, the one that had given them their daughter Vessna, the sacred duties had been performed by Albert Einstein, the custodial technician from the police station. Albert, like all *binnaums,* was sometimes a bit slow on the uptake—to put it mildly—but surely he wouldn't have done something like this behind the back of his friend Sikes. That was also impossible.

He reassembled his thoughts, back to the tense discussion between himself and his wife. "And then . . . and then there's the matter of the transfer of the fetus, from Cathy to the biological father." Little more needed to be said, as far as he was concerned. Beyond all else, this set the Tenctonese apart from humans: the male of the species gave birth to its young. Matt, more than most humans, was aware of the whole Tenctonese birth process; he had actually assisted in Vessna's delivery. Male bonding, even between species, didn't get much tighter than that.

Perhaps—George had to admit it, if only to himself —it was one reason he took Matt's side in this matter so immediately. It was a question of loyalty, as much derived from what he had become here on Earth as those things brought from the Tencton of his ancestors.

"Cathy would've had to arrange for that as well," continued George. "Between herself and the father of the child." The sacred vow between a Tectonese woman and her mate, for him to be there when the time of the fetal transfer came round, was more important than even the sacraments of marriage. For a lot of reasons, but also for the sheer practicality of survival: a Tenctonese female couldn't bring her pregnancy to term, the way a human was able to. Without the father to receive the unborn child, the pregnancy would end with the death of the fetus, and nearly always the mother as well. There was no way that Cathy wouldn't have known about that; such matters were at the core of Tenctonese existence.

"Well, of course." Susan certainly knew not just the mechanics of Tenctonese reproduction, but what all these things meant for Cathy and Matt. "Maybe . . . maybe Cathy simply wants to have a child. And this is the only way she could go about it. Matt can't give her one."

"Susan . . . I can't believe you're saying this." The last wooziness from the sour milk was evaporated by his wife's words. He was left feeling slightly stunned. "These are sacred matters. The holy act of procreation . . . the bond between loving partners . . . those things can't be separated. If it was important to Cathy to have a child, then she should've been the one to end her involvement with Matt—before she ever approached a *binnaum* and a Tenctonese male. Don't you see what Cathy's done by betraying Matt's trust in her? The beginning of a new life is now mired in deception and bad faith. What good can possibly come of it?"

Without answering, Susan turned away, picking up a dirty plate and slamming it into the dishwasher so hard that the racks clattered. She whirled back around to face him. "I don't care about any of that!" The sparks of anger in her gaze had burst into full flame. "All I know is that Cathy's my friend—and that it didn't happen the way you make it sound! She just wouldn't do that."

"All right," said George patiently. "Then how did it happen?"

"I don't know . . ." Susan rubbed her brow. For a moment, as she looked away from him, he saw the anger in her eyes turn into pained confusion. "I just know it didn't happen that way, that's all." She went

61

on staring out the window above the sink, not seeing the house's backyard wrapped in night. Her voice softened. "Maybe . . . maybe nothing happened. I don't know . . . maybe it's like that story they tell here . . ."

"What story?"

"You know. The one the Christians tell. Remember, we took that class together, over at the university extension?"

"'The Bible as Literature,'" said George. "'For Newcomers.'" He mainly remembered getting three units for it, toward the general education requirement of his police science degree.

"That's the one. And there's the story . . . about the virgin birth and all . . ."

He sighed. "Susan . . ." A shake of the head. "I hardly think you can claim that Cathy was a virgin, even before she hooked up with Matt."

"Then you tell me what happened!" Susan picked up a damp dish towel from the counter and threw it at him. "But don't tell me that Cathy cheated on Matt! Because I know she didn't!"

George looked down at the dish towel lying across his shoes. From the dining room, he could hear Vessna's wail; the raised voices must have woken her. He glanced up as Susan strode past him and toward the doorway. A moment later, the noise of the crying infant faded as Susan carried her upstairs.

He reached down and picked up the towel, folded it, and hung it on the rail at the end of the counter. Leaning with his hands against the edge of the sink, he looked at his somber reflection in the dark mirror of the window. This little discussion hadn't gone at all well.

That's what I get, George thought gloomily, *for trying to help people.* He should have known better.

All in all, his batting average could stand some improvement. At this point, with the memory of

Susan's angry words having just about scoured the spots off his head, he honestly didn't know whether he had helped his partner Sikes or not.

A night breeze rustled the chain of the swing set in the backyard, the faint sound of metal rendered invisible by the dark. There was the whole business about his son Buck to think about as well; that was another little family discussion that had ended badly. When he'd told Susan what had happened—about his last confrontation with Buck—he'd braced himself for an over-the-top reaction from her. And he'd gotten it, a whole evening of raised voices, his and Susan's combined, like a duet from a bad human grand opera. He would've been happy if it had ended like one of those, with her sticking a knife in him. Instead, it'd been worse: tears, Susan weeping into the pillow on the bed, over what was happening to their family. While he had stood there, feeling—as one of his partner's colorful phrases put it—like ten pounds of primate excrement. After that, silence had set in between the two of them, that had really only ended tonight, with her angry reaction to the advice he'd given Matt.

He supposed that, without Buck's name having even been spoken, it had been the main reason for his wife being so quick to jump all over him. Susan wasn't usually like that. And, in some ways, he couldn't help believing it was something he deserved. Right now, he didn't even know where Buck was. Though he was sure the kid could take care of himself—not really a kid at all, but a young man now—he still felt a twinge of guilt.

He started to turn away from the counter, to head upstairs and make amends with Susan, or at least try to. Then stopped—he had heard something. Or nothing. He glanced over his shoulder toward the window above the sink.

The rattle of the swing set's chain had stopped, as though the night wind had died. Or someone had reached out and stilled the chain's small motion, with a simple touch of the hand.

George unlocked the sliding door that led onto the patio and pulled it open. His other hand rested upon the gun in the shoulder holster inside his jacket; it wouldn't be the first time they'd had prowlers here.

He scanned across the backyard. Nothing, and no one; nothing but the swing and the barbecue and the tamed-jungle landscaping, the leaves of the philodendrons bobbing like big green clown hands. Nothing that wasn't supposed to be there.

Not a good sign, he told himself as he pulled the sliding door shut. Imagining all sorts of things—if he wasn't careful, he'd be the one making an appointment to see the police department's shrink. He rubbed his eyes, feeling them burn and sting beneath the pressure of his thumb and fingertips. Not enough sleep, and bad dreams when he did get any . . .

The kitchen fell into darkness as he flicked off the light switch. He felt so tired now, it took all his remaining strength to pull himself up the steps, toward the light spilling from the bedroom doorway.

The phone rang. Or it had been ringing for a while; she couldn't be sure. Cathy wondered if she had been asleep, or just so far down in her wordless thoughts that the world outside the limits of her head had faded away and become nothing at all.

It must've been sleep, she decided. She sat up on the couch, her gaze slowly taking in the shadowy forms of the unlit apartment. She had been dreaming and she remembered someone calling her name. That same faceless image, silhouetted in light streaming from behind . . .

"Ms. Frankel?"

Someone *was* calling her name; she shook her head to get rid of the last cobwebs.

The voice came again; it was different from the one she had heard in her dreaming. A woman's voice:

"I'm sorry to be calling you so late, but it is kind of urgent. . . ."

A blinking red light by the telephone clued her in. The phone had stopped ringing, and the answering machine's outgoing message had played through without her being aware of it.

"If you could call us back when you have the chance—"

She reached over to the table beside the couch and picked up the phone. "Hold on," said Cathy. "I'm here."

The woman's voice spoke right at her ear, rather than through the answering machine's tinny speaker. "Is this Cathy Frankel?"

"Yes, it is." She hadn't recognized the woman's voice. "Who's this?"

"I'm calling from the Clinic for Exogenetic Studies; I'm the head research assistant for Dr. Anson Quinn."

"Quinn . . ." The name rang a bell. Then she remembered: Quinn had been the doctor in charge of the intensive care unit, when Susan Francisco and her daughter Emily had been lying close to death from the Human Defense League's toxic bacteria attack. "He's not at the hospital any longer?"

"He left about a year ago. He had already been doing some work with the Clinic, and then he came on full time, to take on some of the . . . more important projects here."

Cathy wasn't sure if that was a good thing or not. Quinn was an excellent physician, specializing in Newcomer physiology. He had basically kept Susan and Emily alive long enough for the cure to the infection to be found. There weren't enough doctors like Quinn around. And she had never heard of this clinic.

"Is there something I can do for you and Dr. Quinn?" She glanced at the clock LCD on the answering machine; the black digits read out well past ten P.M. "I mean, what's this about?"

65

"Actually, it's about you, Ms. Frankel. Your gynecologist gave us a call. He knows about our work, and he told us about your pregnancy."

"Really?" She sat up straight on the couch. "I suppose you know that's against medical ethics. There is such a thing as patient confidentiality."

"We're very aware of that." The woman on the other end of the line made an effort to sound apologetic. "Believe me, there would have been no breach of your privacy unless it was absolutely necessary. And in this case it is."

"What're you talking about?"

"I'm not at liberty to discuss it at this time. But Dr. Quinn would like you to come down to the Clinic's offices tomorrow morning. He needs to see you."

The phone conversation was turning weirder, as though it were something left over from her dreaming. "I don't know . . ." Cathy looked around the end table for her Day-Timer book. "I have a pretty tight schedule tomorrow . . ."

"Ms. Frankel—I don't mean to make this sound more mysterious than it already is. But it really is a matter of considerable urgency. For both you and your child. We wouldn't have contacted you otherwise."

"Oh." The tone of the woman's voice, more than her words, settled stonelike against Cathy's hearts. "All right . . ."

After the woman had hung up, Cathy sat looking at the address she had written down. Somewhere near the university; it wouldn't be hard to find.

She slipped the paper back inside the Day-Timer, then stood up from the couch and walked over to the apartment's largest window. She looked down at the cars parked along the street below, clasping her arms tight around herself as she did so. Even with the apartment's thermostat turned up, she felt suddenly cold. And alone.

She realized what she was looking for, down on the street. Matt's car.

It wasn't there.

"Okay," he muttered. "I've got you this time, you sonuvabitch." Sikes fumbled inside his jacket for his gun. The faceless, silhouetted figure had made the big mistake of coming up on him while he was fully armed. In about two seconds, there wouldn't be light just streaming all around the figure, it'd be streaming through a 9-millimeter hole in the middle of its head as well. "Just you wait . . ."

Whoever the mystery image was, it kept on calling his name. "Matt . . . hey, Matt . . ." A tapping sound also came to his ear, like a fingernail against glass. "What're you doing in there, Matt?"

He got his hand around the gun at the same time as he pushed himself up from the car seat; his shoulder brushed against the bottom rim of the steering wheel. The ugly snout of the gun clanked up against the car's passenger side window. Sikes found himself blinking into, not the eerie ghost light of his dreaming, but the thin, harsh light of a Los Angeles morning. On the other side of the window stood Albert Einstein, the police station's janitor, gazing with wide, startled eyes at the weapon confronting him.

"Jesus, Albert . . ." Sikes rolled the window down; he had already tucked the gun back into its shoulder holster. "Scared the piss outta me."

"Skuh-scared you?" Push broom in hand, Albert shook his head. "What about me?"

"Yeah, I suppose. Sorry about that." He pulled himself upright on the car seat, rubbing sleep grit out of his eyes. He ran his tongue over his teeth; they felt furry, and tasted vile from stale alcohol. A reluctant sobriety had overtaken him, nevertheless. He laid his elbow on the window sill and rolled his head back to look at Albert. "I woulda just winged you, though."

"Baloney." The Newcomer janitor still looked resentful and unmollified. "You had that thing pointed at my head."

There had been a time when he would have considered that to be the most expendable part of Albert's anatomy; his opinion had shifted over the last year or so. "Hey, I said I was sorry."

Albert stepped back as Sikes pushed open the door and got out. "What're you doing sleeping in your car? You have a fight with Cathy?"

If anything, Albert was getting too smart. Sikes nodded as he rubbed the cramp in the small of his back. "You could say so."

"That's why guys sleep in cars. It must be a tradition or something here. I mean, on Earth." Albert picked up the trash container he had just dumped into the bin at the corner of the parking lot. "You wanna tell me about it?"

Sikes followed him toward the station's rear entrance. "I don't want to do anything until I've had some coffee."

Albert poured him out a cup from the pot he kept on the hot plate in the store room. The space was the janitor's little kingdom; Sikes sat on the edge of the rickety cot, the heavy porcelain mug between his hands, and glanced up at the store room's walls. "Hey, what happened to all your stuff?" He remembered there being layers of brightly colored posters and calendars on the walls and Scotch-taped to the ends of the metal shelving units.

"Oh . . ." Albert set the push broom in the corner. He pointed to an overflowing cardboard box. "Most of it's in there. The stuff I wanted to keep, anyway."

"Huh? What d'ya mean?"

Albert wouldn't look him in the eye. "Well . . . I'm not going to be here at the station any longer." Albert picked up another box and began filling it, tossing in a dented clock and a little brass-tinged plastic trophy with WORLD'S GREATEST JANITOR inscribed on its base. "I'm leaving."

"Did Grazer can you?" The coffee turned to battery acid on Sikes's tongue. "That does it. I'm gonna kick his ass—"

"No, no, I haven't even gone in and talked to Captain Grazer about it yet. I mean . . . I haven't told him that I'm quitting."

"Quitting?" Sikes stared at Albert in amazement. "Quitting?"

Albert nodded, looking slightly embarrassed. "Yeah. May and I talked it over last night. I got another job."

"Doing what?"

"I'm going to be a picker."

"Aww, Christ," groaned Sikes. "You can't make any money picking fruit. That kinda work's the pits—literally. I did it one summer when I was a kid, up near Modèsto, and it just about broke my back."

"No, it's not like that. It's something else altogether." Excitement crept into Albert's voice. "Listen . . ."

He listened, and heard all about it. None of it sounded believable, until Albert showed him the bank deposit slip for the check that the Precognosis people had given him. And then a lightbulb had flicked on inside Sikes's head, and he remembered a *Newsweek* article he had read maybe a month ago—he had been waiting for a haircut—and it had been all about this new breed of market researchers. One of the companies' names had stuck in the back of his mind; he remembered thinking that it sounded like a skin disease—the heartbreak of Precognosis.

He went on thinking about it, sipping another cup of coffee, after Albert had gone to Captain Grazer's office to hand in his official resignation form. Glancing up at the store room's walls, now stripped of their accretion of Albert's stuff, made him feel oddly hollow and sad. That emotion, or lack of it, was layered on top of how he'd already felt from the whole business between him and Cathy. Everything he'd gotten used to seemed to be coming to an end.

Place isn't gonna be the same without ol' Albert around. He hunched over the coffee, rolling the cup back and forth between his hands. And right out of the blue—a couple of months ago, the whole world had seemed basically locked down tight. If anybody had told him back then that he and Cathy would wind up splitting, he wouldn't have been able to do anything except laugh. It would've been too ridiculous to even contemplate. He'd been down the turnpike enough times to know the real thing when it came along. Only from the looks of things, this pregnancy and all, he hadn't. Everything his partner George had told him at the bar was true; he had to admit it.

The coffee had gone too cold to drink. He leaned forward and poured it out into the sink with the mops, then set the empty cup in the nearest of Albert's cardboard boxes. His eyes ached as he rubbed them.

Really gotta start getting some more sleep. Maybe now that enough shit had descended upon him, the bad dreams would stop. The Irish portion of his blood had already known that they would turn out to be prophetic. Something horrible coming his way, calling his name . . . figure it out. You didn't need to be a genius like Albert's namesake to work that one out.

One thing still worried him, enough to make his palms sweat. You're spooking yourself, he scolded, but he couldn't get the dismal thought to leave his head.

The worst possible thing had already happened, with him and Cathy. The business with Albert leaving the police station was small potatoes compared to that. The worst had happened . . . and he had still dreamed, last night in his car, about the faceless image with the light streaming from behind, and the voice calling his name . . .

Only it had been louder and closer this last time. So close, that in his dreaming he had almost been able to stretch out his hand and touch the image's shadowed face.

Sikes shook his head, bracing his spine against the chill that tightened across his shoulders. If the dreams kept coming . . . then maybe the worst hadn't happened yet.

He didn't even want to think about that.

CHAPTER 6

"IT'S REALLY . . . REALLY . . ."

Buck Francisco sat on the edge of the sagging bed, watching his sister Emily struggle to find the perfect word. Dusty sunlight slid beneath the tattered edge of the pull-down curtain, revealing where the floor's linoleum had been scuffed through over the years, to islands of dingy black.

"Really glotchy."

He smiled as he leaned back on his hands. "Is that worse than grunge?"

"Oh, way beyond grunge." Emily spoke almost admiringly. She tilted her head to examine the map of brown-edged stains on the ceiling. "That's *sooo* dead. Glotch is . . . glotch is like this."

"Welcome to Glotch Manor, then."

"Hey, there's fur in this sink!"

"Don't blame me. It came that way."

Emily dragged the single wobbly chair over from the room's kitchenette corner. She sat down with her hands in her lap, as though she had been invited to tea. "Well . . . it's kind of interesting. I guess." Her gaze moved around the room's confines once more. "And it is all yours."

"It's all mine. As long as I pay the rent every week." Buck laid his shoulders on the pillow propped against the wall. The room was so small that he could stretch out his hand and touch the stitched leather seat of the motorcycle that took up most of the floor space. At night, the glow of the streetlamps glinted blue off the machine's hand-polished chrome, like liquid electric sparks seeping under his eyelids as he slept. "Same with this thing, Em. Gotta make the payments." He flicked a dust speck off the ridged throttle grip.

"That's where all your money goes, huh?" His kid sister was no fool.

Actually, he knew money wasn't going to be a problem. Emily could honestly go back to their parents and report—if she wanted to risk confessing that she had skipped school to come here and see her brother—that he wasn't starving to death. He'd gotten a warehouse job the day after he'd had his final argument with his father and had stomped out of the house. Newcomers were preferred for that kind of work; he could wrestle around crates twice as heavy, for twice as long, as the average tert. As long as he watched himself, the job would pay just enough for this shabby room . . . and the distinctly non-shabby bike.

Maybe a little shady, though. He'd gotten a good deal on the machine from one of the crazed internal-combustion freaks that infested the building. The stairwells were oil-spotted and shiny-slick from the frames and engines and whole motorcycles being pushed in and out of the rooms all day and all night. Behind every numbered door could be heard the clinking metal sounds of hand tools and, every once in a while, the coughing rasp of a freshly-tuned engine cranking gray exhaust out a window. Buck's machine had been pried loose from a telephone pole, its first owner doing a long stretch in the head injuries unit at the hospital, straightened out, and refitted with even more murderous parts. The frame still shuddered when the speedometer pegged out at a hundred, but one quarter-inch of the throttle past that point and the whole world became glassy smooth, as though time itself had stopped. Nothing but the wind tearing at his face as he laid his chest close to the black teardrop tank . . .

"You're going to kill yourself on that thing," pronounced his sister. She regarded him with disapproval. "I know you are."

"Yeah, I expect you're right about that." Buck watched his own hand smooth along the chrome of the handlebars. "Doesn't matter."

"How come?"

He had to think about that; the words had slipped right out of his mouth. "I don't know," he said finally, and shrugged. "It's different for you, Em. You're smarter than I am—you know how to fit in here."

"Give me a break." Emily rolled her eyes.

"No, it's true." He had started to figure things out. "Maybe it's because you're younger. You don't really remember any place besides Earth—"

"I do, too! I remember lots."

"If you say so." Buck turned his gaze away from his sister toward the window and its bleak view of the decaying buildings that surrounded this one. "Maybe . . . maybe it's just because you're a tough cookie. Inside, I mean. You didn't give up; you're still fighting for what you think this world owes you. That's what makes you different from me."

"Aw, Buck . . . come on. Don't talk like that." She suddenly looked close to tears. "You didn't give up."

His own smile felt sad on his face. "Yeah, I did. And you know why? Because I don't care anymore—that's a big difference right there. I stopped caring a long time ago, about whether there's a place for me in this world. It's their world, not mine."

"That's stupid." Emily's expression was one of disgust. "Just 'cause you had a fight with Dad . . . that doesn't mean you gotta go kill yourself over it. You had lots of fights with him before."

He didn't say anything. Not that there wasn't more to say—the words were right there on his tongue—but because he didn't want to make things worse for her. Why should his little sister have the same bad ideas rolling around beneath the spots on her head? What good would that do? Maybe she really was smarter and tougher than he was; smart enough to *not* know something, to *not* see this world the way he did. Emily had human friends, the same as he'd once had, before he'd realized the truth.

That was what he didn't want to tell her. That the terts were nobody's friends, except to their own kind. In their single, stingy hearts they believed this was their world, and they wanted to keep it that way. They didn't need alien breeds cluttering up the place, grabbing even the littlest pieces of it for themselves. The terts had had a hard enough time getting along with each other, until the Day of Descent had given them somebody new to kick around.

Maybe I should warn her, thought Buck. Prepare her for what she's going to find out someday, no matter what. He wondered if he had already been trying to do that, stick his grim thoughts inside her skull, put the dark lenses with which he saw this world in front of her eyes. She wasn't really such a tough little cookie. Nobody was that tough, to be the same afterwards as she was before she had both her hearts broken. That was the problem with these goddamn humans—they wanted to kill you, but first they wanted to kill your dreams.

And humans like his father's partner Sikes—Emily's would-be Uncle Matt—they were the worst of all because they gave you those dreams and fed them. By acting all friendly to the Newcomers, like there would ever be a way that the differences between one species and another could be overcome. More than friendly, even. There had been a time when he'd been able to think about Sikes being together with Cathy, without feeling nauseous about the whole idea. Now his anger was like a little red coal in the pit of his stomach, that the slightest whisper could fan into white heat.

His sister was watching him with her great big eyes, so he couldn't say anything at all. *You coward,* he thought. She would find out soon enough, the same way he had. What was the point in making that day come along any faster than necessary?

"Hey—" Buck glanced at his watch, then held up his forearm to show the dial to Emily. "I gotta get ready to go to work. I got the swing shift today."

She nodded as she gathered up her backpack from the floor. "So . . . anything you want me to tell 'em?"

"Naw." He knew she meant their parents. "Well . . . maybe tell Mom that I'm doing all right. Okay?"

"Sure." Emily glanced at the motorcycle's sleek and ominous shape, then at him. "And you be careful."

He knew she would be insulted if he told her the same. Or if he walked her out to the corner RTD stop and waited with her for the bus to come. But he watched discreetly from the window of his room, until she was safely aboard and rolling back toward a cleaner part of the city.

Yeah, she's tough. Buck had to smile, thinking about his sister's one-girl expedition all this way just to check up on him. If anyone was going to survive and dig out a place to stay in this hard, ungenerous world, it would be Emily.

He stopped smiling when he thought again about what her chances—what anyone's chances—would be.

Buck took his workshirt from the nail in the wall and pulled it on. The warehouse was walking distance from here, but he'd decided already that he was going to bump the motorcycle down the building's stairs and climb onto it. Maybe a quick blast of pure acceleration would drive his grim mood to the back of his head where he could ignore it and all the attached bad thoughts for a little while longer.

They did everything to her.

She folded her hands across her abdomen, as though to protect the new life forming inside there, and let the medical technicians draw her out of the magnetic resonance imaging device. *Just like being born,* thought Cathy with grim humor. Lying on her back, she blinked at the overhead fluorescent lights. You're in a little tiny place and the next thing you know, you're surrounded by doctors.

"Ms. Frankel?" A nurse, human and young and pretty, smiled down at her. "You can get dressed now."

Cathy sat up, legs dangling over the edge of the MRI platform. She pulled the thin hospital gown closer around herself. "Can I go home?" She felt exhausted from the battery of tests, much more than her own doctor had ever put her through. Most of the procedures had been familiar to her, a few had required hugely expensive-looking equipment that she had never seen before.

The nurse apologized with another smile and a shake of her head. "Doctor Quinn will want to talk to you." She took Cathy's elbow and helped her down. "It won't be long."

A half hour later, she sat in the same mahogany-panelled and book-lined office to which she had first come when she had kept the appointment these people had been so insistent about. On the desk before her was both a plastic-resin cast of a human skull and a multi-colored working model of the Tenctonese dual-cardiac system. Quinn seemed to be covering all the bases at this clinic. Cathy glanced over her shoulder as she heard the door behind her open.

"Well, it's good to see you again." With a thick sheaf of manila file folders in one hand, Doctor Quinn stepped toward the desk. "It's been a little while, hasn't it?" He sat down and spread the folders across the desktop. "Except, of course, you weren't the patient then."

"Oh?" Cathy raised an eyebrow. "And am I your patient now?"

Quinn leaned back in his chair and made a cage of his fingertips pressed together. "It would be best if you thought of yourself that way."

"Thank you, but I already have a doctor."

"True, and he quite properly notified us of your, shall we say, condition." Quinn leaned forward again. "Tell me, Cathy, how do you feel right now?"

"Poked and prodded." She sighed. "Tired and bored. And quite frankly, I'm ready to go home unless someone starts telling me what the hell's going on here."

"Fair enough." The doctor scanned the contents of a couple file folders that he had opened on the desktop. "Our tests confirm what your own doctor told you. You are, in fact, pregnant."

"Whatever." Once more, she felt the mental dislocation that came with the single word. It seemed as if she had stepped into a strange land where impossible things could be true, where the knowledge of what she sensed inside herself had no connection with what had happened in the world outside. "Everybody keeps telling me that, so I guess it must be the case." She reached down for her purse beside the chair. "Can I go now?"

"Please, Cathy—" Quinn held up a restraining hand. "I'm afraid the situation is a little more complicated than that."

She started to laugh, to say something along the

lines of the situation being sufficiently complicated already, when a fingertip of ice touched her hearts. Any variation on the word complications was as much an emotional trigger as the word pregnant. "The baby. Is . . . is it all right?"

Quinn nodded. "The fetus is alive and appears to be at a perfectly normal state of development. Your child isn't the problem, Cathy. You are."

"What do you mean?"

"Your pregnancy is considerably different from that, um, normally seen in a Tenctonese female." He turned around one of the open file folders; with the tip of a pen, he began pointing out details in a blurry MRI scan. "It's all at an early stage, but the indications are that the process is well under way and will continue. What you can see here, Cathy, is that you've already begun to develop a human-like womb, as well as the associated physiological elements. The necessary hormones are being produced; even the connective tissues capable of bearing the increasing weight of the uterus and the enclosed fetus have started to form."

She had seen MRI scans before; it took only a moment for her to accept the notion that what she was being shown was a map of the world contained inside herself—a territory that now held two lives rather than just one. She lifted her gaze to meet that of the doctor on the other side of the desk. "So what exactly does this mean?"

"It means . . ." Quinn tilted his head and drew a breath through his teeth. "It means, Cathy, that the chances are very good of this child coming to term entirely inside you. There will be no need to transfer the fetus to its father, as is normally the case in Tenctonese pregnancies. You will have the distinction of being the first Tenctonese female to actually give birth."

"Oh." Dazed, she sat back in her chair. Inside her shock-numbed brain, she could hear part of her mind idly trying to remember the name of the human author who had advised believing several impossible things before breakfast. The name Lewis Carroll came to her after a moment. Was that from *Alice in Wonderland?* It was what she felt like now. This strange world she had entered seemed to contain one amazing thing after another. "This is . . . something new."

"Indeed." Quinn mused over the MRI scan for a few moments. "It's absolutely unprecedented, Cathy. Though not entirely unanticipated." He opened another folder. "There is more you should know, however. It's part of the reason we had you come in here to the clinic, and we wanted to run so many tests on you. The amniocentesis we performed appears to confirm our initial suspicions. Your child is not Tenctonese. Or at least not completely."

"I don't understand . . ."

"The genetic analysis of the fetus indicates a combination of both Tenctonese and human DNA. The child you're carrying is a hybrid of our two species." Quinn looked up from the folder. "Am I making myself clear? In other words, the child's father is human."

She brought her hand to her mouth, as though she could touch the breath that had suddenly stilled inside her. And then, with equal suddenness, she burst into tears.

"I know it's frightening, Cathy—" Doctor Quinn had reached across the desk and taken her other hand, trying to comfort her. "But we've prepared for this here. You'll get the finest care possible. Everything will be fine—"

Blindly, she shook her head. "No . . . you don't understand—" How could she tell him? Joy had broken free inside her hearts, as though the sun in that strange land had finally risen over the horizon, flooding everything she saw with golden light. "I'm not scared at all."

She pulled her hand free from the doctor's grasp and stood up.

"I have to go—" Wiping the tears from her face, Cathy smiled down at the doctor's wondering expression. "I have to tell Matt!"

He followed the nurse down the corridors of the clinic.

"Look, what's all this about?" Sikes was having a little trouble keeping up with her. He was still out of breath from having sprinted from the car he'd left outside at the curb. The call from the station had made it sound as though some big emergency were going on here, but so far he'd found nothing but calm quiet and the usual faint disinfectant smell of a medical facility. "What's the big deal?"

The nurse smiled over her shoulder at him without breaking stride. "You'll see."

He did see. The nurse stopped at the end of the corridor, pushed open a door and said, "Doctor Quinn's been waiting for you." As soon as Sikes stepped into the office, he saw the white-coated doctor sitting behind the desk. Two chairs in front, one of them empty . . .

Cathy sat in the other one. "Hello, Matt." She smiled up at him.

The door closed behind him. "Okay—" He stood where he was, keeping a tight lid on his temper. If there was one thing he hated, it was being set up. "Whose bright idea was this?"

"It was mine, Mr. Sikes." The doctor folded his hands together on the desktop. "Cathy wanted to go home and tell you, but I thought it would be best for everyone if you came here. There's a lot that all of us need to talk about. Please—have a seat." Quinn gestured toward the empty chair.

"No, that's where you're wrong." Sikes reached back and laid his hand on the doorknob. "I'm already hip to Cathy being knocked up. All right? So if that's all you brought me in to hear about, let's just consider it old news. I'm outta here."

"Mr. Sikes." The doctor's voice turned more commanding. "There's news you haven't heard yet. And it's nothing small, either. So you really should have a seat."

The way the doctor spoke stopped Sikes from pulling open the door. He sat down, looking away from Cathy but aware that she was watching him. And smiling.

Quinn opened one of the folders on the desktop. "Here's the situation . . ."

That was when the doctor laid it all on him. And he was glad he was sitting down.

"Isn't it wonderful, Matt?" Cathy reached over and laid her hand on his arm. "It's a miracle."

"Yeah . . . I guess it is . . ." He still felt stunned, the doctor's words repeating on a tape loop inside his head. He had already accepted Cathy's pregnancy, even her infidelity to him. Shit happened. Cops saw a lot of worse things. But now he had to start all over. He had to rethink everything, working in this new factor—that he was the father of the unborn child. He slowly shook his head. "Jeez . . ."

Quinn spread out more of the file folders' contents, the computer printouts spilling off the edge of the desk. "There really is no doubt about this, Mr. Sikes. If you'd care to take a look at the DNA trace analysis—"

"No, that's okay." He held out a hand to ward off the arcane-looking charts and graphs. The scientific stuff inspired a superstitious dread in him. Cathy understood that kind of stuff; he didn't. "I figure you know what you're talking about."

From where she sat beside him, Cathy squeezed his arm tighter. He couldn't look at her, meet her gaze, but for reasons different than before. Everything else he had to rethink was falling in a domino line. A hollow feeling, that he recognized from so many times before, opened inside him. It always came with the realization that he had been a complete jerk, breaking the hearts of the woman he loved, and who loved him. *Because if I'm the father,* he thought, *then she . . .*

"It's okay," Cathy spoke softly. Just as if she could read his thoughts. She leaned toward him, her shoulder close to his.

"Well, I'm sure the two of you have a lot to talk about." Quinn started shuffling his charts and graphs together, stuffing them back into the file folders. "In fact, there's still a lot we all need to talk about."

Sikes nodded. "Yeah, you're right about that. Like . . . how is this all possible? I mean, I'll accept that it's true and stuff, but . . ." He glanced over at Cathy, then back to the doctor. "I thought that this pregnancy wasn't supposed to be in the cards for human and Newcomer couples. 'Cause of us being like, uh, different species and all."

"That's a good question, Mr. Sikes." The doctor laid his hands on top of the stack of folders. "And it's not one to which we have a complete answer yet. But the possibility of a human-Tenctonese hybrid is something that we've already been investigating here for some time now. To be honest, this is really more of a research facility than a clinical one. I can't go into all the details right now; let's just say that my own studies had begun to indicate certain . . . unsuspected potentialities in a human-Tenctonese relationship such as yours and Cathy's. I had notified other doctors— specialists in Tenctonese physiology—and asked them to be on the lookout for just such a pregnancy." He gave a brief nod toward Cathy. "That's how your condition was referred to me."

"I guess it's a good thing somebody was ready for all this." Sikes took Cathy's hand and held it tight. "Look, maybe we can talk about all the rest of it later.

I think maybe it's been a long day for everybody. And . . . there's some people we gotta talk to. To tell them about it."

Quinn's expression grew somber. "I'm afraid it's not that simple. This is a situation that calls for a great deal of secrecy. As a matter of fact, the necessary security protocol has already been established with the Bureau of Newcomer Affairs."

"Huh?" Sikes gazed blankly at him. "What're you talking about?"

The doctor shook his head. "I wouldn't have thought I'd need to remind you, of all people, about certain less-enlightened elements in our society. Not after what we all went through—not that long ago—with the Purists and the Human Defense League."

"Oh." He sank back in his chair. He had forgotten about the world outside this office.

"I'm afraid," continued Quinn, "that this pregnancy has enormous political implications attached to it. The Purists may have suffered some setbacks in their plans, but they haven't gone away. If anything, they're more active now. Nothing like a human-Tenctonese hybrid has ever occurred before, so we can't be sure of how the different Purist organizations and front groups will react to the notion of interbreeding between the two species. But judging from their past record, I think it's safe to assume that they're not going to be happy. And a few of them will undoubtedly try to do something about it."

Sikes tightened his grip on Cathy's hand. He knew that Quinn was right; there were some mean sonsabitches wandering around in the dark. Starting now, his every thought would focus on keeping them from getting close to Cathy and the child growing inside her.

"Okay." He nodded. "I'm sure as hell not going to argue with you about this. But there is somebody I specifically want brought in on this. Not just because he's my friend, but because he knows how to deal with Purists. And that's George Francisco."

The name brought a thin smile to Quinn's face. "There won't be any problem with that. He's at the top of a very short list for someone to coordinate the security arrangements. I'll make it official with the Bureau."

"Doctor—" The office door had opened, with the clinic's nurse looking in. "You're needed out here right away."

Quinn left the two of them in the office. A few moments of silence ticked away before Sikes could speak. "I, uh . . . really owe you an apology." As if that were all.

"About what?"

"Come on, sweetheart, I feel bad enough already. I'm talking about what I said before. When you . . . first told me, and all. I really screwed that one up."

Cathy leaned across the arms of the chairs and kissed him on the side of his face. "Hey . . ." Her voice was soft at his ear. "You know . . . we wouldn't be here at all—in a doctor's office, talking about me being pregnant—if I didn't love you."

He had to suppose that was true. *Schmuck,* he told himself, *she's letting you off the hook.* Cathy must have her reasons, though at the moment he couldn't imagine what they were; he felt both blessed and bemused, a recipient of unmerited grace.

The office door flew open, interrupting Sikes's meditations. Doctor Quinn rushed into the room; he grabbed Cathy's other arm, nearly lifting her out of the chair.

"You'll have to leave now." The words tumbled from the doctor's mouth. His face had turned pale, expression distraught. "Immediately."

"What's wrong?" Sikes stood and helped Cathy up. He watched as the doctor went behind the desk and hurriedly gathered up the file folders.

"Nothing—there's nothing wrong." Quinn's agitation belied his words. "But please, just go."

Sikes's thoughts were fixed so hard upon Cathy and the baby that the doctor's strange behavior seemed no more than a distraction, like a bird fluttering at a closed window. He let Quinn push him and Cathy down the corridor toward the clinic's front door.

"What should I do now, doctor?" Just outside, Cathy looked back over the arm that Sikes had around her shoulders. "Do I need to make an appointment or something?"

"Everything will be taken care of." Quinn's face was just visible behind the door as it closed. "You'll be contacted."

Sikes led Cathy toward his car across the street. "I wonder what the hell that was all about." He saw Cathy's car parked farther down the block. He'd have to make arrangements to pick it up; right now, he wanted her to be with him. "He knows his stuff and everything, but he's kind of a weird guy. Ya know?" He unlocked the passenger side door and pulled it open for her.

A worried expression crossed Cathy's face as she adjusted her seat belt. "Maybe there really is something wrong." She touched his arm as he slid in behind the steering wheel. "Maybe you'd better go back and—"

He didn't hear what else she said. Her words were swallowed up in a deafening roar, the shockwave of an explosion hitting them like a massive hammer, hard enough to rock the car sideways on its suspension.

Sikes shielded her with his body, a rush of flame heat rolling over his back. With one forearm he gathered Cathy tight to his chest. He could just hear her gasp of shock as he looked back over his shoulder toward the clinic.

Or where the clinic had been.

As the first blackened fragments began to rain down upon the car, a tower of fire, churning with coils of smoke, rose into the sky. Shards of broken glass, scattered across the street, glinted like jag-edged sparks.

In the few seconds before the alarm sirens began wailing, he held Cathy even tighter in his arms, trying to protect her from all the darkening world's harm.

CHAPTER 7

HE ROLLED ON the throttle and felt the engine beneath him respond. The pure, unmediated force of machinery shimmered up his spine. That, and the sharp wind whipping into his squinting eyes, blurred his vision for a moment as he leaned forward over the motorcycle's tank.

On the freeway heading east, toward the obscured hills of the San Fernando Valley, a narrow gap appeared between an eighteen-wheeler and a school bus in the next lane. Buck Francisco shot for the opening, the bike's front wheel jittering on the lane divider bumps. For a moment, the truck's axle churned at his elbow, a row of kids' faces gawked and grinned from the bus's windows above him—then he was through, into a pocket of relatively clearer traffic. He struck the middle of the lane and maxed the throttle, past the motorcycle's built-in shiver and then into pure smooth sailing, miles and miles of faceless asphalt and concrete and steel in front of him. The gentle, high-speed curves of infinite freedom beckoned him onward.

Buck let everything else fall behind him, like the dust of the warehouse stripped away by velocity. When his shift ended—when the whistle blew, as the old-timer terts said, though there was never any actual whistle to hear—he rarely headed off to the nearest watering-hole with the rest of the Newcomers he worked with, to knock back rounds of cheap sour milk while the humans were getting plowed at their own bar farther down the street. The bike was a better intoxicant, one more to his liking. All that he wanted —just to climb onto the machine, its mingled smells of gasoline and oil and neoprene cables rising into his nostrils like a spread of ripe, raw organ meats. And when he hit the starter and the engine came to life, its first tremor coming up through his hands clutching the ridged grips . . . that was when he could turn his head just a fraction of an inch and see the thin trace of a smile on his own face, his reflection shimmering in the small round mirrors at either side.

Right now, more luck came his way, the only kind he valued when he was on the bike: a mini-van full of commuters, terts and Tenctonese jammed in shoulder to shoulder, changed lanes and moved over toward the exit ramp coming up on the right. The business suits, with their monogrammed briefcases and laptop computers, were heading home to their boring ranch-style houses in another one of the boring subdivisions that kept crawling fungus-like across the scraped-raw desert. Much farther and these poor bastards would be trying to get into their downtown L.A. offices every morning, all the way from Las Vegas.

That wasn't Buck's problem. Enough traffic, vans, and station wagons, had peeled off the freeway that it suddenly seemed as if he had the whole road to himself. He didn't have to see anybody around him, human or Tenctonese. And that was the way he liked it.

He leaned closer to the bike's tank, his hands on the grips now level with his ear canals. His eyes watered with the sting of the wind in his face. He rolled on another quarter-inch of throttle, the lanes' dividers blurring into white threads beneath him.

He didn't have to see anyone, think of anyone. Out here, he could just go. Other people might have their problems, but for this brief, shining, eternal moment, he didn't have to bother with any of them. He could just forget . . .

The mountains, the borders of the world, silently watched his knife-cut progress across the empty landscape.

The state, in its cruel wisdom, brought prisoners over from the men's honor farm, to clip the hedges and edge the billiard-table lawns and generally buff up the grounds of the women's facility. *Stupid friggin' losers,* thought Noah Ramsey as the electronically-controlled gate rattled open and he stepped through. With the knot of his necktie tight against his throat and the lawyer-type attaché in his hand, he walked toward the glass booth, straight into the sullen glare of the uniformed guard.

"Special visit, under provisions of the Los Angeles Superior Court, District Ninety-Seven." Noah slid the envelope with the appropriate paperwork through the scuffed chrome trough beneath the central window. He had gone through this ritual dozens of times— Christ, maybe a couple hundred times by now—and still the head guard, always the same one, had to examine every official scrap of paper as though it were the first time. You'd think they'd have learned by now. Strings had been pulled, from way up on high, and there was nothing they could do about it. They had to let him in.

Bored with the examination of the documents, he looked out across the facility's manicured grounds. A squad of prisoners—all humans, he noted—were perfunctorily pruning one of the trees set a safe distance from the fence topped with razor wire. He supposed it was a good idea, cool in its way, for these guys to get to come over to the women's slammer. Even if they didn't catch sight of any, they could still catch a whiff of what they were being deprived of while they were locked up so they'd be ready when they got dumped back out on the street.

Ready for war, thought Noah grimly. The more pissed-off humans there were, tired of being jerked around for fighting against the parasites in their midst, the better. Every increment of anger was like taking the fire underneath a seething pot up another notch. Soon enough, it would boil over.

"Yeah, all right—these look okay." The guard folded the papers with the judge's signature inscribed, stuffed them back into the envelope, and shoved them out to Noah.

"Of course." He flashed the guard his best nonchalant smile. "Why wouldn't they?"

The guard had already picked up the phone to ring up the prison's visitor reception area. His gaze lifted to Noah's face; the eyes narrowed and the expression hardened.

"Listen, punk." The guard spoke softly, one hand covering the phone's mouthpiece. "You aren't fooling anybody here. Believe me, whatever you and your jerk-off Purist buddies are planning, it's not gonna happen."

Noah looked straight back into the guard's eyes. A human like him—it was a shame to see a member of one's own species, made of flesh and blood and guts just like his, who had sold out and gone over to the other side. A tool of the parasites. The guard was easily up into his late thirties, close to twice Noah's age, and his head was obviously stuffed with lies and Tenctonese propaganda. All that crap about peace and brotherhood between the two species. Yeah, right. There had been a time, when he'd first joined the Human Defense League, when he would have flared up and started arguing with the guy, trying to use

91

words like sledgehammers to pound some sense into this moron's skull.

That's what they want you to do, thought Noah as he kept his face a carefully controlled mask. Make a scene so they'd have an excuse to throw his ass out of here and curtail his visiting privileges—they'd love that.

"I don't know what you're talking about," said Noah evenly. "There's nothing we're doing that isn't perfectly legal."

The guard's eyes narrowed into little slits. Radiating suspicion, he studied Noah for a few seconds longer, then turned away. "Guess who's here again," he spoke into the phone. "Yeah, that's right . . ."

Noah didn't mind lying to a poor, deluded creature such as this; such things were necessary, if the human species was to rid itself of the parasites. Everything was justified for the Purist cause. Being lied to would be the least that could happen to this fool. If people— real people, human beings and not parasites—didn't wake up when the time came, then he would have no problem with putting a gun to their heads. It wouldn't be anything personal with this prison guard; he didn't even know the man. But there were others . . . like that jerk cop back in L.A. Noah could feel a spark of brooding anger next to his heart as he thought about the man. Always acting so buddy-buddy, like he'd been some kind of true friend. Like it was even possible to be friends with somebody who slept with a slag woman. The spark flared hotter for a moment. Now there was somebody it would be a real pleasure to put a bullet in between the eyes.

The guard's voice brought him back from that pleasant reverie. "Go ahead." The steel-barred door buzzed and rattled open. "You know the way."

Lockups always smelled the same, no matter where they were or who they held. The odor of mop buckets filled with disinfectant solution permeated the corridors, the cinder-block walls painted institutional green and beige. Noah walked toward the visiting area, the fluorescent panels buzzing overhead. He had memories of being in a place just like this—as an inmate, not a visitor—from the days before he'd wised up and joined the HDL. Back then, he'd just been into getting loaded and making trouble. Now he had a purpose in life.

She was waiting for him, in one of the private conference rooms; that was something else the court orders stipulated, along with a monthly security check to make sure that the cops weren't bugging the tiny space for the benefit of their parasite bosses. A bored-looking female guard unlocked the door and then closed it after him as he stepped through.

"Good afternoon, Noah." Darlene Bryant's words were cool and formal, as they were every time he came to see her. She rested her folded hands on top of the small wooden table. Her thin smile emerged. "How are you?"

She always asked that. "I'm . . . I'm fine." And he was always unnerved by the piercing gaze of her steel gray eyes. He drew back the battered wooden chair opposite her and quickly sat down. He swung the attaché case onto the table and snapped it open.

Without looking up from the papers through which he sorted, he knew that she was still watching him with that same, semi-amused smile. He drew out a thin sheaf of computer printouts and handed them to her.

"Hmm . . ." Bryant nodded slowly as she looked over the neat columns of figures. "Yes; yes, indeed . . ." Her blunt fingernail moved down one of the rows.

Once, that fingernail had been something of a work of art, grown long and then buffed and polished to match the glossy, pearl-like sheen of the others on her hands. Noah had seen the photos, both at the HDL headquarters and in the magazines, of Darlene Bryant in her glamour days. Even with her beauty pageant days long past her, she had still radiated an aura of lacquered perfection. She still retained that icy, regal bearing, though her prison stay had ended her regime of weekly manicures and all the other expensive personal maintenance in which she had indulged. Now, the fingernails and the once-golden hair were cut short; gray the color of her eyes streaked back from her temples. Life in the slams, eased however much by the legal and financial resources of the HDL, had hardened the Purists' leader, stripped away the fluff and designer gowns and ladylike genteelisms. In the standard prison-issue overalls, she looked to Noah like a machine, as cold and efficient as the loaded automatic he kept under his own pillow. The slag-loving authorities didn't know what they had created, what they had called into being, by putting her in a place like this.

"These revenue figures from the southwest divisions seem a little low." Bryant asked for Noah's pen and he handed it to her; she quickly circled some of the numbers on the printouts and scribbled a note in the margin. She favored him with a slightly larger smile as she folded the printouts back into a tidy stack. "I'm afraid not everybody in our organization works as hard as you do, Noah."

The smile and the words and the meaning they held, eased the tension along his spine, as though the handle of a clamp vise had been loosened a quarter-turn. He knew that she had ways to get her approval passed along to her lieutenants in the HDL; since she had taken him under her wing, his rise through the ranks had been greased to the max. Just being her chief courier to the outside world—that was an honor that had been bestowed upon him like a blessing.

He'd have to be ready for the next step. It wouldn't be enough to have mastered the intricacies of the accounting and database systems with which the organization kept track of its worldwide net of supporters. More would be asked of him—much more.

And he'd be ready. He glanced away from the imprisoned leader of the Human Defense League, and down to his own hand resting on the table. He squeezed it into a fist, a weapon hard and crushing as stone.

"Everything else looks to be in order." Bryant finished glancing over the contents of a set of manila envelopes Noah had given her. "Tell McMann and Petrowski that I'd like to have their quarterly reports the next time you come out here."

"Okay . . . I mean, all right; I'll tell them." A little bit of his initial nervousness had ebbed, as it always did when he made his visits. He stuffed the envelopes and printouts back into the attaché case and closed the lid. He knew what she was going to ask about next.

"Tell me—" Bryant leaned across the table, bringing her cool gaze closer to him. "How's the . . . development project going?"

Those words were coded, a subterfuge. Even with the security checks on this little room, some things were too important to risk talking about openly. And too dangerous.

He nodded slowly. "All our, uh, monitoring systems indicate that things are proceeding normally. Or at least without interruption. The project appears to be at the stage that the, uh, interested parties expected it to be at this time. Our sources predict that the project's termination date will be on schedule as well."

It was the same report he had given her a week ago. And it met with the same reaction: a single nod from her, with that same thin smile and her eyes almost closed, as if nothing could have pleased her more.

Those eyes opened again, fixing him with their steady gaze. "And our initial project? How has the follow-up on that been?"

This time, he couldn't keep from meeting Bryant's smile with one of his own. "I don't really think," he said smoothly, "that we've gotten the proper credit for that. At least, nobody has formally charged—sorry, I mean thanked us for it yet." His smile increased to a grin. "Even if they'd like to, nobody seems to be quite able to make the connection yet."

"What a pity." Bryant leaned back in her chair. "Maybe someday . . . when things are different . . . then maybe we'll be able to talk about it. And people really will thank us. But in the meantime, as they say, discretion is the better part of valor." She wasn't smiling now. "So it's important that we all stay . . . silent. Understood?"

"Of course." There was no way he could be made to talk. And as for the others, any HDL members who had actually taken part in the so-called initial project —they weren't likely to open their mouths, either. Why risk a murder rap?

She stood up from the table and signalled with an imperious wave of her hand, visible through the tiny window behind Noah, that the visit was over; the female guard outside began unlocking the door.

"Take care, Noah." Bryant looked back at him as the guard led her away. Another thin smile showed on her face. "And don't forget those quarterly reports."

Down the long green-and-beige corridor, as he headed toward the reception area, he thought about the things of which he had just spoken with Darlene Bryant. Different words meant different things.

The initial project had been the blowing up of Doctor Quinn's clinic. He hadn't been part of the operations team that had done the job, but he knew something about it. The doctor had been a parasite-loving traitor to his own species; he'd deserved to die. There hadn't been a piece of Quinn left after the explosion that couldn't have fit into a shoebox. Good riddance, as far as Noah was concerned.

And the development project? There was something developing, all right; Noah's thoughts turned grim as he watched the reception guard filling out the forms to check him back out of the prison. There was an embryo developing, nearly four months along—he didn't really know how big that would make it. It was growing in the belly of some slag bitch back in L.A.; she and the government thought it was all such a big secret, but it wasn't. The HDL had it sources, closer than any of the parasites or their lickspittle human toadies realized.

Watch and wait; that was what the leader of the Purists had decided they should do. For now. Noah wondered what Darlene Bryant's plans were; so far, she hadn't told anyone. But she'd have to, soon enough. Five more months, and the horrible cross-breed bastard would be born . . .

The gates clanged shut behind him, and he started across the parking lot of the women's prison. Whatever the plans were, he'd be ready. She'd promised him. There was no way he wasn't going to be part of this.

The spark of anger at the core of his being pulsed with a familiar, even comforting heat. That stupid cop, the one who'd tried to come on all buddy-buddy with him—what a laugh, to know that jerk was the father of the unborn little mongrel. That was too good; it was perfect. Killing two birds with one stone, as the old saying went . . .

Noah smiled to himself in satisfaction as he dug the car keys out of his pocket. They were all going to find out.

Five more months? *I can't wait,* he thought as he slid behind the steering wheel.

"So—any new leads?"

It took a moment for the words to register, to break through the layer upon layer of thoughts encumbering his head. Sikes looked up and saw his partner standing by the desk.

"Nada." He reached out and tapped his fingertip against the computer screen. "I've been combing through these databases again, the ones the Feds sent us, and there ain't diddly in 'em." Sikes could hear the

disgust in his own voice. He and George had been working every angle now for months, and they weren't any closer to making a collar than they had been the day after Dr. Quinn's clinic had been bombed. "Anybody with that kind of explosives expertise and Purist connections was either out of the country or has an alibi you couldn't break without a papal dispensation."

George shrugged. "You know . . . there always is the possibility that the Purists weren't involved. That somebody else might have done it."

"Yeah, right." He could barely believe that his partner had just said something so bone-ass stupid. "And everybody in the HDL might have decided to go out for the Betty Crocker Homemaker of the Year Award, too—that's just about as possible." He gestured angrily toward the screenful of names. "C'mon, George, we know it must've been one of these clowns."

"Oh?" George had sat down at his own desk and begun sorting through the various folders stacked upon it. He didn't look up. "And just how do we know that so exactly?"

You're really getting on my tits, thought Sikes, temper simmering. The room was so silent he could hear the fan at the back of the computer and the dull tick of the vein at the corner of his forehead. He missed the bustle and clutter of the squad room, with all the other detectives and uniform cops coming and going and smarting off to each other. That was how tight the security lid that had come clamping down because of Cathy's pregnancy was—the LAPD brass, along with the Bureau of Newcomer Affairs, had shoved him and George into this back room by themselves, even pulling their computer terminals off the station net. He supposed it was all necessary— Quinn's clinic going up like the Fourth of July proved that—but still, the morgue-like feeling in here oppressed Sikes. Plus all this time one-on-one with his partner—it was going to be a race to see which would happen first, Cathy popping the kid or him diving across the desks and strangling George with his own necktie.

"How do we know? Get real." Sikes shoved back his chair. "Who the hell else could it be? Who else would want to blow up a medical clinic for Newcomers?"

Another shrug from George. "Perhaps there were other individuals who didn't like Dr. Quinn. Perhaps he had enemies that we don't know about."

"Okay, then how's this—I know in my frickin' guts that it was those goddamned Purists. Satisfied?"

"Really, Matt." George raised an eyebrow. "If that's the kind of answer you gave on your Detective Two orals, I'm not surprised you haven't gotten your promotion yet."

That was still a sore point between them; Sikes managed to ignore the dig. "All right. If you're so smart, then you tell me who blew up the clinic, if it wasn't the Purists."

"Oh, there's no doubt in my mind that it was the Purists. Almost certainly someone associated with the HDL was involved. Those Federal databases prove it." George gave a slight smile. "Think about it, Matt. How many names are there on those lists? Total, that is."

He glanced at the tally figures at the bottom of the computer screen. "Right around three hundred. That's just the most likely ones. If I widen the search categories another step, it'd probably go up to five hundred, maybe even six."

"Say three hundred, then." George leaned across his desk. "What would be the statistical probability of that many individuals having ironclad alibis, even if none of them had anything to do with the clinic bombing? Any time before, that we've had to check out a group as numerous as that, there's always been a dozen or so that we had to investigate before we could eliminate them as suspects. Now, we're dealing with the fact that every single one on our lists is already out of consideration."

Sikes nodded, getting the point. "Yeah, you're right . . ."

His partner continued. "What could possibly account for this apparent anomaly? The only thing would be that they were all warned ahead of time that the clinic bombing was going to happen, and that they should put all their mules in a safe place."

That last one puzzled him for a second. "You mean 'cover their asses,' George. But you're right; that must be what went down." It was the only explanation that made sense.

"Unfortunately," said George, "if that is in fact the case, then it means the situation is much worse for us. The indications would be that the Purist groups have not only tightened up their internal organization considerably, but they've also reached a new level of cooperation with each other. To enforce an order such as this, the HDL would have had to achieve a state of dominance over the other Purists, right down to the tiniest splinter groups. We've never seen that before. In the past, there had always been a few loosened cannons who went their own way, regardless of what the HDL tried to put out as an official line."

"Good call." Sikes glanced again at the long scroll of names on his computer screen. "That would explain why they were all lying so low—I mean, we hadn't heard a peep out of most of these jokers, for months before the bombing. They weren't disbanding or giving up, like we'd hoped; they were getting their act together."

"They do seem to have managed," said George drily.

"And we haven't gotten a leak one from any of our own contacts inside the HDL." That had been another source of puzzlement for him; a big part of police work had always consisted of following up on tips from informants, and tracking the Purists' activities had been no exception. This time around, in the weeks and then months since Quinn's clinic had gone up, there had been nothing. "So we gotta assume they've managed to identify all our people and cut 'em out of the loop."

"Exactly." The tone of George's voice was somber. "That's happened before. What's worrisome now is that the HDL appears to be handling their security differently. Their previous reactions to finding an informant in their midst were nearly always violent— we lost a couple of good sources that way. But at least we'd know that they had been found out and we could develop other contacts. But this time, none of our people have even been touched. That points to the HDL leadership having become much more sophisticated in how they handle these matters. They've reached a new stage in the learning curve—we're not going to get much help in the future from their mistakes."

Sikes felt a little tick of excitement inside himself, a detective's rush of adrenaline, from the picture suddenly becoming clearer. The bitter mockery, the feeling that he had been banging his head against the computer terminal with no results, lifted from his soul. Granted, he should have seen all this for himself, without George having to go through a point-by-point explanation. His only excuse was how tired he'd gotten these last several weeks, feeling as if he were right at the brink of physical and mental exhaustion. There was all the business of worrying about Cathy and taking care of her, none of which was made any easier by the necessity of her being tucked away in a secured location, as safe as possible from the reach of the murderers who had blown away Dr. Quinn. That had to be rough on her as well, being just about entirely cut off from the outside world—about the only one of her friends who knew where Cathy was, and could come and see her, was Susan Francisco, and that was only because her husband headed up the team whose job it was to keep Cathy and the baby inside her alive.

He rubbed his forehead, as though he could reach inside and get the blood moving inside his brain again. Here was his partner, busting his ass the same way he was, and he'd jumped down George's throat for no reason at all. Fatigue and frustration did that, made anybody cranky and mean.

"Uh, George . . ." With a sigh, he looked across the desks. "I'm like sorry I been getting on your case so much these days. You know how it is."

"Certainly." George gave a brief nod. "There's no need to apologize, Matt. We're all overworked." He leaned forward, his gaze growing sharper. "Have you been getting adequate sleep?"

"Yeah, I guess." He shrugged. "I mean, you know me; I've always kept kinda erratic hours. Plus lately . . . jeez. You remember how it was when Susan was pregnant with your kids—wait a minute. That's right, you wouldn't know about that." He had to keep reminding himself that Cathy's pregnancy was a first in Tenctonese physiology, with her bringing the kid to term rather than handing it off to the father. After having gone through all that with George and his youngest, little Vessna, he was now even happier that he was a human rather than a Newcomer male. It had been enough to get used to the notion of Cathy being pregnant; there was no way he could imagine himself in the same condition. "Whatever. Anyway, don't worry about me. I'll be fine."

"Are you certain there's nothing else?" George's scrutiny became almost clinical. "Frankly, you haven't been looking all that well lately."

He wondered what George suspected. Because there was more, but nothing he wanted to talk about. Not to his partner . . . not even to Cathy. Other things that kept him from getting a night's sleep. Or if sleep did come, something that jerked him up from the depths in a cold sweat. Those dreams . . . that figure with its outstretched arms, face all in shadow as the light streamed from behind . . . whispering his name . . .

"No." Sikes shook his head. It had taken an effort of will to keep hidden the shiver that had crept up his spine, just remembering last night's vision. "There isn't anything else." The same damn thing, again and again, but with one difference: each time he had the dream, the figure came closer than before. Soon he'd be able—in his dreaming—to touch it. And see its face revealed.

"Well, if you say so." George went back to shuffling through the files on his desk.

"You know, now that you mention it . . ."

George looked up.

"These last couple of months," said Sikes, "you haven't been looking all that great yourself."

"I don't know what you mean." George had visibly stiffened, even beyond his usual tightly buttoned demeanor. "I feel perfectly healthy. Fit as a violin."

"You mean fiddle."

George frowned in puzzlement. "I thought they were the same thing."

"They are, but . . . never mind. I'm not joking around." Sikes scrutinized his partner across the desk. "I've been meaning to say something about this for a while now. Are you sure you've been getting enough sleep?"

"I'm very well rested, thank you." The irritation in George's voice was apparent. "Your concern is noted and appreciated. However, in my case at least, there's nothing to worry about."

But there was; he could see it in George's eyes. Or he would have been able to, if George had looked straight back at him. The way he usually did—for him to turn away, as if he were hiding something, convinced Sikes that something was wrong.

Maybe . . . if he's not getting any sleep, either . . .

George was busy tapping away at his keyboard, his gaze intently following whatever was on the computer

103

screen before him. He really did look tired, Sikes decided. And more than that. Almost . . . haunted.

He looked away, toward the computer on his own desk. The screen had blanked itself, leaving a dark mirror to hold his reflection, the empty glass like a boxful of night. The same night had started to seep through the blinds over the room's high windows; he glanced over his shoulder and saw the cold blue glow of the station's parking lot lights come on.

Sikes wondered what his partner's dreams were like, what George saw when he went home and closed his eyes . . .

He turned the bike around at a gas station, out in the middle of nowhere. Under the sputtering fluorescents, Buck filled the tank while a human in greasy overalls and a Caterpillar cap watched.

"That oughta do it." He hung the nozzle back on the pump and screwed the motorcycle's gas cap down. "Get me home, at least." Buck extracted a ten from his wallet—leaving only a fiver and a couple of singles until payday—and held it out to the attendant.

"Ya goin' back to the city?" The guy wiped his hands on a black-stained shop rag before taking the money. "That where ya goin'?"

Buck laughed. "Where the hell else?" Not that it was any of this tert's business.

The attendant slowly turned and looked away, toward the distant mountains edged by the night's first stars. When he brought his gaze back around, Buck could see that he had loony eyes, like someone who had spent too much time staring across the empty desert.

"Ya know . . ." The attendant's words drawled out slow. "Ya could just keep goin'. Just as long as you wanted to. There ain't shit stoppin' ya."

Buck kickstarted the bike, revved the engine to a roar and then brought it back down. "Yeah, well, maybe I will some day. But not right now."

The attendant looked disappointed, as though he were the prophet of a new religion who hadn't found any takers. "Why not?"

"I don't know." He zipped his jacket against the cold wind that had begun to pick up, then turned the bike away from the gas pump. "Maybe I still got things to do."

That was a stupid answer, thought Buck as he leaned over the motorcycle's tank, the white line of the highway shimmering in the headlight beam. Why did he tell the guy that? There wasn't anything—or anyone—that kept him in L.A. Not anymore. So why?

No answer. He rolled on the throttle, letting the speed of the machine and the enveloping night silence the thoughts inside his head.

CHAPTER 8

HE WAS GLAD when his partner went home for the night. George's head had gotten so crammed—with thoughts and fears and memory scraps, the bits and pieces left from his bad dreams—that another person's presence was almost unbearable. To even begin to sort things out, he needed this room at the station all to himself, with the buzz and murmur of the regular cop work safely removed to the other side of the closed door.

You could have been easier on him, thought George as he gazed unseeing at the computer screen on his desk. He knew he must have come across as stiff and pompous—like an uptight, button-down Newcomer police drone—when he had been talking to Matt. He supposed he came across that way because, deep down in his hearts, that's what he was. And then lecturing his partner about how to do his job, what could be logically induced from the mountain of airtight Purist alibis . . . and worse, that crack about Matt's still not passing the Detective Two orals. That had been completely uncalled for. Matt was a saint to put up with him at all.

Dropping his elbows onto an open file folder, he rubbed his aching eyes with his palms. Past the room's door and down the station's hallway, some drunk was yelling in the booking sergeant's holding tank; the muffled words sounded angry and demented. That person was lucky. His problems could be sorted out, for the most part, with a good night's sleep. George wished the same could be said for himself. It had been a long time since sleep, when he could get it, had had any beneficial effect.

"Everybody's got their problems," he spoke aloud to the empty room. It sounded more like the kind of vaguely ungrammatical thing Matt would say, some mournful piece of Earthly ethnic wisdom. George slumped back in the chair, blinking and refocussing his eyes. He supposed it was true. He should listen to Matt, instead of the other way around.

The temptation to go home, to try and get some sleep, was almost overwhelming; cumulative fatigue weighed on his shoulders and rolled down his spine like the coils of a lead jacket. He could hope that the dreams of the light-silhouetted figure, the shadow that spoke his name, wouldn't make its usual visitation. There had been a couple of times in the last few months when he had been able to achieve some degree of unconsciousness, waking up in the morning without being haunted by what he had seen, by his own name whispered as the light slid through the figure's outstretched hands . . .

George shook his head, half in denial and half to jog himself back awake. It wasn't worth the risk. Besides, he still had work to do.

He looked down at the photos tucked into the pocket on one side of the folder. Now here was somebody with problems . . . or looked at another way, someone whose problems were over.

The photos had been taken at the autopsy performed by the coroner's office on the late Dr. Quinn. They weren't pretty.

Lois Allen, the department's top forensics specialist, had done the autopsy herself. It had been over two months ago that the medical examiner had come to this station and delivered the results and analysis, complete with the stack of photos, that alone indicated how high a priority the clinic-bombing case had. The ME had wrung out every scrap of data possible from the fragmentary—very fragmentary—remains of Dr. Quinn. Science had confirmed the obvious: Quinn had died instantly, torn apart by the force of the bomb. When he had gone back into the clinic after rushing Cathy and Matt outside, he had apparently searched and found where the bomb had been hidden in a service closet. Perhaps he'd had some notion of being able to defuse it, keep it from going off. Movies gave people ideas like that, as if there would be some big red wire that one could pull loose from a cluster of red dynamite sticks, and everything would be fine. Quinn had discovered otherwise.

Identification had been positive. The doctor had played football as an undergraduate, right up to his senior year when a cheap shot had taken out his left knee, the intricate bones splintered beyond repair. A replacement joint, surgical steel coated with Teflon, had been installed. Under a microscope, the serial number from the Swedish prosthetics manufacturer would be visible. One of the photos that Lois had taken was a blow-up of the battered metal that had been found in the clinic rubble; the number etched upon it matched the info that had been faxed to the station from the factory in Malmö. George had wondered if the artificial knee would be buried along with the rest of the bits and pieces of the late Dr. Quinn. Would that be the human way of handling the situation?

He slid the photos back into the envelope in which they had come from the coroner's office. There was something that bothered him about them, but he hadn't been able to figure out what it was yet. Perhaps the sheer clinical gruesomeness of them, the way the numbered tags on each scrap matched up with the paragraphs in the ME's report. In a just universe, a sentient creature shouldn't wind up reduced to charred tissue and bone fragments. If nothing else, it proved the murderous nature of the Purists; they didn't just seek to kill the Newcomers, they had now turned against their own species, against anyone who didn't agree with them. The Purists had enough hatred in their bowels for everybody on this planet.

They'll never go away, thought George gloomily. The wicked were always among us, to paraphrase one of the humans' holy texts. One didn't have to be a saint, human or Tenctonese, to realize that truth.

His eyes and the brain behind them ached. He knew he ought to follow Matt's example and go home, to his own wife and family, and try to get some rest. How much good was he accomplishing here, burning himself out this way? Every lead on the Purists and whatever they might be planning had come to a dead end. The only thing he and the rest of the Bureau of Newcomer Affairs security team could do now was wait and see what Darlene Bryant's thugs did next. Most of what a police detective did was wait, trapped in a little pool of light while evil circled closer in the darkness beyond . . .

He pushed away the autopsy file on Dr. Quinn, as though it contained—for a moment—all the cruel things in the world, that he wanted to forget. His hand reached toward the other corner of the desk for the phone; he'd already decided to call and let Susan know he'd be home soon. Maybe he could spend some time with their baby Vessna before Susan put her down for the night. And with Emily, though she'd probably be deep into her homework by now. He could find out if she'd had any more communication with her brother. He knew she was sworn to secrecy about going to see Buck, but she had ways of letting her parents know that things were going all right with him. And that'd been a big help, George admitted to himself, in smoothing things out between himself and Susan. They had talked it over, more than once, and Susan had agreed that their son needed the chance to take care of himself for a while—at least, until things got less hectic. Maybe after Matt and Cathy's baby was born; then he'd be able to get himself transferred from this security assignment, and they could concentrate on putting all the pieces of their own family back together.

A fraction of an inch away from the phone, his hand stopped. A mental circuit had sparked complete, as his eye had caught sight of something else on his desk that he had shoved beneath the stack of paperwork that filled his In basket. Another folder, thinner than the one with Dr. Quinn's autopsy report and photos; a corner of the single sheet of paper that this folder held peeked out, just enough to remind him of what it was.

One minute passed, then another, before George drew his hand away from the phone. Slowly, he pulled out the folder from where he had hidden it at the bottom of the pile. His hearts trembled in his chest as he flipped open the folder, and looked at the sheet of paper inside.

Perhaps I'm dreaming again. He closed his eyes, trying to will that explanation into reality. *Yes . . . I went home and had dinner, and played with my kids. I'm at home, not at the station. And I went upstairs to bed, and I'm really lying beside my wife. And I'm dreaming all this.*

He knew he wasn't dreaming. With his eyes still closed, he had picked up the sheet of paper; he could feel it in his hands. He didn't have to see it to know what was printed on it, the words framing the image at the center. A piece of his dreaming, even though this was real, and the other . . .

Was what? He no longer knew.

He folded the piece of paper where it had been creased before, then again, so it was small enough to slip into his shirt pocket.

From the hook behind his desk, he pulled his jacket off the hanger where he had carefully placed it before, brushing the lapels smooth from force of habit. He one-handed the buttons as he headed for the door.

I should have called Susan anyway, he thought as he switched off the room's overhead lights. He knew it was going to be a while before he reached home.

A long while.

He ran into his old friend in the hallway of the station.

Literally ran into him; George was preoccupied, his thoughts a million miles away. Albert had to grab onto George's arm to keep him from falling.

"Sorry; my apologies . . ." George mumbled the words in a distracted manner. "Very clumsy of me . . ."

"That's okay." Albert stepped back, then reached out to brush a speck of lint from the shoulder of George's suit jacket. Glancing down, he saw with a pang of guilt how scuffed and in need of a shine George's shoes were; that was the kind of thing he used to take care of, back when he had still been the station's janitor. Not because it had been part of his official duties, but because he'd been so proud of George and what an important person he was— certainly the most important Newcomer that Albert was acquainted with. People had gone from the LAPD to the mayor's office; Albert was sure that would happen to his friend George someday. But not with shoes in that condition. He wished he had brought his shine kit with him this evening.

"George, it's me." Albert had suddenly realized

that George hadn't recognized him at all. George stepped to one side of the corridor and continued on his way. "It's Albert!"

Frowning, George looked over his shoulder at him, then blinked as though he had just woken up. "Albert . . . yes, of course." He shook his head, an embarrassed half-smile appearing on his face. "Now I really am sorry. I just don't know where my mind's at these days." He turned back and shook Albert's hand in both of his. "It's good to see you, Albert. How have you been?" George took a step backward, spreading his hands out as though in amazement. "You look great!"

"Yeah . . . uh, thanks." He had to look down at himself to make sure. "I guess I do." He poked with one finger at his own double-breasted suit, then glanced back up at George. "May bought me this." The suit's fabric was of a perfect dove gray, soft as air against his fingertips. May and Mr. Vogel's incredibly thin personal assistant, a human named Brian, had dragged him to a shop on Rodeo Drive, where they had been the only customers for a whole hour of having his measurements taken and trying things on. That'd been fun enough, until he and May had gone home and he'd seen the sales slip for the one suit the shop's tailor had gotten ready for him, and he'd realized that the amount was bigger than any paycheck he'd ever brought home from the station. He'd nearly fainted, like back at the fancy restaurant where Vogel and Dierdorf had hired him. Now there were six more suits like this one, hanging up in his closet. "May said I needed it. Because of, uh . . ." Now he felt embarrassed. "Because of me being important and stuff. That's what she said."

"Nonsense." George laid a hand on his shoulder. "You were always important, Albert. Remember that."

"Maybe . . . maybe we could get together some-time." Albert looked with more concern than hope at his friend. Truth was, George didn't look so good; he looked all run-down, as though whatever he was thinking about so hard was an invisible ton of lead pressing upon him. "Maybe you and Susan could come over for dinner. May and I have a bigger place now. It wouldn't be so cramped, like before. And, and May's been taking these gourmet food preparation lessons over at the Tenctonese Cultural Center—you should see what she can do with buffalo spleen—"

"That's a good idea, Albert." The faint smile on George's face was still there, like the flag of a defeated army. "Susan and I would love to come over." He gave Albert's shoulder a squeeze. "We'll do that sometime. I promise."

"No, no—I mean like soon." His worry over the state of George's health had grown. "Like . . . maybe tomorrow night." He wondered if George just wasn't eating right these days; maybe that was it.

"Sorry." George shook his head. "I'm pretty busy right now. Work and all. Perhaps—"

"Or the night after that," Albert said anxiously. "Anytime this week would be great."

Another shake of the head. "I don't think so. But soon." His hand fell away from Albert's shoulder. "Good seeing you again." The last remnants of the smile faded as the preoccupied look settled behind George's eyes like a dark cloud.

Albert watched in dismay as his friend, head down and shoulders hunched, headed toward the station's exit. *I should've been able to help,* he thought glumly. *Since I'm supposed to be so smart.*

"There you are!" Another voice called out to him. "Been looking all over for you."

He turned and saw Captain Grazer, hand outstretched and with a big smile on his face, striding from the opposite end of the corridor. The smile was bigger than any Albert could remember seeing when he had still been mopping the station's floors.

Grazer seized Albert's hand and pumped it. "How

113

you been? I was starting to think that maybe you'd forgotten how to find the place." Grazer rolled Albert's lapel between his fingers. "Hey, nice suit. Come on, let's go back to my office."

"I was wondering . . . ." Albert resisted the captain's tug at his arm. "Do you know . . . is there something wrong with George?"

"Huh?" Grazer looked past him, to where George could be seen going out of the station. "Ah, that's just how you get when you're a workaholic like him. He likes it that way. Come on."

In the captain's office, Albert sat in the big chair pulled around in front of the desk and watched as Grazer pulled a bottle of sour milk from the bottom drawer. Albert recognized the brand. He'd recommended it to one of Precognosis's clients.

"Care for a nip? Supposed to be the good stuff." Grazer held the bottle up. "At least, I hear that's what you told the folks. Me, I wouldn't know." His smile widened, becoming even more ingratiating. "I'll just stick to the single malts for now."

"Thanks . . . but no." Albert shook his head. "I drove over here."

"No more riding the bus for you, huh? That's great. I sure hope you passed your driver's test—" Grazer laughed as he stowed the bottle away. "I'd hate to have to arrest an old pal!"

"I got my license. I studied."

"I'm sure you did; just kidding." Grazer picked up the cigar from the ashtray on his desk. "What kind of car you got?"

He shrugged. "I don't know. They gave it to me. The people I work for did." He searched his memory but couldn't come up with anything. "It's a new one," he said helpfully.

"Yeah, well, you make sure they gave you a nice one. Don't let those bastards cheap out on you. You deserve the best." Grazer leaned back in his chair, eyes narrowing as he meditated on the cloud of smoke he had just exhaled. He pointed with the cigar toward Albert. "You know why I asked you to come here tonight?"

He didn't, but he hadn't let it bother him. Nowadays, people were always asking him to go someplace or another. It was one of the pleasant parts of the job—he got to see a lot of different places and meet people who acted happy to see him. "No, you didn't tell—"

Grazer interrupted him. "It's the future," he said, his voice going deep and mysterious-sounding. "That's what it is. That's what you deal in, don't you, Albert?"

"I guess so . . ."

"Well, Albert, so do I. That's one of the great things about police work, isn't it?" Grazer didn't wait for an answer. "Detective work, like some of those little things you did for us. It's all basically the same principle that's involved. We analyze the past—a crime—so we can create the future: the arrest of the criminal. And thus we go from a state of potentiality to one of actuality."

"Gosh." Albert wasn't sure he knew exactly what Captain Grazer meant, though a lot of it sounded like stuff that Vogel had talked about. The future and everything.

"Tell me, Albert—" Grazer leaned across the desk, bringing the glowing tip of the cigar closer to Albert's face. "Did you get that package I sent you?"

He nodded. The smoke from the captain's cigar made his eyes water.

"Did you look through all that stuff in there?"

"Well . . ." He felt even more uncomfortable. It was always interesting getting a package delivered to you, and one from an old friend—he had thought that maybe it was some kind of present from everybody at the station, or maybe something of his that he had forgotten to pack up and take with him when he quit. But instead the box had held a book, a big fat one with a glossy cover and Captain Grazer's photo on the back, and a dozen audio cassettes. He had tried reading the book, but hadn't been able to get through even the first couple of pages; it was full of that same kind of language, stuff about the future and making possible things real. The cassettes were even more disappointing. He had hoped they would have music on them—he had gotten to like human music nearly as much as an old Tenctonese *visahooli*—or maybe a good mystery novel read aloud, like some of the tapes May had gotten him for when he was driving around in the car. But instead, they had all been full of Grazer reading stuff from his book in a carefully intense voice. Albert had fast-forwarded through a couple of the tapes, and there had been some even weirder stuff, all about closing his eyes and 'visualizing' the future, like it was some place you could go visit. He had tried doing what Grazer's voice on the tapes told him to do, but had wound up falling asleep.

"That's okay," said Grazer. He tapped the ash from his cigar. "I know you probably haven't had a chance to get through more than, say, the first ten or twelve chapters. Rome wasn't built in a day, Albert. GIT is a big concept; it's understandable that it takes a while to get a grasp of it. Especially for somebody of your . . . well, your particular talents, that is. That's why I put in the set of tapes for you. Great, huh? Technology in the service of actualizing the future. So easily assimilated, you hardly have to pay attention at all. Like having your head turbo-charged. I knew you'd like those."

"Um . . . yeah." Albert nodded slowly. "They were . . . really great."

"Thanks. A lot of thought went into them. A lot of work went into the whole package, Albert. I've been working on GIT for a long time. Years, Albert, years. I like to think of it as my contribution to humanity—and Newcomers, too, of course. A breakthrough in conceptual dynamics, a whole new system of organizing the processes of sentient effort.''

Albert nodded. He recognized some of those phrases from the little bit of the book he had been able to read. He didn't want the captain to think he wasn't paying attention to all these ideas. *They probably really are good ideas,* he thought. Since Captain Grazer had them and all.

"But it's hard, Albert. It's hard.'' Grazer had swivelled his chair around so he could gaze out the window behind him. The streetlights had come on and the tall downtown buildings glowed in the distance. "Now I know how Napoleon must have felt. Or Oppenheimer. Any of those genius-type guys who were so tragically misunderstood in their time.'' The expression on Grazer's face turned dark and brooding as he puffed at the cigar. "The world doesn't appreciate real breakthrough ideas like this, Albert. Not at first, anyway.'' He swung the chair back around. "But that's why I asked you to come here tonight. Why I wanted to talk to you. I think . . .'' He punctuated his words with jabbing motions of the cigar. "I think there's a way we can help each other, Albert . . .''

"Oh.'' He had started to get a suspicion of what else the captain was talking about.

"Yes, indeed . . .'' Grazer nodded, his gaze turning inward to some glorious vista that—for the moment at least—only he could see. "That's part of what GIT is all about. People helping other people. To evolve, to grow . . . to bring the future into reality. The way you can help me, Albert . . .''

He hoped he was wrong. He hoped the captain wasn't going to ask him what he was afraid would be the case.

"Yes . . . the future . . .'' Grazer leaned back in his chair, filling the air above himself with blue-gray smoke. "You and me . . . it'll be great . . .''

Albert felt his hearts sinking inside himself. He

wished his friend George were here, or just somewhere around in the station. He could talk to him, and George would tell him what he should do.

But George was gone. He felt like he was all alone in Captain Grazer's office, like he was drowning here inside his expensive suit. The captain was still talking but he couldn't really hear anything that was being said, as though all those grand words were a transmission from another planet, too distant to make out.

The future, Albert thought worriedly. It was coming faster than he was ready for.

The door was at the end of an alley. In an abandoned section of the city's old warehouse district, where the switch lines running off the railroad tracks had rusted from disuse. Dry brown weeds sprouted up from the broken bottles filling the cracks in the asphalt, the roads that freight trucks had once rumbled down. A night wind dragged a scrap of yellowed newspaper against George Francisco's legs as he locked the car door. He kicked the newspaper free and it tumbled away, close to the litter-strewn sidewalk, like a ghost bound by gravity and words.

With his hand still on the car's door, he looked carefully around the area, examining the darkness for possible traps. He was on his own; he had told no one that he was going to this place. There would be no way of calling for backup once he walked away from the car. Whatever happened here—and he had no idea yet of what it would be—he would have to handle on his own.

As he walked toward the door, the alley's damp brick walls pressing toward him on either side, he spotted the faint light seeping across the battered sill. The light was the same cold-ice color as the narrow strip of stars he could see above himself.

"Greetings, brother." The door had been pulled back a few inches even before he could knock upon it with his raised fist. He realized that someone had been watching him from the moment he had gotten out of the car. The face of a Tenctonese male peered out at him. "Enter," said the man, "and be at peace." The man stepped back into the building's dim light, drawing the opening wider.

The interior smelled musty, as of air that had been trapped inside an empty warehouse years ago. George looked up and saw bare wooden beams spotted with ancient pigeon droppings; a broken skylight had been covered up with plywood, now warped and crumbling at the edges from L.A.'s infrequent rains.

Behind him, the door was pushed closed. Sealed into the warehouse's quiet, he could detect faint sounds at the limits of his hearing, the whisper-like breaths of others somewhere in the darkness farther on.

"You are new to the Way."

A statement, not a question. George looked over at the Newcomer standing beside him. "Yes . . ." He fumbled inside his jacket for the piece of paper that he had taken from the file on his desk. His hands shook as he started to unfold the single sheet. "I came . . . because of this . . ."

"That's all right, brother. You don't have to show me." The other Newcomer laid his hand on George's arm. "It doesn't matter how one finds the Way. All that matters is that you have found it." The other's eyes shone with fervent conviction. "Come with me."

He was led to the far reaches of the warehouse, past a thick curtain that had been hung from the ceiling to the oil-spattered concrete floor. The other man drew back a corner of the heavy cloth and motioned for George to step through.

On the other side, he found what he was looking for.

His eyes had already adjusted to the darkness. He could make out row after row of Tenctonese, both men and women, seated on benches cobbled together from rough wooden planks; toward the crude elevated stage that had been built at one end of the space, there were more of his people, kneeling and gazing up at the figure standing before them.

The same figure whose image had been printed on the piece of paper, still folded and tucked away in the pocket of his jacket. The image that had brought him here, to this secret place of devotion.

He had seen the same image before, in his dreaming.

The shadowed figure raised its arms, light streaming from behind, past the outstretched hands.

Even before the figure spoke, George felt the gaze of the hidden eyes search him out, finding him and peering into the farthest recesses of his soul.

You have come to Me. The voice spoke inside him. *I have waited for you . . .*

George closed his own eyes, but could still see the figure silhouetted by light.

He knew that now there would be no waking from the dream.

CHAPTER 9

"HEY, YOU ABOUT ready to go?"

From the doorway, he peered back inside the safe house; there was no sign of her. Sikes turned back around to the uniformed cop standing on the front steps, heaved his shoulders and sighed.

The cop nodded sympathetically. "It was the same way with my old lady; we got three kids, and every time with 'em it was the same." He gestured toward the two bulging suitcases beside him, packed with Cathy's things. "Some women, the time comes and they go into the maternity ward with enough luggage, it's like they're going on some Princess Cruise liner for three months." He gave a philosopher's shrug. "But you take Garlinski back at the station—each time his wife went in, she took like one robe, her lipstick and mascara, and one of those romance paperbacks. Like she needed that, right? Go figure."

Sikes didn't listen to the other guy's words of wisdom. They interfered with the attempt he was making at remaining cool. No need to be a jerk about all this, he'd told himself. He was trying to be sympathetic even, seeing it from Cathy's viewpoint. That wasn't so hard, given that he had gone through this whole going-to-the-hospital business before, at least from the male side of it. He had even been through the process when the hospital hadn't been reached in time, twice in fact, in the back of a patrol car when he'd still been in uniform. The quickie medical course he'd gotten as a rookie at the police academy had covered the basics of an emergency delivery, and the rest hadn't been exactly brain surgery. He'd been lucky, though; those two women had been so easy, his part had been more like playing a utility infielder, hands poised to catch a ground ball skipping between the bases, than having to act like an obstetrician. Though he had been hoarse for a week afterward each time, from shouting over the patrol car's radio for backup. He'd never been so glad in his life to see a paramedic's van come pulling up.

"Yeah, you're right," Sikes told the uniform cop. "They're all unpredictable that way." With his ex-wife, when they'd still been married, he'd wound up coming out of the hospital carrying in one hand the single overnight case she'd already packed before her water broke, and their newborn baby slung in the crook of his other arm. Now his daughter Kirby was a sophomore at UCLA. Time didn't fly, at least not by flapping its wings; instead, it got itself shot out of a cannon.

He leaned back inside the doorway and shouted. "Hey, Cathy, where are you? We got folks waiting on us."

"Just a minute!" Her voice echoed through the safe house's sparsely furnished rooms. They had never really moved into the place, in the sense of putting pictures on the walls and stuff. "I'm still looking for something."

"Don't worry about it, pal." The uniform cop gave him a knowing smile and wink. "Let her take her time. This is all standard operating procedure."

Yeah, right, he thought. Sikes knew that if he were still hooked up with his ex-wife, he wouldn't be worried. 'Standard operating procedure'—what the hell was that supposed to mean, right here and now? Those two women pulling their flying champagne cork numbers in the back of the patrol car—that had been within the realm of S.O.P. They'd been human women, after all. Happens all the time; there were lots of cab drivers who had stories like that. Even when he'd gotten stuck helping his partner George pop out his baby Vessna, that was normal, too. These things were supposed to happen that way.

"Found it." Cathy came out of the house's back bedroom, her third-trimester tummy preceding the rest of her. She held up a tiny Walkman. "Hey, I know what kind of Muzak they play over those hospital systems. I'd go nuts listening to that stuff all day long." She tucked the folding headphones with their trailing cord into the top-front pocket of the floral print maternity overalls she was wearing. "Now I'm ready to go."

The sight of her walking with that tilted-back posture pregnant women used to balance themselves triggered more memories from the days when he'd been married. He sometimes caught himself thinking, he and Cathy were as good as hitched. They'd even talked about whether to just go ahead and formalize the whole arrangement—especially now that there was going to be a kid who'd presumably need a last name and all—and if they did, whether they should have a Celinite ceremony or one in the church. He'd been a lapsed Catholic for so long that either ritual would probably seem foreign to him. Maybe after his and Cathy's kid was born, they'd finally do the deed. Better late than never, he figured.

"You sure?" Sikes nodded toward the suitcases outside the house's door. "Maybe that little thing won't be enough; maybe we should check out whether we could get a grand piano shipped into the hospital."

"Matt—come on. That's not fair." With both hands, Cathy kneaded the small of her arched back. "I'm going to be in there a long time." Both her expression and her voice started showing signs of irritability. "Maybe you should go flat on your back for a month, and we'll see if you wind up getting bored or not."

He knew she had a point there. Cathy was only eight months along, and there was every indication that she was going to take the pregnancy to full term. Doctor Friedman, the head of the medical team that the Bureau of Newcomer Affairs had put together after Dr. Quinn's untimely death, had told them both that from all appearances Cathy's condition seemed perfectly healthy, with no imminent complications. If the baby was growing inside a human female rather than a Tenctonese, everything would have been considered normal. But since none of the doctors could even explain how it had been possible for her to get pregnant, let alone develop all the internal physiology to develop the fetus this far along, they had decided to err on the side of caution and take her into a secured ward of the hospital now. Everyone was waiting for her: the doctors on the inside, the police guards stationed outside the doors.

She must feel like some kind of experimental test subject, thought Sikes—not for the first time. Cathy was already well into a territory that nobody else—no Newcomer female, at least—had ever entered. An odd realization had come to him when Cathy's condition had first started to show: that as much as the whole Tenctonese species had become part of life on Earth, and in his life more than that of most humans, he had never seen a pregnant Newcomer woman before. Nobody had, of course; Cathy was the first ever. He supposed a lot of human women went through that phase—his ex-wife had—of staring at themselves in the mirror and thinking, *Great, I've gotten myself knocked up. Now what?* But at least the human women were always able to comfort themselves with the notion that umpty-ump billions of other women had had the same thing happen to them and they'd all gotten through it more or less intact. Of course, some didn't, but the odds were still basically pretty good. But for Cathy . . . who could tell? The BNA doctors could poke at her and run their ultrasound gizmos all over her round, pumpkin-like belly, and pop her in and out of their CAT scan machines like a frozen dinner going in the microwave, and they still wound up shrugging their shoulders and saying everything seemed fine and normal—if she were human instead of Tenctonese.

Another odd thought stepped through familiar territory inside his head. Just looking at Cathy, as she fussed with one of the straps of her maternity coveralls—she was still different, in that way that must have been part of the reason he had found her so attractive, the whole exotic trip of her being from some other world. There had been a time, when he had first started getting to know her, that he had despaired of getting past all the difficulties that were involved in a relationship with a Newcomer; it had been hard enough just being able to accept working with George Francisco as a partner. *They really are different from us,* he thought again. How could they not be? Yet at the same time, there was a part of Cathy that had become just like that of a human female— she might as well have become human, for all the difference it made now.

"Matt . . . hey, Matt." A hand waved in front of his face. "You still with us?"

He blinked and saw Cathy smiling at him. He gave his head a shake, trying to free it of the web of thoughts that had come tangling out of the back reaches of his brain.

"Yeah, okay . . ." His own smile flashed a sheepish embarrassment in turn. Sikes knew it really didn't do any good to think about this stuff, at least not now when they were still in the middle of it all. He had enough on his mind just taking care of immediate business. Not just seeing Cathy through this pregnancy jazz, but those other, less pleasant things he had to worry about. His smile faded. The Purists were lying low, but he knew in his gut that they would never be satisfied with having blown up Quinn and his clinic. They were just biding their time.

He reached down and picked up the suitcases, letting the uniform cop lead the way to the unmarked car at the curb. The warm L.A. sunshine rolled over the sidewalk like a shimmering wave. Sikes noted with grim satisfaction how both this cop and the one sitting behind the wheel kept a constant visual scan of their surroundings. When all the joking around was done, they were still on duty, still working the top-level assignment they had been given, making sure that one pregnant Newcomer female arrived at the hospital safely.

Sikes felt better when he had gotten the suitcases stowed in the car's trunk. Now his hands were free, to grab Cathy if necessary and shove her behind himself for protection, and to reach inside his jacket for his own gun.

The street remained wrapped in its suburban quiet. The uniform cop, who had gotten in beside the driver, looked over his shoulder to the car's back seat. "All set?"

"Sure." Sikes nodded. Beside him, Cathy sat with her hands folded across her rounded abdomen. "Let's get rolling."

Another unmarked car pulled out after them; Sikes glanced back and recognized two plainclothes officers in the vehicle; it was all part of the security arrangements.

"Don't worry so much." Cathy reached over and squeezed his hand. "Everything's going to be all right."

"Hey, I know that." He leaned back beside her,

trying to look relaxed. "It's like that crack Zepeda over at the station is always making. That from what she's seen, pregnancy's rough, but with a lot of support from the woman, the man will get through it just fine."

Cathy gave him a smile; that was enough to ease some of the tension out of his shoulders. If he closed his eyes, he knew he would be in danger of falling asleep. That wouldn't give a very good impression to the two cops sitting up front. Officer Zepeda's joke had more truth than not in it; he wondered if every expectant father wound up feeling this loaded down with fatigue, or whether it was just the cumulative result of his own sleepless nights catching up with him. Those goddamn dreams . . . that light seeping past the shadowed figure's hands . . . his own name whispered . . .

He jerked awake, the back of his head snapping against the car's seat. Neither Cathy nor the two uniform cops had noticed his little stumble into unconsciousness.

Turning to the window beside him, Sikes concentrated on scanning the traffic on the road, looking for anything suspicious. He clenched one hand into a fist, using the pump from his arm muscles to keep himself alert.

It'll soon be over, he told himself. *Nothing to worry about. Everything's going to be just fine . . .*

She wished he had stayed longer.

"Don't worry—" Nurse Eward smiled gently at her. "I imagine he'll swing back by tonight. He looks like the type who would."

Cathy sat in the middle of the hospital bed with the pillows propped up behind her, feeling faintly irritated. Not about Matt having to leave—she knew he had other things to take care of, that he couldn't stay with her all of the time—but about her own being here. Considering all the time she had spent in hospitals for her job, her career, she supposed she should have been used to it by now. But all that had been on the other side of the relationship between patient and staff. *The warden rather than the prisoner,* Cathy thought grimly. The thought of there being armed guards just outside the doors of the ward depressed her even more, though she knew in the rational part of her mind that they were there to protect her, not to keep her from escaping.

"I suppose he will," said Cathy. She wasn't worried about that. "Hey, don't mind me, Paula. I'm just having a mood attack." That was to be expected as well. So now I know what it feels like to be pregnant. All the way pregnant, that is, from start to finish. She had more sympathy for human females, and Tenctonese men, than she'd had before this had all come about. It was a new experience for a Newcomer female, and not one that she was sure she would unreservedly recommend to others. Maybe when it was all over, she'd feel differently about it. In the meantime, she was covering new frontiers in the consciousness of Tenctonese women: this was what it felt like to be a lump, not just that light and airy creature of one's previous existence, but something heavy and earthbound, with a belly swollen all the way out to there and an aching back and a *trés* charming flatfooted stance . . .

"Well," said the nurse, "it must be a hell of a mood. You look like you're about ready to murder someone."

"It'd have to be somebody slow enough for me to catch." Cathy lay back against the bank of pillows. On the wall beside the bed a television protruded on a hinged metal arm; on the screen a Tenctonese talk-show hostess poked a boom microphone toward a group of scowling teenage Purist wannabes, their acned faces as spotted as the skulls of the people they hated so fiercely.

The audio on the TV was already turned down; she was glad when Nurse Eward reached across her and switched off the picture as well. "We don't need that." The nurse went back to sorting out and plugging in the room's vital signs monitors.

Cathy tried to relax. The nurse's presence was something to be grateful about, a thread of continuity that had run through her pregnancy from the first day she had been told of it. Paula Eward had been the head nurse at Dr. Quinn's clinic, she had been there when the doctor had told Cathy what all the tests had revealed, the still-unexplained miracle. She had been so happy when she had finally understood that she had wanted to jump up and fling her arms around the human woman with the short, no-nonsense dark hair and just a few incipient streaks of gray peeking from beneath the white nurse's cap, just hug her from sheer delight. There hadn't been time for that, not then; for poor Dr. Quinn, there had been no time at all. After he had shoved her and Matt out the front door of the clinic, he'd just managed to get Paula, the only clinic staff on duty that afternoon, out the back way. The explosion, when it hit, had knocked her sprawling across the asphalt of the small parking lot behind the building; for a couple of weeks afterward, she had worn bandages over her scraped-raw palms and forearms, and another for the flash burn left on the side of her neck.

It's no wonder she hates them, thought Cathy. She had seen the same tight-lipped expression come over the nurse's face, triggered by something on the evening news or a picture on the front page of a newspaper. Anything to do with the Human Defense League or any other Purist group got the same silent reaction, Paula's eyes narrowing with contempt. Over the last several months, Cathy had pieced together just how devoted Dr. Quinn's nurse had been toward him; she had worked a long time with him. And now to think of him as a small collection of barely identifiable remnants in the coroner's office . . . They would've killed her as well. That was another grim realization. It was just as Matt had told her, that the Purists had entered into that stage of fanaticism where it no longer mattered to them who they killed, just as long as somebody died for the sake of their warped beliefs.

Cathy knew it was also the reason why Paula Eward had agreed to continue the supervision of her medical care, even after they both had come so close to dying in the bomb attack on Dr. Quinn's clinic. Nobody would have blamed the nurse if she had dropped out after that traumatic event; it would have been enough for most people. Instead, Nurse Eward had acted as a one-woman transition team, using her expertise in Newcomer medicine and her knowledge of Quinn's research to bring the BNA doctors up to speed with their new patient. That was her way of fighting back, Cathy had figured; her way of making sure that the Purists didn't win.

"We need to get a blood sample." Nurse Eward turned back toward the bed. "Won't take but a minute . . ."

She watched as the nurse expertly slid the needle point under the skin. The clear syringe filled slowly with pink liquid—her blood at least was still Tenctonese, no matter what was happening someplace else in her body.

"Ouch!" The needle stung as the nurse drew it out.

"Sorry." Nurse Eward pressed a bandage over the tiny wound. "I usually do better than that."

Cathy managed to smile at her own flash of irritability. "I thought pregnant women were supposed to get all mellowed out, from those endorphins in the brain and stuff."

"Well . . ." The nurse shrugged. "Back when I worked straight obstetrics, I did have a few patients who were slightly more—shall we say?—zoned than you are."

"Just my luck." She laid herself back against the pillows. "All of the work and none of the fun." Gazing up at the ceiling, Cathy shook her head. "Now I know what humans mean when they say God couldn't be a woman—She would never have thought up a system as stupid as this."

"Probably not." Nurse Eward carried the tray with the blood sample toward the door. "Get some rest. You've got a lot more work ahead of you."

"Yikes."

When she was alone in the room, Cathy found herself staring at the acoustic tiles above her, unable to sleep. A month to go—a minute trace of apprehension lurked behind her thoughts. She'd had vague ambitions, since her people had come to this place where everything had suddenly seemed so possible, of becoming famous, of doing something no one—no Tenctonese woman, at least—had ever done before.

It wouldn't be too much longer now, before all those ambitions came true, whether she was ready or not.

"Hey, nice of you to show up." The words were heavy with sarcasm.

The squad car's door slammed shut behind him. George looked up and saw his partner Sikes striding down the path that led to the hospital's entrance.

"I'm sorry, Matt." Just inside the tinted glass doors, a couple of officers in uniform were already standing guard; he recognized them as being part of the BNA security detail. "I came over here as soon as I got word that you had taken Cathy in." George rubbed his brow, as though to erase his own confusion. "I really must have lost track of time; I didn't think the infant was due yet. Unless . . . is Cathy all right?"

"She's fine, you genius." Matt walked past him toward the driver's side of the car. "At least she's still got all her wits about her. For Christ's sake, George, you're only about a month off; Cathy's not due to pop for weeks yet." He yanked the door open and slid in behind the wheel. "Come on, get in. We got other business to take care of." Leaning across the seat, he peered up through the passenger side window. "What, you so spaced that you've forgotten you're still working as a police detective?"

He shook his head. "No . . ."

"Then act like one, already. Jeez." Matt pushed open the door, and it hit George's leg. "Look, get in or I'll drive over to the women's prison by myself; I don't have a problem with that. But the department might wonder what the hell you're doing these days to earn your big Detective Two paycheck." Matt drew back behind the steering wheel, watching with grumpy satisfaction as his partner got into the car.

As Matt drove, swinging the squad car up the curving ramp onto the freeway, George sat stiffly beside him, hands on his knees. "I know I really do owe you an apology, Matt." He gazed straight ahead through the windshield as the dense traffic parted to either side and disappeared behind them. His partner always drove too fast for his liking, at least when there wasn't an actual emergency that would have required turning on the siren. "I've been preoccupied these last few months . . ."

"Oh, think nothing of it, pal." Sikes one-handed the steering wheel, his other elbow stuck out the rolled-down window. "It's not like you oughta have any reason for thinking I don't have time for doing your job and mine. Hey, all I got on the burner right now is that my main squeeze is gonna have a kid, which is just something that no female of her species has ever done before, but what the hell—there's a first time for everything, right?"

"Matt, it's not difficult for me to discern that you're annoyed with me—"

"Annoyed? Annoyed?" Sikes barked out a harsh laugh, then hit the top curve of the steering wheel with his fist. "Like I got enough time to be annoyed with you! I just stuck Cathy in that hospital and there isn't a single doctor in the place who can tell me whether she's gonna be alive ten minutes from now, let alone in a month when they wheel her out of the delivery room!"

George flinched as his partner came close to side-swiping a gasoline truck. "Please, Matt, I understand how you feel. I know that an impending birth can be a considerable generator of stress . . . for everyone involved." He tried a wan, conciliatory smile. "After all—I've been there, in a way that I'm sure we'll agree is impossible for you."

"Get bent." Sikes's scowl grew even darker. "You popping a kid is like normal, okay? For Cathy it's not, and you can't tell me otherwise. Remember, pal, you were the one I told about all this, about Cathy even getting pregnant in the first place, and you didn't think it was possible. Instead, you gave me just about the worst friggin' advice anybody could've thought up—"

"Let's not go through all that again. I was wrong; I've already apologized for what I said then about you and Cathy. How was I to know? As you just put it, this has never happened before."

"Yeah, well, it's never happened before that a partner of mine has just completely flaked out the way you have. Where the hell have you been the last couple of months? Even when you show up at the station, George, it's like that spotty head of yours is still out in the ozone somewhere." Sikes was practically standing on the accelerator now. "What gives? You were supposed to be in charge of the security arrangements for Cathy—hey, I asked the Bureau guys to bring you in on this—and you've been just about totally vacant on the whole thing. I've had to do everything—I'll be holding Cathy's hand, trying to keep her from busting out in tears, and my brain's running around like a rat in a rain barrel, worrying about whether some HDL hit team is climbing in through the windows!" He jabbed a finger toward George. "Fat lot of help you are!"

"Matt . . ." He tried to reach past his partner's hand, to get his own on the steering wheel. "Perhaps you should let me drive." Whatever truth there might have been in the comments about his mind being elsewhere, he was still conscious of every near-miss that Sikes's driving produced. The car's mounting speed blurred the freeway traffic on either side. "Seriously . . . you're upset . . ."

"Oh, real good, Sherlock. There's a great example of that fabled Newcomer brainpower we keep hearing about." Sikes cut the wheel hard, slamming the squad car around a White Gold tanker that had suddenly loomed up in the center lane. "You're so on top of things, why don't you tell me who we're going to see? I'll bet you don't even know!"

George reached between the seats and pulled up the emergency brake handle; at the same time, he yanked the steering wheel to the right. The squad car swerved and fishtailed, finally coming to a stop on the freeway's narrow shoulder space. Dust slowly settled as the other cars and trucks flung themselves hurtling by.

"As a matter of fact, I do know." He dug into his coat pocket and came out with the yellow memo form that had been routed from the department's legal office. "I got the same notice that you did, Matt; that's why I came over to the hospital to find you. The Bureau of Newcomer Affairs finally managed to get a judge's order allowing us to go and talk with Darlene Bryant. We probably have only a few hours before the Human Defense League attorneys find some other way of slamming the door in our faces. So that's why we've got our pack animals in such a hurry. There—are you satisfied now?"

"Asses," muttered Sikes sourly. "Asses in a hurry. And no, I'm not satisfied." He shoved the gearshift into neutral and pushed himself back into the seat. "Look, George, if you got something else cooking—something else going on that you haven't told me about—hey, that's fine. Whatever. But you're gonna have to face up to the fact that it's cutting into your other duties. You don't wanna be part of this security detail thing, just say so; we'll go back and tell it to Grazer, he'll deal with the BNA and get you reassigned. But I'm not coming off the detail with you, man. I can't; we're talking about protecting the woman I love, ya know?"

George nodded. He couldn't say anything; sitting in the squad car, with the traffic roaring by a few yards from him and his partner, he felt oddly disassociated from the scene, as though Sikes's words were being radioed in from a long distance away. Somebody named George Francisco was listening to those words, or making a show of listening to them, but it wasn't him anymore. Sikes was right; his mind really was somewhere else. Someplace more real than this, a world whose contours of force pressed more urgently about him . . .

He clenched one of his fists, concentrating, summoning himself back to this time and place. For a moment, he had been in danger—as he always seemed to be these days—of slipping away, drifting off just as his partner had accused him of doing, dropping the thread of the words being spoken to him. And picking up another one, heavy and solid as a chain around his skull, with no words other than his own name being whispered aloud, no vision other than light streaming past the hands of a shadowed image.

"I'm sorry," spoke George. If he just bore down, kept the mental pressure on, he could keep the fragile little world around him from dissolving into mist. *This is insanity,* he told himself. He knew that, but it didn't help. There was so much at stake in that other world that kept drawing him away; everything depended upon what happened there—but he couldn't tell his partner that. "You're right . . . of course you are." He reached over and laid his palm on Sikes's shoulder. "There is something . . . but I can't discuss it now. Soon, though. I promise you that."

Sikes peered at him, the angry expression replaced by one of genuine concern. "Are you all right, George? I mean, what the hell's going on with you?"

"Don't worry about me, Matt . . . it's nothing . . ."

"Jesus H. Christ; if one more person says 'Don't worry' to me, I'm gonna deck 'im." Sikes shook his head in disgust. "Maybe you oughta take a coupla days off or something. Just go home to your wife and kids and just . . . relax. Then you'll be able to—"

"No!" His partner's suggestion filled George with alarm. "No, I can't do that. It's too important—"

"What is?" Suspicion moved behind Sikes's gaze. "What're you talking about?"

He said nothing. Biting his lip, George turned and stared out through the windshield.

"You wanna know something?" Sikes drummed his fingertips across the top of the steering wheel. "I think you're cracking up. I really do. The pressure's on me, and you're the one falling to pieces. I always knew you were a sympathetic kind of guy, but boy . . . this is really something."

"I'm fine." The words grated from George's throat. "As I told you before, you have no reason to worry about me."

"Right. You oughta check yourself out in the mirror some time, pal. You look like death in a mayonnaise jar—jeez, even your head spots are faded! Isn't that a Newcomer thing, like a dog having a dry nose?—the next stop's the pet cemetery?"

"No," said George testily, "it's not. And I find the comparison offensive."

"Suit yourself." Sikes gave a shrug. "But you look like you haven't gotten any more sleep since the last time I got on your case about it."

He glanced from the corner of his eye at his partner. What did Sikes know? "Perhaps you're correct . . ."

His words came slowly from his mouth. "My sleep hasn't been . . . very good lately . . ."

"George, that comes with the territory. Cops don't sleep like babies—they see too much bad stuff, right? So deal with it, already." Sikes spread his palms outward. "Take a pill. Or start hitting the sour milk a little harder; a nightcap now and then isn't going to be considered like major dereliction of duty." He slapped a hand against his own chest. "Hey, I don't sleep too good. I wasn't sleeping too good *before* I found out about Cathy being pregnant." With a deep sigh, Sikes shook his head. "These goddamn dreams I keep having . . . they're about to drive me nuts . . ."

His spine went rigid. George kept his voice flat and expressionless, to avoid revealing the sudden shock that had pierced him. "What . . . what kind of dreams?"

"Ah, stupid stuff." With one hand, Sikes rubbed his eyes. "Nothing I'd probably even remember, if I didn't keep having the same one over and over. Just creepy: it's like I'm someplace where it's all dark, only there's light coming from over there, behind some big dude who's got his arms stretched out like he's about to take a swan dive off the high board, and I can't see his face and I hear him whisper my name and then I wake up in a puddle of sweat. Man, I must be getting old; I must be losing it if that's all it takes to scare the bejeezus out of me."

He knows, thought George. *He's seen it.* At the same time, it was obvious that Sikes didn't know; he didn't know what the visions meant. The truth beyond what he had seen was still hidden; the great revelation had not yet been made to the human mind. But still . . . for Sikes to have even gotten a glimpse of the light, to have heard the voice of the one who had come again . . .

It meant that the time was close at hand.

Closer than he had hoped, than he had feared . . .

A faint noise, part electronic and part mechanical,

came from the close, insubstantial world of the squad car. It took George a few seconds to discern and then recognize the sound of the police radio's telefax unit. It stopped, and he heard Sikes tearing off the printed strip of paper.

"Aw, shit . . ." A sour disgust filled Sikes's voice. "That's just great."

George pulled himself back from the deep abyss of his thoughts. "What's the matter?"

"We just got the word from Grazer." Sikes glared at the curling slip of paper in his hand. "The HDL lawyers have already filed for an injunction." He glanced at his watch. "We're going to have to step on it if we're going to get any time at all with Bryant, before we get yanked out of there." Sikes crumpled up the fax paper and threw it down on the car's floorboard, then shoved the car back into gear.

His partner's angry mutter had only filtered partway into George's consciousness. "It's not important," he said softly.

"Huh? 'Not important?' What're you talking about? We got zip for leads right now. If we can't squeeze something out of Bryant, then we've got no way of even beginning to figure out what the HDL's planning."

The dream and the vision it contained still filled George's thoughts.

"Someday," he said, "you will understand. It will all be made clear to you, Matt." He closed his eyes and let the squad car's sudden acceleration push him back into the seat. "And it will be soon."

CHAPTER 10

HE WAS GREETED by a smile. And that only made him feel worse.

"Albert!" From behind the parking-lot-sized mahogany desk, Vogel rose up, leaning forward with his big hand outstretched. The Precognosis CEO grabbed Albert's hand, squeezed and pumped. "Hey, it's good to see you! How you been?" He sat back down in his high-backed leather chair and gestured toward the slightly smaller one across from him. "Have a seat. Did you just get here? Would you like something sent up, a little refreshments maybe? How about a tray of those little ranch-style kidney nips—you're the guy who recommended them, remember." Vogel grinned and winked. "Hey, and those things are flying out of the stores. If Hormel wasn't so happy with your services, we wouldn't be able to get any of them at all!"

"Uh . . . no, no, thanks. I'm not hungry." Albert shifted uneasily in the chair, as though Vogel's ebullient mood was about to smother him. He felt more

139

queasy than hungry, even though he had only picked at his dinner last night and his breakfast this morning, to the point that May had started to worry aloud that he might be sick. "Please don't bother—"

"How about a drink, then? Little early in the day, I know, but still . . . all part of the job, right?" Vogel laughed, then reached into a cardboard box behind the desk; he came up with a bottle, unlabelled except for a number scrawled on a piece of sticky tape. "The White Gold people sent this over just yesterday." The contents of the bottle shifted lumpily around. "Their latest brain wave—floral-scented soured milk! Genius concept, huh? Newcomers are traditionally big on the ol' nature trip, and there aren't many who don't go in for a blast of the curds now and then, so why not combine the two?"

"I don't know . . ." The odor from the uncapped bottle had hit Albert; it reminded him of some of the heavy-duty janitorial products he had used back at the police station. "Smells kinda . . . strong."

"Think so?" Vogel's frown was reflected in the glossy curve of the bottle. He reached for a memo pad. "Is that what you want me to tell our clients?"

"No . . . maybe. I don't know." He felt confused, as though his boss had sandbagged him as soon as he had walked into the plush office. "Let me think about it." Maybe other Newcomers would like this stuff; right now he honestly couldn't tell. His head was so full of the merry-go-round-like chase of his worries, he couldn't get any vibrations from the bottle and its mute contents.

"No problem, Albert; take your time. Want to take it home, sample it later? No? Suit yourself." With a slight air of disappointment, Vogel slipped the bottle into the cardboard box, then swung back around in his chair. "So then, what can I do for you, Al? That car running all right?" His toothy grin widened. "You don't need another one already, do you?"

"It's . . . it's fine." Talking about the car made

Albert squirm in his own chair; a pang of guilt stabbed through both of his hearts. Everybody here at Precognosis was being so nice to him—this was the second car they had given him, even more wonderful than the first. He knew they must get them free from the people who made them as part of the reimbursement for his market predictions, but still, Vogel could've kept the cars for himself rather than passing them on to him. When this last one had shown up at his and May's new house, with a big red ribbon wrapped around the gleaming metallic body, he had sat down in the middle of the circular driveway and just stared at it, holding his hands out in front of him as though to absorb the heat of some new sun. He didn't even know what make it was, though he had found an owner's manual in the glove compartment that he and May had eventually figured out was written all in German. Finding out what each button on the dashboard did was still a matter of trial and error. What else could he tell Vogel? "It goes . . . really fast." He assumed that there were gears beyond third, but so far he'd been scared to determine that for sure.

"It damn well should," said Vogel. He laughed, wagging a finger at Albert. "Now don't you go wrapping yourself around some telephone pole with that machine—you're too valuable to us. Anyway, if it's not the company wheels, then what is it you wanted to see me about?"

He could feel his feet swelling with nervousness. There was one advantage to being Tenctonese; nobody could see that sign of his emotional state, not unless it got so bad that the soft leather of his custom-made shoes actually split open.

"Well, I wanted, uh, to talk to you . . . about something new." It had all seemed straightforward when Captain Grazer had told him—coached him, really—about what to tell Vogel. Now all those words seemed to have drained out of his head, and he had to scrabble around with what was left, like scattered pebbles on a barren field. "I mean . . . a new product. That is, I mean, something that's not on the market yet." Albert shrank back in the chair. "So it's, uh, something new. I mean . . ."

"New things are our business, Al." Vogel nodded slowly. "That's what we're all here for. So which of ours are you referring to? I thought we'd gotten a report from you on everything we had pending. Let's see . . ." He sorted through the In basket on the desk. "According to what we got here, you nixed the pilot show for that cable sitcom—boy, I sure agree with you on that one; what would be so funny about a wisecracking headcheese, for Christ's sake?—and you gave a thumbs-up on the new fall colors for the SpotSheen cosmetics." He winked at Albert. "Sure your wife didn't help you on that one? Just kidding." He dropped the report forms into the basket. A puzzled frown appeared on his face. "Except for that new stuff from White Gold that I just showed you, I'm not aware of any other prototypes or mock-ups that we'd have on hand yet. Is this something that Dierdorf brought in?"

"No—" Albert shook his head. "It's not from one of our clients. It's, uh, something that I found." His shoes felt like two vises now. "And that . . . I thought you should see."

Vogel rose partway from his chair, so he could peer over the desk. "Is that what's in the shopping bag?"

"This?" Startled, Albert reached down and grabbed the brown paper bag that he had carried into the office with him. He held it to his chest, fighting the impulse to jump up and run with it out to the parking lot. "Uh . . . yes. Yuh-yes, it is." *Think!* he shouted at himself inside his head. What had Captain Grazer told him to say? "It's . . . uh . . . really important. A buh-buh-breakthrough in . . . in . . . in everything." He couldn't believe he'd just said that; he rummaged

desperately through his scattered thoughts. "In like
. . . communication . . . and doing stuff . . ."

"Really?" Vogel looked impressed. "All in that one
bag?" He stretched out his hand. "Can I have a look?"

Slowly, Albert peeled the bag away from his chest
and gave it to the human who was his boss. He knew
there was no turning back now; he'd have to see it
through. The only comfort for his guilt-flayed soul was
that he was at least keeping his promise to his friend
Grazer.

"What is all this?" Vogel had started pulling the
various items from the bag. "Tapes?" He peered at the
label of one of the cassettes.

"There's a couple of buh-books in there, too."
Albert pointed down into the bag. "They kinda explain everything."

Vogel already had one of the volumes in his hand.
"Let's see . . . 'Grazer Intellinomics Training.'
Sounds . . . interesting." A doubtful undertone fil-
tered through his voice.

Albert clenched his fists, squeezing them between
his legs and the sides of the chair. Now his head felt as
though it were about to explode as well. If only he'd
been able to talk to George—or if he'd had the
courage to tell his wife May what Captain Grazer had
asked him to do—then he wouldn't feel so helpless
and alone now. Somebody would have told him what
he should do; they might even have told him that
bringing Grazer's tapes and books into the
Precognosis offices was the right thing, the best thing
for him and everyone else. But he just didn't know.
He was only a *zabeet;* how could anyone expect him to
figure out these things?

"Looks like some kind of motivational program."
With his elbows on the desk, Vogel leafed through the
book. "Seems very . . . psychological." His frown
curved deeper. "Not sure I catch some of these terms
this fellow uses . . ." With a thumb and forefinger,

Vogel pulled on his lower lip, brow creasing. "Grazer . . . Grazer . . . wait a minute." He glanced up at Albert. "Now I remember. Wasn't this guy your old boss, back when you were with the police department?"

He nodded dumbly. All was lost; how could he have ever hoped to fool the head of a whole company?

"Well, well, well . . ." Vogel rocked back in his chair, regarding at arm's length the cover of the book. "That puts everything in a whole new light."

He had been afraid of that. Inside, his hearts began a slow, tortuous dive toward the pit of his stomach. How was he going to tell May what he had done, and what the inevitable consequences for his sin would be? They'd probably make him give back the car and everything else. Would he and May be able to afford the cramped little studio apartment they used to have? After screwing up like this, he wasn't likely to get his old broom-pushing job back from Captain Grazer.

"I—I can explain . . ." He couldn't, but he knew he had to say something. "It was all . . . all . . ." *It was all Grazer's idea*—that was what he wanted to say, and it was the truth besides. He would never have come up with the notion by himself, of coming in here and saying all those wonderful things about Captain Grazer's books and tapes. He didn't even know what they were about—just listening to one of the tapes had made his head throb with all the strange words and ideas—and he had still wound up telling poor Mr. Vogel all those lies. His new boss, who had trusted him. He deserved to be fired.

The words failed him. Even now, he couldn't betray his old friend.

"There's nothing to explain, Albert."

"No . . . I guess not . . ."

Vogel held the book up, higher than his head. "This is wonderful!"

"Wuh-what?" Albert gazed at the human in astonishment.

"It's a whole program, isn't it?" Vogel pawed excitedly through the tapes spread out on his desk. "It's a package—that's great!"

"What do you mean?"

Vogel spread his hands wide above the GIT materials. "The marketing, and the merchandising potential—it's all built in. I see it all now—this Grazer's a genius. It all links up. A person buys the first tape, or reads the book, and he's in for the whole ride. He'll buy them all. And then of course there'll be spin-offs—more books and tapes, advanced courses in GIT, a lecture series—this guy comes across pretty good behind a microphone, I bet—seminars, a TV series—public broadcasting stations go for this kind of stuff like you wouldn't believe." Vogel shook his head slowly in admiration. "This . . . this is a franchise that's worth a fortune." He started to reach for the phone on the desk. "Tell you what. I'm going to get on the line to that cable network we've done so much work for, and give them some idea of what we've got here. The conglomerate that they're a part of also has a major publishing division." He excitedly waved the phone around. "Hell, if they don't go for it, we'll start up our own publishing company to get this out on the market!"

Albert hunched in the chair, as though Vogel were about to spring the lever of a giant trap. "But . . . but how do you know if it's any good?"

"Pardon me?" Phone in hand, Vogel gazed blankly at Albert for a moment, then radiated a beatific smile. "Albert," he said softly, "come on. How do I know? Because you brought it to me. Your track record for predictions is up in the high ninety-nines right now; you haven't made a duff call in months. There isn't much in life that could be more of a sure thing than this. Maybe what you got has started to rub off on me—I can feel this one, myself." Vogel shrugged. "Hey, and besides—this Grazer fellow's got to have something on the ball, right? He's the one who first figured out how bright you really are, what kind of talent you have, started you cracking those cases for the police. So he's no slouch, the way I see it." He punched buttons on the phone, then leaned back in his chair. "Trust me, Al. This is going to be great."

Keeping his silence, Albert watched his boss. In his head, a new set of realizations had begun to blossom. He wasn't going to be fired for having come in here and telling a bunch of lies to Vogel. He had pulled it off, at least for now; Vogel had believed everything he had said, just the way Captain Grazer had told him it would happen . . .

And that meant—it was something he would have to think about for a long time—that Mr. Vogel wasn't any smarter than he was. Not really; not in the way that mattered. *Or he would've known,* thought Albert. *That I was lying to him.*

Maybe nobody was smarter than he was. Or to put it another way, maybe there was nobody, human or Tenctonese, who was smart at all.

It was a realization that didn't make him feel any better. He sank back into the chair's depths, seeking shelter from the cold wind that was already stripping away the familiar lineaments of the world.

As they strode down the corridor, their footsteps ringing off the drab institutional walls, he turned to his partner and said, "Look—you've really got to help me along with this one. Okay? I really need you, pal."

Sikes watched for the effect his words had on his partner. *Shit,* he thought in disgust. George's face remained a wall as impenetrable as those of the women's prison surrounding them. *Earth to friggin' George Francisco—wake up!* He felt the anger rising in his throat. *Doesn't hear a word I say. Still off on his own trip, whatever the hell that is.*

When they were a couple of yards away from the interview room, Sikes suddenly wheeled around, slamming the butts of his palms into the other man's shoulders, hard enough to rock George back a step.

"Matt—" Startled, George blinked wide-eyed at him. "What . . . what's wrong . . ."

"Don't give me that crap." Sikes leaned right into his partner's face. He kept his voice low, but let the words rip with fury. "You wanna veg out while we're rolling along in the squad car, fine; I can live without your sparkling conversation. But so help me, if you space out on me while we're in that room and I'm trying to crack that Bryant bitch open, I promise you I'm gonna go upside your head so hard it'll make your spots fly. You'll look like an egg by the time I get done with you." He took a step back. "Got me?"

He expected—even hoped for—some kind of a reply, for the Newcomer detective to defend himself. Or better yet, a full-out argument, anything to get George's blood pumping. But instead, George just slowly nodded his head.

"Yes, of course, Matt . . ." The voice was scarcely more than a whisper. "Whatever you say . . ."

"Aw, man . . ." Sikes turned away. "I give up." He could see that he would have to carry this whole show by himself.

Darlene Bryant was waiting for them inside the interview room. She sat behind a plain wooden table, idly toying with the pack of cigarettes in front of her. One eyebrow—significantly less glossy and artistic than Sikes remembered from before—arched as she glanced round at the two police detectives. "My gentlemen callers seem to have arrived," she drawled to the prison matron standing beside the door leading back toward the cell blocks. "I'm sure they won't mind if you excuse yourself now."

"Yeah, don't worry." Sikes nodded to the matron. "If she gives us any trouble, we'll slap her around a couple of times before we give her back to you."

"Pity my attorneys couldn't have heard that remark." She glanced over one shoulder as the matron withdrew, the heavy steel door closing behind her. A tomblike silence settled over the tiny space and the three figures—two human and one Tenctonese—that it contained. "I'm sure they'd find that attitude very interesting. And profitable."

"Good thing they're not here," said Sikes. He and George pulled back the two chairs on their side of the table and sat down. "I'm surprised you didn't have 'em lined up outside like a wall for us to get over."

"Don't indulge in too much self-congratulation." Bryant slid a cigarette from the pack and lit it, then tucked the lighter back into the breast pocket of her faded, ill-fitting overalls. "I told my legal staff to ease up—just for a little bit, that is. Just so you could come in and talk with me."

Sikes glanced over at George and saw his partner's nose wrinkling.

"Must you?" George fanned the drift of cigarette smoke away from his face. "There's not much ventilation here."

"Precisely." Bryant indulged in a malicious smile. "I don't enjoy being at such close quarters with a parasite such as yourself, Detective Francisco. So you'll have to excuse me if I engage in a little—shall we say—fumigation." She flicked ash from the tip of the cigarette. "So get used to it."

Glad something brought him around, thought Sikes. He turned back toward Bryant, studying her as though looking for pressure points, some way of cracking her steel facade. She looked even tougher and more determined than when he had encountered her before, on the outs. That was to be expected; a lock-up either hardened people or broke them. He would have put money on Bryant being one of those who didn't break. With the aging beauty queen veneer stripped from her like a discarded chrysalis, she had emerged as a laser-eyed, toxic creature.

"I always heard smoking was bad for a woman's looks."

She turned her narrow gaze toward Sikes. Her hatred was a palpable force, unrelieved when she let a corner of her smile return. "Is that why you came here? To get beauty tips for your little slag girlfriend?" Bryant folded her arms, one hand holding the smoke aloft. "Has her 'delicate condition' made her that ugly in your eyes?" She shook her head in mock sadness. "And all this time I thought you really loved her. Everyone to his own taste, and that sort of thing."

Sikes felt his face tighten. "What do you know about her?"

"Oh please, Detective Sikes—must we engage in all these little pretenses? As if you would have any other reason for pestering away over the last six months or more to get in here. And as if it were possible to keep something like this a secret from me." The angle of her smile showed that she was relishing every word she spoke. "My followers and I have sources of information that you can't even begin to imagine. Isn't that why you wanted to see me? To find out what I know?" Another flick of ash. "Good thing you took the slag to the hospital. Getting close to the delivery date, aren't we? Perhaps I could arrange to have a nice little floral arrangement sent over."

He hesitated a moment before saying anything back to the woman. A rhythm had been established a long time ago, a way of working in these kinds of interrogation sessions; now would be the time for George to cut in, verbally hitting the subject from another angle. Things like that had a cumulative effect, chipping away at the defensive armor concealing the truth they had been sent to discover. Bit by bit, the target would be trapped, cornered, and exposed. But it took both of them working together to do it . . .

From the corner of his eye, he glanced over at George. His partner gazed straight ahead, as though looking through Bryant to the wall behind her. *Shit*—

he kicked George's shin underneath the table. *Get with it!* he silently yelled.

"You know . . ." George slowly turned his impassive, unnerving scrutiny toward Sikes. "Miss Bryant is right. Time . . . the time is near . . ." His voice echoed spookily in the small room, a pronouncement from afar having been delivered.

Bryant studied George with amusement, then glanced over at Sikes. "What's his problem?"

"Just can it," Sikes replied savagely. "We're the ones asking the questions; you get to answer them." Though what chance there was of pulling that off now, he didn't know. The whole process had gone way out of his control. Not only had George failed to pick up on the rhythm of picking away at Bryant's defenses, he had obviously winged out on that same weird trip he'd been on before. *Great time for it,* he thought with bitterness. The sonuvabitch couldn't even pull it together for this much—what the hell's going on? And in the meantime, Darlene Bryant was sitting there, smirking at both of them. "Look, you wanna brag about how on top of things you are? Fine—why don't you start by telling us what you know about the bombing of Dr. Quinn's clinic. I'll bet you got some prime bits on that one."

"Bombing?" Bryant widened her eyes with faux innocence. "I'm shocked by the insinuation you seem to be making. You've displayed before an irrational prejudice—and a personal one, at that—against anyone trying to resist the parasites' encroachment upon our world; I suppose that has something to do with your own obvious preference for the company of these creatures. Now I have to wonder if you've let that mania overwhelm your professional standards. Why ask me about the bombing of this so-called clinic? Here I sit in prison—largely as a result of the lies you and others have told about me—yet somehow you imagine that I'm to blame for some incident out in the free world. Or perhaps you'd like to think that I climbed over the fence and planted the bomb myself, and then ran all the way back here in time for the evening population check? I'm flattered that you think I'm still capable of such athletic endeavors. I do try to keep fit but after all, Detective, there are limits."

The woman's sarcasm grated on Sikes's nerves. "Cut the crap, Bryant. We all know you don't even have to step out of your cell here to get what you want done on the outs. You're still running the HDL—you've got your little messenger boys trotting back and forth to get your orders practically every day."

"And that really bothers you, doesn't it?" A cold sense of triumph glittered in the woman's eyes. "It rankles your ass that the Human Defense League and all the other Purists didn't just wither and blow away in the breeze." Her voice turned as ugly and harsh as her words, ones that she would never have used in her previous genteel incarnation. "That's what you really wanted, isn't it? So the parasites with whom you're so buddy-buddy—these creatures that you're so happy to climb into bed with—would have a free hand in taking over this world. Nobody to oppose them, no one to get in the way of the plans they have for the human species—plans that traitors such as yourself are all too willing to be a part of. Well, deal with it: we didn't go away. We're still here. We will be fighting the parasites and their collaborators until every single one of them is dead."

"So I take it you're admitting that you ordered the hit on Quinn's clinic."

"Did I say that? Really, Detective, even if I had done so, I would hardly be trapped so easily into confessing responsibility." Bryant contemplated the burning tip of her cigarette for a moment. "Though in this case, I can afford to be quite honest with you. The HDL had nothing to do with the destruction of the clinic. Of course, we weren't entirely displeased that it happened; the late Dr. Quinn was singularly loathsome in his dedication to the welfare of the parasites."

"Really expect us to believe that?" Sikes gave a snort of disgust. "The HDL is the only Purist organization capable of pulling off an operation of that scale."

"Perhaps so." Bryant nodded slowly. "But you reveal just how blinded you are by your own preconceptions. Anything happens that's not to your liking, that threatens your precious slags, and you come running to blame the Purists. Well, let me tell you something." She leaned across the table, her voice lowering in pitch. "You can peek up my skirt all you want to, but you're not going to find what you're looking for. Quinn and his clinic deserved to be bombed out of existence, but we didn't do it. There's more going on here than you even have an inkling of. You're wasting your time trying to pin this one on the HDL. Quinn had enemies—forces opposed to what he was trying to accomplish—that even he didn't know about. If he thought he could just blithely go along, trying to cross humans and parasites, and nobody would mind . . . well then, he was certainly proved wrong, wasn't he?"

In silence, Sikes gazed at the woman, trying to figure her out. Logically, he knew that she was lying, attempting to deflect their investigation from the most likely suspects. There really were no other possibilities besides the HDL. Of all the Purist organizations, they had over the years made the least effort to conceal the violent nature of their opposition to the Newcomers. They had never had any objection to wholesale murder before—after all, Bryant was doing time for her involvement in a scheme to spray a lethal, Newcomer-specific bacteria over the entire Los Angeles basin—so why should they have any scruples about blowing away one man they despised so thoroughly?

At the same time, as he contemplated Bryant's smug expression, his gut told him something different. His cop instincts, honed to distinguish between lies and the truth, had their red needle swung all the way over to the other side of the dial. Sikes would have pawned his back teeth to put a bet on any horse he had this strong a feeling about. The former beauty queen might be radiating a malevolence just short of weapons-grade plutonium, but she also seemed to be telling the truth, at least as far as the clinic bombing was concerned.

Too weird, mused Sikes. And even scarier. Because if it hadn't been the HDL's thugs sneaking around with little ticking packages, that meant somebody else was out there in the dark, somebody the authorities hadn't even had a glimpse of yet. Another Purist outfit? A group that had both the will and the means to pull off a bombing—maybe a splinter group from the HDL, a bunch who couldn't put up with Darlene Bryant's high-handed leadership? Sikes gnawed away at the problem, already sensing that approach led up a blind alley. Bryant's ill-tempered little diatribe had seemed to suggest some other, entirely different source, somebody not even aligned with the Purists. *Quinn had enemies that even he didn't know about . . .*

If that were the case, it would mean starting all over again, from scratch, without the benefit of already knowing who their most likely suspects would be. And there wasn't time for that, Sikes realized with a sinking heart. Enough time had elapsed for the unknown enemy to regroup its forces and get ready for an attack on another target. First the clinic, and then . . .

Time had been ticking away, measured by cells dividing and reforming, slowly building the embryonic life inside Cathy, giving the unborn child eyes and a quickening heart—perhaps two?—and delicate, perfect fingers. If the murderers of Dr. Quinn were waiting for anything, he knew that it would be the birth of that infant, the mingling of his and Cathy's blood lines. These shadowy figures hated the yet-to-be-born as much as the innocent ones already walking on this world's surface.

A sudden noise interrupted Sikes's bleak meditations. The door behind Bryant swung open. A human male in a three-piece Brooks Brothers suit stepped past the prison matron into the interview room. Sikes recognized the man from the times he had seen him in court.

"All right, that's it," said the HDL attorney. He thrust a sheaf of official-looking documents toward Sikes. "This little session is at an end. We're not living in a police state yet, much as you'd like that."

He paid scant attention to the rest of the attorney's blather, having heard most of it before. Something about the previous judge's order being set aside, appellant's right to privacy, the state's failure to show compelling need—

"Whatever." Sikes pushed aside the injunction papers. "You can send those over to the department; I don't wanna look at them. We were just about done here, anyway." He glanced over at Bryant. "Nice seeing you again, Darlene. Maybe if you stay on your best behavior, you'll get out of here before your hair turns completely gray."

George was still gazing ahead of himself, lost in whatever thoughts had come to preoccupy him. Maintaining his air of abstraction, he stood up when Sikes nudged him in the shoulder.

"Come on," said Sikes. "I really need a change of air." He pulled open the interview room's other door, without even looking over his shoulder to see if his partner was following him out.

On the outskirts of the city, he finally spoke up. All the way back from the women's prison, George had been aware of Matt, simmering—almost boiling over, actually—with a barely controlled anger. He supposed that was only to be expected. Matt stared straight ahead through the windshield, scowling darkly at every vehicle that came within his line of vision, cranking the steering wheel and punching the accelerator, working the squad car through the dense lanes of traffic. He knew better than to say anything about the quality of his partner's driving.

He had come up from his own deep, wordless meditations, as though rising through an unlit ocean, emerging at last into the small bubble of air held by the car. Everything that had happened at the prison, that confrontation with a vector of evil named Darlene Bryant, and before, when Sikes had actually blown his top and started shouting at him, passed in his memory like a filmed reenactment on television. He could see someone who looked like himself, and whom others addressed as George Francisco, but he knew somehow it really wasn't him. His soul, the innermost part of him, was still somewhere else. A place where he lifted his gaze toward the light streaming past a shadowed figure's outstretched hands . . .

One true thing had been spoken in that airless room that had held Sikes and Bryant and that empty creature who bore his own name and face. The human woman hadn't intended to say it that way, but he had heard and known the meaning behind the words. She's right, he remembered telling Sikes. The time is near.

"Matt . . ." His voice, so little used recently, sounded strange in his ear canals. He cleared his throat and spoke louder. "Pull the car over."

"Huh?" Sikes glanced at him. "Now what?"

"Pull the car over," he repeated. "And stop."

Sikes rolled his eyes upward, but did as George had requested. The freeway traffic roared past the car.

"So we're going to have a little conference, right here?" Sikes rested one of his hands on the steering wheel. "Sure, why the hell not? You spend so little time these days in the same world as the rest of us, I suppose I have to grab whatever chance comes along to get two words in a row out of you."

He ignored the comment. There was no point in explaining; not now.

Sikes's anger turned to puzzlement, then alarm, as he watched his partner open the passenger side door and step out. "What the hell you doing, George?"

Everything seemed clear and bright now, as though a great calm had descended upon his soul. Even the roar of the freeway traffic sounded as gentle as a stream tumbling over water-smoothed rocks. He reached into his coat and extracted his wallet.

"Here—" George plucked out his Detective Two identification and held it through the window toward his partner, his former partner; that was all ended now. "I won't be needing these anymore."

"What!" Sikes stared at him in astonishment. "Are you crazy?"

He tossed the ID onto the empty seat. "Give Captain Grazer my apologies for not giving proper notice. But soon he'll understand as well."

As he turned and walked away, the wind from the traffic fluttering his coat and trousers, he could hear Sikes scrambling out of the squad car.

"You're outta your mind!" Sikes shouted after him. The driver side door slammed like a cannon shot. "You don't need sleep, you need a friggin' brain transplant!"

George knew that he if he looked back over his shoulder, he'd see the human that his been his friend red-faced, his teeth clenched with anger.

"Fine!" Sikes's voice cut through the noise of the vehicles rocketing past. "Go ahead, crap out on me—I should've known you'd do it some day!"

Enough of his twin hearts remained behind that the human's words stung him. But there could be no turning back. Not now.

He kept his head down and continued walking along the freeway shoulder and toward the destiny that had been revealed to him.

CHAPTER 11

"ALL RIGHT, NOW—bear down. Breathe through your mouth."

She looked past the doctor and the rest of the white-masked faces, toward the ceiling of the delivery room. "I *have* been pushing." In Cathy's ear canals, her own voice sounded more peevish and annoyed than anything else. There was no pain so far, or at least not much. She wondered precisely what anaesthetic had been in the epidural the doctors had given her. Would it have been what human women usually got, or a Tenctonese dosage? Maybe, given the circumstances, a little of both.

So this is what it's like, thought Cathy. This last bit seemed to be mainly hard work; she supposed that was why they called it labor.

"Won't be much longer now." The surgical mask slightly muffled Nurse Eward's voice. She leaned over and wiped the beads of perspiration from Cathy's brow. "We're not quite at the home stretch, but pretty soon."

"Did Matt get here?" Cathy raised her head from

the pillow to look around. The delivery room looked like a convention of every doctor and scientist the BNA had ever sent over to take a look at her. So much for privacy; she had already wondered why they didn't just put the whole show on television—who was there left to let in on the big secret? "I don't see him—" She was sure she would have recognized him, even behind the sterilized disguises.

"We called him, right after your water broke. He knows just where you're at in the process." The nurse gently pushed her back down. "Don't worry—I'm sure he's on his way. With the siren on and everything."

"That's typical." Cathy figured she had earned the right to complain about all the same things that human women did. The dutiful father-to-be puts in all that attention and time—she had gone full-term, the complete nine months—and then when the pay-off comes, he's nowhere to be found. "If he doesn't get here soon, I'm going to have to do everything myself."

"You're not quite on your own," Nurse Eward said drily.

She rode out the last of the contraction, a fairly mild one, and shook her head. "Yeah, you're right; being alone isn't the problem around here." Her reply was tinged with irritability. "Am I crowding you folks? Maybe I could wait in the hallway until it's over."

Nurse Eward turned toward the lead doctor. "Perhaps we should've given her a general anaesthetic."

"Here it comes." She pointed to the television screen. "I knew it was going to be on again."

Buck Francisco already felt strange, sitting beside his kid sister Emily on the sofa in his parents' house. It had been his house as well, a long time ago—not even a year, but it seemed a lot longer than that. So much had changed—not in the house; it was still full of the overstuffed tert furniture that their father preferred, sitting in the middle of the bright washes of color that their mother had splashed around during her return-to-Tenctonese-culture period—but in himself. He still couldn't figure out whether those changes came out to either a gain or a loss.

"Where's Mom?" Buck glanced toward the kitchen.

"I told you—she took Vessna out to the park. She does that every Wednesday afternoon, there's like an infant play group or something. Now be quiet." Emily punched her small fist into her brother's leg. "You gotta pay attention to this."

". . . strange new cult sweeping through the local Newcomer population . . ." The voice from the TV went louder as Buck picked up the remote control from the coffee table and thumbed the volume button. He recognized the human on the screen, talking into a microphone with the station's call letters around it, as a news reporter for whom their father had always had an acute dislike. The screen didn't have the word "live" in the corner, so it had to be a rebroadcast. "Clashes between the group and followers of the traditional Celinite religion have been on the increase over the last several months, but never on a scale like today's events." The camera angle turned slightly away from the man, taking in a scene full of paramedic vans and police black-and-whites. Heads were being bandaged by the people in the white outfits, while the uniformed cops were busy leading away those who had already been handcuffed.

"Big deal," said Buck. His sister had called him up—he'd had to go down to pay phone in the hotel's seedy lobby to talk with her—and had carried on like there was some big emergency. All that just to get him to come over and see this? It was old news already; he'd heard over the radio that morning about the mini-riot out in the city's warehouse district. There was always some kind of action like this happening somewhere in L.A.; he figured that was what urban life was basically all about. "Em, you can't get all torqued about every little thing you see on the news."

"Shh!" Her forefinger pointed toward the screen. "Look!"

He looked. What he saw rocked him back against the sofa cushions.

"With me now," said the TV news reporter, "is George Francisco, formerly of the Los Angeles Police Department. Mr. Francisco is one of the 'Bearers of Light,' as the adherents of the new cult call themselves—"

Buck's eyes widened. "What the . . ." He leaned toward the television screen.

In that little world of colored dots behind glass, his and Emily's father stood beside the reporter. Instead of the necktie he always wore in public, a knotted cord dangled a small amulet at the front of their father's bare white shirt.

"Mr. Francisco—" The reporter had turned toward him. "You seem to have become the spokesman for this new cult—"

"It's not a cult." Their father's voice was stern, unfazed by the human's media-juiced mannerisms. "We are merely those who are fortunate enough to have received the light of truth."

"Okay . . ." The reporter nodded in a show of amiability. "It seems, however, that the followers of the Celinite faith—which is, I'm sure that most of our viewers are aware, considered to be the orthodox faith of most Newcomers—seem to have taken some pretty strong exception to the growing popularity of your, uh, group's beliefs. Would you agree that that seems to be the case here today?"

The shot cut to what Buck assumed was an earlier clip depicting a shouting match degenerating into a frenzy of wrestling and flying punches that filled the street. A Tenctonese woman shouted "Heretics!" and clopped one of the new cult's members over the head with a picket sign. The clip ended, and the shot went back to the reporter and George Francisco.

Buck and Emily's father hadn't lost the public

relations skills he had picked up while working for the police department. "These are very unfortunate incidents," he said gravely. "We hope to cooperate fully, both with the authorities and with our brethren who have not yet shared in the light with us, to make sure that there are no further repetitions of this kind of violence. After all, this is a situation that affects everyone in our community, Tenctonese and human alike—"

"That brings up something I'd like to have you confirm, if you can." The reporter thrust the microphone closer to the other's face. "Is it true that there are human members of your group? That is, who have shared in this, um, 'light' experience, as you put it?"

A nod. "Yes, that's true. This truth, the message that has been brought to us, is for all people, of whatever blood. The time has come. There shall be a new birth that will bring us together as one . . ."

There was more, but Buck scarcely heard it. The inside of his head was buzzing by the time the piece ended and a commercial came on. A smiling pitchman on a yacht decorated with sultry, bored-looking women in microscopic bathing suits held up a book and a couple of audiocassettes and started rattling on about them with an even more palpable religious fervor.

Emily took the remote control from her brother's limp hand and switched off the TV. He glanced over and saw that her eyes were shining with held-back tears.

"Wow." He continued to stare at the empty screen. "When . . . when did all this come about?"

His sister shrugged. "I guess about a month or so ago. That was when Dad stopped coming home. 'Cause he was spending all his time with those Bearers of Light people."

"You're kidding." Buck stared at her in astonishment. "He's like . . . left you and Mom and the baby? That's impossible. He wouldn't do that."

"Well, he did." Emily's voice sounded small and fragile. "He and Mom had a big argument about it, the last night he was here. It wasn't much of an argument, since she was the only one shouting, and like crying and stuff; I couldn't hear what Dad was saying. And then when it was all quiet again, I came down from my bedroom and she was all alone in the kitchen. She had her head down on the table . . . and she was crying . . . and when she looked up and saw me standing there, she grabbed me and hugged me so hard and she was still crying . . ." Emily's voice wavered, then broke at the same time her own tears started to flow. "Oh, Buck—" She grabbed his arm and leaned her face against his arm. "I don't know what's happening . . . I don't want to know . . ."

"Hey, come on. Come on, Em; everything'll be all right." He managed to get his arm around her shoulders and held her against his side. "Don't . . . don't worry." With his other hand, he brushed away the tears on her cheek. "Did Mom tell you anything? About what Dad had told her about all this?"

"Yeah . . ." Emily nodded. "I guess she knew I was scared and stuff. So she tried to tell me—but there wasn't much she could say. 'Cause Dad had told her that this was just something he had to do. Mom said he couldn't explain it to her, either. It's like all a big mystery, with these Bearers of Light and everything. He'd had a vision; that was what he told her." She rubbed her damp face with the flat of her hand. "Mom told me we didn't have to worry about money, at least not right now, even though Dad had quit his job. He'd made arrangements so that everything would be okay; there's like interest coming from all their savings and stuff at the bank. I mean, I was a little scared about that, when I thought about it." She looked up at her brother. "'Cause you hear about other people joining these cult things, and they have to give all their money, and their house and their car and everything to 'em—I guess it's different with this Bearers of Light

163

thing. I was kinda glad when Mom told me that much was going to be okay, that we weren't gonna have to go to a shelter or like starve to death or something."

"Yeah, I bet you were." Buck shook his head, still finding the whole bit hard to believe. "And you say all this started a month ago? I mean, Dad joining this cult—why didn't you come tell me before now?"

"I didn't know how . . . I didn't know what to say. That's why, when I saw this on the news this morning, I phoned and made you come and see it. So you could see it for yourself." Emily's voice turned softer. "I couldn't tell you."

"Oh, man . . ." He looked up at the ceiling. This was all too much. He felt a little guilty, whether for not being home when it all happened or because somehow what his father had done was because of him, he didn't know.

A strange, illogical thought came into Buck's head. With all this, and with the effect it must be having on his mother and his sister Emily—he found himself wondering how his father's human partner Sikes must feel. George Francisco's work with the police had meant nearly as much to him as his own family, and the two police detectives had been such good friends. For him to just quit and walk away from all that . . . what could it mean?

Poor Matt, thought Buck. He felt an edge of sympathy for the tert. That would be one more person trying to figure it all out.

He went through the contents of the truck, checking once again all the equipment that had been assembled over the last few weeks. Noah Ramsey knew he was being obsessive, but he had reason to be. This was the big one, the one for which he and the other HDL team members under his command had been gearing up for a long time.

"It's looking good, Ramsey." One of the assault technicians followed him through the truck's interior.

The older man had actually served with the legendary Marc Guerin, the hero of the human race for whom the HDL's top commando unit was named. "This is all going to go down like a greased torpedo." A humorless smile moved across the man's face. "They'll never know what hit them."

"That's the plan, all right." Noah looked across the weapon racks mounted on the truck's walls, silently ticking through the checklist he kept in his head. Everything was locked and loaded, ready to be grabbed, safety catches thrown off, and employed with deadly force. The tech's words echoed in his thoughts: *They'll never know . . .*

"Any last words from Bryant?" The tech leaned against the open rear doorway and folded his arms across his chest. He was still in lean, hard-muscled shape, despite his gray hair and sun-grizzled visage. "Something to send the boys off with?"

Noah glanced over his shoulder at the man, then swung his gaze back to the row of automatic rifles in front of himself. He had to wonder if the other was mocking him, making some kind of point about his tight relationship with the HDL's imprisoned leader. He had been aware that there might be resentment from a few of the team members for some time; his status as Darlene Bryant's protegé, combined with his relatively young age, could easily rankle the older veterans of the Purist campaigns. Their attitude would change, though, after this action. He had sealed a vow in his heart that the team would pull it off, or he would die leading the attempt. A certain grim pleasure came from the contemplation of being a posthumous hero, like Marc Guerin.

He shook his head in reply to the tech. "There's no need for that." Noah laid his hand for a moment against the black phenolic stock of one of the assault rifles. "She knows we've got everything under control."

The team's communications tech appeared in the

truck's rear doorway. "We've located that Sikes guy," the comm tech shouted to Noah. "Picked up a trace on his car—looks like he's headed to his own apartment, where he was living before the BNA stuck him in that safe house."

"Probably just going back to pick up something he forgot before." That was one more thing Noah could cross off his mental checklist. "Okay, keep an eye on him—he could be real trouble if he turns up at the hospital before we move in."

"You're right about that," said the assault specialist. He watched the comm tech return to his bank of radio monitors, then looked back around at Noah. "I've had run-ins with Sikes before. He's nobody to mess with, if you can avoid it."

Noah shrugged. "We can deal with him. Just like we're going to deal with all the rest of them."

"Ah." The tech nodded, a half-smile appearing on his face. "I suppose so. You got a launch time for this little operation?"

"That's not up to me." He looked at his own hand, the fingertips curving along the bright metal of the rifle's trigger, then turned his somber gaze to the tech. "It's all up to the woman in the delivery room."

He turned the key in the lock, pushed the door open an inch, then stopped. Through the narrow space, Sikes could see no one inside; the apartment he had shared with Cathy appeared empty. But past the dull rhythm of his own heartbeat, he could hear another person's breathing. Someone waiting for him.

"Please—" The unseen person's voice came to his ear. "Come in. We don't have much time."

Cautiously, Sikes put his hand inside his jacket, his grip closing about the gun in the leather shoulder-holster. He hadn't come all this way, summoned by a mysterious phone call, just to walk into a trap.

With his elbow, he shoved the door open wider. He saw then the chair that had been dragged out from the kitchen space, and the man sitting in it. His fingers loosened on the gun, as he realized that what the voice had told him over the phone was true.

"You're alive." Sikes had stepped into the apartment and pushed the door shut behind himself. "It's you . . ."

Dr. Quinn gave a single nod. "My apologies . . . for having let you believe otherwise for so long." He shifted uneasily in the chair, as though made uncomfortable by being trapped within the room's walls. "The deception was, however . . . necessary."

All the apartment's curtains were drawn, a diffused afternoon sunlight was barely able to creep among the shadows. Sikes stepped further toward the center of the room, stopping a few feet away to study the apparition returned from the dead. Though over half a year had passed, he remembered the doctor well enough to make the identification, even with the apparent changes the man had undergone. Quinn's hair was cropped short now, a virtual prisoner's cut, and steely gray; one side of his face and neck was mottled with scar tissue. Sikes knew that was the aftermath of the clinic bombing. The doctor's usual white coat was gone, replaced by a denim jacket and a pair of faded jeans with a tear at the left knee. *Hard travelling,* thought Sikes. The man looked like somebody who had been hiding out in tough places, the harder and more unlit the better for his purposes.

Noticing Sikes's scrutiny, the doctor managed a thin smile. "I found out," said Quinn, "that it's not easy being dead. Or let's just say it would've been easier if I actually had been that way."

"You pulled it off as far as we were concerned." Sikes leaned against the counter separating the kitchen from the rest of the space. "Our coroner's office doesn't make very many mistakes; the medical examiner thought she had a nice little box full of your bits and pieces." A note of grudging admiration tinged his voice. "How'd you do it?"

"Does it matter?" Quinn folded his hands together in his lap. "I am, after all—or I was—in much the same business as your coroner. Bodies, whether live or dead, are a commodity to which doctors often have access, and I had been making my plans for quite some time in advance. I knew what the coroner would be looking for, and I provided it; the explosion made the resulting evidence more convincing. The corpse whose remains were mistaken for mine was one of those poor nameless and homeless individuals that usually wind up on the dissecting tables at medical schools; I implanted an artificial knee-joint identical to my own, and kept it preserved at low temperature in the clinic until I would have need of it. Perhaps if your coroner's office had had the time to examine the evidence more thoroughly, they would have noticed that the serial numbers on the knee-joint had been altered to match mine. I had to engrave the numbers under the microscope; the factory in Sweden stamps the numbers before sealing them under a bio-inert resin."

Sikes nodded slowly. "Yeah, I remember my partner saying something about the photos from the coroner looking fishy—just something wrong about them. I guess we should've looked harder."

"I'm glad you didn't. It's been hard enough pulling off this little ruse even without the police knowing I had gone underground. Not that I would have been averse to you knowing; it's just that these secrets have a way of being found out by people with considerably less interest in my personal well-being."

"You mean the Purists? Darlene Bryant and her bunch?"

Quinn smiled ruefully, then shook his head. "I wish the HDL were all that I had to worry about. They are something of a known quantity, and you and the rest of the police manage to keep an eye on them. I discovered, however, that I had other enemies about whom you knew nothing."

The doctor's words triggered a memory inside Sikes's head; Darlene Bryant had said almost the exact same thing. Bit by bit, the pieces of this jigsaw puzzle were beginning to fit together. With Quinn sitting right here in front of him, he had already been able to get over the shock of the ostensible dead coming back to life; that process had begun when he had heard Quinn's voice over the phone at the station, telling him to come to the apartment—and not to tell anyone else.

It showed how crafty and hard the doctor had gotten while on the run, though Quinn obviously hadn't been any slouch before the clinic bombing, when he'd still been making his plans to go underground. And it wasn't just the knee-jobbed corpse kept on ice to throw off his eventual pursuers; he must have palmed Cathy's key to the apartment during the exam at the clinic; then made a copy and gotten it back into her purse without her noticing. A good thing the doctor wasn't a criminal by nature: he had all the instincts for it.

"So you're alive, and you're here," said Sikes. "You wouldn't have called me if you didn't have something to spill. So let's not waste time; we might as well get right to the big questions. You knew the clinic was going to get hit—who planted the bomb if it wasn't the HDL?"

"That question would be easier to answer if you knew who was behind my clinic in the first place." Quinn leaned forward in the chair. "What do you know about the *Sleemata Romot?*"

"The Tomorrow Foundation?" Sikes knew enough Tenctonese to translate the words.

"That's right. They're the ones who provided the financial backing for the clinic."

"I know a little about it. A group of wealthy Newcomer businessmen . . ." He shrugged. "I talked to a couple of 'em after the bombing. Struck me as being the kind of solid citizens who write nice fat donations for all kinds of things. Everything seemed to check out with them, so we didn't poke around any further along those lines."

"Those 'solid citizens' are very good at appearing to be nothing more than that. It's how they got to be so rich," said Quinn. "The *Sleemata Romot* was funding me to the tune of several million dollars a year, and I still wouldn't trust them out of my sight. The foundation members had their own agenda, which wasn't quite the same as mine."

"And what was that?"

"There was a time . . ." Quinn's voice fell low and musing. "A time when I did think they were interested in exactly the same things I was. When they first contacted me about the research I had been doing into the possibilities of crossbreeding between humans and Tenctonese—this was a few years ago. My research was at the most preliminary, almost purely theoretical stages, but somehow these men had found out about it; only later did I learn of some of the less than savory methods they had for obtaining information. But at the beginning, all I could see was the research grants they offered me. With that kind of money I could become possibly the world's leading authority on Tenctonese physiology, even if the crossbreeding research turned out to be a complete dead end—"

"Wait a minute." Sikes held up a hand to slow the doctor down. "You already had some idea, even before Cathy showed up at your clinic pregnant, that something like that was possible?"

"Of course." Quinn nodded. "In medical and research circles, there had been talk of this for some time now. Nothing was ever made public—the Bureau of Newcomer Affairs kept a pretty tight lid on any such speculations. But the evidence was there, mostly in the areas of genetic mapping and microsurgery. At a fundamental level, humans and Tenctonese share more characteristics than had previously been thought, enough to even suggest that both species are derived from a common genetic stock."

"You're losing me," said Sikes. "'A common stock' —what're you talking about? Look, doc, Newcomers and humans don't even come from the same planet."

"Really? And how do we know that for certain? For those of us who were investigating the core material of Tenctonese physiology, the things we discovered forced some fairly radical notions upon us. The alien species that enslaved the Tenctonese may have genetically manipulated the original breeding stock hundreds of thousands of years ago, before the dawn of human history—and that breeding stock may have been taken from the human species or its ancestors here on Earth. Human cultures and the Tenctonese all have ancient myths and legends revolving around a fall and expulsion from a golden, Eden-like primeval state—perhaps those are all derived from ancestral memories of these traumatic events. And if that's the case, then what has happened to Cathy is not a mutation or adaptation of normal Tenctonese physiology, but a reversion to an original human childbearing capability. What we're seeing might be an instance of an artificially-derived genetic branch returning to its root stock."

"Jeez." Sikes didn't know whether he should be appalled or not at the doctor's blunt scientific language. Somewhere in all this talk of genetics and crossbreeding was the woman he loved. It didn't matter to him whether she was entirely different from him or somehow part human. "But . . . but you can't prove all this . . ."

"You're right." The half-smile showed on Quinn's burn-scarred face again. "Proof, in the scientific rather than the legal sense, is a rare commodity. But as far as this theory goes, there is at least one piece of very compelling evidence. When your and Cathy's child is born, it will not be the first cross between humans and Newcomers. There's already been another one."

"Oh." He felt stunned by this news. *Another one*— what did that mean? "Was it . . . you know . . . born healthy?"

"Very." Quinn's smile grew slightly wider. "A completely healthy little girl. I've been following her progress for quite some time. She's a bit older than you might expect; she was born about a year after the Newcomers' Day of Descent, the crash-landing of the slave ship here on Earth. The Tenctonese mother of the child isn't alive, however; she didn't die of any complications from the birth, but from some long-standing injuries suffered in the ship's landing. This is why I was so confident when I first talked to Cathy that she would be able to bring her pregnancy full-term and deliver a healthy infant. The process of developing a human-like womb, as well as all the other necessary changes for carrying the fetus, is based upon internal elements that are already present in microscopic form—you might almost say 'embryonic'—in normal Tenctonese females."

"Yeah, but guys like me—human guys, I mean— there's been quite a few of us sleeping with Newcomer women for a while now. And out of that whole batch, you've got what? Two pregnancies? So something else must be going on for Cathy to get knocked up by me. What's so special about us? Was I taking too many vitamins or something?" A joke, but with a serious intent behind it.

"I don't know . . ." Quinn's expression shifted, his gaze turning toward the dim light seeping through the curtains. "There must have been some kind of trigger —something that kicks in on the biochemical level, with a cascading physiological response, but I haven't been able to determine what it is. That's what all my research was oriented toward finding out. So you can see how important Cathy's pregnancy is; it's our first opportunity to observe almost the entire process resulting in a human/Tenctonese hybrid birth." He glanced back over at Sikes. "If I had been able to continue my research—if the clinic hadn't been destroyed—I might have been able to answer that question for you by now."

"That's the other big question, then, isn't it?" Sikes knew he was on a roll; a police detective didn't often get a chance to grill somebody back from the dead. "Like I asked before—who bombed the place if it wasn't the HDL?"

"Isn't it obvious?" Quinn emitted a bitter laugh. "The *Sleemata Romot*—the Newcomer businessmen who were funding me—they did it. Not personally, of course; they don't like to get their hands dirty. But they paid to have the bombing done."

"Huh?" Puzzled, Sikes tilted his head to one side. "That doesn't make any sense. These people bank-rolled your research, and then they blew it up? Why would they do that?"

"They funded my research because they wanted to control it; there were things that they were afraid I would find out, that they wanted to make sure that no one else ever heard of. And when I did in fact discover those things, they pulled the plug on me. I had been aware, of course, that I had to be careful, that some of my preliminary findings had made them uneasy, so I didn't tell them everything. But somebody on my staff—I still don't know who—was funnelling them information. And when the time came, when they decided that they had heard enough . . . that was when the *Sleemata Romot* also decided that I was too dangerous to let live. I had found out too much."

"Your research? What the hell could you have found out that they'd wanna make burnt kibble out of you?"

"I discovered the truth, and I had the data to back it up. And it was what they were afraid all along would turn out to be the truth. That a human/Tenctonese crossbreed is not a true hybrid, with equal genetic material from both parents. Essentially, the resulting child from such a mating is a genetically pure human child with perhaps some minor Newcomer-like physical characteristics. Not just the gestation process, but the resulting infant as well appears to be a reversion to what I've theorized is the original human matrix. That's what happened with the first child who was born to a human/Tenctonese mating, and I believe it will be the same with the child born to you and Cathy." The doctor leaned forward, his gaze fastening hard upon Sikes's eyes. "Do you see now why those wealthy Newcomers who were funding me would be afraid of what I had discovered? These are men who are absolutely dedicated to the future of their people —and I had found something that could mean the end of the Tenctonese species. Not by the crude violence of the Purists, the mass murders that Darlene Bryant and her ilk would be only to happy to perform—but by the simple, gradual process of interbreeding between humans and Newcomers. If the biological trigger could be found that allows a viable pregnancy to result from a human/Tenctonese mating, and that trigger became universal, then with every such mating and pregnancy, a small portion of the distinctive Tenctonese genotype would be eliminated. According to my research, the children resulting from such pregnancies would all revert to a basic human genetic makeup. With each generation of such children, the Tenctonese—as a species separate from human— would progressively die out. Given a continuous rate of interbreeding between human and Tenctonese, eventually there would be no Tenctonese left; they would have been completely reabsorbed into the human genetic stock."

"I get it," said Sikes. "And that's what got the wealthy Newcomers who were funding you so upset. They could deal with the HDL putting a gun to their heads easier than they could with what you had found out."

"Exactly. As I said, these men are dedicated to the

cause of the Tenctonese people. The forces of innate
biology may be slower than what the HDL would
prefer, but in the long run they're surer and even more
final. The foundation would have shut me down a long
time ago, destroyed all the records of my research, if I
hadn't been holding something else over their heads."

"And what's that?"

"The child," said Dr. Quinn. "The living result of
the first successful human/Tenctonese mating. A little
girl—she's about seven years old now. The Bureau of
Newcomer Affairs doesn't know where she is . . . but
I do." An expression of grim satisfaction appeared on
Quinn's face. "As a matter of fact, I'm just about the
only person who does know where she is."

"I see." A situation like that, Sikes realized, would
make a perfect trump card for the doctor. "How'd you
pull that off?"

"Come on; do you really expect me to confess all
my slightly illegal actions to you? Let's just say that
I've had resources of my own for some time and that I
realized early on how valuable this little girl could be.
I acquired her—is that a polite enough way of putting
it? I prefer it to 'kidnapping'—and have kept her very
safe and very comfortable. She's probably been safer
at the hiding place I created for her than if I had left
her in the care of the BNA. Of course, the girl has been
useful to me as well: I informed my wealthy Newcomer businessmen that if any attempt was made to shut
down the clinic and my research, or if there was any
threat against my own life, then the arrangements I
had already set into place would reveal the little girl to
the world, along with all the data about her nature as a
human/Tenctonese hybrid. Everything would be
made public about the possibility of crossbreeding
between humans and Newcomers. That was my insurance against these men trying to stop my research."

"Something must've gone wrong. The clinic was
bombed anyway."

"They were told . . ." Quinn's face darkened into a scowl. "Someone must have told them—someone I trusted. They were told where the little girl was hidden, and I lost her. When I found out that she was gone, that the hiding place had been broken into and the girl stolen from me, I knew that I didn't have much time. I was in the midst of making my final arrangements, completing the preparations I had already made, when I was contacted by Cathy's doctor and told about her pregnancy. That complicated things a great deal. If the news of her pregnancy had been made public, her life wouldn't have been worth two cents; the men who had been funding my clinic could easily arrange to have her killed. I figured that the only way she could be protected immediately was if I saw her and brought her on-line with the Bureau of Newcomer Affairs; the security the BNA could arrange would be better than nothing. Unfortunately, I had even less time than I had thought: you and Cathy were there at the clinic when I found out that the bomb had already been planted. I just barely managed to hustle you both out and arrange the evidence that would indicate my own death." Quinn laid his hand against the burn scars on his face. "As you can see, it came close to not being an imposture at all; I imagine your coroner's office would've had a hard time accounting for two sets of body fragments in the clinic's ruins, each with a artificial knee joint with the same serial number." He took his hand away, like removing a partial mask. "I crawled out of the flames at the rear of the block while the fire engines were still pulling up out front. I wasn't in great shape then, but I survived. But being officially dead has definite advantages—no one's caught up with me yet."

"Maybe so, but you're taking a risk getting hold of me and telling me all this." Sikes studied the man sitting in front of him. "Why now?"

Quinn was silent for a moment, rubbing his hands

together nervously. "I have reason to believe . . . that my ruse has not been entirely successful. My enemies may already have discovered that I'm not really dead. And if that's the case, they won't stop until they've rectified the situation."

"Okay, so you wanna come into protective custody. You're talking to the right man."

"No!" Quinn's head snapped back, eyes flaring wide. "That—that's out of the question! There's no way I can turn myself over to the authorities. I can trust *you*—but the others, the rest of the security detail, the BNA forces, they may already have been compromised. My enemies can be anywhere . . ."

Sikes knew he was hearing the voice of madness, that the doctor's life on the run had injected a streak of irrationality into his thinking. "Look, you don't have to worry," he said as soothingly as possible. "I'll personally guarantee your safety—"

"You're more of a fool than I thought." A spark of anger showed in Quinn's eyes. "You still don't understand how powerful these people are. I didn't come here for your protection—I came here to warn you. Cathy is still my patient—I was a doctor when she came to me, and I still am; I'm responsible for her well-being. I haven't lost track of time—I know her baby is due any day now. Better you should worry about her, and your child, than about me. I can take care of myself—I've done a pretty good job of it so far—but Cathy and that child will be in far more danger. My enemies will be their enemies, and they'll know that another human/Tenctonese crossbreed has been born. How long do you think they'll wait before they come seeking your child's death?"

The doctor's words chilled Sikes's blood. "We're already doing everything we can to make sure Cathy's safe—there's armed guards all over the hospital we've got her at. Whatever hit squad these people send out, they'll have to get through me and a whole other troop

177

of police and BNA agents before they'd be able to lay a
hand on her. And when she pops that kid, it's going to
be inside more security measures than Fort Knox."

"I'm glad to hear it." Quinn's voice was tinged with
sarcasm. "But these people know how to bide their
time, then strike. Since the bombing of my clinic,
there've been months of peace and quiet—long
enough to lull you into thinking there's nothing to be
concerned about. If you fall into that trap, you'll wind
up regretting it."

"Yeah, well, thanks for the advice." Sikes pushed
himself away from the counter. "But right now, I'm
afraid you don't have any further choice in the matter.
You're a material witness to a whole string of crimes,
including the attempt on your own life. If we're going
to shut down the people responsible for this bullshit,
we're going to need you in custody." He reached down
to take Quinn's arm.

The doctor scrambled to his feet, knocking the chair
over behind himself. "No!" he shouted, face contorted with anger and fear. "I told you!" Quinn
grabbed the fallen chair by one of its armrests and
swung it in a wide arc, catching Sikes across the chest.

Caught off-guard by the blow, Sikes fell, landing
hard on his shoulder. He pushed himself partway up
in time to see Dr. Quinn bursting out of the apartment's front door and into the building corridor
beyond.

"Stop!" Catching himself against the doorframe,
Sikes spotted Quinn climbing out of the window at
the end of the corridor, onto the fire escape outside.
"Goddamn it, don't be an idiot!"

The metal grids of the fire escape racketed beneath
Sikes as he pursued Quinn down toward the alley.
With a screech of rusting iron, the hinged ladders
pulled away from the brick wall with each impact of
his and the doctor's weight.

He almost had him—the collar of Quinn's jacket
was an inch away from Sikes's grasp as he swung

one-handed around the last grid's support pole. Quinn hesitated before jumping the few feet down to the litter-strewn asphalt; his eyes widened as he looked back up toward his pursuer . . .

A red flower blossomed on Quinn's forehead. That was what it looked like to Sikes, but for only a moment; the sharp report of the rifle shot slammed against his ears as he watched Quinn fall away from him, the stunned and baffled look in the doctor's eyes already fading. The fire escape grid caught Quinn's heel, and he dangled upside down for a few seconds, blood forming a pool just inches below his shattered head; then the weight dragged the lifeless foot from the shoe and the corpse fell.

With one hand on the iron rail, Sikes looked down at Quinn's crumpled body. Even before he heard the next shot, he had already ducked and rolled against the wall of the building; bits of rust flew, exposing bare metal, as the bullet hit the spot where he had just been crouching.

Flat on his stomach, he rooted inside his jacket for his own gun, drawing it out as he spotted the car with dark-tinted windows at the alley's mouth—whoever was inside it had stationed themselves so they could cover all the exits from the apartment building. Before Sikes could aim and get a shot off, the rifle barrel lying on top of a partly rolled down side window was snatched back inside; the car's tires smoked and squealed as the unseen driver punched the accelerator. By the time he had hit the ground and run up the alley to the street, the car had swung around the next corner and disappeared.

He walked back toward the corpse and stood looking down at it. Sirens were already wailing in the distance; a couple of apartment windows had been shoved open, his neighbors checking out the scene below and quickly dialing 911.

Zepeda was in the first squad car on the scene. With the red gumball lights flashing around the alley walls, she and Sikes watched the other officers holding back the crowd gathering on the street. "Hey, isn't this what's-his-name?" She pointed toward the body at their feet. "The doctor that got blown up a while back?"

"Yeah, it's him." Sikes felt disgusted with himself. He'd had another piece of the puzzle in his hands, and had lost it. "The guy's name was Quinn."

"Busy fellow," said Zepeda with mock admiration. "Not enough to get killed once—he's gotta do it twice."

"I better get back to the station." Sikes shook his head wearily. "This is gonna take a lot of writing up."

"Forget that noise, man. I'll cover you for a while. You're not even supposed to be here."

"What're you talking about?"

"The dispatcher's been trying to get hold of you for hours. You got other business to take care of." Zepeda gave a quick laugh. "Cathy got rolled into the delivery room—and she can't sit there with her legs crossed forever, waiting for you to show up."

He barely heard the last few words. He had already turned away and started running toward the yellow tape sealing off the alley.

CHAPTER 12

"YOU HAVE DONE well, brother. Your labors serve to bring light into this darkened world."

He heard the words spoken to him, words of both praise and blessing, and nodded. George Francisco knew that the things he sought were closer, almost within reach of his hand. That had been the purpose of his labors. Soon enough—he could feel the moment approaching—the light would wash over him like the wave of a rolling ocean.

"I have tried," said George simply. He sat on a folding chair in one of the little rooms that had been scrabbled together from plywood and salvaged building materials, miscellaneous scraps of acoustic ceiling tiles and cheap hollow-core doors. The spaces had been carved out of the back sections of the warehouse that still served as the center of the new faith. From here, the message that had been bestowed upon his blood, and upon the blood of all other people on this earth, radiated outward. Soon all would receive it. In the meantime, any word spoken above a whisper passed through the makeshift walls as though they had no more substance than the air itself. "I'm glad," he said, "if what I've done has met with the approval of the initiated."

"More than that." The other Newcomer in the small room was one of the original Bearers of Light; he had first dreamt the word well over a year ago, and had become a disciple to the One who had brought the message. "There are more than your brethren who are pleased. Your efforts have been noticed . . . at the highest level." The Bearer smiled gently. "By that One, of whom we can be aware of none greater."

George nodded, keeping his silence. This was what he had worked for. The faith of the Bearers of Light had gained its initial converts from among the lower ranks of Tenctonese society, the outcasts and failures, those who had found little success on this world's hard, unforgiving surface. For such as them, it was easier to receive the light, let it transform their souls. Their hands were empty; they had less of the world's glittering illusions to let go of. Unfortunately, they had less skill in working the machinery of public knowledge, the interlinked network of press conferences, media feeds, spin control, image polishing. These things had to be mastered if the Light was to reach into every dark corner; it was a measure of the fallen state of both the Tenctonese and human species, that the message could not just simply be presented and accepted by those who most desperately needed it. The Light had to be sold, as if it were a spiritual intoxicant more heady than the finest soured milk.

That was why he had been sure he would rise among the brethren. They needed someone like him, a man of accomplishment in the world's complicated dealings. His public relations skills had been honed in the administrative workings of the Los Angeles Police Department; he'd had to scramble and push to make sure his talents were acknowledged. Before he had accepted the Light, his hearts had contained ambitions greater than just being a Detective Two; the LAPD had been a stepping-stone for political achievement before. Deep inside himself, where no one else could see, he had entertained fantasies of standing at a podium topped with news station microphones, while flashbulbs went off in front of him like exploding stars. *My fellow citizens . . . this is the beginning of a new era . . .* The words had changed from time to time, but not the feeling they had given him.

Those dreams had been a long time ago; some other George Francisco, it seemed now, had watched them behind his closed eyelids. Another dream had come, over and over, that had changed him into the being he was now. A Bearer of Light . . . one who had heard and listened to the message . . .

His only regret was that there had been no way he could make his wife Susan understand—the things that had happened, and what he had to do about them. He missed her, and his two little girls, and even his son Buck, whom he'd already lost to the entrapments of this world. The hope he kept inside himself was that the Light would bring them—soon—together once again. Then Susan would understand everything he had done.

"There will be more troubles," mused the Bearer of Light who sat before George. "How can there not be? What has now been brought into this world produces its own enemies, those who resist the message freely given them, those who have placed their souls in the service of the darkness. Yet there are many among our people, and among our human brothers, who are simply confused or afraid or unable to believe that such a gift is theirs for the taking. For those, a soft voice, a voice without wrath or strident argument, a voice such as that is a comfort in these and the times to come. Such a voice will bring us many friends, and draw more into the reception of the Light." The Bearer smiled and nodded. "That voice is yours. You have proved it by your deeds. The message cannot be

183

carried by your voice—there is only one who can do that—but the way can be made straight and clear by you." The Bearer's gaze turned sharper. "Is that something you wish?"

He was taken aback by the other's question. What did the Bearer know . . . or suspect?

"I wish . . . for the Light to be seen, and to be received by all." George brought his voice down to little more than a whisper. "It is a great honor to me, if there are those among the Brethren who feel that I help accomplish such a task."

"As I said, by more than your brethren. You have received the Light, you have been in the presence of the messenger—but only at a distance, in the company of the faithful. But now . . ." He regarded George with even more respect than before. "Now that One has asked—commanded—to see you in person. In private."

Nothing, thought George. *That was what this man opposite him knew.* "When?"

"Right now. Immediately." The Bearer of Light rose from his chair. He bowed his head, as though to one whose eminence in their shared faith had now exceeded his own, and gestured toward the door. "I am to take you to him."

At last. For a few seconds, George turned his consciousness inside himself. With steeled deliberation, he composed his soul, eliminating any unvoiced words that would be unseemly in the presence of that greater Light. Then he looked up toward the other. "I'm ready."

The other Bearer led him toward the rear of the old warehouse, through the narrow corridors and past the maze of tiny warrens into which the high-ceilinged space had been carved. Few of the Brethren were allowed to venture this far into the sanctum; silence wrapped around George, as though with each step the building's interior were multiplying itself, its central point the seed of an expanding universe. Mottled sunlight fell upon him; he looked up and saw a skylight clouded with ancient pigeon droppings, the broken panes mended with rain-warped cardboard. The day's radiance was dimmed to that of an underwater cavern.

"Here." The Bearer stopped before a door of rough, unpainted wood. He stood back to let George approach it. "The One who brought us the Light awaits you."

He entered into darkness, deepened to absolute black when the door was closed behind him. George's eyes adjusted slowly; the faint radiance he saw in the distance could almost have been illusory, a trick of his own expectations. Then the voice spoke to him.

"It has been a long time. Centuries, perhaps." The voice was the same one George had first heard in his dreams. "Or it could be only a matter of a few minutes since we were last together."

The light was a flame no bigger than a thumbnail, shielded by a hand cupped around it. The burning match was brought close to the wick of a candle stubbed onto a small, barren table; the room filled with the shifting glow.

"Centuries or minutes—it really doesn't matter." George looked at the figure sitting on the edge of a raised pallet, a thin army-surplus blanket draping from it to the concrete floor. "You and I are both the same, Ahpossno, and yet different from what we were then."

He had spoken the name, the name of the dead, a name that he had believed would never again be spoken to the living. It was one thing to see that figure in his dreaming, where the dead and the living had always been able to walk around in the dark spaces inside his skull; seeing that same figure on the raised platform before the mass of the faithful, the Bearers of Light, had seemed to George like more of that dreaming, a place and time separate from the real world. But now there sat before him a living man removed from dreams, a man of his own Tenctonese blood, a man leaning forward to drop a burnt-out match onto the table with the other charred fragments like it.

"Yes . . . that was my name. I remember it." The man wore a simple cassock of rough cloth, its hood pushed back to show the pattern of his head spots. He looked round from the candle flame, toward George. The face was out of shadow now; he appeared more haggard than before, fleshless skin tightened upon the bone beneath. His eyes were ancient things, the gaze as bright and piercing as it had been in that other life, but now deepened with unnameable visions. "Ahpossno . . . that name is no more. The man who bore that name is dead. After all . . ." A thin smile lifted a corner of his mouth. "Did you not, George Francisco, kill that man? It was by your hand that I died."

"Yes . . ." George nodded slowly. "I did kill you." That had been another time, another world. Memory, that lay beneath dreaming, rose up inside him, blotting out for a moment the small room and the figures it contained.

. . . the air tensed with the mounting vibration of the shuttle's engine. The craft rose higher, its shadow spreading beneath as the sheriff and the deputies emptied their guns at it. Sparks glanced off the shining metal.

Sikes dug into his jacket pocket. His hand came out, not with his gun, but with an object no larger than a pocket flashlight. With his vision still blurred, George recognized it when the red glow illumined Sikes's hand. It was what Ahpossno had used to bring down the Purists' helicopter. Sikes raised his hand, pointing the object straight at the shuttle; the device's slighter note was almost drowned out by the shuttle engine, as Sikes kept his thumb pressed upon the trigger switch.

In the sky, the shuttle faltered, its noise dipping in

volume and pitch. The craft hung suspended, blotting out the sun, then dragged lower as Sikes continued aiming the jamming device.

"No . . . !" George lurched to his feet. He swung his hand against Sikes's fist. The impact knocked the jamming device loose, sending it tumbling down the face of the dune.

The shuttle's noise shrieked to a higher pitch. The craft trembled for a moment, then bulleted into the sky. A glint of fire remained, the sheriff and his deputies shading their eyes to watch it. Then a spark, that became lost against the sun's glare. The sky was empty.

Sikes, his face contorted with fury, grabbed the front of George's shirt, keeping him from slumping back to the ground. "Why?"

George broke away from him; he stumbled toward the unconscious figure of Cathy.

"I had him!" Sikes shouted after him. "I was gonna bring him down! You know what you've done?"

He looked over his shoulder. "Yes . . . I couldn't let you interfere—I had to fight Ahpossno. He had to take the Serdsos."

"What're you talking about?" Sikes stood in front of him.

"It's filled with the bacteria that the Purists tried to use. I took the Serdsos to the your lab, Cathy; I knew you still had a supply of the bacteria there, for your work. I drilled a small hole, and filled the hollow space inside with the bacteria." He smiled, then winced as a sudden pain caught him. "You don't have to worry about me—I followed all the necessary handling precautions. The hole is covered with a thermal-release patch; its pores will open just from Ahpossno's handling of the Serdsos. By the time he reaches his mother ship, he'll be completely infected—and unconscious. There'll be no way for him to tell the others the truth about what he found here. Even if there's no bacteria left to infect the others, they'll believe that this planet is

contaminated, and that all the slaves must be dead . . ." He paused, the effort of his words beginning to show. *"They won't come here . . ."*

Sikes caught George before he fell . . .

Another time. That had held a dead man, a man he had killed. He had given the *Chekkah* Ahpossno his *Serdsos,* the facetted crystalline sphere that was the embodiment of his own soul, let it be taken from him, the combat between enemies seemingly over—and by doing so, had landed the last blow, the fatal one.

It was by your hand that I died. Perhaps that was true. Because the figure sitting on the thin pallet before George was Ahpossno—but someone else as well. A figure transformed, made anew; a figure that could move inside dreams and visions as easily as in the world of daylight and substance. Had death done that for him?

"There is much we need to talk about," said Ahpossno, the messenger and bringer of light. His somber gaze held George fast in its grip. "Much that I need to tell you. And then . . ." Ahpossno nodded slowly. "Much that needs to be done."

"Yes . . ." George gave a nod in agreement. Unnoticed by the other, he slipped his hand inside his jacket pocket and felt the cold metal weight hidden there. His fingers and palm settled tight upon the gun that he had carried into this sanctum. The colder metal of the bullets chilled his blood. "There's a lot left to do."

"Okay, here it comes." The lead obstetrician bent forward, the other doctors as close behind him as they could get without crowding. "Easy now . . ."

From where Sikes stood, up by the head of the delivery table, he couldn't really see what they were doing, which suited him fine, though he wouldn't have told Cathy that. He had gone through that trip with his daughter by his then-wife, down by the raised stirrups like some kind of backup shortstop, and it hadn't been an angle on the process that he'd really enjoyed. When push came to shove—so to speak—he was just as glad to be over here holding Cathy's hand, wiping the perspiration from her brow and trying to recall all the right Lamaze coach phrases. His mind had gone blank and all he could remember was what the coxswain had kept shouting that one summer he'd rowed for the LAPD's amateur sculling team. Somehow, he didn't think yelling "Stroke . . . stroke . . . stroke!" through his face mask was going to help much.

Cathy broke off her panting breaths to give a small moan, which made him feel even worse. He could disregard the fact that if she squeezed his hand any tighter, she would crush the bones inside it—if she popped the kid all right, that was all he was asking for.

He had gotten there just in time, slamming his car into the hospital's locked and secured parking lot— the guard at the gate had been watching for him and had waved him straight in—then leaving the car right at the building's curb and sprinting inside, past all the other guards who knew who he was and why he was running so fast. The nurses had gotten him into his sterile green scrubs and mask, and into the delivery room in five minutes flat.

There was some hubbub among the doctors down at the other end of the table. Sikes craned his neck to try and see what was going on, but the sheet over Cathy's legs blocked his view. The calm murmur of the doctor's voice seemed to indicate that nothing was going wrong . . .

Then everything seemed to happen at once, so fast that he was left dazed; he heard another voice, that wasn't his or Cathy's or any of the doctors or nurses, that wasn't even words but just a shrill piping little cry. And then, as though it were a jump cut to a memory of that other delivery room, the lead obstetrician was showing him and the woman whose hand he held something all wrapped up except for a small, wrinkled red face. The infant's eyes were squeezed closed, as though displeased with whatever turn of events had brought it here.

"There you go." The doctor leaned forward, tilting the bundle in his arms so that Cathy could see. "A healthy baby boy."

Sikes watched as she let go of his hand and, smiling, reached up to touch the baby's face.

Real time started up again, and he knew he wasn't in some memory loop from the past. It had all happened right now. Hovering protectively over her —she looked exhausted but happy—he turned his own head, regarding with dumbstruck amazement the tiny stranger before them.

The team's communications technician came around to the front of the truck. With one hand on the side of the truck cab's open door, he looked up to where Noah Ramsey sat. "Just got word from inside the hospital." The comm tech's voice was calm and matter-of-fact. "The brat's been born."

Noah pulled himself back from the deep field of his thoughts, turning his gaze away from the windshield and toward the comm tech. "Is it alive or stillborn?" Everything—whether the team went ahead with the mission or not—depended on the answer to that question.

"Lemme make sure." The technician held the earphone tighter against the side of his head, repeating Noah's query in a soft murmur to the microphone angled at his throat. A moment later, he glanced back up. "She says the baby's fine. The doctors are still checking it out, but everything looks stable so far."

"Good . . ." He slowly nodded. The assault tech and the rest of the team were standing around by the rolled-down door of the industrial garage space that served as the mission's staging area; Noah looked over at the group of men in service fatigues. He knew that they were just waiting for the word from him.

"So what's it gonna be?" With the back of his hand, the comm tech pushed the mike away from his mouth.

It only took a second to decide.

"Take the operation code from standby to alert." Noah enjoyed the sensation of the words in his mouth, clipped and efficient. "We'll be moving out on my command."

He watched the comm tech striding over to the team with his orders. He set one hand on top of the truck's steering wheel and squeezed it into a fist. From this point on, everything that would happen was already wired into place.

The gun stayed in his jacket pocket, hidden but ready for use. He had brought it here to use, to this place, this small room that held the unfolding mysteries of the past.

George felt the gun warming against the hand he kept upon it, the heat of his blood seeping into the inert, potential metal. It would be a part of him, an extension of his arm and brain and will, when he drew it out, lifted it, and aimed.

"You have not gone mad. You are not suffering from some delusion." The figure sitting on the thin pallet put his own hand on one of the loose sleeves of the cassock he wore. "Before you is that man you killed, that one who bore the name Ahpossno. Look." He drew back the sleeve, exposing the bare skin of his forearm. Along its underside, from the wrist to the elbow, was an elaborate tattoo, etched in deepest black, studded with bright specks of imbedded gold. "You see? The emblem of the *Chekkah.* That was how you knew what I was before. Can you now have any doubt as to my identity? Or rather, the identity of this body that my spirit still inhabits."

His hearts clenched at the sight of the tattoo, the insignia showing a high rank in the ruthless military elite that had served the alien slave-masters. A man bearing such a mark had been feared even by the cruel

Overseers who had earned their traitors' privileges by whipping obedience out of their fellow Tenctonese. A mark such as the one inscribed on Ahpossno's arm had been earned at the cost of others' lives; in a just universe, that mark would exact the penalty of death for the one who bore it.

Once before, George had executed this man, had brought about his death through his own desperate cunning. To save his own people, to keep the slave-masters from finding them again, bringing their whips and shackles to this bright world. He had no objection to killing the man again.

"How did you . . ." Before that sentence could be passed, he had to know. "How did you come here again? Alive?"

"Why am I not dead?" A grim smile showed on the other's ravaged face. "Is that what you ask?" He turned his gaze away from George, toward the wavering candle-flame; he raised his hand before it, as though to study the nature of his own resurrected flesh. "I did die; the one whom you knew as Ahpossno, the warrior of the *Chekkah,* died. He is no more. The one you see before you bears his scars, some of his memories—and none of his soul." He glanced back around at George. "How could I? Souls, whether they are contained in a *Serdsos* or not, souls belong to the Tenctonese and to humans . . . and I am neither of those. Not any more." His voice hushed to little more than a whisper. "The one you see before you has been transformed into another order of being, different from either Tenctonese or the humans who are more of your brethren than you realize."

He supposed that was true. Once dead, neither Tenctonese nor human rose again. Not in this world.

"I died, and my corpse, sealed in a coffin containing its own vacuum, was jettisoned from the *Chekkah* mothership." The candlelight shone dully through Ahpossno's fingers. "The ship's officers, my commanders, did so to prevent the contagion with which you had infected me from spreading to the others aboard. Perhaps they succeeded; it is impossible to tell. The mothership returned to those stars from which it came, far from this system. I believe that you at least accomplished what you set out to do; it will be a long time before this world is investigated by the slave-masters again. So my death accomplished a great deal; you have no reason to regret that act, George Francisco."

"I regret," he said, "that it was necessary. But there was no other way."

"You speak the truth. To do that which must be done, even at the peril of one's own soul . . . that requires a great strength. You could have made a *Chekkah* warrior." Ahpossno brought his hand closer to the candle, as though to touch the flame. "But no matter; the enmities that divided us no longer exist. The loyalties that once were mine, the oaths that I had taken in allegiance to our masters—those died at your hands as well."

"And what replaced them?"

"The Light." In Ahpossno's eyes, the candle-flame's reflection glinted. "The Light that I have brought to you, and to all your brethren, both Tenctonese and human. I found it there, out in the cold and the darkness, out where the *Chekkah*'s mothership had abandoned my lifeless form. Beyond the limits of these planets' orbits, where the sun is no more than another faint star. My corpse drifted there, in that endless silence . . . can you believe I remember that? Some cold spark, not alive but not yet dead, must have remained inside my body, perhaps down at the sub-atomic level, some place that forms the ultimate basis of consciousness. Perhaps in that nonmaterial substance that humans and Tenctonese alike call the soul. That also makes little difference now. In that cold, in that dark, in that silence, the spark that remained, the infinitesimally small thing that was no longer me but was not yet what I was to become—that spark burned and changed, until it was brought back into the realm of the living."

George listened to the other's voice in what seemed as great a silence as that of deep space. "But how . . . ?"

"Before the Day of Descent, as our people on this world call it—before the slave-ship crash-landed here —the ship was already in grave danger of breaking into pieces; if it had, everyone on board, you and your family included, would have died out in space. The navigational crew did what they had to in order to leave the bulk of the slave-ship intact enough to survive impact upon this planet's surface. In deep space, the crew had begun jettisoning as many nonessential sections of the ship as they could. Many of those abandoned sections of the ship are still out there; some have drifted even farther away, toward the stars. One of those sections was an autonomic medical unit; it incorporated our slave-masters' most highly developed medical technologies. The unit was designed to operate under extreme emergency conditions, when there would be no one capable of directing its actions. It came to life—the life that had been programmed into it by its makers—when its sensors detected my corpse floating in empty space. Through the steel of the chamber in which I had been laid, that small spark was detected; that is how finely honed the sensors were, that the medical unit could detect the last bit of cellular decay. Detect it and seek it out, then reach with its uncoiling arms and bring the dead inside, to light and warmth. That is where I woke, where I found myself, inside that nurturing machinery, in the womb of a non-living thing that had been cast off just as I had been. It was there that the non-living, the machine, brought the dead back to life."

"No machine can do that . . ." George slowly shook his head in disbelief. "The dead can't come back."

"You doubt the evidence of your own eyes."

Ahpossno lifted his hand, palm outward, displaying the *Chekkah* emblem on his forearm. "Is this not proof? Or this?" The hand turned, fingertips touching his jaw. "You recognized me, didn't you? You recognized me even when I walked inside your dreaming. Even when you couldn't see my face, when I was a thing of shadows, you knew who I was. You knew, but you were afraid to say my name, even to whisper it to yourself."

The other's words struck George like a blow from his fist. "I—I couldn't say it. Because you were dead . . ."

"Perhaps I still am—the part of me you can see, at least. Here." Ahpossno reached out and grabbed George's hand, the one that wasn't hidden inside his jacket pocket with the gun, and pressed it against the cassock, over his chest. The rough cloth was all that could be felt; there was no beating of the twin hearts underneath. "You're right, of course; nothing can bring the dead back to life. The slave-masters' machines couldn't do it. But something else happened to me out there, before the autonomic medical unit found me. The change had already happened. Something . . . unknown . . . had entered the seed, transformed it, bathed it in the Light that you have never seen." He fell silent, folding his hands together. "When I awoke, I knew I was dead . . . and alive. What had been Ahpossno had died, just as you willed it. What lived was a new thing. A creature of Light."

"And now you've brought that Light to us." George could feel his grip tightening upon the hidden gun. "Whether we want it or not."

"If you knew—if you really knew—what it is that I've brought to this world, you would want it. Because I found something out there, something that changes all we know."

"Really?" A bitter skepticism tinged George's voice. "And what would that be?"

"Listen to what I have to say. When I awoke inside

195

that autonomic medical unit, out in deep space—when I awoke with the new life that had been given me—I searched the unit's data banks, and I found out why it had been jettisoned from the slave-ship, before it ever came close to Earth. There were Tenctonese aboard the ship, slaves such as yourself, but with a high level of scientific and medical training; they were an elite group, much as the *Chekkah* are. The research in which they were engaged served the aims of the slave-masters, the genetic manipulation of the Tenctonese people, to make our people into even stronger and more dependable workers. At least, that is what they were supposed to have been doing for their masters; in fact, as I discovered in the records aboard the autonomic medical unit, these Tenctonese slave-scientists had been using the unit's facilities for clandestine research into the basic genetic structure of Tenctonese physiology—research that had been forbidden, upon pain of death, by their masters. Nevertheless, the scientists had discovered a way of triggering a change in the Tenctonese reproductive processes, a reversion to what the scientists had theorized was the original genetic stock from which our people had been developed thousands of years ago. Just as this discovery had been made, however, the slave-ship's navigational malfunctions that would result in its crash-landing upon this world had already begun. The slave-scientists, not wanting to risk their discoveries being lost, had taken advantage of the situation and had initiated the jettisoning of the autonomic medical unit containing all the records of their research. It was already too late for the scientists themselves; they had been betrayed to the Overseers for having engaged in the forbidden genetic studies, and had been put to death before the slave-ship landed here. Thus, there was no knowledge among the Newcomers on Earth of what the scientists had discovered about their own genetics and reproductive processes."

"I find it hard to believe," said George, "that something so fundamental to our people—something that defines our very nature—could be so completely suppressed."

"But then, it wasn't." Ahpossno gave his gentle half-smile again. "I found it—as perhaps I was meant all along to find it. My destiny and the destiny of the Tenctonese people . . . those have become intertwined, in a way that the slave-masters who first sent me to this world could never have imagined." His voice softened, became more deeply meditative. "Though I still have cause to wonder . . . there should have been another way that this knowledge was given to our people, even before I came bearing the Light. One woman upon whom the scientists had performed their research remained on board the slave-ship, after the autonomic medical unit had been jettisoned; the scientists had managed to conceal her identity, so the Overseers wouldn't be able to find her. She should have survived the crash-landing, the Day of Descent; with the change that had been made in her, and the coming together of the two bloods, the Tenctonese and the human . . . then all should have been revealed, even back then. It was destined to be known."

George gazed at him in puzzlement. "What are you talking about?"

"Is it not obvious? You have seen it happen already with those whom you know and love. It is possible for Tenctonese to mate with humans, to bring forth a child that is a mingling of both our peoples. Your friend, the human Matthew Sikes, and the Tenctonese woman who shares his life—they have such a union. And I have made it possible for them to have a child together."

"You?" The other's words stunned George. "But . . . but how?"

"There is much that I can do. Or rather, the being that you once knew as Ahpossno, that one who died but did not die, who was transformed into what you see before you now—to that being, great powers have been given. Powers beyond your knowing." A cold glint of light appeared in Ahpossno's eyes. "I knew that I was no longer the same creature as before, that I could do such things as I willed—as had been given to me as my destiny. And I knew as well what had to be done. When I realized the truth, the implications of what I had discovered aboard the autonomic medical unit—that Tenctonese and humans were not two separate bloods, but one originally, and that they could be made one blood again—I saw that I could bring peace to the warring tribes upon this world. If our people and the humans became as one, and they saw that it was, there would be no cause for hatred between them. We would be as brothers, with the same blood running in our veins."

The words had rolled out in the other's voice, like the speech of ancient prophets. For a moment, George closed his eyes where he stood, hearing the echo of what had been spoken. *One blood . . .*

A vision came to him, that he had not seen before in all of his dreaming. A few seconds passed before he recognized it as something that had happened in reality, that he had seen with his eyes open. Rough wood nailed into the shape of a cross, a crude thing wrapped in rags—where had that been? He recalled both himself and his partner Sikes looking at it in disgust; the same twinge of anger moved inside his gut. Now he remembered; it had been propped up on the front lawn of a Newcomer like himself, the Purists had put it there to show how much they hated anyone who wasn't the same as themselves. They had soaked the rags in blood, making it even uglier and more loathsome, a shining red pool collecting at its base.

Then the vision changed, from memory to something that Ahpossno's words had called forth. The blood-soaked cross was no longer a hideous and mocking construction, but radiant, transformed into a new splendor. Light streamed from it, as though it

were a jewel illumined from within, banishing the
darkness that had surrounded it. The blood was no
longer that of some slaughtered animal, but a substance that had just been called into creation. Blood
that was neither Tenctonese nor human, yet both at
the same time. *The same blood running in our
veins . . .*

He pushed Ahpossno's words out of his thoughts.
He had come here with a purpose; nothing was going
to make him forget that.

"I owe your friend Matthew my thanks." Ahpossno
spoke again, his voice low and calm. "More than
anyone besides yourself, he served to bring about my
transformation—though I know that like you, he
would have been satisfied with my death alone. His
intent is not a matter of consequence; he is a man of
honor and courage equal to yours. What better choice
could there be then, to help bring the Light into this
world? Such was my resolve. I had sufficient training
in my previous existence, so that I could override the
autonomic medical unit's programming; there were
enough fuel cells remaining in its navigational system
that I could direct it here. The journey took time, but
the dead have plenty of that. Planetfall was out in the
desert, not far from where the slave-ship had come
down on the Day of Descent. No one saw me, which is
as I wanted it; before I revealed the message that I had
brought with me, there was one simple task that I
wanted to accomplish. Even before I set foot on the
ground, while I was still above the Earth's roiling
clouds, I reached down—not with my hand, but with
my soul, with the spark of light that had grown so large
within me—I reached down and touched . . . not
Matthew, but the woman he loves. Cathy. I had
learned from the data banks that the Tenctonese
slave-scientists had left aboard the medical unit, what
could be done and even how—though they didn't
have the powers that I do. I reached down, I tried, but
I was still not close enough; there is a limit to the

powers that have been given to me. I had to come closer; I left the medical unit out in the desert—I no longer needed it—and walked. Here, into the city. The souls contained by their two bodies sleeping together guided me to them. I stood beneath their window in the night, and reached up to them; now it was possible. I even entered their dreams, as I did yours. But the touch of my soul went elsewhere inside Cathy. A simple thing, a spark within her body that needed to kindled . . . and thus the change was made. There was now a part of her, deep inside, that was no longer merely Tenctonese; it was human as well. As it had been from the beginning of both our peoples. Her womb was now capable of accepting his seed—that was all that was necessary. Matthew and Cathy already loved each other . . . the rest would follow as a matter of course." Ahpossno showed his gentle smile again. "As I'm sure you know."

George studied the figure seated before him, trying to detect the signs of madness. "You're saying that it was you . . . that you made Cathy's pregnancy possible. Through some kind of . . . magic." He pronounced the last word with distaste, his innate rationality rebelling at the thought. "But can you prove it?"

"Proof? I would have thought by now you would have learned that certainty is hard to come by in this universe." Ahpossno gestured toward the candle on the small table. "You see a flame burning, and you assume it must exist, that your senses do not lie to you. You see a dead man in front of you, a man that walks and speaks as you do, yet without hearts beating inside his chest—you see it, but that is something you have difficulty believing. So then, what proof could I possibly give you?"

"Oh, I believe that you're alive, all right . . ." George slowly nodded. "I don't know how it came about, if this story you've told me is true or not—but I can see that the man I killed is here again." He tightened his grip and pulled his hand from his jacket pocket, revealing the gun. "But what can be killed once, can be killed again. If that's what it takes." He raised the gun, aiming straight toward the center of Ahpossno's chest.

The figure seated on the pallet looked up at George. And smiled.

"All right—" Noah turned toward the assault tech. "Let's hit it."

The assault tech gave the signal, a quick drop of his arm. Bright sunlight flooded into the garage as the steel door was racked up. The team member operating the controls at the side of the door stepped back as the first unmarked van rolled past. As it cleared the building it slowed enough for the man to scramble into the back, helped up by the others already inside. From where he stood, Noah had a glimpse of their black combat gear, anonymous and ready for violence as the weapons arrayed along the van's interior.

At the curb, the van turned right onto the street, heading past the empty delivery vehicles and lots fenced with barbed wire that filled the city's industrial zone. A few seconds later the second of the two vans with its cargo of hardened HDL commandoes rolled out of the garage, turning left instead. The carefully drawn plans called for them to rendezvous at the hospital's target site.

"Looks good." Noah checked his watch, synchronized with those worn by the rest of the team. The tip-off from their source inside the hospital had come less than five minutes ago. "We'd better get our asses in gear, too."

"You're the boss." The assault tech pulled himself up behind the wheel of the truck. He started the engine as Noah scrambled up beside him.

Once outside, Noah waited until the truck had gone a block away from the garage; then he leaned out the passenger side window and thumbed the button of the small metal box in his hand. He felt the wash of heat against his face as the building went up, flames roaring out of the open door, then bursting through the roof in a churning fireball. A few seconds later, he could see people rushing out of the nearby buildings, alarmed by the roar of the explosion; they stopped in their tracks and stared at the fiercely burning ruins, shielding their faces with upraised arms.

"There—" Noah turned back around in the truck's cab. "That oughta keep some of 'em busy for a while." As the assault tech drove farther away from the area, Noah expected that it wouldn't be long before they heard the first sirens racing toward the scene, fire engines and police black-and-whites converging. That was part of the plan as well; now, not only were the signs of what the HDL assault team had been putting together in the garage effectively erased, but a distraction had been created, which should draw at least part of the LAPD's forces away from the hospital.

He touched the automatic slung at his hip, and felt a heart-speeding pump of excitement. Everything was happening at last, everything he had been waiting for.

The smile made him hesitate. The smile, and the absolute calm the other man radiated. They spoke of knowledge greater than any George possessed.

"I'm sorry I cannot act surprised." Ahpossno's gaze moved toward the gun, then back to George's face. "Is that what you wanted? But I knew you would come here, intent upon this deed. When I told the other brethren that I wished to see you, I instructed them that no search was to be made of your person. Nothing was to impede your progress toward the destiny you had chosen for yourself."

"You knew that I was coming here to kill you?"

"How could I not?" The shoulders inside the cassock lifted in a slight shrug. "I have walked inside your dreams, George Francisco. I know more of your thoughts and fears and hopes than you do, despite your efforts to turn your soul into a mask capable of concealing your intentions. The pain that you inflicted upon your own wife and family, the abandonment of them and your embracing this new faith, your apparent commitment to the Light and all you've done to help spread the message—who could doubt your sincerity? And no one does. Except for the one who can see more deeply into your soul, into what you truly believe." Ahpossno's gaze sharpened, piercing George like a lance of steel. "You believe that I am a being capable only of evil. That I bring only suffering and death to the Tenctonese people—"

"And isn't that the truth?" Anger flared inside of George. He squeezed the gun more tightly in his fist. "Even if I were to believe everything you've told me—how you came back from the dead, what you found there, how you made Matt and Cathy's child possible—why should I alter my decision? It is death that you bring us; you've as much as said so. Are you so blind that you can't see it? What you want to accomplish, this making one blood, one species, out of the Tenctonese and the humans—that would be the death of our people. We would no longer exist. Everything: our culture, our faith—our true faith, not this sham you've created—that would all be over. If what you say is true, we would eventually be reabsorbed back into the human species . . . or into some common species that both we and the humans were derived from. You would destroy us as surely, as completely, as the Purists would like to, if they could. And I'm not supposed to think of that as evil?"

"There are others who believe as you do." Ahpossno's gaze had saddened, as though weighted with grief. "Not just the Purists, but others of the Tenctonese race as well. They don't understand, and neither do you. This is the only way possible for any of us, Tenctonese or human. None of us will survive; the hatred and fear that divides our species will consume us. We can become one blood again, or we can lie in our separate graves. There is no alternative. That is the Light I have brought to this world. It is the way out of this trap that the slave-masters put us into, so many thousands of years ago."

"I don't believe that." The weight of the gun had dropped George's hand a few inches while he had listened to Ahpossno. The renewed determination in his hearts brought the weapon back up, its muzzle on a straight line into the other's chest. "And I'm not going to let it happen. I came here on my own; I quit the police so I would be able to do what I knew I would have to. I'm not bound by the oaths I took to uphold the law."

"You are bound by laws greater than those." In silence, Ahpossno looked upon him, and the unwavering gun in his hand, then spoke again. "Go ahead, then. How can the dead be afraid of death?"

He squeezed the trigger. He willed his finger to tighten upon the tiny curve of metal, to send the bullet crashing into the other's chest. He willed the simple action, the entire force of his being concentrated into the muscles of his forearm, the tendons that contracted his fist . . .

Nothing happened. His hand stayed frozen, motionless upon the weapon rendered useless.

"You see?" Ahpossno's voice became a whisper once more, as though speaking in the dreams that held this smaller world. "There is part of your soul that knows I am right. Your will is mine, if I will it so. And I have work here yet to do."

He closed his eyes, the gun a cold weight that he tried to crush in his grip but couldn't. With an anguished cry, George threw the gun away. Blindly, he turned and pushed through the door behind him, stumbling out into the corridors beyond, fleeing from the gaze that had pierced his innermost being.

They let him hold his son for only a few minutes. Then the baby was whisked away from him and

Cathy. "We need to check out a couple more things," the lead obstetrician told Sikes. "Just to be absolutely sure there are no problems."

"'Problems?'" Sikes followed the doctors to the corridor outside the delivery room. He heard his own voice rising with a sudden anxiety. "What kinda problems are you talking about?"

"Hey, calm down." The obstetrician gave him what was meant to be a reassuring thump on the arm. "Don't worry. This looks like one healthy kid, all right? And I should know, I've had a lot more experience in this business than you." The other doctors, along with the cart the baby was riding in—it looked unnervingly like a chrome version of the cart with which the inter office mail deliveries were made at the police station—were already heading toward the double doors at the end of the corridor. "Just relax and catch your breath. I'll probably be right back out in about ten minutes or so and we'll have a lot to talk about then." The lead obstetrician turned away and followed the scrub-clad parade.

"She's taking a rest," said the nurse barring his way in to see Cathy. "A well-earned one."

He was finally allowed to sit down in the obstetrician's office, and given a Styrofoam cup of brackish cafeteria coffee. On the other side of the door, he heard footsteps and indeterminate voices, and all the other slightly mysterious noises that hospitals emit when somebody is sitting in a room by himself and wondering what the hell is going on. Sikes stripped off the green outfit and the face mask that had gotten looped around his throat, and pitched them on top of the obstetrician's file cabinet. He sat leaning forward, alternately sipping the coffee and wishing he hadn't.

"There you are . . ." The office door swung open and the obstetrician strode in, carrying a sheaf of assorted papers, computer print-outs, and X-ray sheets under his arm. "I was afraid you might have gotten lost."

"Yeah, right." Sikes set the coffee down on the corner of the desk. "So what's the verdict?"

"Same as I told you before." The obstetrician shrugged. "Most parents should be so lucky. Your son's as healthy as the proverbial horse."

"Okay . . ." He nodded slowly. "That's cool. But, uh . . . like what is he? I mean . . . I didn't really get a very good look at him back there in the delivery room. You guys snatched him out of my arms like he was an intercepted pass or something; next thing I knew, you were in the opposite end zone with him." Sikes made a vague, confused gesture with both hands. "So is he a human kid, or is he like Cathy, or what?"

"Well . . ." The doctor started to spread the papers out on the desk.

"Don't give me 'Well,' just tell me."

The obstetrician sighed. "Mr. Sikes. A lot is going to depend on some pretty extensive lab analysis of the tissue samples we took from your son—don't worry, they were little tiny samples. We'll be doing a full genetic workup on the boy, but that's going to take a few days just to get the preliminary data. This infant —your child, Mr. Sikes—represents an unparalleled scientific opportunity for scientists all over the world; we'll be working for years on all this information—"

"Hold it." Sikes leaned across the desk. "Just wait a minute, doc. If you think you're going to stick some kid of mine in a laboratory somewhere and wire him up with electrodes, lemme tell ya, that ain't gonna happen."

"Please." The obstetrician held up a hand against Sikes's fury. "We have absolutely no intention of doing anything like that. After all—" A disarming smile appeared on his face. "That would be unethical, wouldn't it? Believe me, if anything interferes with you and Cathy and your baby having a perfectly normal family life together, it won't come from any kind of research being done. All right?"

Sikes nodded. He knew what the obstetrician was

talking about. The hospital, with its guards at every door, was a little bubble of safety. The big bad world, with all its maniacs and murderers, lay outside. *Shit,* he thought sourly. *We'll have to deal with that when the time comes.*

"Anyway," continued the obstetrician, "I want you to understand that what I'm telling you now is just based on our first examination of your son. Here, take a look at these." He handed a photo, then a second one, across the desk. "We just took these."

The first Polaroid showed the same red, squinty face Sikes had seen in the delivery room; in the second, the small head had been turned to one side. "Looks like a baby, all right." Actually, it looked more like a shaved and boiled monkey, but he had thought for a long time that that was what all newborns looked like.

"If you look closely—" The obstetrician leaned over the spread-out papers and tapped the photos with a ball-point pen. "You'll see that's there an interesting cross of human and Newcomer characteristics. Underneath this fine, dark hair that the baby was born with—he gets that from your side, of course—there's a light scattering of Tenctonese-like head spots. They're more visible here, where they taper down the neck and a little farther along the spine. Also in the profile shot, you can see the formation of the ear. The *pinnae*—that's the outer ear—is almost entirely absent; the distinctive Tenctonese ear canal shape is there, but with an actual opening rather than a membrane covering . . ."

Sikes nodded as he listened to the doctor's description. Somehow it all sounded perfectly fine to him. He supposed that was an indication of how used to the appearance of Newcomers he had gotten over the years—more than 'used to,' in the case of Cathy. So there didn't seem anything wrong with a combination of her looks and his. "What about the, uh, stuff on the inside? Like his heart?"

"Your son has a single heart, completely human in structure from what we've been able to determine so far, not the Tenctonese double heart. In fact, physiologically this infant seems to be almost entirely human; if there is any significant difference in either the gross internal or cellular makeup, we haven't found it yet. Of course, we've just started looking. But it does raise some interesting possibilities about what we'll find in the genotype analysis: either this child is essentially human in nature, with very little genetic donation from its Tenctonese parent, or the Tenctonese genes are largely recessive when combined with the dominant human genes . . ."

Once again, he found himself listening to the obstetrician with fading attention. The baby was all right, healthy and sound; that was all that mattered. Sikes felt as if some iron coil that had been wound up tight inside himself for over half a year had suddenly been allowed to relax. There was stuff he was going to have to tell these doctors, about what Quinn had told him before being killed right in front of him, but that could wait. Right now, all he wanted to do was find whatever room they had taken Cathy to and, even if she were asleep, just sit there beside her bed.

"Look, doc, maybe we better talk about some of this stuff later. Like tomorrow, maybe—"

That was when all hell broke loose. The sound of an explosion—a big one, and close, right inside the hospital—slammed into his eardrums, with enough sudden shock to almost knock him off his chair.

"What the—" Sikes's ears were still ringing as he gripped the chair arms and pushed himself up. Across the desk from him, the obstetrician stared in unfocussed surprise, eyes wide and mouth gaping open. Sikes shoved the chair away and dove for the office door.

Turmoil filled the corridor outside, the light of the overhead fluorescent panels dimmed by pungent smoke. Through it, Sikes could make out the milling, white-coated figures of the hospital staff, and the darker shapes of several guards running past the central nursing station. A shot rang out in the distance, echoing along the walls like thunder; a guard fell and tumbled with the bullet's impact, stopping at the feet of one of the nurses. Her scream was blotted out by the sharp percussive blast of an impact grenade; the glaring light flash came from far enough away that Sikes wasn't blinded, his vision filling instead with a static overlay of wavering, purplish after-images. Shielding his eyes with his forearm, he ran toward the intersection of the corridors with his gun drawn from inside his jacket.

He spotted the others then, a half-dozen men in black combat gear, faces masked with terrorist-style balaclavas. Concealed by the explosion's smoke, Sikes braced himself flat against the wall, just as one of the black-clad figures raked a burst of automatic rifle fire across the stunned and blinded guards. The intruders hadn't caught sight of him; he kept his spine and the back of his head to the wall, watching as the group's apparent leader fanned the rest out across the area.

Something had gone wrong; the shriek of alarm sirens had already started to cut through the air, but Sikes knew that more guards, drawn from their posts throughout the building, should have been pouring onto the scene. The security arrangements must have been broached from the inside; either the automatic lock-down panels had been triggered, sealing this floor off from the rest of the building, or the HDL hit team—he knew instinctively that it must be a Purist operation—had already taken out the other guards.

An electric charge shot up his spine as he saw one of the intruders coming back down the corridor on the other side of the nursing station. The man had his assault rifle slung in one hand; the other was gripped tight on Nurse Eward's elbow as he hustled her along. In the nurse's arms was a cloth-wrapped bundle . . . just big enough to be a newborn infant.

Force of will kept Sikes against the opposite corridor's wall; his impulse had been to hurl himself forward, straight toward the sonuvabitch who was endangering his son. The coldly rational part of his mind told him that he would be cut down in seconds by the rest of the HDL team; even if he could get off a shot of his own, it was too much to risk with the child and the nurse in the middle of the action. Sikes ground his teeth together in impotent fury, the gun sweating in his grip.

He crouched down, silently creeping toward the wall's corner. From this angle, he could see only a tight wedge of the space around the nursing station, but he was close enough to hear the men's voices.

"Okay, we got what we came for." The leader's voice was only slightly muffled by the balaclava over his mouth. "Let's get out of here."

He'd heard that voice before, but he couldn't place it. Shifting a few inches away from the wall, he kept himself close to the floor, gun poised ahead.

"We're getting out, all right." A harsher, deeper-pitched voice answered. "But this brat's not going anywhere."

His heart thudded in his chest as he raised his head. He could see, just past the counter of the nursing station, the tallest of the group of intruders shoving the muzzle of a rifle against the bundle in Eward's arms.

"What the hell are you doing?" The group's leader gripped the other's forearm. "You know the orders Bryant gave us. We're supposed to take it out of here alive—"

"Bryant's lost it." The sneer in the man's voice was easily discernible. "She's been locked up so long she doesn't know what's going on anymore." He shoved the other's hand away. "Something like this doesn't deserve to live."

The group's leader grabbed the rifle's muzzle, wrestling it away from the small bundle. There could be no waiting now. Sikes aimed and fired, steadying the gun in his doubled fists. The bullet caught the man in the angle between his neck and shoulder, knocking him back from the nurse, the assault rifle flying in an arc behind him. One hand reached out and clawed across the group leader's face; the fingers snagged the eyeholes, tearing the thin cloth away as the man fell.

Sikes had no time to see the leader's face. The rest of the assault team had snapped alert at the sound of the gunshot. He rolled into the safety of the corridor's other wall as a quick hail of bullets spattered across the floor where he had been.

"Go! Move it!" The group leader pushed Nurse Eward, the baby still clutched in her arms, toward one of the other corridors branching away from the station. "Get 'em outta here!"

One of the assault team backed slowly behind the others, keeping Sikes pinned down with a few more shots. A moment later, he heard the man turn and run after the rest of the team. Sikes scrambled to his feet and broke for the nursing station, diving behind its counter as one more bullet pinged against the wall an inch from his head.

A couple seconds of silence, then he lifted his head above the level of the counter. The HDL assault team was nowhere to be seen; at the far end of the corridor, a heavy security gate had rolled down, blocking the exit. Nurse Eward stood on the near side of the gate, beside the alarm system's control panel.

Gun in hand, Sikes ran up to her. "Where are they?" Before she could answer, he bent over the control panel, studying the array of lights on its surface. The green sections on the chart of the hospital's floors showed the sections that were still unsecured; if the assault team reached one of those points, it would be a straight shot to the outside of the building.

He heard a noise of metal next to himself; he turned and saw Nurse Eward scooping a discarded assault rifle from the floor. She raised and pointed it at him. "Don't worry about them," she said with a thin smile.

Eward's finger tightened on the rifle's trigger. The weapon emitted a sharp click, but nothing else. Her expression changed to one of fury. She gripped the rifle by its muzzle and swung it clublike against the side of Sikes's head.

One shot was all he managed to squeeze off as the rifle butt slammed into his skull. The blow knocked the gun out of his own hand. Through a shockwave of white light, he saw the outside edge of the nurse's sleeve rip open, a flower of blood springing from the wound. But it wasn't enough to stop her from crashing the rifle down upon him once again, an impact that pushed him to the edge of fading consciousness.

His darkening vision caught Nurse Eward slapping her open hand down upon the security controls. The alarm system cut off in mid-scream, the lights on the panel flashing to complete green. The gate rattled back up toward the ceiling.

With the last of his strength, Sikes rolled up onto his knees. "No . . ." He could see Eward running toward the HDL assault team, waiting for her just a few yards away. The leader held the infant, Sikes's son, in the crook of one arm; he wrapped the other around the nurse's blood-spattered shoulder and hurried her away with the rest of the team. "Don't . . ." Sikes stretched his hand out toward them.

He collapsed, pitching forward into blackness. His chest struck the floor, his fingertips still clawing at the unyielding surface.

CHAPTER 13

THE TV WAS on down in the lobby. It sat on a platform made of scrap plywood and bits of two-by-fours hammered together with more violence than skill; the maladjusted set shone through the screen made of chicken wire. Every face that popped up looked green, standing next to its own wavering pink ghost.

"Man, these bastards oughta get cable." One of the hotel's long-term residents slumped down in a broken-bottomed chair, the upholstery so dirt-greasy that it shone like imitation leather. "This shit sucks." He fingered the dog bottle inside the paper bag propped on his lap.

All the lobby regulars nodded or murmured agreement. The group included a couple of terts so old they looked like they were made of crumpled-up paper that had been smoothed out over skeletons of wire coat hangers. Buck got the creeps every time he caught sight of one of them clanking down the hallway with a chrome walker wrapped with duct tape, or hunched over a paralyzed checkerboard with his equally senile buddy. Most of the lobby regulars gave off enough of an air of slow decay to make them seem like semi-animate pieces of the crumbling building itself.

Man, who wants to end up like that? Buck had stopped blowing every spare cent of his paychecks on his motorcycle, and had begun putting away a little bit from each toward the deposit and first-and-last on an apartment of his own. He knew that places like this were more like roach hotels than ones for people; if you weren't careful, you could wind up checking in and never getting around to checking out.

An empty beer can hit the TV's protective mesh and fell clattering to the lobby's worn-through linoleum floor. With his foot on the first of the stairs, Buck glanced over his shoulder at the noise. In the crook of his arm was a small bag from the corner liquor store, with his usual lunch of micro-waved spleenfurters and liver chips.

"Hey! Knock it off!" A warning voice shouted from the clerk's window, covered with the same chicken wire. "No trouble!"

The parolee who had thrown the can—there were a lot of those, both tert and Newcomer, in the hotel as well—turned and scowled at the cage-like opening. "So change the channel already, Ab-dool."

With a shrug, the clerk picked up a remote control and aimed it at the TV. Nothing happened. "Batteries dead," he announced. "Watch the news. Might learn something."

"Aw, man . . ." The parolee slouched down in disgust. "We could be watchin' some good-lookin' stuff over on the stories . . ."

Buck could see that the early news broadcast had come on. Out of habit, he stopped and watched. A moment later, he had walked away from the stairs and back toward the center of the lobby, where he could get a better angle on the set.

"Who the hell are these jerk-offs?" The dog-bottle man gazed with bleary hostility at the screen overhead. "Whuz their problem . . ."

"Hey, shut up." The food in the paper bag was growing cold, but Buck didn't care. "I'm trying to listen."

"Yeah, well, you can go and . . ." The other's drunken mutter faded away.

The voice of the newscaster—it was that same obnoxious tert that he had seen before, talking with his father about that weird new cult—crackled and buzzed out of the TV's minuscule speaker. Buck could just barely make out what was being said. But the face on the screen was quickly identified by him, even through the smeared, streaky off-colors. It was his dad's former partner on the police force, the human that Buck's sister Emily called "Uncle Matt." He didn't look happy—in fact, Sikes looked really pissed-off, scowling darkly as he shoved away the microphone that the newscaster thrust in his face.

On the TV screen, the image cut back to a full-face angle on the newscaster; behind him was a milling crowd of other reporters, cameramen, and police officers. "That was Detective Matthew Sikes of the Los Angeles Police Department—" The newscaster spoke with one hand cupped to the earpiece at the side of his head. "Obviously a very angry man, angry and upset over what has happened here . . . if we could just get another shot . . ."

With the newscaster's rapid-fire voice as counterpoint, the camera lens swung over to a multi-story building; it took Buck a moment to recognize it as one of the downtown hospitals. Something heavy had obviously gone down. A big section of the fence surrounding the parking lot had been knocked flat, and the guard booth at the entrance looked as if it had taken a mortar round. Pieces of metal and wood were scattered all over the asphalt, along with the broken length of the barrier arm. Lengths of shiny yellow tape, with the words *Police Investigation—Do Not Cross* were strung all around the scene. Flashes of red from the squad cars' roof-mounted gumballs pulsed like open wounds.

The camera zoomed in for a close shot on the front of the hospital. *Sheesh,* thought Buck, the newscaster's squawky voice fading from his awareness for a moment. They had creamed the place. Serious damage was apparent: a side entrance to the hospital had been completely blown open, leaving a big gaping hole framed with twisted girders, like something from old file footage out of Beirut or Bosnia. The camera angle tilted, moving up the side of the flank of the building, showing a section of windows on the fifth floor that had been blasted out, with dark scorches and smoke marks all around the frames.

Static from the TV's ancient innards rendered the newscaster's words indecipherable. Buck turned to one of the lobby regulars slouched in a chair. "So what happened?"

"Eh, some kinda stupid horseshit." The man shrugged. "Somebody like blew up this hospital or something, just to steal some baby. Like a kidnap thing."

"Whose baby?"

"That dude's." The man lifted a raw-knuckled hand and gestured toward the screen. "No, not that guy; the other one they showed. The cop." A scowl crossed his face. "Man, I remember that bastard from back when he was in uniform. Chased me down an alley and caught me with a whole cash register till. Shit, I was just outta the slams, and he still wouldn't cut me a deal. Sonuvabitch . . ."

One of the older regulars chimed in. "Yeah, it was that detective guy. It was his girlfriend or something, she was in the hospital to have their kid, and she did, and then all of a sudden there were all these masked guys with bombs and guns and all, and they snatched the kid right out of there. And now they're gone, man."

"Huh." Something about all this didn't make sense.

Buck knew that Sikes' girlfriend was Cathy Frankel—and she had been his only girlfriend for a while now. The last time he had seen the two of them together, back at his parents' house, Cathy and Sikes had been giving off serious couple vibes, Monogamy City. It was hard for Buck to believe that his dad's partner would have been keeping some human number on the side. But then who else could Sikes have had a baby with?

The TV's sound cleared up for a few seconds. ". . . police spokesmen have so far refused to release the name of the woman . . ." The camera angle was back to the newscaster with his microphone, dramatically posed with the damaged hospital in the background. ". . . still unexplained . . . why such extensive security arrangements were already in place . . ." Static blotted out some of his words. ". . . or who the still unidentified group of attackers . . ." Pause. "This is Mike Bollinger, signing off from . . ."

On the screen, the station's anchor desk popped up, with a human female and Newcomer male looking concerned and well-groomed. "Thanks for that report . . ." The camera closed in on the woman. "Police investigators have released a portion of videotape from the hospital's internal security cameras . . ."

The screen went to blurry black-and-white, showing a skewed cubist scene, an intersection of corridors viewed from above and to one side. Numbers showing the date and time flicked by in the corner of the tape's image. Two men wearing cliché terrorist masks seemed to be wrestling over a small cloth-wrapped bundle and a high-powered assault rifle. Suddenly, the bigger of the two men fell back, his neck spattering blood as it was struck by a bullet that came from somewhere out of the image's frame. His clawing fingers caught the other man's mask, tearing it open as he collapsed toward the floor. The other's gaze snapped toward the point that the shot had come from; at that angle, the security camera had a perfect three-quarters profile of the unmasked face.

"Hey . . ." The murmured word escaped from Buck's lips as he watched the TV in the hotel lobby. *Wait a minute*—His thoughts were louder inside his head. *I know that guy*—

The screen went back to the anchor desk, a woman holding a sheet of paper, the freeze-frame shot of the young human male floating in a box to one side of her. "Police request anyone . . . information . . . contact . . ."

"Speak up, bitch!" A wadded-up hamburger wrapper bounced off the screen. "Can't hear ya!" The lobby regulars, or at least the younger ones, sounded a chorus of guffaws. A few seconds later, the station's weatherman was standing in front of a big map, poking at smiling sun emblems.

"What's the matter, son?" One of the old guys in the chairs turned and looked up at Buck. "Look like ya seen a ghost."

It was worse than that. He had seen a memory.

Noah . . . Slowly, Buck nodded to himself. That's who it is. The face on the TV screen that had been revealed when the terrorist mask was pulled off. He and Buck had once been friends, a long time ago, in what seemed like another world by now.

"Here." Buck dropped the bag with his uneaten lunch into the lap of one of the lobby regulars. "Chow down." He didn't even notice whether the guy was human or Newcomer, into raw organ meat or not. Around the end of the month, when the public assistance checks ran out, some of the hotel's residents were grateful for anything to eat at all.

Zipping up the front of his jacket, Buck headed for the lobby door and the motorcycle he'd left parked out at the curb. He had business to take care of.

* * *

The door to the office closed behind him, silently and inexorably. Across a sea of perfect oyster-shell carpet, Albert looked toward his boss's desk, a shining mahogany yacht afloat in all that space. The yacht's captain didn't look too happy.

"Albert." His name was spoken by Mr. Vogel with all the weight of disappointment that the ancient Earth deity Jehovah might have shown when He'd discovered that his first two sentient creations had been picking fruit off the wrong tree. More sorrow than anger, though enough of the latter to be scary, Vogel even looked like an Old Testament illustration out of the textbook they'd used in Albert's Intro to Human Culture night-school class. "Thank you for making the time to come in and talk with me." Vogel heaved a sigh, shoulders lifting and then falling. "Have a seat."

"Is there . . . anything . . . wrong?" He had to fight to keep himself from cringing as he perched on the edge of the chair in front of Vogel's desk. *Of course there's something wrong!* he shouted at himself, inside his head. He even knew what it was, why Vogel had called him in here. What was worse, he had known a long time ago, from the beginning, that it was all going to wind up like this. And there had been nothing he could do to stop it from happening. It was like being bolted hand and foot to the ground, and helplessly watching an enormous stone, that he himself had winched up into the sky, falling toward him.

Vogel slowly shook his head, not to indicate No, but to further display the tonnage of the griefs that oppressed him. "Albert . . ." The gaze of the sad eyes shifted to his hand softly tapping a single sheet of paper on the desk's surface. "How could you? How could you have done this?"

"Wuh-what?" But he knew.

"Let's not play any more games, Albert. It's too late for that." Vogel picked up the sheet of paper in both hands; by the expression on his face, he might have been looking at the death sentence of everyone he had ever known and loved. He lowered the paper to look straight at Albert. "G . . . I . . . T." He slowly spelled out the initial letters. "The Grazer Intellinomics Training. The tapes and everything else from your old friend, Captain Grazer." Another shake of the head. "That was wrong, Albert. You shouldn't have done that."

"I duh-don't know what you mean . . ."

"Come on." The underlying thread of anger rose in Vogel's voice. "I sent you all the figures on that project. The sales, the projected sales . . . the projected losses."

"Well . . ." Albert shrugged nervously. "Haven't there been other things that I predicted, that didn't work out? I mean, that didn't make money? You said my track record, it was like ninety-nine percent or something. So don't there have to be times when I'm wrong?"

"Oh, sure; we've never expected you to be perfect, Albert. Though we've always been glad that you almost were. But what happened with this GIT thing isn't just a matter of being wrong. It's much worse than that."

Vogel was right, of course; Albert remembered wincing when he had looked at the figures that had arrived in a slim Federal Express envelope. You didn't have to be a genius—you could be a *binnaum,* in fact—to see that that multi-digit numbers with minus signs in front of them added up to a lot of red ink. His wife May had looked over his shoulder at the financial report, and he had heard her give a small gasp of shock and dismay. She didn't know everything about his involvement with GIT—how could he have told her?—but she at least knew that he had recommended Grazer's tapes and books to his employers at Precognosis, so they had something at stake in their success. Or failure.

"Maybe," said Albert, "you could take something out of my salary until it's all paid back. Muh-maybe you could take everything you pay me." He supposed he could always get another job as a janitor, to tide him and May over until it was all sorted out, however long that would take.

"We pay you an awful lot of money, but we don't pay you that much. It's not just the money that Precognosis invested in this GIT project, it's the guarantees and indemnities that we gave to the cable and satellite broadcast companies, the publishing houses, that CD-ROM group we brought in on this. We made assurances to a whole slew of people and organizations about the absolute profitability of this venture. Essentially, because of the predictions you gave us about the future of your friend Grazer's stuff, we put ourselves on the line for everybody's start-up and operating costs. And those people are just now sending their bills in to us. The deficits that have shown up in the accounting are nothing compared to what we're going to be hit with in the next few months."

Albert shifted uneasily in the chair. "My wife and I have some money saved up. And there's that car you gave us—we could sell that . . ."

"Forget the money, Albert." Vogel gazed at him from beneath the dark, overhanging storm clouds of his brow. "The money isn't even the real issue— though it's bad enough. There's a bigger problem involved. We trusted you, Albert. We did everything we could for you. And this is how you pay us back."

He couldn't say anything in reply. He wanted to be dead, to have disappeared from this room and completely off this planet.

Vogel picked up the sheet of paper again, though he had obviously read it through many times already. "This whole business with the GIT stuff—it's not a matter of the sales performance coming up to your predictions. You weren't even close; your forecast was one hundred eighty degrees off. We can't even *give* these goddamn tapes and books away. They're a dead dog; the market for them is zip. And the video stuff? They test-ran the first half-hour segment in Pittsburgh and it came in last for its time-slot, behind a Venezuelan soccer match and a public-service documentary on how to floss your dog's teeth!" Vogel shook his head. "But let's not get started on the grisly details. Let's just say that we here at Precognosis were so shocked by how off-the-mark your predictions were, that we decided—no, we were forced—to have some outside investigations done. And what we found out . . ." He emitted another sigh, even deeper and more tragic. "It was definitely not to our liking."

Albert shrank farther back into the chair.

"What our investigators found was a gentleman named Marty Balfe, who runs a small print shop and bindery in downtown Los Angeles. As a matter of fact, Mr. Balfe produced the first run of GIT publications, before anyone other than your friend Captain Grazer got involved with the promotion and sales of these things he'd written and recorded. The printing had been done largely on credit; Mr. Balfe was still holding some fairly substantial IOUs from Grazer, and he wasn't too happy about it. So he wasn't averse to spilling the beans about the business dealings between him and the captain. Apparently, a few months ago Grazer had assured Mr. Balfe that he would get all the money that was coming to him, inasmuch as Grazer had found a sure-fire way of making GIT into a roaring commercial success. Grazer even told Mr. Balfe how this was going to come about, that he had a close personal friend who was the chief 'picker' for a major market-research and prediction firm, and that he had convinced this friend to tell his employers that GIT was going to be the biggest thing since sliced bread. And of course, after that everything would be easy; the whole world would rush out to buy these wondrous products, Mr. Balfe would get paid the money owed him plus interest, and everybody would be rich and happy. Except it doesn't seem to have worked out that way, has it?"

"No . . ." With his voice small and mournful, Albert shook his head. "I guess not . . ."

"Because your friend Grazer," continued Vogel, his voice turning to thunder, "overlooked one small factor. Namely, that his goddamn tapes and books are total crap. God Himself could come down out of the sky and recommend these things, and people still wouldn't buy them. So they're not very likely to do it based on the recommendation of ace picker Albert Einstein, are they?"

Albert decided it would probably be better if he didn't remind Vogel that he had looked at Grazer's stuff when it had first been brought into this office, and had said all kinds of nice things about it. It would probably just make Vogel even angrier.

"We trusted you, Albert." A look of wounded bafflement appeared on Vogel's face. "Everybody here at Precognosis figured how the hell could one of you special dim-bulb Newcomers ever have enough on the ball to be anything except perfectly honest with us? And then you turned around and hosed us like this, Albert. We never thought you'd even be capable of pulling off a number like this."

"Well . . ." He managed a shrug. "I won't do it again."

"Oh, you got that right." Vogel tossed the sheet of paper back onto the desk's surface. "You're not going to be doing anything—good, bad or indifferent—for Precognosis anymore. That's why I called you in here, to tell you that our need for your services is at an end."

That puzzled him. "But I'm still a good picker, aren't I?"

"You're the best, Albert. Even with figuring in this GIT disaster, your successful prediction rate is still way up in the nineties. We could probably all go rolling along forever, getting more picks from you, the way you did before this whole mess came along. But there's a problem. In dealing with our clients, we haven't been just selling them your predictions; we've been selling them your reliability. And now, we don't have that to sell anymore. There's only two ways to explain what happened, and neither one of them looks very good. If we tell our clients that you picked this GIT stuff to be a big money-spinner and it turned out you were completely, one-hundred-percent off-base, everybody is left wondering when you might do that again. And if we tell them that you were dishonest with us, that you gave us a bogus prediction to help out one of your old friends—then that's even worse. That's why we're not going after Grazer for the damages he's caused us. If we're going to keep Precognosis going as a market research and prediction firm, we can't let it get out that our top picker entered into a conspiracy to defraud us. That would make us look like idiots. How could we get any clients to hire us in the future if it looks like we can't even run our own company without taking it in the shorts?"

Reliable—that was what George had used to say about him, back when he was still mopping the floors at the police station. And that was something he'd been proud of, that everyone could always count on him. It was better even than being smart, or good-looking, or anything else people could be. And now— since he knew that what Vogel said was true—now he wasn't reliable anymore. What he had been, he wasn't anymore. Albert frowned, trying to figure out what that meant. If he wasn't that, then what was he? Or was he anything at all?

From somewhere in the office's echoing immensity, Vogel's voice continued. "We're in the process of drafting the corporate press release that we'll be sending out to all the business papers and trade journals. Basically, what the announcement will say is that in order to pursue other avenues of endeavour, blah blah blah, Mr. Albert Einstein has resigned from his position as chief market prediction analyst, and that all of us here at Precognosis wish him the best of luck, every success, et cetera, et cetera."

"Does that mean . . ." Albert tried to figure out the rapid string of words. "Does that mean I'm fired?"

Vogel gazed at him in silence for a moment, then sighed one last time. "You can keep the car, Albert."

"Hey, I thought there were going to be trees and stuff up here." With one hand, he shaded his eyes against the flat yellow sunlight. The landscape was just as flat, but a deracinated brown, as though the sun had baked it to the distant horizon. "This is kinda . . . harsh. You know?"

"Get with the program, man." Standing beside Noah was the member of the HDL assault team who had driven the truck all the way north from L.A. "This part of Oregon is high desert, from here into Idaho. You want trees, you gotta head west." He slammed the door of the truck cab shut. "You think it's mean-looking now, you oughta be up here in the winter. There's some snowstorms come barrelling across the flats, you think you got hit by a runaway deep freeze. Need a snowplow just to get around to your front gate and check your mail."

Noah and the other man walked around to the rear of the truck. "I can believe it." His boots crunched into the dry sand and gravel. "Jeez, this really is the middle of nowhere. Why the hell would Bryant have a camp put up here?"

"That's exactly why." The assault team member flipped open the latch above the truck's bumper. "Out here, there's no one to come snooping around what you're doing. And that's the way the people in these parts like it. You don't poke your nose in their business, they keep theirs out of whatever you're doing. And that's the way we like it."

The segmented door went clattering up, revealing

the truck's interior. Sunlight bounced off gleaming chrome surfaces and white enamel. The space was filled with as much equipment as the truck that had been used for the raid on the hospital, and then stripped and abandoned, but this array of gear wasn't weaponry. The rear of the truck looked like a segment of the hospital itself, scrubbed and sanitized, and crammed into the cargo area. A compact replica of a neonatal ward, but set up for just one infant. The most important baby in the world right now, at least as far as Noah and the rest of the Human Defense League were concerned.

Nurse Eward looked up from the high-tech cradle in the middle of the space. "It's about time," she said irritably. She still wore the white uniform she'd had on when the raid had gone down. "I was about ready to start climbing the walls in here."

The woman's voice grated on Noah's nerves. She had dropped all the pretense of concern and warmth, the masquerade she had carried out for so long. There was no denying that it had worked: Eward had been the HDL's deep agent for a long time, first in Dr. Quinn's clinic and research facility, then in the heavily guarded hospital ward that had been set up for this baby to be born in. Everything that the authorities, the Bureau of Newcomer Affairs, and the LAPD, had done to ensure the child's security had been reported out to Noah and the other planners of the raid. Thanks to Eward, everything had gone smoothly, right up until Noah's second-in-command had flipped out and tried to kill the kid. Noah had been relieved when the radio newscast they had heard on the way up here had stated that the man had died from the bullet he'd caught in the action; that was one less loose end to deal with, one less way the police might have been able to figure out where they had gone. Noah figured he could put up with Eward's newly-revealed abrasiveness for as long as they all had to hole up in this godforsaken place.

226

He reached a hand up to assist her, but she knocked it aside and jumped down from the back of the truck without help. "Somebody else can take care of this kid for a while." Eward pointed a thumb over her shoulder. "I'm sick of the brat." Carrying a small suitcase of her own things, she headed for the group of low, single-story buildings at the center of the camp's fenced area. In the distance, the points of the razor wire topping the wire mesh glittered like small knives.

"You heard the lady." Noah glanced around at the other HDL members who had gathered around. "We got the kid here alive; let's see if we can keep him that way."

Two of the men climbed up into the truck and lowered the chrome cart out to the others. The bundle inside the cart emitted a weak cry; two small pink fists fought the air.

"Hey! You can't just put him out in the sun—jeez!" Noah held his arm over the cart, to shade the baby's face. "What're you trying to do, make a raisin out of him?"

"No skin off my ass if this little mongrel dies." One of the other men shrugged, displaying his lack of concern. "Maybe it would've been less hassle if you had let it get plugged back at the hospital."

"Can that crap." Noah shot a narrow-eyed glare at the assault team member who had spoken. "Bryant gave us our orders, and we're going to make sure they're carried out exactly the way she wants. Got it?"

Another shrug. "You're the boss."

"That's right." With his other hand, Noah gestured toward the jeeps and off-road vehicles, all painted in desert camouflage, that filled one corner of the fenced compound. "One of you go over there and bring back a tarpaulin—now. I'm not gonna stand here like this all day."

While he waited for the tarp to be fetched, Noah looked down at the small face in the shade of his upraised arm. During the raid and in the switching of vehicles immediately afterward, and during the long drive up here from Los Angeles, there hadn't been time for him to get a good look at the baby. He remembered its face being redder before, but then that had been within just a few hours of it having been born. Now its face was more of a mottled pink, the skin appearing soft as rose petals. Damn thing looks almost human, thought Noah. He could just see the light dusting of spots beneath the fine wisps of hair on the scalp, and the way the infant's ears, what there was of them, was more like a Newcomer's than like his own. But other than that . . .

The baby's small eyes opened, as if it knew somebody was right above, looking down at it. The pupils were two tiny flashes of blue; for some reason, Noah hadn't been expecting that. He frowned, feeling puzzled but without knowing why. The miniature hands —just like a human baby's, right down to the almost microscopic white flecks of the fingernails—made disjointed semaphore gestures, the face puckering and the hiccupping gasps turning into a faint wail. Noah wondered when had been the last time that Eward had fed him.

"Ugly little shit, ain't it?"

Startled, Noah turned and saw one of the other assault team members with a smirk on his face and a wadded-up green tarp under his arm.

"I don't know about that—" Noah's arm had started to ache from being held so long over the cart. "If somebody didn't know, they might think it was one of ours. Human, I mean."

"Yeah, well, I think human kids are pretty ugly pieces of work, too." The man handed the tarpaulin to Noah and walked away.

He organized a procession with himself and another assault team member holding the tarp over the open cart and pushing it across the gravelly, weed-stubbled ground toward the buildings that looked even scruffier and more neglected the closer they got to them. A couple of dusty windowpanes had been broken out and replaced with flattened cardboard boxes, warped and made ancient by the bleak landscape's sun and rain.

"What did this place used to be?" Noah studied the complex with growing distaste. Behind him, the short parade of team members carried the rest of the supplies and equipment from the truck. "I mean, before the League took it over."

"Gun club." The other man smiled evilly at him across the tarp. "So if a few rounds get let off now and then . . . nobody around here gets too excited about it. Convenient, huh?"

Noah pushed open the door of the main building with his boot. When the cart had been rolled inside and the tarp tossed back out onto the wood-plank porch, he looked around the space. It had the appearance of a low-rent bachelor pad gone seriously downhill, a place where a group of men had been living with no one to get on their case about their general slobbishness. The pent-up air had the aroma of sweat-stained clothes piled into the corners and the charcoal-like scent of burnt food on an encrusted stove. He couldn't see the kitchen, and assumed it was somewhere in the rear of the building. A couple of doors opened onto sleeping areas, with a few broken-backed Army cots and sleeping bags strewn in a haphazard non-pattern on the bare floor.

"Jeez, this place smells like the zoo or something." Noah shook his head in disgust. "How can you guys stand it?"

"So it's not the Ritz." One of the other men shrugged. "It doesn't have to be. We're not going to be hanging around here that long."

"We'll be here as long as we need to. And that decision is going to come from Bryant." The camp's disorder offended Noah, from a strictly military viewpoint. It radiated carelessness and a slackening of standards—and these men were supposed to be an elite corps, the best that the human race had to offer in its struggle against the alien filth. Right now, the place didn't look like much of an advertisement for the wonderfulness of humanity. "So okay, how many people we got up here now? With the crew that was already here, plus the team that came up with the truck—let's see, that makes twelve of us, right?"

The other nodded. "Plus that nurse."

"Her job's full-time already, looking after this kid." Noah pointed to the cart. "But we don't need her anyway; we got plenty enough manpower already to get this place pulled together. And as long as I've been put in charge here, that's the way it's gonna be. So round up the rest of the men, I don't care if they're sacked out or what, and have 'em all here in fifteen minutes. We'll get a duty roster drawn up—"

"What about Aalice?" A small group had already gathered in the room. One of them stood with his arms folded across his chest. "You gonna have her pitch in? She's big enough to swing a broom."

Another man snickered. "Yeah, she oughta earn her keep."

"Alice?" Noah didn't understand. "Who's Alice?"

"Not 'Alice'—*Aa*-lice." The man put a slight drawl on the first syllable. "With two A's."

"Okay, fine," said Noah with growing irritation. "Whatever. So who are you talking about?"

"You mean nobody's told you about her?"

"Nobody's told me squat." Noah glared at the other men. "So somebody better let me in on it right now. Who's this Aalice?"

As if in answer to his question, he heard the door open behind him. A little girl peered around it; she looked to be about five or six years old, dressed in faded jeans with the cuffs rolled up and a t-shirt with some cartoon character on the front. Noah watched as the girl caught sight of the chrome cart in the middle of the room; her eyes widened, then she ran over and looked down at its tiny occupant.

"It looks just like me!" The girl turned around, a smile of delight on her face. "Just like me!"

"That's Aalice," one of the assault team members said simply.

He had already figured that out. And Noah had to admit the little girl was right: she could have been the baby's older sister. The ears, that were like a human's and a Newcomer's at the same time, and the head spots that were just visible beneath light blond hair . . . it was all there.

Nobody had told him that there was another one, another hybrid child. And now here he was, in charge of both of them.

He wondered what that meant, what Bryant might be planning. An odd, uneasy worry moved in Noah's gut. He didn't like surprises.

"What's the deal?" He turned toward the closest of the other men. "What's going on? Who is she?"

"Hey, don't jump down my throat, buddy." A smug grin showed on the assault team member's face. "Isn't it obvious? She's our other little guest here. That's why we've been running a crew up here for the last year or so. Just to keep an eye on her—and make sure nobody else knows about her."

"And she's a hybrid? Like the baby, I mean?"

"Just look at her." The other man gestured toward the child. "You got any doubt about it?"

Noah looked back toward the girl. Half human, half Newcomer—part of him could believe it right off the bat, just from the visual evidence. Another part of him was pissed off that he hadn't been told about her before.

The little girl walked right up to him and tilted her head back to look him in the eye. "I'm glad you brought him here," she said. "They told me it was a boy. What's his name?"

"I . . . don't know." He was taken aback by the girl's forthright manner, like that of a miniature adult. "I don't think he has one yet."

"Oh." Aalice looked disappointed for a moment, then brightened. She reached out and touched Noah's hand. "Then maybe we can think one up."

"Yeah . . . I guess so." Noah felt the other humans' gaze weighing upon his back. He glanced over his shoulder and saw the men watching him, as though waiting for him to do something. But he didn't know what.

When he turned his head around, he saw that the little girl had gone back over to the cart. She reached down and carefully stroked the baby's cheek.

Noah still didn't know what to do. Or what was going to happen.

CHAPTER 14

SHE TOLD HIM everything he needed to know.

"And then—you're not going to believe this—Cathy got pregnant." Emily drew herself upright where she sat on the couch, radiating the triumph of someone who can impart secret information. "With Uncle Matt's baby. I mean, Uncle Matt's the father of the baby. Isn't that wild?"

"How do you know all this?" Buck regarded his sister with suspicion. "Did they tell you all this? Maybe you're making it all up."

"Hey—" Emily looked offended. "Nobody has to tell me stuff, for me to find it out." She gestured at the living room and all the rest of their parents' house surrounding them. "I live here, right? I hear Mom and Dad talking all the time—well, I did when Dad was still living here . . ."

"You little snoop." He saw again what a good international spy his kid sister would make some day. It was a real advantage to have a source like her, right on the spot like this. "What were you doing, putting your ear to their bedroom door?"

"Well . . . if I'd had to, I would've." Emily's expression turned to one of slight embarrassment. "But I didn't! You know how Dad's always complaining about how flimsy the walls are in these new houses, and how he was going to put in soundproofing so he and Mom wouldn't be able to hear the CD player in my room—"

"Maybe he should put it in." Buck smiled at her. "I'll remind him about it, the next time I see him."

Right now, the house was empty and quiet, except for him and his sister talking. He had come over here on the sly, straight from the hotel, the memory of the news broadcast he had seen on the lobby's crappy TV still fresh in his mind. He had parked the motorcycle a couple of blocks down the street and walked the rest of the way, so the noise of its barely mufflered engine wouldn't alert his mother, just in case she had been at home. He really only wanted to talk to his sister Emily.

As it turned out, nobody was in the house except her. And she had some good news for her brother—excellent news: their dad had come home, just that morning—what could be better news than that? And he had swept up their mom, his wife, into his arms—to use the words of Emily's soap-operatic account—and had carried her away, taking the baby with them to the nearest park. They had a lot to talk about. "They were like reconciled," Emily had announced, her face all wide-eyed and glowing. "It was better than a TV show."

Buck was glad to hear that his father had come to his senses and knocked off that crap with that stupid cult, those Carriers of Flashlights or whatever they called themselves. Though now he had to wonder if their dad had been up to something else all along. Maybe he had just been acting, pretending to have joined up, all as part of some police investigation. Buck wouldn't have put that past his father. From what Emily had told him, their dad still had a lot on his mind—maybe the investigation hadn't come off the way he had hoped—but at least he could go back to being a full-time, living-at-home husband and father. That accounted for the newly reunited Mr. and Mrs. Francisco going off to the park, to have some time together; having the baby with them wouldn't cramp their style as much as having Emily the spy around. Maybe when they got back, they would see if Emily wanted to do a sleep-over at a friends's house; even if that would interfere with her checking out the progress of her parents' reconciliation, the all-night gossiping potential would be too attractive for her to resist.

"Anyway, that's the story." Right now, Emily sat on the couch beside her brother, her legs tucked up under herself. "Neat, huh?"

"Yeah, that's cool, all right." The amount of happiness that his sister radiated had almost made Buck forget why he'd come back here to the house. He had some snooping of his own to do. Fortunately, it was the kind that Emily could help him with. She had already filled him in on the business with Sikes and Cathy and their hybrid, half human and half Newcomer baby—that had taken some doing, getting his mind around that concept. But he'd had to admit that all the other signs pointed that way: the stuff he'd seen on the newscast about the raid on the hospital, all the top-secret security measures that had been in place there—not that they had helped much—plus what he'd already known about Matt and Cathy's relationship with each other. Buck had seen the way the human police detective looked at his Tenctonese girlfriend; you didn't have to be a detective to figure out that the guy was totally gone on her. It made more sense to accept that a way had been found for humans and Newcomers to have kids together, than to believe that Sikes had been cheating on Cathy and had gotten some human female knocked up. And if there had been a human/Tenctonese baby in that hospital, that sure would explain the guards that had been stationed there.

"Listen, Em——" He had just been struck by a thought. "Maybe you shouldn't get your hopes up too much, about Dad being able to spend a lot of time with Mom and you and Vessna. That stuff that was on the news—about the raid on that hospital—that's heavy business. Because if that was Matt and Cathy's baby, then Dad isn't going to take time off to just sit around here with you guys. Once he finds out what's happened, he's going to shoot right down to the police station and pitch in with whatever investigation's going on with that kid."

"Yeah, you're right." Emily's face clouded. She frowned, deep in thinking. "Dad's not going to leave Uncle Matt hanging there, even if they're not partners anymore."

"Okay . . ." Now came the delicate part, convincing his sister of the wisdom of what he wanted to do. "So if we can help Dad sort this all out, and get that baby back where it belongs with Matt and Cathy, then the sooner everything'll be back to normal. Right?"

"Yeah, I guess." Emily shrugged. "I don't see what there is we can do about it, though."

"You just gotta back my play on this one. Do you know Dad's password for his computer? The one he's got in the den?"

"Maybe . . ." She regarded him with suspicion. "Why?"

"I got a hunch about somebody who might've been involved with the hospital raid. Somebody I used to know. If we can get into Dad's files, I can find out for sure."

Emily mulled it over. "Okay," she said at last, sliding off the sofa. "Let's do it—before they get back."

In the den, Buck watched as Emily flipped on the computer's power. He pulled up another chair beside her at the desk. "The password is W-G-V-W-S-G," she said, punching the keys one by one with her index finger.

"What the hell's that?"

"It's the letters of Vessna's name, transposed one more letter down in the alphabet, then two more letters, and so on."

"How'd you know that?"

"It's easy." Emily sat back, waiting for the computer screen to clear. "Dad told me that was how he used my name for his password on the computer terminal he used at the police station. So one day when he wasn't home, I came in here and fooled around 'til I got it right." She shook her head, as though in mild disgust. "Really—it didn't take very long."

The interface for the police department's on-line data bank came up on the screen. Buck leaned forward and pulled the keyboard away from his sister. With a few quick keystrokes, he got into the search function, then typed in RAMSEY, NOAH. A few seconds passed, then the face of his one-time high school buddy appeared. The image rocked him back in the chair. It was the same Noah, but different as well; he'd changed, and not in any way that seemed good. The young human's eyes glared defiantly out at the lens of whatever camera had taken the photo—it looked like a standard LAPD mug shot—and the insignia of one of the Human Defense League's paramilitary units showed on the points of his shirt collar. His dark hair had been cropped short enough to reveal a healed-over scar along the side of his head. It looked like Noah Ramsey hadn't been shy about getting into the kinds of street fights that these Purist thugs were known for.

"Oh, this is a nice-looking guy, all right." Emily's voice was thick with sarcasm. "And you used to know this person?"

"Yeah . . ." He sighed and slowly shook his head. "Used to be a friend of mine, actually." Buck felt as if that had been a million years ago. They had fallen out over one of their teachers, a human woman named Marilyn Houston—and the difference between the way she had felt about him and about Noah. That had been a real mess, one that he still couldn't pull up out of his memory without a pang to his hearts. What had happened between him and Marilyn had been just impossible, with no solution except for her to quit her teaching job and move out of Los Angeles to some-place back East. *If you call that a solution,* he thought bitterly. He'd wound up losing her and his buddy Noah. He'd heard that Noah had started running with a rough crowd, but he hadn't known that it had gotten this bad, that Noah's jealousy and wounded pride had warped his mind to the point of him joining up with those Purist sonsabitches.

But that was what seemed to be the case. Buck scanned the ID file and rap sheet that filled the other half of the computer screen. From just about the time that Buck had lost touch with him, Noah had been getting into some serious trouble. The LAPD's hate crimes unit had Noah down as joining the HDL a year ago, though there might have been some involvement before then. But once the connection was official, Noah had fairly quickly stopped brawling and banging heads in the HDL's so-called 'peaceful demonstrations,' and had begun rising in the League's ranks. Right up to the top, becoming the main courier for Darlene Bryant herself, bringing her orders out from the women's prison where she was stuck and making sure that the rest of the Purists snapped to and did as they were told. If that was the level at which Noah was dealing, then it stood to reason that he would have been put in charge of a heavy-duty operation like the raid on the hospital and the kidnapping of this human/Tenctonese baby.

"You know, I think you're right," said Emily. "That was the guy they showed on TV, the one who got his face mask torn off." She looked away from the computer screen and toward her brother. "So now what're you going to do?"

"I don't know." Buck flopped back in the chair. He hadn't worked it out any further in his head. "So now I've established that someone I used to know is one of the jerks who swiped Matt and Cathy's baby. That doesn't tell us where they took the kid or what they're planning to do with it." He rubbed his chin, trying to figure out what his next move should be.

"Maybe you could just tell Dad. Or you could get hold of Uncle Matt down at the police station and tell him. I mean, that's supposed to be their job, tracking people down and stuff."

"Yeah, I guess so . . ." He didn't consider the notion with much enthusiasm. What would that accomplish, besides giving the police a name to hang on a videotaped face? *Big deal,* he thought. Their computers were probably grinding that out already, using some high-powered scan-and-match program. An obscure and irrational sense of guilt moved inside him, as though he had let down just about everybody he knew. Noah Ramsey had been his friend, but he hadn't managed to keep him from becoming some kind of Purist stormtrooper or preventing him from hurting innocent people like Matt and Cathy. "I wish there was something else I could do . . ."

"Come on, Buck . . ." Emily laid her hand on his shoulder. "Don't beat yourself up over it. There's only so much you can do. Or that anybody can do."

"You're right." He nodded. What his sister said was true, but that didn't stop the feeling in his hearts. "Still . . ." He turned away from the computer screen, looking around the small office his father had put together in the den, as if something there could give him a clue.

Over by the telephone, a red light blinked on top of the answering machine.

"Hey, somebody called Dad." This phone, he

knew, was on a separate line from the others in the house; like the computer terminal, it was for police business only.

"I know; I heard it ringing in here just before you came over. So that was maybe an hour or so ago."

Without knowing why—he didn't even have a hunch, just a lack of anything else to try—Buck reached over and hit the message button.

"And you call me a snoop." Emily folded her arms across her chest. "Dad would flip if he knew you were doing this."

"Yeah, and that's why you're not going to tell him. Now be quiet, I want to hear this."

The tape in the machine whirred into rewind, then stopped. Another click, then a voice emerged from the machine's tiny speaker.

"Uh . . . Detective Francisco? Are you there?" The taped voice paused. "I really need to talk to you . . ."

Buck sat bolt upright. "Hey! That's him!"

"That's who?"

"That's Noah Ramsey! I recognize the voice!"

Disembodied, the words unwound into the room. "It's really important . . . so if you're there . . ." Another pause. "Shoot. Look, uh, my name is Noah Ramsey . . ."

Buck nudged his sister. "See, I told you it was him!"

"I know that you're Matt Sikes's partner, so this is something that you should be pretty interested in." Frustration seeped into the voice on the answering machine tape. "It's about what happened at the hospital . . . and that baby and everything . . ." The words suddenly rushed faster, the voice edging up a notch in tension. "Look, I can't say any more right now—I'll have to try and get ahold of you later—" With a sharp click, the connection had been broken.

"Wow." Emily gazed at the answering machine in amazement. "Why would he have called here?"

"You heard him. He wanted to talk to Dad."

"Yeah, but about what?"

"Jeez, who knows?" Buck shook his head. "Maybe him and the rest of the bunch who took the baby want to negotiate a ransom payment. Or maybe he just wanted to screw around with Dad's and Matt's heads." Even as he spoke, he knew that none of those possibilities seemed right; the sound of Noah's voice on the tape had sounded too weird, scared, and anxious. As though something had gone wrong—but what? "What he wanted to talk about isn't as important as figuring out where he was calling from."

"You must not watch very many cop shows on TV." His sister looked at him with exasperation. "Otherwise you'd know that it's not very likely he called from wherever they've holed up. Even Purists aren't that dumb."

"But if we could figure out the general area . . . that might help."

"Well, why didn't you say so? That part's easy." Emily slid off her chair and went over to the phone stand. She lifted a strip of paper that curled out of a smaller device next to the answering machine. "Dad's got one of those caller ID gizmos; you gotta be a policeman to have one in California. It's really neat—look." She pointed to the last string of numbers on the narrow paper. "See, that's the number of the phone that this Noah guy called from."

Buck peered at the number. The Area Code was 503. "Where's that?" It wasn't a California prefix, he knew. "Where's a phone book?"

"Why do it the old-fashioned way?" She went back over to the computer and started punching away at the keys. "Boy, it'd take you forever to find out anything." Noah Ramsey's mug shot and rap sheet disappeared, replaced by a crawl of digits. "Okay, here we go." Emily put her fingertip on the screen. "According to this, 503 is the Area Code for the state of Oregon."

"He was calling from Oregon?"

"So?" Emily shrugged. "They gotta be somewhere. And it's just up north."

"Okay, okay—but where in Oregon?"

"Give me a minute, will you?" She leaned forward, studying the computer screen. "Let's see . . . this says that the number is for a pay phone—that makes sense; that's where a call like that would come from—and it's in a little town called . . . hold on . . ." She drew back, her voice indicating triumph. "In a town called Vindoma. Ever hear of it?"

"Course not." Buck put his head next to his sister's, looking closer at the screen. "Is there a map on this thing?"

"Sure." She punched more keys. A couple of seconds later, a red circle flashed around the point where two almost perfectly straight lines crossed each other. "There it is."

"Man, that's the middle of nowhere."

"What did you expect? They're not going to go hang out at the mall."

Buck reached over and switched on the printer hooked up to the computer. "Give me a hard copy of that map." When the printer had ejected the sheet of paper, he glanced over it, then folded and tucked it into his shirt pocket.

"What're you going to do?" Emily perched on the chair and watched him. "Are you going to go up there?"

"Maybe." He zipped up his leather jacket. "But not right away. Listen, when Mom and Dad get back, don't tell 'em I was here. And super don't tell Dad that we got this stuff off his computer."

"Are you kidding?" Emily rolled her eyes. "You want to get into trouble, you can do it on your . . . wait a minute." She grabbed his forearm. "Their car . . . I can hear it in the driveway! Quick—you gotta get out of here!" She turned off the computer, then jumped down from the chair and pushed her brother toward the living room.

Buck was out the sliding glass door and onto the patio as he heard a key sliding into the lock in front of the house. A moment later, he had scrambled over the back fence and through the oleander bushes on the other side. With a glance over his shoulder—no one appeared to have seen him—he started walking, hurrying toward his motorcycle down the street.

"Where did you go?" The little girl looked up at him, from where she sat on the building's wooden front steps.

Noah hesitated before answering. "Who says I went anywhere at all?" He knew he had to be careful.

"Nobody." The girl named Aalice shrugged, her shoulders lifting inside the faded shirt that was slightly too big for her. "I just know you did. I see everything that happens around here."

"I bet you do." He looked around the fenced compound to see if any of the other HDL members were nearby. As far as he could tell, they were all still over at the main building, grousing and grumbling about the duty roster he had instituted just a few hours ago. It didn't seem to have gone over too well, that their slobbed-out vacation was at an end per the orders of this young upstart who had been put in charge of the operation. Noah had caught some pretty venomous glances shot his way, along with some muttered comments that came close to mutiny. By this point, he didn't care. As long as they were too afraid of Darlene Bryant to actually do anything about their supposed grievances, he was in the clear. At least for a little while longer . . .

He sat down on the step beside Aalice. The building was the smallest one in the compound, in such bad shape that it had no official use; Aalice had taken it over for her private hideaway and make-believe castle. Noah had checked it out—the little girl had actually invited him inside, to show it off—and had found, underneath a roof so full of holes that the bright sunlight made an abstract checkerboard across the warped and dusty floor planks, a dirty blanket in one corner and a pair of dolls in outfits even more ragged than hers. The HDL members who had been assigned the cake job of guarding the world's first hybrid human/Tenctonese child hadn't busted their asses making things pleasant for her here.

From this angle, he could see across the compound to one of the uncurtained windows of the main building. Inside, Nurse Eward was visible, moving around as she prepared the infant's formula. She at least was going about her tasks in an adequately professional manner; if anything happened to the baby, it wouldn't be from lack of care.

If anything happened . . .

The phrase chilled Noah's thoughts. He'd already had a peek inside the heads of some of his fellow HDL members, the ones who had been on the hospital raid team and the ones who had already been stationed up here at the camp. It had been more of a view than he'd really wanted, or been prepared for; first that crack about it being better if he'd allowed the infant to get blown away back at the hospital, and then some other remarks equally repellent. If he'd known he would be working with guys as irrationally bloodthirsty as these, he would have asked Bryant to give him any other assignment besides this one. It was one thing to put a bloody cross up on some Newcomer's front lawn, or throw a few punches in a demonstration that just happened to turn into a riot, or jump some slag who was on his own and rough him up enough to put him in the intensive care unit—all slags were scum anyway, who deserved that kind of treatment. Even assassinating the big important parasites, the ones who were masterminding their species' takeover of the planet . . . that was just defending one's own species, the human race who were the rightful owners of this world. Even the big scheme, the one that the legendary Marc Guerin had died in, that had wound up putting Darlene Bryant behind bars—that one had been so big that it still seemed abstract and theoretical to him. He knew that if that one had gone off the way it had been planned, every Newcomer in the Los Angeles basin would have been killed, but it was hard to translate that into specific, one-by-one deaths; he had never even really tried to work it out in his thoughts. But to sit around and cold-bloodedly speculate about killing this particular baby, even if it was half slag, or this particular little girl sitting next to him on the step . . . a sour taste seeped under his tongue. He was beginning to wonder if the other HDL members were right in their heads. The one comfort was that he knew Bryant wasn't as cracked as some of her troops. She was too smart to order innocent children's deaths. What good would murders like that do for the Purist cause? The HDL was still struggling to bring the rest of humanity over to their cause, to get them to see the dire necessity of driving the parasites off the planet once more. Killing off kids would be a public relations disaster; it would make the HDL look like a bunch of bloodthirsty maniacs. *That's why Bryant picked me,* thought Noah. *She knows she can trust me. I can see the big picture, just like her.* It was up to him to keep these thugs in line.

"Did you go out there?" Aalice pointed toward the raw landscape beyond the compound's fence. "I wish I coulda gone with you. It's boring here."

He looked over at the little girl sitting next to him. She didn't seem like the hybrid monster that he would have expected from the mating of humans and Newcomers. More like a kid with funny ears—they didn't look weird or anything, just different—and a wild case of freckles that were just visible underneath her fair blond hair and down the back of her neck. And a bit of a mouth on her—he wondered where she had gotten that from; it certainly couldn't have been from having deep conversations with a bunch of HDL members who seemed to be more into drinking beer and cleaning their guns than anything else.

"Yeah, you're right." He nodded. "This place kinda sucks."

Compared to the other places she had been in her brief career, this was probably the worst. Noah had already heard most of her life story, or at least as much of it as Aalice could remember. She had latched on to him almost as soon as he had shown up with the rest of the hospital assault team and the baby; it couldn't have taken much for her to figure out that he wasn't as mean as the others at the camp. Since then, she had been chattering away to him at every opportunity. That showed how lonely it was for her in this out-of-the-way dump.

There had been other places that had been more fun for her. She remembered a house with a big backyard, that had even had a swimming pool and a fence so high that nobody could see over it. She had been there a long time, with Dr. Quinn coming to see her a lot and checking up on her. That Nurse Eward had been there a lot of the time as well, but Aalice had never liked her much. She had never gotten to go anywhere, but at least it had been more interesting there than in this place.

"And he's the one who gave me my name," she'd told Noah. She seemed oddly proud that it was spelled with two A's. "That's 'cause I was the first one." She knew all about being a human/Tenctonese hybrid, the only one until this new baby had shown up; Quinn had explained it to her. And in his research files, she had been labelled as "Case AA." Noah supposed that if Quinn had started a file on the infant before he'd been killed in the clinic bombing, it would have been labelled 'Case AB.' But a real live kid couldn't be called something like that; thus the "Aalice" name. "Like in Wonderland," she'd told Noah. "But different." She had then glanced around the compound and the desert beyond the fence. "This isn't Wonderland, either."

There wasn't much else to the story. She didn't

remember her mother and father. Dr. Quinn had told
her that they were both dead. He had been about the
only family she'd had, or anything close to it. "He was
always real nice to me," she had told Noah, her voice
turning sad. It had been typical of the HDL members
at the compound to have taken some sadistic pleasure
in telling her that the doctor had been killed. She had
cried and cried, huddled up by herself on the blanket
in this empty building, so they wouldn't see her. Still
red-eyed and wet-cheeked, Aalice had crept back over
to the main building to find something to eat, and had
overheard her keepers talking some more about Dr.
Quinn's death.

"They didn't do it," she had told Noah. She meant
the Human Defense League. "They came in and took
me away. That nurse lady told them where I was at,
but they didn't, you know, blow up that clinic and
stuff. That was those other people, the ones they call
the rich slags—you know, the ones that the doctor
was always getting money from, for the clinic—
they're like real rich Newcomer businessmen; that's
what they say." She had pointed over to the compound's main building. "They were talking about it,
about how they had, like, sent pictures of me and stuff
over to the businessmen, to show they had me and the
doctor didn't anymore. So it was those businessmen
who went and blew up the clinic and killed the doctor,
and everything." Aalice had frowned, trying to work
that last part out in her mind. "I don't really understand why, though. He was real nice."

Noah had understood. He had already heard, from
Bryant herself, about how Quinn had been getting the
funding for his research from the *Sleemata Romot,*
and how the wealthy Newcomer businessmen didn't
like the notion of human/Tenctonese crossbreeding
any better than the HDL did. So to steal Aalice from
Quinn's safekeeping and then tell the Newcomers
about it had been a neat way of getting them to do the
HDL's dirty work. There was a disturbing irony in the

notion that this interaction between the rich New-comers and the Purists who hated them so much would result in the death of the one person who had been doing the most to bring the two species together. At one time, Noah would have thought that the doctor had gotten what he'd deserved; now he was beginning to wonder about that.

He was also beginning to wonder what he was getting into, sticking up for Aalice and the baby. The muttering from the other HDL team members had been getting louder and uglier. He had started worry-ing if he would be able to hold everything together until Darlene Bryant's orders reached them about what to do next. A little panic attack had set in, triggered by something he would never have expected to happen or to have such a major effect on him. Noah had wound up taking one of the Jeeps from the ones parked in the corner of the compound; he had told the other men that he was just going out to get familiar with the surrounding area . . .

But he hadn't done that.

Something had happened, something unforeseen, and he had taken the Jeep and gone out the gate topped with barbed wire, and he had driven the five miles down the narrow asphalt road to the nearest town, a hole-in-the-wall crossroads called Vindoma. There wasn't much more than a post office and a gas station with a little store attached. But there had been what he was looking for, an old-style phone booth hooked up next to the pole on the other side of the town's single street. It took him a few minutes to get the information he needed from the Los Angeles directory assistance operator, but he had managed.

He had been afraid to get Matt Sikes's number and call him up—how could he, when he'd just helped steal the man's baby?—but he remembered that Sikes's partner was a Newcomer named George Fran-cisco. That was the number he'd dialed, but he'd gotten an answering machine rather than a living voice. That had rattled him, but Noah had gotten even more unnerved when he'd glimpsed out of the corner of his eye another off-road vehicle rolling down the street; he'd had a quick stab of fear that the other HDL members from the camp had followed him out here and had spotted him in the phone booth. He'd realized his mistake—it was just a pickup truck with one of the local townspeople at the wheel—but by then he'd already slammed the phone back onto its chrome hook.

Driving back to the HDL compound, he had shouted at himself inside his head. *What the hell were you doing? Jeez, what were you thinking of?* It had all been too weird, as though somebody else had stepped inside his skin for a few minutes, making him think and do things that he never would have otherwise.

That had all happened a couple of hours ago, and now he was back here inside the compound's fence, sitting on a splintery wooden step with this strange little girl. She leaned her head against his arm.

"You'll take me out there, won't you?" Aalice gazed at the bleak landscape past the gate. "The next time you go, I mean."

It took a little while for Noah to find his voice. The weird feeling came over him again, of being somebody else, somebody who wasn't a Purist, somebody who didn't want to kill all the slags in the world.

"Sure," he said finally. "I'll take you out there."

The little girl was silent, and he remembered what had happened, the small event that had preceded his taking the Jeep and driving out to find the phone booth in the small town. He closed his eyes, thinking about it.

He had gone inside the main building to check up on how Nurse Eward was taking care of the stolen infant. Everything had looked fine; she was over talking with some of the others, and the baby was making little gurgling noises where it lay in the hospital cart that now served as its cradle. Noah had stood beside the cart, looking down at the baby, aware of the other HDL members' gaze on his back, their silent watching. He had reached down and pushed aside the edge of the blanket next to the baby's face. And that was when it had happened . . .

One of the tiny hands had seized hold of Noah's finger. Just a newborn, with barely enough strength to grasp anything—but it had.

The baby's hand had held on, with the soft yet insistent force of a living thing, a life that had just started.

"I was told that I'd find you here."

Sikes turned, looking back toward the door of the shabby room. "Here" was a crummy flophouse room with a single-burner hot plate on top of a battered dresser. The faded blooms on the peeling wallpaper looked as if they had died in a previous century. The room was the end of the trail that the late Dr. Quinn had left behind him. The rent receipt had been found in his wallet when the coroner's office had finished with the body.

Standing in the room's open doorway was Sikes's partner. *Ex-partner,* he thought with more than a trace of bitterness. It had been a while since he had last seen George, and a lot had happened since then.

Sikes turned back toward the room and its dense clutter. He stood with his hands on his hips, feeling as though the tension inside him were about to snap his spine in two. He didn't have time for whatever loony trip George might be into now. "Look, whatever your problem is, I can't deal with it now. There's lots heavier shit that's come down, so why don't you just take a hike back to your wacko friends, and stay out of my way."

"Matt . . ." From the doorway, George stepped into the room. "I know about your child. I know that it was kidnapped from the hospital—"

"Yeah, well, you were always were a great detective,

weren't you? So you know as much as was already reported on the TV news." Sikes shook his head in disgust. "That's really bright of you."

"I know more than that," said George softly. "I know how it came to happen, that you and Cathy were able to have a child together. I know more about that child than you do."

"Like what?" He snapped his gaze back around toward the other man. A wild anger rose inside him. He was almost at the point of vaulting across the room and throttling the answers out of George. "What're you holding out on me—"

"As I believe your words were meant to indicate, there isn't time right now for a lot of discussion. Perhaps later, when the child has been located and returned safely to you and Cathy—then we'll have a lot to talk about." George walked to the center of the room, next to Sikes, and looked around. "If there are any clues to be found here, the two of us will be able to dig them out faster than you would on your own."

"What's that supposed to mean? You're done being a religious fanatic and now you're a cop again?"

George looked straight into his eyes. "I don't know if I'm anything at all, Matt, other than somebody who was once your friend. And as for being a fanatic, religious or otherwise . . ." He nodded slowly. "That's one of the things we'll have to talk about when the time comes. There's more to that story than what I previously led you to believe. If it's any comfort, you weren't the only one to whom I lied. My wife, my children—but there were reasons for what I did. And they've let me try to make it up to them. That's what I'm asking from you."

Silence filled the room. The impulse to shout at George and order him to get out was still inside him, but another feeling had opened as well. Sikes wished it were true, that George saying it and his believing could make it that way, could make them partners once again. He needed George, now more than ever.

The rage in his heart, that could have burst loose and struck down the bastards that had stolen his son—that rage was mixed with fear as well. A fear that he would have to return to a different room, one that was all in scrubbed and soothing tones of beige, shuttered against the light of day; a room that held a sobbing woman, the mother of that stolen child, his own Cathy. The time might come when he would have to go back there to the hospital and tell her that there was nothing he could do, there was no way to bring their son back, it was already too late . . .

It would be simple to believe him. Not just because Sikes wanted to, but because the voice and the words had sounded like the old George, as though his partner had come back from the dead. Not all zoned and drifting off into some vague ethereal trance, but locked right into real time and the real problem in front of him.

In front of us, thought Sikes, nodding to himself. That did it. He'd made his decision.

"Okay." He looked straight back at George. "You're on. Let's get started."

George pulled off his jacket and laid it over the back of a rickety chair. "What exactly are we looking for?"

"Beats the hell out of me." Sikes prodded an empty cardboard box with his shoe. "There's already BNA agents swarming all over the hospital and at some burned-down garage they figure was used for the raid's staging area—they haven't found anything yet that'll tell us where those sonsabitches headed. I came here just hoping that there might be some clue in Quinn's stuff. He had more of a line on what was going on behind the scenes than anybody else."

Five minutes later, with a good portion of the room's contents searched and tossed out into the corridor, they found a slim laptop computer tucked into a canvas duffel bag full of unwashed clothes. Sikes popped the lid and quickly examined the machine.

"Damn. There's no hard disk in this thing." He'd flipped the power switch and gotten nothing more than an initial prompt on the flat screen. "Quinn must have kept everything on floppies." With one hand, he rooted futilely through the duffel bag. "Come on, give me a hand looking for 'em."

His partner made no reply, but took a couple of steps over to the other side of the room. George picked up the hot plate from the top of the battered dresser. "There's no cord on this rather primitive cooking device." He ran his hand over the wall's surface. "And this wallpaper would show scorch marks if it had been used over here. With his thumbnail, George pried between the hot plate's blackened top area and the chrome surrounding it. The two parts separated like a clamshell. From the space inside, he shook out a pair of floppy disks onto his palm. "Here we go."

"Let's hope the good doctor didn't have a password set up." Sikes placed the laptop on the dresser and fed the first disk into it. "Or worse, all that encryption jazz."

"It's been my experience that security measures such as those are employed by people who stay in one place. People who are on the run, as Quinn was, don't have time for such things."

Bending close to the computer, heads almost touching, they scanned down the directory that appeared on the screen. "Jeez," said Sikes. "He's got his old tax returns on here."

"Force of habit." George ran a fingertip down the glowing lines. "None of these look very promising. Try the other disk."

Sikes swapped the disks. He punched in the directory command.

"Great! These must be Quinn's research files. A great big batch of 'em." Sikes hit a few more keys. "And we're straight in. The good doctor may have been paranoid about a lot of things—and with plenty

253

of reason—but it was nice of him to leave this unlocked."

A couple more keystrokes, and the first segment of the file appeared on the screen. The two men began to read.

An hour later, they were finished. The last glowing lines had scrolled to the top of the screen. For a moment longer, the two men were silent, then George reached out and tapped a key. The screen went blank.

Sikes rubbed his eyes, burning with the effort of that much high-speed scanning of information. A new fear gripped his heart, rendering him incapable of speech, nearly beyond rational thought. Time had been racing before; now it rushed toward a destination, the fate of his child, that he hadn't a glimpse of before . . .

"Come on." He felt his partner laying a hand on his shoulder. George's voice was soft, trying to extend comfort in a world that had suddenly become even more terrible and relentless. That was all that Quinn's notes had given them. "We'd better get back to the station. Maybe the others have found something. Maybe there's still time . . ."

"You're right." With a sweep of his arm, Sikes sent the laptop computer crashing off the dresser and onto the floor. He gazed down at the machine with all the rage and frustration that had been unlocked from his heart. "Let's go." He spun on his heel and headed for the room's door. He could hear George following him as he broke into a run in the corridor.

"I need to see Detective Sikes."

A face turned toward him. "How'd you get in here?" The face regarded Buck with suspicion, then relaxed. "Wait a minute, you're George Francisco's son, aren't you? Say, where's your dad been the last couple of months or so?"

"What?" Buck was still partially deafened by the roar of his motorcycle's engine and the wind noise past the helmet he now carried slung under one arm.

He wasn't sure he had heard this police detective right. Why wouldn't the man know about his father's resignation from the department? "Look, I don't have time to talk about that now. I just really need to see Matt Sikes. It's important."

"Everything's important. Right now more than usual." The police detective, a human—Buck had seen him before but couldn't recall his name—shuffled through a stack of messy file folders he had against his chest. "The heavy shit's really come down, kid. Which means you're outta luck if you wanna get hold of Sikes. He's got a lot more important things on his mind than hearing whatever you got to tell him."

Buck looked around the station's offices, this room with his father's old desk in it and what he could see of the spaces beyond the doors and hallways. The place was busier than he had ever seen it before, on any of the occasions he'd come down here to talk to his father. To the unfamiliar eye, it would have looked as if sheer chaos had broken out, with all the detectives and uniformed officers quick-striding or even running from office to office, or hunched over their desks and computer terminals, then shouting questions and orders to each other across the room. The station vibrated with tension, as though the inadequate air-conditioning itself had become infused with the psychic atmosphere of a Pentagon war room in full swing. Buck had seen the station in crisis mode before, though; it didn't faze him. He knew that this was the full-court press that the department and its people would swing into for one of their own. If Matthew Sikes's stolen baby wasn't found alive and well, and the scumbags who'd taken it weren't slam-dunked into the station's holding cells so hard that their tert heads split open, it wouldn't be for lack of every lead, suspect, or scrap of clue being followed up on.

And that was why he was here, though he seemed to be having a hard time convincing this particular bull-necked brick wall of that. Buck had decided that it was better to get the info he had straight to Sikes, rather than getting hold of his own father and telling him. He knew that Sikes would be right in the middle of the investigation on the hospital raid—it was his kid that had been taken, after all—whereas Buck's father might be completely out of the loop. When George Francisco had resigned from the LAPD and broken up his partnership with Sikes, it had apparently not gone down on the friendliest of terms. With the kind of temper that Sikes had in the best of times, let alone a high-pressure situation like this one, if Buck's father tried to tell him where the call from Noah Ramsey had come from, the chances were good that Sikes would blow him off before the crucial data could be passed along. Or else it would take forever for his ex-partner to get through to Sikes and tell him—and right now, time was at a premium.

The other factor that had entered into Buck's calculations was that he knew Matthew Sikes was no dummy. He had sufficient smarts to be able to recognize what the phone call info meant, and he was wired into the center of the police and BNA web that would be able to make use of it—it'd be total gung-ho city once Sikes got the word.

If he got the word. That was starting to seem unlikely.

The cop he'd been talking to had turned away, which was just as well; Buck didn't feel like hassling with him any more. Before anybody could stop him, he zipped down the aisle between the desks, stopping at the one he knew was Sikes's—it faced onto the one his dad had always used. He grabbed a blank sheet of paper and a pen, leaning over to quickly write out a note.

"Hey!" The detective had turned around and caught sight of him. "What're you doing? Authorized personnel only—you're not even supposed to be in here."

"Just leaving," Buck folded the paper, scrawled SIKES—THIS IS IMPORTANT! and left it in the center of the desk where it would be seen right off. "Keep your hair on."

He walked past the detective without saying anything else. When he hit the street outside the station, he didn't hesitate. His mind had already been made up about what to do next.

Buck climbed onto his motorcycle and kicked it into roaring life. Wheeling it away from the curb, he headed for the nearest freeway on-ramp, that would get him onto I-5 heading north.

The police detective shook his head. He could hear, coming from outside the station, the roar of a motorcycle engine, loud and then fading into the distance.

In his arms, he still had the suspect files that Detective Sikes had requisitioned. He walked down and dropped the files on Matt's desk. There were enough of the manila folders to cover the desk's surface, hiding beneath them anything else that might have been there.

The detective started back toward the files room. He still felt annoyed at that kid barging in, especially without his father George being around. People had to realize that there was work to be done here.

CHAPTER 15

IT HAD BEEN getting worse and worse, a threat gathering over the last twenty-four hours, like storm clouds massing at the horizon, heavy and dark. Something was going to happen—he could tell just from the sound of the others' voices, without even being able to hear the words they whispered to each other. Voices, and then silence, when Noah looked over his shoulder at the other HDL team members, his gaze would be met with ones of mute resentment and simmering disdain, the dark clouds reflected in the depths of their hooded eyes. Silence, and then the voices again, whispers and mutterings as he walked away. Laughter as well, harsh and mocking, and words that were just loud enough for him to make out, as they were intended to be.

"Slag lover . . ."

Noah kept on walking, past the wooden front steps of the compound's main building, where a knot of six or seven of the HDL members—the men who were supposedly under his command—sat in the motionless air of the high desert's early evening. A couple of

258

them had been knocking back cans of beer, though he had put out an order forbidding alcohol as part of the general tightening up of standards. They didn't even bother attempting to hide their petty rebellion, and he knew better than to push them on it. The fiction of the HDL's elite commando units, and their commitment to strict military discipline, was wearing pretty thin— dangerously so. All Noah could hope to do was keep open mutiny from breaking out, at least until Darlene Bryant's next orders came through and the two children were moved on to some place where they would be safer.

He kept walking, boots scuffing through the loose gravel and sand, his spine and shoulders rigid as a shield. Whatever words the others shot at him, he had to let them bounce right off. *Stay deaf,* Noah told himself for the hundredth time. *Don't show a thing.* His head, though, felt as though it were about to explode from the sheer pressure building up inside. He wondered how the hell he had gotten into this situation. When he had found the Purists—or when they had found him—and he had signed on with the HDL and taken the blood oath to protect his own species, it had been like coming home at last after a lifetime of wandering through the world alone and friendless. To be hooked up with a bunch of people— people like him—people who thought the same as he did, who could see what was happening to the world that was their birthright, and who were willing to lay down their lives to drive the parasites back where they had come from. He'd had a family at last, brothers in a common cause. That was why he'd poured every scrap of energy into the organization, given up everything else; if he had shot up through the ranks, until he was Bryant's personal right-hand man, he had figured that it was only in recognition of his faith, his desire, his will, put in service of the one shining goal that united them all . . .

Yeah, right, Noah thought bitterly. He kicked a

pebble out of his way. Something had sure deep-sixed that shining vision. He couldn't even begin imagining what was going on inside some of these guys' heads. By now they would have offed the baby they'd stolen, as well as the little girl Aalice, if he hadn't been there to stop them, to keep them in line with Bryant's orders. Noah shook his head as he gazed out through the fence topped with razor wire, and across the landscape of rock and dry scrub. He couldn't get with the trip these sonsabitches were on. He hadn't signed on with the HDL in order to murder kids. And these weren't even slag children, at least not totally; Aalice and the baby were both half human. Didn't that count for something? He would have thought that the other team members would at least be slowed down by that consideration. Instead, they were just getting more and more pissed off that he was standing between them and the two children they wanted to kill. *Sonsabitches* . . .

He reached the wooden front steps of the ramshackle camp building that the little girl Aalice had claimed as her own private hideaway. The realization had come to him some time ago that the other HDL members, the ones who had been up here supposedly guarding her, probably let her have the place—it wasn't much more than an extended shack, ready to fall over in the next stiff breeze—just so they wouldn't have to look at her. Though why the sight of the hybrid kid should irritate them so deeply, Noah still hadn't figured out.

Pushing open the squeaky-hinged front door, Noah looked inside. Dust motes hung in the parallel slices of light that penetrated the boards nailed over the broken windows. On the blanket in the corner, Aalice lay curled up asleep, an arm protectively clasping to herself the battered doll that was one of her few playthings. Her mouth was slightly parted, cheek against an old sweater rolled up for a pillow, her breath slow and regular. In the partial light, Noah could have mistaken her for a completely human child. Or one that's all Newcomer—he frowned, the unbidden thought puzzling him for a moment. The next thought troubled him even more: he found himself wondering if it made any difference what the little girl was.

He didn't wake her up. Instead, he wandered back over to the camp's main building, still feeling a crawly sense of unease across his tensed shoulders, his head crammed with things he found impossible to sort through.

Inside, Nurse Eward was tending to the stolen baby. The milky scent of the warmed formula was just discernible. From where she leaned over the baby's cart, Eward glanced over her shoulder at him, but said nothing. He ignored the look of mute resentment in her expression, as the buzzing sound of a cellular telephone's ring cut through the room. Nobody was sitting at the equipment-laden table that served as the camp's link to the world beyond the fence; Noah figured that the comm tech must be hanging out somewhere with the rest of the team members.

The ring was cut short as the small fax machine switched on. A few more electronic noises, then a sheet of paper began to slowly uncurl from the slot. Noah stood beside the table, tilting his head to read the upside-down words. Before the print-out was halfway through, his heart had jumped a beat, then raced faster. When the single page was finished and the telephone connection broken, Noah reached down and picked up the curved sheet of paper. With a carefully maintained aura of calm, he folded it and tucked it into his shirt pocket.

"What was that?" Nurse Eward's voice came from the other side of the room.

He turned away from the communications table, meeting the woman's suspicious gaze. "Nothing special." He shrugged, then started toward the door, making sure that his pace was not too fast. "Just routine business." He walked past Eward, then outside, pulling the door shut behind him. Only when he was well away from the main building, and with none of the others in sight, did he pull out the fax sheet, unfold it, and quickly scan across its message once more.

The message was addressed to him. It came straight from Darlene Bryant, via one of the HDL attorneys that shuffled in and out of the private visiting area at the women's prison. A slight tremor passed from Noah's hands to the fax paper as he read. When he got to the end, he slowly lowered the sheet of paper and gazed sightlessly across the compound's empty grounds to the bleaker desert beyond the fence. He felt as if a space equally as hollow had been carved out of his guts.

The fax he held was the death warrant for the little girl Aalice and the stolen baby.

Inside Noah's head, the words of the Human Defense League's leader marched and chanted, like an idiot army. The hollowness inside him grew larger, as though it were capable of swallowing him up, a black hole he wished he could vanish into. The bleak realization came to him, that he had made these words possible, had helped summon them into being, and that they were inevitable. He had known all along that Bryant's orders for the two children's fate would come and what they would be. There was no other possibility. He had been lying to himself when he had thought some other outcome would be arranged. Their deaths were sealed, just as if he had done nothing to prevent them from being killed back during the raid on the hospital. It was just a matter of timing and public relations. Bryant had weighed everything and in her cold judgment had decided it was better to exterminate Aalice and the baby out here, where nobody could see what happened to them, or find their bodies—find them and analyze them and reveal to all the world what the two children had really been . . .

We can't let monsters like these live—Bryant's words were tiny black elements on the curling fax paper. *Not because they're part parasite—but because they're nearly all human.* That was the secret that couldn't be revealed: a mating between a Tenctonese and a human produced a child that was genetically human. The few remaining physical differences—the trace of head spots, the altered ear pinnae—mattered little, if at all. The fax spelled out, in quick, brief sentences, what Bryant and the rest of the HDL top command had already known about Dr. Quinn's research. The doctor had proved, by his genotyping of the first Newcomer/human hybrid, the little girl Aalice, that the human strain was the dominant one, almost completely eliminating the contribution from the Tenctonese partner. There was nothing to be feared from matings between Newcomers and the human species; the only result would be children that were in essence human.

Nothing to be feared . . . and everything to be lost, for the HDL at least. Bryant had hinted about these things to him before, the real reasons for the League's existence, but Noah had always dismissed them from his thoughts. But now—because he had vindicated her trust in him and his abilities—now she had come right out and said it. Admitted it right in the fax that he held in his trembling hands . . .

The Newcomers were only a pretext. The reason that the HDL existed was power. And nothing else.

To the HDL, the existence of Aalice and the stolen baby, and the implications they had for the relationship between humans and Newcomers, was their worst nightmare come true. If the Newcomers were to be seen as essentially human—not alien parasites, but a branch that had once come from the same root—and if matings between Newcomers and humans would result in nothing more than the Newcomers being reabsorbed into one genetic stream again . . . then there would be no way for the HDL to stir up hatred between the two groups. No longer two, but one people; brethren reunited. And with no hatred, there would be no reason at all for the HDL to exist. And no reason for people to listen to an aging beauty queen like Darlene Bryant, no way for her to grasp power in her hand . . .

Noah had learned his history well enough; Bryant had even encouraged him to read up on the HDL's illustrious—her word—predecessors. The grasping of power required an enemy, something to be labelled as evil, to whip up loathing against. The Nazis had known how to do it; there had even been those in the top ranks of the Third Reich who'd admitted they had no feelings one way or another about the Jews, but had found them useful as a way of bringing their own followers to heel. A cold, calculating evil, one that knew the road to the city of power was paved with murder.

Cold evil, cold logic. In the middle of the high desert of eastern Oregon, Noah felt his skin chilled by a wind that stirred no dust at his feet. The time had come and embraced him, the time when the evil he had served claimed him for its own. The harsh landscape faded from his vision; he saw Darlene Bryant turning toward him and smiling, her eyes two mirrors of polished darkness, smiling and saying, I know who you are. You're one of us. Bryant had looked into his heart and had judged him to be the same order of creature that she was, wanting the same things, capable of doing whatever was necessary to get them.

Eliminate the two children, the fax's concluding orders had read. *Instructions on disposal of the bodies to follow.*

Noah folded the paper and tucked it back into his shirt pocket. No thoughts moved inside his head, as though the words themselves had been rendered numb. He started walking toward another of the camp's low buildings.

The little girl was still asleep on the blanket in the corner. The light sifting through the boarded-up windows had changed its angle, touching a corner of Aalice's face. He stood gazing down at her, one minute and then another passing. *Instructions to follow* . . . Words that weren't his own turned inside him. *Disposal of the bodies* . . .

He knelt down and prodded the girl's shoulder. "Hey . . ." His voice was kept low. "Come on, Aalice, wake up."

"Hm?" She lifted her head and sleepily regarded him. "I was dreaming . . . I dreamt you took me out there." Aalice pointed to the cabin's open doorway and the desert beyond the fence.

"Yeah, well, that's where we're going." Noah stood up, reaching down to help her to her feet. "We're going for a drive."

"Really?" Her face lit up.

"Sure thing." He found it easier to speak now that his decision had been made. "But we gotta keep it quiet, okay? It's kind of a . . . surprise thing. So I don't want the others to know just yet."

"Oh." Aalice peered more closely at him. "I get it. I'll be quiet as a mouse."

She knows the score, thought Noah. This kid had been up here a lot longer than he had, and she wasn't stupid. She could have figured out a long time ago that her survival might depend upon reading out the situation around her.

"Are we going right now?" asked Aalice.

He nodded, his brain still working through the details. There was more to worry about than just him and the little girl. He glanced around the empty room, then back down to the blanket at his feet. "You know, we're going to be gone for a while. Maybe you should bring your doll along . . . you wouldn't want it to get lonely back here." Aalice picked up the doll and stood beside him, waiting. "Here—" He reached down and gathered up the blanket. "Let's wrap her up so she doesn't get cold." Aalice let him bundle the doll in the folded blanket, then held it against herself when he gave it back. "Okay, now we gotta go over to the other building and pick something else up. Now you just do whatever I tell you, all right?"

Aalice said nothing, but gave a nod, her eyes wide and serious.

Crossing the compound, Noah saw a bunch of the HDL team members clustered near a wooden pole to which they had nailed a broken-through ten-gallon can; they were shooting desultory hoops, knocking back the beers in their hands with more enthusiasm. Some of the men had stripped off their shirts, their shoulders and backs damp with sweat. All of them turned their sullen gazes toward Noah and Aalice, then away with muttered comments and ugly, snickering laughs.

In the compound's main building, Nurse Eward was standing at one of the windows, smoking a cigarette. A litter of ground-out butts lay around her feet, smears of black ash marking the floor's wooden planks. She glanced over her shoulder as Noah and Aalice came inside. "What do you want?"

Noah pushed the little girl ahead of himself. "The kid said she was hungry."

"So get her something to eat, already." Shaking her head in disgust, Eward turned back to the dust-clouded window. "Christ, do I have to do everything around here?"

He stopped with Aalice beside the chrome cart from the hospital. "Hey, is everything all right with this one?"

The nurse's slit-eyed gaze turned his way again. "Why the hell shouldn't it be?"

"I don't know. It just looks . . . kinda sick." In fact, the infant bedded down inside the cart looked perfectly healthy to him. It opened its eyes and gurgled, as though recognizing the face above it; the tiny hands clutched and waved in the air. "Maybe you better come over here and check it out."

Eward angrily threw down her cigarette and stomped over toward them. With one hand, Noah protectively nudged Aalice behind himself. He stepped back so the nurse could lean over the cart.

"What're you talking about?" With unfeeling, clinical precision, Eward ran a hand over the infant's brow, using the ball of her thumb to pull one of its eyelids open wider. "This thing's healthy as a horse."

"That's a relief—" Noah said nothing more, but reached out and grabbed the woman by the hair at the back of her head. She gasped in surprise as he jerked her away from the cart. His other fist arced upward, catching her on the point of her jaw. The blow rolled her eyes back in their sockets; she collapsed limp and unconscious when he let go of her.

"Wow . . ." Aalice breathed out the syllable. "That was cool."

"I told you to be quiet." He leaned down and grabbed Eward under the arms. Her head lolled as he dragged her into the building's kitchen area and out of sight. A glimpse out the window as he came back showed him that the rest of the HDL members were still out by their makeshift basketball court. Noah took the doll from Aalice's grasp and slipped it from the folded blanket. A few seconds juggling act, and the doll was tucked inside the hospital cart. The wriggling infant lay in the crook of his arm, swaddled and concealed. He knelt down in front of Aalice. "Okay, now you have to carry the baby." The bundle, bigger than the doll had been, filled Aalice's arms; she had to lean back to balance her two-handed grip on it. "You got it?"

Aalice nodded gravely.

He led her out the building's front door, hoping that the infant would stay quiet until they were well away from the other HDL members. One end of the blanket dragged on the ground as Noah put his hand on Aalice's shoulder, carefully pushing her toward the other side of the compound. He had debated with himself about whether to stuff a bag full of the infant's supplies, then carry it out himself, but had decided against it. There were some plastic jugs of water in the Jeep he was planning on taking; that, plus the couple cans of formula he managed to cram into his jacket pockets, would have to do. If they got away clean from the compound, it wouldn't be long before he would have the baby someplace where it would be taken care of. And if they didn't get away, a whole case of formula wouldn't make any difference about what happened next, to the baby, Aalice, and him.

Several yards away, a few of the HDL members glanced over at the small parade, then turned back to their hoops. Noah watched them from the corner of his eye—none of them appeared to suspect anything wrong.

As soon as they were around the corner of the next building, Noah took the blanket-wrapped infant from Aalice's arms. They were out of the angle of the others' sight; with one arm tucking the squirming baby against his chest, he took Aalice's hand and pulled her at a quick trot toward the cluster of vehicles parked at the compound's far corner.

With the blanket for cushioning, he made a nest for the baby in the space behind the driver's seat of the Jeep. A bungee cord looped between one floor bolt and another was just slack enough to keep the baby secure. The small face wrinkled; it was annoyed by all the fussing around, but not enough to start crying yet.

Noah dug the formula cans out of his jacket and tucked them underneath the driver's seat. As he turned the key in the ignition, he put his other hand on top of Aalice's head and pushed her down below the level of the passenger side door. "You gotta keep down," he told her as the engine caught and roared to life. "It's a game."

"No, it's not." She looked offended as she crouched beside him. "I know what's going on. We're escaping."

"Sure as shit." He slammed the Jeep into gear and punched the accelerator.

Noah could see in the mirror as the HDL members turned and watched the dust cloud zoom past them. He knew that even these bastards weren't so slow as to not be able to figure out that something was up.

At the fence, he slammed on the brakes, jumped out and pulled back the gate. He could hear voices shouting in the distance. He glanced over his shoulder and saw running figures, a couple others coming out of the main building with the nurse supported between them.

He scrambled back into the Jeep. "Hold on!" Beside him, Aalice yanked her seat belt tight around her waist. The Jeep's wheels spun gravel, then they were outside the compound, laying a rubber track on the road before straightening out.

In the mirror, he saw the larger, heavier vehicles starting to roll. He knew that they would be able to catch up if he stayed on the narrow strip of asphalt; it took only a second for him to make his next decision. With a jerk of the steering wheel, he slung the Jeep off the road, heading across the high desert.

CHAPTER 16

WHAT HE WANTED—needed, really—was sleep. He could feel it right down in his bones, the overwhelming desire to just steer the motorcycle over to the side of the road, switch off the racketing engine, and then lay his weary body on the ground. If he did that, he knew he would be unconscious in a matter of seconds, the bright sun pressing down on him like the covers of the softest bed imaginable.

You go for nearly twenty hours straight, thought Buck, *and that's what you get.* It was a miracle that he hadn't become even loopier than he already was. His spine felt as if it had become fused into a permanent curve from the hundreds of miles of being hunched over the bike's tank. From the center of Los Angeles, straight up I-5 like a ground-hugging rocket aimed due north, and then once he'd crossed the state border into Oregon, the long diagonal northwest—he'd stopped only to fill the motorcycle with gas, shoving down into his own gut bags of organ-meat snacks from the stations' vending machines. The California Highway Patrol had picked him up on their radar somewhere around Fresno, but he'd managed to elude them, turning the bike onto a service road paralleling the interstate and switching off his headlight, gunning through the dark until he lost his pursuers somewhere behind.

That was as close as he'd come to getting caught, which would have put a serious crimp in his elapsed time. Buck didn't know if the road cops in Oregon were better or worse, but there definitely seemed to be fewer of them once he got into the bleak wilds east of the main highway. Once he'd started heading in the direction of Idaho, it had been more or less a straight shot all the way to Vindoma.

The fatigue faded from his system when he saw the sign posting the outskirts of the little town. He had finally reached his destination. He rolled on the bike's accelerator, hurtling down the narrow two-lane road.

There was so little to the place that Buck almost shot out the other side before he realized it. He had to jam on the brakes and fishtail the bike to a halt, his own dust settling around him. A half dozen or so terts, the drivers of the battered pickup trucks parked over at the combined gas station and general store, glanced his way. They appeared only mildly curious. It took Buck a moment to remember that he still had his helmet on—the locals had no way of knowing that he was a Newcomer. A yellow hound lying in the dust by the gas pumps barely managed to lift its head and sniff the air; then it rolled over in slow motion, resuming its noontime slumber.

A few minutes later and he had located the phone booth, snug against the utilities pole a few yards away from the store. The number was the same as the one that the Caller ID device in his father's home office had read out; his little sister Emily's electronic detective work hadn't sent him all this way for nothing. Leaving his motorcycle parked beside the phone booth, Buck headed toward the store, his legs stiff from the long ride.

The place was obviously the town's de facto social center. The humans who had been outside had retreated into the store's cooler shade. A couple of them had popped open beers, leaning themselves against the counter with its antique cash register and rack of tobacco snuff cans, or sitting on top of stacked fifty-pound bags of animal feed.

A human woman, blond hair tied back with a rubber band, rested her sun-burnt arms on the counter. "If you need gas," she said, pointing back out the door, "go ahead and pump it yourself. Just let me know what it comes to."

"Actually—" Buck pulled off the helmet. "I need some directions." He dangled the helmet at his side. "I'm trying to find some people up here."

"Look at that." One of the terts nudged a companion next to him. "It's one of those . . . whatchacallem . . . Newcomer guys." The man's face filled with an almost childlike delight. "You know, like they have over in the big cities." Another poke to the ribs sloshed the beer in his friend's hand. "Ain't it?"

"For Christ's sake, Charlie." The woman behind the counter winced in embarrassment. "Simmer down." She slowly shook her head as she looked back toward Buck. "Don't pay him any attention. His idea of the big city is La Grande."

"Yeah, well, at least I watch something on the tube besides the flippin' Oprah show." Charlie pointed to Buck. "He *is* one of them Newcomers. Remember, it was on all the news years ago, when they came down from outer space?"

"I came up here from Los Angeles, actually—"

"Same difference." One of the other humans snorted a laugh into his beer can.

He didn't have time for the locals' attempts at light conversation. "Look, I'm in kind of a hurry—"

"Like I said, fella, don't let these clowns ring your chimes." The human woman tossed a wadded-up bar towel at the men.

"The whole point, of what I was trying to say," continued the one named Charlie, "is that we've just never had one of these folks come around here before. That's all."

"But that ain't true." The man beside him lowered his beer. "You seen that little girl those fruitloops out in that camp have got. Remember? You thought a coyote had got one of those spaniel pups you been trying to breed, and we went looking for it out by that big old fence they got. And we saw her, we saw that little girl." He pointed to Buck. "I mean, she was kinda like him . . ."

"Wait a minute." Buck had no idea what girl the terts were talking about, but it might still be a lead. "Who do you mean? What camp?"

"Oh, there's a bunch of out-of-state jerks been hanging out in that old gun club up the road." The local spat on the floor in disgust. "Real unfriendly types . . ."

"Yeah, about all they ever do is come in here and stock up on cases of beer." The woman shook her head. "I don't need their business, if they can't even be bothered to say good morning to folks."

"But do you know who they are?"

"Funny thing is," said Charlie, "when they first came around here, I thought they were all like veterinarians or something. 'Cause if you ever heard them talking, all they'd ever go on about was how they were going to get rid of all the parasites. And I thought, shoot, if that's what they want to do, they oughta start by going over and deworming all those mutts Ernest has got in his backyard—"

"Hey!" One of the other men looked offended. "Those dogs are pure-breds!"

"Yeah, right . . ." Charlie and the rest got a laugh out of that.

"Please—" Buck had caught the word parasites and knew what it meant. "There's a camp or someplace where these people are at? How do I get there?"

A few moments later, with the locals' directions locked inside his head, he had fired up the motorcycle and was headed out of the town, not even taking the time to put the helmet back on.

So where's Matt and the rest of those guys? wondered Buck as he leaned forward, wind tearing at his eyes. He had been half-expecting to see Sikes and some other LAPD, along with special units from the Bureau of Newcomer Affairs, swarming all over this territory. By now, everything should have been over except for the mopping-up. The authorities had faster ways of getting on the scene than bone-tailing it on a motorcycle from the middle of one state to another. What happened to the message he'd left for Sikes at the police station? Either the detective hadn't gotten it, or he'd decided it was a joke and had wadded it up and thrown it into the trash can at the side of the desk.

Typical, thought Buck. Any time people wanted to get something done, they always wound up having to do it themselves. The only problem now was that his own plans hadn't actually extended as far as what he was going to do when he got here. *Now what?* He didn't know.

Something caught his eye, in the distance off to the side of the road. A cloud of dust, raised by some kind of vehicle tear-assing across the flat landscape. It didn't look that big—maybe a Jeep or another small four-wheel-drive. Wherever it was headed, it was going flat-out; the driver had the thing bouncing across dry gulleys and cutting off the tops of scrub-crested rises without a touch on the brake pedal.

The cloud of dust was more complicated than Buck had thought at first; he saw now that there were at least two or three other vehicles chasing the first one. He brought the motorcycle to a stop at the side of the road. As he watched, the high-speed caravan headed farther out into the desert.

He turned his gaze in the direction from which the vehicles had come, marked by the slowly settling dust.

On the other side of the road, he could just make out the glistening points of a high chain-link fence topped with razor wire. That must be the one, he figured, that the local back a the gas station's store had told him marked the perimeter of the camp. A gate hung open in the center of the fence.

Something was going down; that much was obvious. The only thing valuable enough to inspire a pursuit like that would be the infant the Purists had stolen from the hospital down in L.A. Maybe somebody, whoever was in the Jeep in the lead, had just swiped the baby from them—that would explain why the other vehicles were chasing so hard after their moving target. But who would've done that? Somebody else must have figured out that this was where the HDL assault team had brought the kid, and gotten here before he had come rolling onto the scene.

The mysteries tumbled inside Buck's head without answers. But he didn't need to know who was in the Jeep, as long as he was sure that the person had Matt's and Cathy's stolen baby with them. That was reason enough to swing into action.

From inside his jacket, Buck fumbled out the creased map that he'd used to get himself from the Oregon border to this empty territory. The tiny dot marking the town of Vindoma was circled in pencil. Right now, he and the bike were parked on the thin line leading east from the town. The Jeep and its pursuers were cutting across the blank space to the south. Another line showed on the map, running on a diagonal from the town's dot. That looked to be the Jeep's destination. In the open country, it appeared to be gradually pulling away from the slower vehicles behind it. If the jeep had enough of a lead by the time it hit the road farther south, it would have a chance of outdistancing the others entirely, maybe reaching the next town farther down the line before they could catch it.

A chance, not a sure thing—Buck knew he couldn't

leave it at that. Whoever was driving the Jeep—if they had the baby with them—might need some help. The motorcycle he was riding wasn't cut out for off-road travel. He'd be left behind in the dry brush and gravel if he joined the chase from here . . .

Buck wheeled the bike around and accelerated back toward Vindoma, and the other road branching off to the south.

"We made it!" Up ahead, he could see the black strip of asphalt, the road at the crest of a gravel-strewn rise. "Hold on!" Noah pressed the accelerator flat against the Jeep's floorboard. As the wheels bit into the loose ground, he shoved the gearshift down a notch. Rocks spat out from beneath the tires as they bounced and jostled upward.

"I don't see 'em," announced Aalice, twisting herself around in the passenger side seat. The Jeep was still swaying on its suspension where Noah had stopped and swung about on the road bisecting the desert. Holding a hand above her eyes, Aalice scanned back the way they had come. Through the settling dust, the Jeep's tracks could be seen, almost ruler straight except where he had swerved around clumps of dry brush or gulleys too deep to slam across. "You musta lost them."

"Yeah, maybe . . ." Noah craned his neck, looking above the little girl's head, his gaze searching the dry landscape for any sign or motion. The other road, that he had swung off from out by the HDL camp, was lost in the distance. He'd had one piece of luck during the chase: a few miles back, he had glanced at the mirror, just in time to see his two lead pursuers, the fastest of the off-road vehicles behind him, smash into each other. The side collision had been enough to send one vehicle spinning out of control on the sand, and the other rolling over and coming to rest upside down. Before he'd had to swing his attention back to the terrain in front of the Jeep, he had caught a glimpse of the third vehicle in the pack behind, a slower modified truck, putting on its brakes to avoid plowing into the others. "For now, at least." The HDL members might still be back there, sorting things out, but eventually they would pick up the chase again—and he wasn't going to sit around here waiting for them.

Noah put the Jeep back into gear, picking up speed as he headed east toward the Idaho state border. He had a vague memory from the map he had looked at back at the camp, of a couple of small towns along the Snake River—those would be closer than anything here in Oregon. With this much of a lead between them and their pursuers, there was at least a chance of holing up in one of the towns and calling for help. He pushed down on the accelerator pedal, the asphalt ribbon winding faster beneath the Jeep.

"How's the baby doing?" Without loosening his grip on the steering wheel, Noah gave a nod of his head toward the space behind the seats. During the wild, bumpy ride through the desert, the infant had started wailing—Noah had taken that as a good sign—but had quieted down since they had gotten on to a paved road again. "Maybe you should take a look."

"Okay." Aalice undid her seat belt and scrambled onto her knees, peering over the back of the seat. "How ya doin' down there?" She extended a forefinger as though to tickle the baby under the chin. "You having a good time? Huh? I am." A gurgling coo came in reply, and Aalice flopped back around on the seat. "I don't know—looks okay to me. Might be hungry, though." She frowned, sniffing the air. "Or something else."

"That'll just have to wait." He shook his head. "I'm not stopping out here to take care of the small stuff." The sooner he reached some place where there were other people, Noah figured, the sooner somebody who knew what they were doing could take care of both kids. His job was just to get them there alive.

Hardly more than a mile had ticked by when Noah heard another sound, a faint, distant edge cutting through the barely mufflered roar of the Jeep's engine. He leaned his chest close to the steering wheel, the corner of his brow touching the bug-splattered windshield as he peered up at the blank sky trying to see if there were a plane overhead. He saw nothing, not even a cloud, just the sun's harsh, eye-stinging glare. Only when he dropped his gaze down to the mirror on the left front fender did he spot the black flyspeck growing slowly larger in the center of the road behind. It took him a moment to decipher the image as a motorcycle gradually gaining on them, the rider tucked low against the tank to cut wind resistance, face hidden by the gauges at the center of the bars.

"What the . . ." Noah lowered his head, trying to get a better view in the jittering mirror. A motorcycle —he wondered who the hell that could be. If it were a cop, the siren would have been switched on by now, and the blue or red lights, whichever they used up here in Oregon, would have been bouncing off the mirror into his face.

And if it wasn't a cop—that left only a single possibility, and it wasn't a good one. There hadn't been a motorcycle among the vehicles at the HDL camp. Maybe there had been some other League member off-site, in one of the other little towns scattered down the highway, that the others hadn't told him about. And when he had busted out of the camp with the baby and Aalice, maybe they had called the guy out, whoever he was, and set him racing down the road to intercept them.

It didn't look good. Whatever the apparition on the motorcycle represented, Noah didn't feel like taking any chances. He kept the accelerator stomped to the floorboard, pushing his sweating grip against the curve of the steering wheel and willing the Jeep to go even faster.

"Shit," muttered Noah. He'd glanced at the mirror

again; the motorcycle and its rider were closer, catching up faster than he'd expected. The bike obviously had some high-powered guts; the roar of the engine snarled even louder, revved to its maximum pitch. In the mirror, the motorcycle's headlight shimmered in the sunlight like a rounded jewel. Noah felt his brow creasing as he studied the reflected image: he could just see now the rider, a face with eyes hidden behind the silvery lenses of aviator-style sunglasses. There was something about that face, as though he could almost recognize the person, somebody he had known from another life, another world. How could that be? He took one hand from the wheel and rubbed his own burning eyes. Even weirder, he had thought he could tell that the guy on the back of the motorcycle was a Newcomer, the pattern of head spots just detectable at the edge of the forehead above the sun-spattering glasses.

Minutes grew out of sweating seconds, with Noah urging his strength into the wheel. A glance at the fender showed the motorcyclist's image filling the mirror, the machine and its rider now only a few yards behind.

"What're you gonna do?" Anxiety tinged Aalice's voice.

He glanced at the little girl sitting beside him. "Don't worry—I can take care of this." He didn't know whether he was lying or telling the truth.

Another glance showed the mirror empty. At almost the same moment, the howl of the motorcycle's engine sounded right next to him. The noise jerked his gaze around, and he saw the motorcycle right next to the Jeep, the two vehicles matching speed. The rider peered into the jeep's open side.

A dizzying puzzlement swept across Noah, as though the combined roar of the two engines had fallen away, the straight-line chase across the desert taking place on some strange kind of wrap-around movie screen. A tiny bit of the past now seemed more real to him. He recognized the face of the motorcycle's rider, but couldn't understand why it should be here.

"Pull over!" Through the noise of engines and the rushing wind, Buck Francisco's voice shouted like that of a highway patrolman tagging some hot-foot freeway commuter. "Come on—you got to stop!"

"Shove it!" he yelled back. Anger pulsed through Noah. There wasn't time to think, to figure out why Buck was here, what it meant. Maybe it wasn't Buck on the motorcycle, maybe it was a hallucination, some scrap of memory that the adrenaline of the chase had sucked up out of his brain—right now, there was no way he could be sure. The only thought that remained in his head was to keep driving, the accelerator pressed flat. He was going to get his precious cargo to the next town up the road, or die trying.

The figure on the motorcycle, whether it was Buck Francisco or someone else, took a hand from the bars and reached into the Jeep, grabbing for the curve of the steering wheel; the bike's footpegs were almost close enough to scrape paint from the jeep's metal. Noah took one hand off the wheel and used it to shove away the rider, giving him a straight shot into his leather-jacketed shoulder, hard enough to send the motorcycle wobbling and dropping several yards behind before the figure on its back managed to wrestle it into line.

"Noah—listen to me!" The motorcycle had caught up again; the rider's face was only a few feet away from Noah's. "I came here to help you!"

"Yeah, right! Like I'm gonna believe that!" He gave a quick twist to the steering wheel, aiming the left fender toward the bike. The rider didn't swerve away, but instead leaned into the Jeep, hooking one arm around the steering wheel and ignoring the blows that Noah pummelled into the side of his face and neck. Noah couldn't dislodge him; the rider held on, pulling himself farther into the Jeep, lifting himself from the motorcycle's seat and letting the machine fall away from beneath him. The bike toppled and struck the asphalt in a pinwheeling flurry of sparks.

He could hear Aalice beside him, screaming something, perhaps just his name. There was no time or space for anything except his own panting breath and that of the rider clambering between him and the Jeep's windshield. Noah's forearm had shoved the sunglasses away from the other's face—it was Buck, there could be no doubt of it now. Buck had managed to get one foot against the door's open rim, boosting himself inside and getting another grip on the steering wheel. Desperate, without thinking, Noah balled one hand into a fist and launched a hard jab into the pit of the other's abdomen. A grimace of pain clenched Buck's face, breath expelled through his clenched teeth, but he didn't let go of the steering wheel. The collapse of his weight pulled the wheel to one side, sending the Jeep lurching crazily onto one side's screeching tires.

Noah grabbed the wheel with both hands, trying to pull it around against Buck's grip upon it. Too much; he could feel the seat belt cutting into his own stomach as the Jeep went out of control, the tires breaking traction and lifting from the road's surface.

As the Jeep toppled toppled over, he saw Aalice's terrified face, the chrome ends of her unfastened seat belt rising up like bright snake's heads. Noah let go of the wheel and grabbed the little girl, holding her close against his chest as the Jeep's inverted roll brought it crashing against the dust and gravel beyond the road's edge.

"You idiot! You could've goddamn killed us!"

He could hear the voice shouting at him, but didn't know from where it came. Buck crawled out from beneath the overturned Jeep, shaking his head to clear his vision.

The roll bar had taken most of the impact, preventing major injury to everyone who had been inside. Or at least he hoped so—his spine and ribs ached, but nothing felt as if it were broken. He slowly managed to get to his feet.

Noah stood nearby, one arm wrapped protectively around the shoulders of the little girl next to him. She watched Buck stand up, her eyes round with a mixture of apprehension and curiosity.

"Way to go, Buck—" The anger in Noah's voice had lowered to disgust. "Where'd you learn your circus tricks?"

"Yeah, well, it's great to see you, too." Buck wiped gritty dust from his brow. "Who's this?" He pointed a thumb toward the little girl.

"My name's Aalice." Her voice piped up in the desert's silence. "With two A's." She smiled, taking a step forward and laying a fingertip against the side of her head. "Look, I'm like you. See?"

"What—" Buck saw now the Tenctonese-like head spots beneath the girl's pale hair. The ears as well; those were also like a Newcomer's.

"Jeez, get with it." Noah's words were like some memory flash from when he and Buck had been in high school together. "The kid's a hybrid, half human species and half Tenctonese. Like the baby—" He stopped, his expression changing to one of sudden alarm. "The baby!" Noah sprinted past Buck and toward the Jeep.

"It's in there?" Buck turned and ran up beside him. At the overturned Jeep, Noah had already reached inside, quickly tugging at the straps securing a swaddled bundle behind the empty driver's seat. A moment later, he stepped back as Noah cradled the squirming infant in his arms.

"Looks okay . . ." Bending his face close toward the baby, Noah cautiously stroked its brow. A tiny, piping wail came from the toothless mouth.

"How would you know?" Buck reached out and tugged aside the corner of the blanket, so he could see the baby. "What're you, a doctor or something? The only time you were in a hospital was when you came running in with your happy little band of kidnappers." He reached to take the infant out of Noah's arms. "Here, give it to me."

"No—" Noah twisted away, holding the bundle closer to himself. "I don't even know what you're doing here. And you're the jerk who just about got us all scraped across the friggin' highway! If it hadn't been for you, we would've been practically to the next town with this baby. Instead of bouncing it around on its head—"

"Look, I came here to help—all right?" His anger rose along with the volume of the infant's cry. "I'm the one who caught the phone call that you made. That's why I'm here."

"You? I wanted to get hold of your father—he would've been of some use, at least—"

"Let's not get into what's going on with my dad, all right—"

"Oh, for heaven's sake." The little girl Aalice had marched up, pushing her way in between Buck and Noah. "What are you two clowns arguing about? Gimme that." She stood on tiptoe and lifted the baby from Noah's arms. "There, there . . ." She cradled the infant, bringing her face down close. An annoyed glance shot toward Buck and Noah. "It's hungry. It needs to be fed."

"Okay, okay—" Noah held his palms out in a placating gesture. "There's formula and stuff in the Jeep; I'll go get it."

Buck looked down at the girl. "What do you know about taking care of a baby?"

She looked offended as she hoisted the infant higher in her grasp. "I watched the nurse—the one they had back at the camp." She tilted her face away from one of the small hands waving from the bundle. "And I'm a very fast learner."

"I guess so." He figured it must be the Tenctonese in

the little girl's genetics. "Hey, Noah—hurry it up, will ya? I don't want to hang around here all day." Buck laid a hand on Aalice's shoulder. "Maybe we should go over there to the shade." He nodded toward the Jeep. "You want me to carry the baby?"

Aalice shook her head. "I got him."

Over by the Jeep, Noah had straightened up, a can of infant formula in one hand. He didn't turn around as Buck and Aalice approached, but continued shading his eyes with one hand, gazing across the vehicle's underside and toward the road beyond.

"What's wrong?" Apprehension moved along Buck's spine.

"We've got company." Noah took his hand away from his brow and pointed. "They've caught up with us."

Buck leaned his hands against the bottom edge of the Jeep's fender and looked where the outstretched hand indicated. A long dust cloud was settling in the distance, out in the barren countryside. Closer than that, where the strip of road diminished to the horizon, another vehicle could be seen, a dark speck growing larger with each second and heartbeat. "Who's that? Your friends in the HDL?"

"Look—" Noah turned a slit-eyed glare toward him. "I don't need you getting on my case about my being hooked up with these guys. I know it was a mistake, so just back off, all right?"

He made no reply; even if there had been time to argue about the point, Buck could see no reason to. Another memory flash had unreeled inside his head, something he'd viewed on a blurry TV screen in the lobby of a run-down hotel: the image of Noah Ramsey preventing another member of the hospital assault team from blowing away Matt's and Cathy's baby, the baby that the little girl Aalice was holding right now. Plus, Buck knew, he'd put his ass on the line by scooping the baby and Aalice out of the HDL camp and hitting the road with them. So if Noah's brain hadn't been ratchetted down too tight when he'd gotten involved with these Purist bastards, at least he'd tried to make up for it since.

"Fine," said Buck. "We can talk about all this some other time. Right now, what are we going to do about these guys?" He pointed back toward the road.

"Frankly—I'm not in the mood for letting them get any closer." Noah ducked his head and upper torso inside the upside-down Jeep and rummaged through the other articles that had been strapped to the floorboard. He re-emerged holding a high-powered rifle complete with a telescopic sight. "There's nothing I feel like talking about with this bunch." Noah shoved an ammo clip into place, then laid the barrel across the Jeep's underside, bringing his face tight against the scope's eyepiece. "Keep your heads down."

The rifle shot brought a howl from the baby. Crouching down, Buck peered through the Jeep's interior. Either Noah was a natural marksman or the HDL had put him through some kind of field training; the windshield of the approaching vehicle shattered and flew apart, specks of glass flying bright in the desert sun. Buck watched as the vehicle swerved crazily, its tires smoking against the strip of asphalt as the driver slammed on the brakes. It came to rest turned sideways, half off the road and onto the gravel shoulder. He could see the men who'd been inside the vehicle scrambling out and taking cover behind it.

"There," said Noah with grim satisfaction. "That oughta give 'em something to think about for a while." He ducked down beside Buck and Aalice when a the sound of a distant rifle-shot was followed instantly by the ping of the bullet hitting the other side of the Jeep.

Buck leaned his shoulders against the sun-heated metal. "Is there another gun in here?"

"No." Holding the rifle to his chest, Noah gave a shake of his head. "This was the only one I had time to stash."

"How much ammunition you got?"

A sudden volley of shots, from more than one weapon, raked the ground at either end of the Jeep. Holding the baby tight, Aalice pressed herself closer to Buck.

Noah pointed to a couple more clips he had laid out on the ground. "That's it."

"Oh, that's great." Buck shook his head. "We just got the one rifle, this many bullets—and there's how many of those guys? With how many guns?" Another shot and clang of metal made him duck instinctively. "Boy, I don't recall you being any whiz at math when we were in school, but I didn't know you were this bad at it."

"You're such a genius, then you figure out what to do."

"Could you open this for me?" Between them, Aalice held up one of the cans of formula. "I might as well feed the baby, while you two sort it out."

Feeling somewhat surreal, Buck managed to get a bottle assembled for the infant. Aalice winced every time another bullet hit the other side of the Jeep, but the two children stayed quiet otherwise. *The kid must trust us,* thought Buck, watching her tend the baby. He wished he felt as confident of the outcome as she appeared to be.

"Maybe if we can hold 'em off until dark—" Noah fumbled a new clip into the rifle. "Then we might be able to sneak away. We could reach the next town or something."

Keeping his head low, Buck leaned closer to Noah. He didn't want the little girl to hear him. "I don't think we're going to get that chance." He pointed toward another section of the road. "Check it out."

In the distance, a couple of figures had moved away

from the vehicle that Noah's rifle-fire had pinned down. He narrowed his gaze at the scope's eyepiece, trying to follow their movements. "What do you think they're doing?"

"Probably circling around us." Looking over his own shoulder, Buck studied the terrain behind them. A low rise sloped up from the desert floor. "So they can get a clear shot from another angle."

"Wait a minute. They stopped." Noah lowered the rifle. "Now what?"

His hearts thudding in his chest, Buck took the risk of bringing his head above the level of the Jeep. He looked past one of the rear tires; in the distance, the pair of HDL members who had moved away from their vehicle had taken a position in the gully at the road's edge. Eyes straining, he could just discern the actions of the two men.

"They're setting up something," said Buck. "It's got legs like a tripod, but it's not—"

"Damn!" Noah gritted his teeth. "They must've brought out some of the heavier armaments they had stashed back at the camp—"

The words were hardly out of Noah's mouth before a hollow whump sounded from the roadside. A streak of light, trailing brown smoke, shot in a low arc toward them. It hit the ground with a louder explosion a few yards away; flame blossomed in a churning column, stray fragments of fire raining in a wider pattern. The incendiary smell hit Buck's nostrils at the same time a sharp-edged wave of heat pulsed across him and the others.

"They're just getting their range—" Hunched over with the rifle, Noah watched the small group of HDL members below the road's edge, then turned toward Buck, his face set grim. "Get out of here! Take the girl and the baby—start running—go on!"

Without thinking, Buck took the infant from Aalice, holding the small bundle against his chest;

Noah's command had struck him as hard as any of the bullets plowing up the desert around them. "What is it? What's going to happen?"

"Don't you see?" With the rifle barrel, Noah gestured toward the distant road. "They're aiming for the Jeep—the next shot will be right on the gas tank!" With his free hand, he gave Buck a hard push in the shoulder. "Go on—get out of here!"

Buck grabbed Aalice by the arm, yanking her to her feet, just as the sound of another projectile was heard. He glanced up and saw the trail arcing at a higher angle, reaching its highest point, then curving back toward the ground. With the baby cradled against his chest, he turned and started running, dragging the little girl only a step behind himself.

He heard and felt the explosion, but didn't see it. A fiercer heat struck their backs, sending him and Aalice sprawling forward in the loose sand; he rolled against his shoulder, protecting the baby. Pulling himself up on one knee, he looked back and saw the Jeep transformed into a blackened hulk, the frame and tires roiling with flame and dense, inky smoke. A few feet away, Noah lay face down, his HDL uniform ripped and charred. One hand clawed futilely toward the rifle that had been knocked from his grasp.

Instinct made Buck take one step back toward the burning Jeep, to try to help Noah. Then he saw the other men running across the road, their weapons held before them. The first bullets lanced into the sand at Buck's feet.

He still had hold of the baby; with his other hand, he scooped up Aalice beneath her arm. Clutching his burdens tight against himself, he ran. His feet dug into the pebbly gravel of the nearest rise, his hearts pounding in his chest as he tried to reach the crest and the safety of the other side . . .

Another shot seemed louder than all the rest. It was wrapped in silence that expanded outward from a sudden, almost painless impact at the back of one thigh. Keep running, he told himself, but somehow he couldn't; something was wrong, the earth and his own body had dropped beneath him, and he was falling.

The bullet's shock had spun him around, so he landed on his back. He could hear the baby crying, as though from a long way distant—but it was still there in the crook of his arm. He couldn't see Aalice.

Farther away, there were more rifle shots. He tried to push himself up from the ground but couldn't, collapsing back against the loose sand. For a moment he closed his eyes, wincing against the sun's glare.

A shadow fell across him; Buck could feel it. Bigger than a man, big enough to set all the earth around him into eclipse. A shadow that roared, a loud mechanical *thup thup thup.* He'd heard that sound before, but couldn't remember what it was . . .

Then he opened his eyes, and saw it hovering in the sky above.

Behind him, the gunshots were still audible as he ran. Some of the Human Defense League thugs had stood their ground when the helicopter had appeared overhead, turning their guns up toward it. From the side hatch of the chopper, the BNA agents and the members of the LAPD's security team had returned fire, pinning down the HDL members and sending a smaller group of them scattering from their open position on the roadside. As the helicopter had settled several yards away from the burning Jeep, Sikes had vaulted out even before the struts had touched ground. The wind from the blades whipped up a storm of dust around him. Head down, he was just barely aware of George right behind.

The figure on the ground was still conscious. Sikes recognized him as soon as he bent down and pulled him over onto one shoulder; the uniform's charred fabric smeared ash into Sikes's palm. "Where are they?" Sikes's urgent shout cut through the desert air. "Where'd they go?"

Noah Ramsey could barely speak. "There . . ." he breathed, one arm flopping toward the footprints leading away from the Jeep. His eyelids fluttered closed as Sikes lowered him back to the ground.

"There they are!" George stood beside Sikes and pointed toward the spot where the tracks ended, near the crest of a low rise. Lifting his head, Sikes could see another figure splayed out, with a smaller one, a child, kneeling next to it.

Behind them, the gunshots died out as the police and BNA agents rounded up the last of the HDL members. A little girl gazed wide-eyed at the two men who came running toward her.

Blood had soaked into the earth around Buck, from the bullet wound in his leg. With one hand, he had managed to roll himself onto his hip. "Matt . . ." A weak, slightly delirious smile passed across his face as he held up a squalling bundle. "I think . . . this belongs to you . . ."

Sikes snatched up the bundle, bringing it close before his eyes. With one hand, he brushed back the edge of the dust-soiled blanket. The tiny face that he had seen so briefly at the hospital in Los Angeles was puckered and reddened, his eyes squeezed shut as the toothless mouth emitted its gasping wail.

As he held his son, hands pressing the warm bundle against his own chest, he could see the little girl standing a few feet away, her silent, watchful gaze taking in everything that happened. His partner George knelt down beside Buck, stanching the flow of blood with a wadded-up handkerchief.

"You'll be all right." George's voice was controlled and soothing. "We brought a full medical team with us. They'll take care of everything."

"Don't worry . . . about me . . ." Buck laid his head back against the ground. "The baby . . ."

"He's fine." A wild joy surged through Sikes. He turned the bundle slightly in his grasp to show the others. At the bottom of the rise, he could see the white-suited doctors racing up toward them. "All that stuff that Quinn had in his notes—it's not true! The baby's fine!"

The wail suddenly choked off. In Sikes's arms, a sharp convulsive shudder twisted through the bundle. He looked down and saw the tiny eyes had snapped open, the centers of the pupils filled with trembling black space. The small face had drained deathly white, the mouth gulping for breath. He watched in horror as a pinkish bubble, the color of Tenctonese blood, burst at the corner of the baby's lips.

"Give him to me—" The lead doctor had appeared in front of Sikes, with the others behind. He reached to take the bundle from Sikes's arms.

"No!" Sikes backed away from the wall of faces that circled before him. His grip tightened, pressing the baby even closer against himself. He shook his head. "No! you can't have him!"

"Matt . . . please . . ." George stretched his hand toward Sikes's shoulder. "Give them the baby. There's still a chance . . ."

"Nobody's taking him!" The wall forced him back another step. He could hear his own voice shouting out of control, the empty landscape shrinking toward the tiny, trembling thing he held. "Nobody . . . get away!"

His partner grabbed him from behind, pulling his arms back as the doctor snatched the baby from his grasp. The shouting turned wordless and incoherent, his struggling desperate enough to topple both him and George onto the ground.

"Matt . . . don't . . ." George's weight and strength pinned him down. Sikes reached past the figure above him, hands clawing futilely toward the doctors rushing the small, fragile creature toward the helicopter. "You can't take him . . . you can't . . ."

The world that had been so small, a space that he could hold in his arms, opened around him. A world that was once more vast, echoing . . . and empty.

CHAPTER 17

"THERE WASN'T ANYTHING we could do . . ."

She sat with him, with her husband, on the edge of their bed. With the house and its rooms all around them, spaces that had seemed empty when he hadn't been there, even with the voices and sounds of their children still present. The emptiness had been in her hearts, Susan knew. For now, although she realized there were still so many things left to be taken care of, for now all that mattered was that he was with her again.

"Nothing anyone could do." Despite all that he had done, a tone of weary defeat sounded in George's voice. He had stopped halfway through tying his shoelaces, as though that small task was momentarily beyond what remained of his strength.

Susan pressed herself close to him, her arm around his shoulders, head bent toward his, trying to give him some of her strength, of what they shared between them. And listening to him, though she had already heard it all. But listening because she knew that he had to talk it through again.

"Doctor Quinn was right." George slowly nodded, his gaze resting sightless on the bedroom's distant wall. "We knew he was. That was his job, after all—to know all about what happens with matings between humans and Newcomers. And what happens to the children . . . the babies." His shoulders lifted, followed by a deep sigh. "He knew because he had seen it happen before. With the first child, the first hybrid infant. Maybe that one would've been named Aalice, if it had lived more than a few days."

She said nothing, feeling a chill against her own skin, grief for a baby that had died so long ago, less than a year after the Day of Descent, when the Tenctonese people had stepped onto the soil of this world. A baby that had had no chance to live, that had been doomed from the beginning by the conflict inside its own small body.

"That was what Matt and I found in Quinn's research notes . . ." George's voice was little more than a whisper in the bedroom's silence. "That was what made poor Matt even more desperate to find his and Cathy's child . . . before time ran out. Before the doctors could at least try to save it." He squeezed his hand together, the knuckles bloodless. "Quinn knew it all along; that had been the whole point of what he had been trying to do, to find a way around the essential instability of a Tenctonese/human hybrid. He called the condition 'inter-genetic warfare.'" Another slow nod. "It could never be. We should've known it was too much to hope for. With a cross between humans and Tenctonese, the result isn't a true reversion to an original, common stock. The human genetics are dominant for only a little while after the birth of a hybrid. The Tenctonese genetics eventually reassert themselves. That's what happened with Quinn's 'Case AA,' the first Tenctonese/human child. That's what happened to Matt and Cathy's baby. The genetic systems are too different from each other; they can't co-exist in the same body. How did

Quinn put it in his research notes . . ." George closed his eyes. " 'With catastrophic loss of homeostasis and death the inevitable result.' When Matt and I read that . . . we both knew what was going to happen. We just didn't want to believe it."

"George . . ." She tenderly rubbed the back of her husband's neck. "You have to stop torturing yourself about this. You said it yourself, there was nothing you could do."

"I know." He turned his head, gaze meeting hers. "But there was just so much that I didn't see—that no one saw. Even the little girl, the Aalice that was up there in the HDL camp. They should've known that she wasn't real . . . that she wasn't a hybrid at all. Just a human child, that's all. What made her different— that was all Quinn's doing. It was something he thought he had to do, so he would keep on getting the money for his research from the *Sleemata Romot*. They didn't know that the real Aalice, the first child born of a mating between a Tenctonese and a human, had died just a few days after it was born. Quinn had developed his skills at making one thing appear to be another—that was how he was able to fake his own death. But Aalice—the Aalice that he created—she came first. An orphaned human baby—we haven't been able to track down who her real parents might have been—that Quinn surgically altered, the restruc- tured formation of the external ears, to give her the appearance of being a human/Tenctonese hybrid. He even found a way of changing the distribution of the subcutaneous melanin of her scalp and along her neck, so she would have something of the head spots of a Newcomer. So she would be at least a little like us." George nodded. "Quinn was thorough, all right. No one but him knew that the real Case AA had already died; he was completely successful at substi- tuting his Aalice for that one. And of course, she didn't know. When she grew up, she believed what he told her, that she was the first child ever to be born of human and Tenctonese parents."

"Perhaps . . . he meant well." Susan had heard the account before, and was still trying to make sense of it. "He thought he was doing the right thing."

"Everybody means well." Her husband shrugged. "Well, maybe not everybody. There's always people like Darlene Bryant and her bunch that you have to take into account. People try to do the right thing, and then they run into other people with evil in their souls. That's when things get messy."

She laid her head against his shoulder. "That's when people like you have to go to work."

"True." George moved away from her, so he could turn and hold her, gazing for a long moment into her eyes without speaking. Then he let go and bent down to finish tying his shoes. A moment later, he stood up. "I know you understand. There's some things I have to go take care of."

"All right." Susan looked up at him and managed to smile. "I'll be here waiting for you."

"I've been waiting for you." The figure on the empty stage turned, bringing his solemn gaze across the warehouse's echoing space. "I knew you would come here."

George walked past the folding metal chairs that were still strewn about the area. As before, dust-clouded sun leaked through the broken skylights above. But now there were no rapt faces of adoring worshippers, Newcomers and humans alike, directed toward the object of their faith. The messenger who had brought the Light was a solitary man now, unencumbered by that fierce radiance.

"What did you tell them?" He stopped at the edge of the stage. "All of the others—the believers. The Bearers of Light. What did you say to them?"

"What could I say?" Ahpossno was dressed in plain

street clothes now, a faded pair of denim trousers and a corduroy jacket over a white shirt. The prophet's flowing robes had vanished as well, as though the costumes of a travelling production had been packed away with the scenery flats. "I told them the truth. As I had told them the truth before. Or what I thought was the truth." Ahpossno looked down at his empty hands, as if searching for something there, then again toward George. "You must believe me—I did not lie to them . . . to anyone. I believed. The Light, the truth . . . I believed. Because . . . for a little while at least . . . it was true."

The words came haltingly, as though each were a heavy stone that had to be lifted and set into place. George felt a wave of sympathy for the other man. He knew what it was like to try to explain things beyond understanding.

"The truth . . ." Ahpossno looked up toward the warehouse's skylights, to the dirt smeared with pigeon droppings. "I told them all to go home, to pick up their lives where they were before I came amongst them. If those who had been my followers wanted to believe I was a liar, that everything I had told them before was a lie, that was all right. If anger would comfort them, then they should have anger. If they had wanted to bury me beneath the stones of their wrath, I would have accepted that as my due. I would only have wished that at some time to come, their anger might have transmuted itself to forgiveness." He brought his gaze back down. "But . . . and here is a mystery, George . . . there was no anger. No rage at my having misled them. There was . . ." Ahpossno smiled wanly, ruefully. "There was disappointment. We had all wanted to believe it was true. We wanted it so much."

"Here—" George reached a hand up toward him. "Why don't you come down from there? It'll be easier. To talk."

When he had helped the other down from the makeshift stage, Ahpossno laid a hand on his shoulder. "Perhaps it was hardest on you, George. Because you didn't let yourself believe—though I know you wanted to. I could see that in your soul."

They walked through the empty warehouse, toward the great doors swung open at the front. The city's distant traffic noises gradually became audible.

"Do you know . . . everything?" As they walked, George looked over at Ahpossno. "Everything that happened? To Matt and Cathy's baby?"

"Of course." Ahpossno nodded, slowly and sadly. "I knew as soon as it happened. As soon as the baby . . . died. I felt it. Just as if the hearts had been torn out from my chest. That was when I knew that I had not been in possession of the truth . . . not the whole truth. I had only a part of it, a piece of the Light. That was true, but it was not enough. What I had learned—out there—" He pointed toward the spaces beyond the warehouse's skylights. "The power that had been given to me—that was true. I could make it possible for a Tenctonese and a human to have a child together; I walked inside Matt and Cathy's dreams—as I walked in yours—and I made it happen. I made her womb capable of nurturing his seed, of making a new life from what their love for each other gave to it. That was my doing. The Light, my power." He shook his head. "But not enough. I could bring the child into being, but I could not make it live . . . I could not give it life beyond a few days. Just like the first one that died all these years ago. Some things are not possible. There is not power enough, no light sufficient, to bridge such differences. Perhaps humans and Tenctonese were one blood, one species, millenia ago. But in this time we are not so."

They stepped into the daylight outside the warehouse. George looked at the figure beside him. "What are you going to do now?"

Ahpossno tilted his head. "Isn't that up to you?"

He frowned. "Why would it be my decision?"

"You are a man of the law, George—of this world's law. As you always were, even when you came amongst the Bearers of Light. You have duties toward that law. Is there no crime I have committed, for which retribution must be exacted? I would make no effort to resist your taking me into custody. Consider: disturbances of the peace, violation of the civil order . . . or perhaps a more personal crime. I did, after all, grievously invade Matt and Cathy's privacy." Ahpossno gave a small smile. "I also entered this country without proper documentation. No small matter, these days."

"Given the circumstances, I think that can be overlooked." George shook his head. "I'm not going to take you in. There's the law, and then there's . . . other considerations. You did a great service to your own people once; many would have died if it hadn't been for you. And now, what you've tried to accomplish for both the Tenctonese and the human races . . ." He shrugged. "It wasn't done with malicious intent. That's what I see in your soul."

Ahpossno regarded him for a moment. "You realize, George Francisco, that you have taken it upon yourself to be a judge of the law."

"I guess I'll just have to accept that responsibility. At least this time."

"Very well." He clasped George's shoulder with one hand. "Perhaps one day my wisdom will be the equal of yours. Until then . . ." He dropped his hand and turned away.

George called after the figure walking down the street. "Where will you go?"

"That hardly matters." Ahpossno had stopped and glanced back at him. "I will be among my people."

He watched the figure until it had disappeared in the distance, lost in the maze of buildings at the city's edge. A few moments later, he took his keys from his pocket and walked over to the car he had left at the curb.

Waiting was the hardest part. It had always been bad enough just visiting someone in the hospital, but now he was definitely getting bored and ready to split. Buck heard somebody coming down the corridor beyond his room's numbered door, and hoped that it was one of the doctors with the paperwork to spring him out of here.

"Hello, Buck." It wasn't a doctor, but his father, leaning around the edge of the doorway. "Care for a visitor?"

"Sure. Come on in." He pointed to the side of the bed. "There's a chair over here."

"Thanks." His father sat down, glancing over at the white-plastered bandages in which Buck's left leg was immobilized. "Quite a job they did on you."

"Yeah, it's mostly because of the bone chip." He leaned back against the bed's pillows. "If the bullet had been over another quarter-inch, the doctor told me, it would've been a lot worse; I'd be in a cast for a long time." Buck shrugged. "As it is, I'm going to be hobbling around with a cane for a few weeks. That's what they said, at least."

"Well, you're right, it could've been worse." Buck's father nodded toward the doorway. "I was just over at the secure ward, checking up on Noah Ramsey."

"Oh yeah? How's he doing?"

"Not bad. He's had to have some skin grafts, but there's been no complications with those. He'll be fine . . . in a lot of ways. Noah's still going to have to face kidnapping charges, as well as some others, but since he's turning state's evidence against Darlene Bryant and the rest of the HDL, the Bureau will recommend clemency to the court. Plus there's plenty of testimony—your own, for instance—about what he did to get the children away from the Purists. If he serves any time at all, it'll be minimal."

"Sounds fair. The next time you look in on him, give him my regards." From the bed's slightly elevated vantage point, Buck studied his father. For a moment, his gaze had drifted away, an abstracted expression on his face, as though he were going through that whole trip again that Emily had told her brother about. Buck figured he should go easy on his old man; he knew that his father had been through a lot lately. "So . . . what brings you around here? Something on your mind?"

His father looked back around at him. "There might be. Your mother and I were wondering what your plans were."

"Don't have any." Buck shrugged. "Go back to work, soon as this leg's all healed up. I've got a little money saved up. It should last me until then."

"We thought that perhaps . . . you might want to move back home with us, instead of going back to that hotel where you've been living." His father held up a placating hand. "Just until you're completely up on your feet. The food's bound to be better, if nothing else."

"Yeah . . ." Buck smiled. "You know, I might take you up on that one."

"Good." His father nodded. "We'll get your room ready." He fell silent again, without making any move to get up from the chair.

"Is that it?"

His father regarded him for a moment. "About your going back to work . . . I mean, where you were working before. I've been wondering—is that what you really want to do? Moving boxes and crates around?"

"Suits me for now." Buck folded his arms across his chest.

"Seems to me to be kind of a waste. Of your talents, I mean."

"Maybe," said Buck. "But there's not really anything else I'm interested in at the moment."

300

"Oh." His father made a show of mulling that over. "I thought perhaps everything that happened— everything you did—perhaps that indicated some- thing else."

"Like what?"

"Well, when you think about it . . . you did the right thing. Without hesitating. You sort of went to the rescue."

"Didn't seem to do much good. The baby still died."

"You can't blame yourself for that." His father leaned forward in the chair. "Even if Matt and I had found that note earlier, the one you left at the station, and we had gotten up there to help you sooner, it wouldn't have helped that child." He looked down, studying his own hands. "What matters is what you tried to do. That your instincts were to help and you followed through on them. You did what you could. Somebody like that shouldn't be just shifting crates around for a living."

"Wait a minute." Buck peered more closely at his father. "I'm getting the feeling that this is all leading up to something. All right, what is it?"

From the inside pocket of his suit jacket, Buck's father took a thin packet of folded papers. "The police academy here in the city is going to be taking applica- tions again. The physical tests won't be for another three months or so; your leg should be all healed by then . . ."

"What?" He stared incredulously at his father. "You want me to try to get into the LAPD? Is that what this is all about? No way." He gave a quick, harsh laugh. "No flippin' way am I gonna be a cop."

"Buck . . ." Still holding the folded papers, his father spoke softly. "A cop is what I am. And I'm not ashamed of it."

"Yeah, well, that's the difference between you and me. One of the differences."

"I became one," said his father, "for the same reason you went up there to eastern Oregon. So I could help people."

He made no reply. He couldn't think of one.

"Well, your mother and your sisters are waiting for me to come home." His father stood up. "Tell you what. I'll just leave these with you." He dropped the papers on the little table beside the bed. "You'll make your own decisions."

After his father had left, Buck shook his head, still amazed. *My old man must still have a few screws loose,* thought Buck. For his father to consider that there was even a chance of his going for something like that . . .

Minutes passed, without the doctor coming around. From the corner of his eye, Buck glanced over at the papers on the table. Another minute passed before he unfolded his arms from his chest and reached over to pick up the police academy's glossy recruitment brochure. Bored, he flipped through the pages.

Still no doctor.

He went back to the first page and started reading.

When the doctor finally came into the room, he didn't notice. The doctor had to speak his name twice before he looked up.

He brought her home.

Already, he'd gotten rid of all the baby things. He'd boxed them up and taken them over to the Salvation Army thrift store for them to sell to people who did have babies, or who would have them some day. Sikes knew that wasn't in the cards for him and Cathy.

"Everything seems so quiet here." She looked around the apartment as Sikes brought in her suitcase and set it down. Cathy pulled open the blinds over the big living room window and looked out at the alley and the brick wall of the next building over. "You know, you don't realize how noisy hospitals are, until you really have to spend some time in one. There's always people going back and forth, and carts full of stuff, and voices out in the corridor . . ." Her own voice faded, then she glanced over her shoulder and smiled at him. "It's amazing that people get any sleep there at all."

Sikes kissed her on the brow, then held her by both shoulders so he could look at her. "I'm glad you're home."

He busied himself in the kitchen area, making her a cup of liver extract tea, while she put away the things she had packed and taken with her to the hospital. That seemed a long time ago. A lot had happened since then. Sikes leaned against the counter, waiting for the kettle to boil. There had been a time, not too many days ago, when he'd thought he would be bringing Cathy and their new baby back here. All that might as well have happened in another life.

"Thanks." Cathy sat with him on the couch, her feet curled up under herself, and sipped from the cup he had brought her.

From the beer he dangled in one hand, he took another swallow. "Yeah, well, you're welcome." The apartment's silence settled around them again.

He had to nearly finish the beer before he could say anything more. There were things that he and Cathy had to talk about; they might as well start now.

"I guess . . ." He spoke softly, watching his thumb rub the dark green top of the bottle in his hand. "I guess I really wanted to believe it was true. That you and I . . . you know . . . that we were going to have a baby together." He shrugged. "Not just because of us, that it'd be ours and everything. But maybe because of what it would've meant . . . to everybody." He glanced over at her. "That Newcomers and humans would maybe get along with each other better. Because of them really being the same. People like us having kids together—I thought that would prove it

303

was true. But now . . ." He shook his head. "Now we still gotta deal with humans and Newcomers being different from each other."

Cathy held the cup in both hands, gazing down into it. "Is that so bad?"

"No . . . no, it's not." Sikes frowned, trying to find the right words. "Funny thing is . . . I've been thinking, because of all the stuff that's happened . . . and you know, I finally decided it wasn't so bad. About my people and yours being different from each other. It's just one of those things, like I said, that we gotta deal with. Maybe it would've been nice if we'd all wound up blending into one species. Or maybe not. Who knows? But it doesn't look like it's going to happen, so we'll just have to learn to get along with each other the way we are."

"I don't care about that . . ." Cathy set the cup down on the coffee table. She took his arm in both hands and leaned her head against his shoulder. "As long as you and I get along all right."

He turned her face up toward his and kissed her—for a long time—then held her close against himself. "There's something else I wanted to talk to you about. Something important."

"What's that?" She didn't raise her head from where it rested against his chest.

"Well . . . even though you and I aren't going to be having a kid together, that doesn't mean . . ." He took the last sip of the beer, then set the bottle down on the floor beside the couch. "The thing is, there already is a kid who's kind of a cross between a human and a Newcomer. Not really, but in a way she is . . ."

"You mean that little girl?" Cathy lifted her head. "Aalice?"

Sikes nodded. He knew that Cathy had met the girl, had even talked with her for a bit, at the hospital when the BNA agents had brought her in to be checked, to make sure she hadn't been hurt during all the action out in the desert.

"I was talking to the social worker who's been assigned her case." He tried to keep his voice casual, low-key. "Poor kid doesn't have any family. So it's going to be pretty much foster homes for her. Unless somebody . . . you know . . ." His throat tightened a notch. "Puts in to adopt her . . ."

Cathy moved away from him, sitting upright on the couch. She turned and gazed straight into his eyes, until he knew, without any more words having to be said.

"Okay . . ." Sikes rubbed his sweating palms against his trousers. "I'll go down and make an appointment with the social worker tomorrow. For both of us . . ."

This time, it was her turn to kiss him on the brow. He closed his eyes, still trying to catch his breath.

He saw him coming down the station's hallway. And Albert smiled and waved. "Captain Grazer— hi!"

The captain's stride slowed, a wary expression forming on his face. "What're you doing here, Albert?" He had stopped right next to him; he reached out and fingered the lapel of Albert's suit. "I thought Precognosis had let you go . . ."

"Oh, yeah. I'm not with them anymore." He still felt a little embarrassed talking about it, about how badly he had screwed things up for those people. Besides, he didn't have to explain that to Grazer. The captain knew all about what had happened. "I've got my own company now."

"What?" Grazer stared at him in amazement. "You? You're kidding." He glanced around at the detectives and uniformed officers milling through the police station, then pushed open the door of his office. "Maybe you'd better come in here and tell me about it."

Albert sat in the chair in front of Grazer's desk,

swivelling a little from side to side and feeling good. Things really had worked out for the best, after all.

"So what is it you're doing these days?" Grazer sat forward, leaning across his desk with his fingertips pressed together. "You still doing the market prediction stuff?"

"Naw . . ." He shook his head. The necktie he wore snugged his collar close against his throat. His wife May had him put on a tie every morning, except on the weekends, telling him that he was a businessman now and he had to look the part. "I didn't want to do that any more. Plus . . . you know . . . it wasn't real likely anybody would listen to me anymore. Not after what happened with your tapes and books and stuff—"

"Please." Grazer winced. "Don't remind me."

"So at first I thought maybe I could just come back here, to my old job, and sweep the floors and clean up like I used to. But I found out that while I was gone, the police department had switched over to contracting their building maintenance to outside janitorial services. So I didn't know what I was going to do." A smile came across Albert's face. "Then May said, why couldn't I do that? She meant, why couldn't I have a janitorial service company? 'Cause after all, it's what I know best, isn't it? So we took our savings and we sold that big house we had when I was working for Precognosis and we bought just a little one—it's real nice, though—and we took all the money and bought what we needed, a couple of vans and all the cleaning equipment. And I hired some people! Can you believe it?" He shook his head, still amazed at it himself. "So May keeps the books and does all the paperwork, and I do the supervising and put the bids together for the jobs we go after. And you know what? I just won this one! I won the janitorial contract for this station—isn't that funny?"

"You're right . . ." Grazer sat back in his chair, looking slightly stunned. "It's hilarious."

"I'm glad you feel that way," said Albert. "It means I'll still be coming in and out—you know, taking care of things—and I'll be able to see you and all the rest of my friends here at the station. And sometimes one of my employees might call in sick and I won't be able to get a replacement for him right away, so I'll just have to roll up my sleeves and pitch in with a mop and bucket myself—it'll be just like old times!"

"Sure will." Grazer nodded slowly, as though deep in thought. "Listen, Albert, there's something I gotta tell you. All that business with those books and tapes of mine—I really owe you an apology for dragging you into that mess. Plus—and this is the important part—I think I finally learned my lesson from that. I was spending more time on that GIT stuff than I was running this station. I was really letting things slide here for a while. Though funny enough, it kinda worked out the right way, at least regarding George Francisco. His resignation from the department was sitting on my desk the whole time, and I never even looked at it, let alone did anything about it. So as far as the LAPD was concerned, he never really quit at all—we just knocked off some of his accumulated vacation days, and that was it." Grazer looked straight across the desk and into Albert's eyes. "Anyway, what I'm trying to tell you is that I've restructured my priorities, so to speak; I'm just going to take care of police business from now on. So it means a lot to me that you're going to be on the ball here, and that this is going to be the cleanest goddamn station in the department. You got me?"

They shook hands, standing beside the desk. "My crew will be out here first thing tomorrow." Albert tilted his head toward the office door. "Those hallway floor are going to take a lot of work. They're filthy."

"Yeah, well, that's your business. Do what you have to." Grazer clapped him on the shoulder. "Too bad you had to give up that car those guys at Precognosis bought you. That was one snazzy piece."

"Oh, I didn't get rid of the car . . ."

"You didn't?"

Albert shook his head. "May and I decided to keep it. 'Cause it was all paid for and everything. Plus she thought I needed to—what'd she say?—I needed to project a prosperous image. For my business." He pointed to the window. "It's parked right out there."

He watched as the captain drew back the shades and looked outside. The jewel-like red gleam of the car, brilliant under the L.A. sun, seemed to radiate onto Grazer's face.

"What a pretty machine." Grazer's voice was a murmur of admiration and deep, heart-felt longing. "What a *pretty* machine . . ."

Two Blood-Curdling Novels Based On
The Bestselling Computer Game

DOOM™

HELL ON EARTH
52562-X/$4.99

KNEE-DEEP IN THE
DEAD
52555-7/$4.99

By Dafydd ab Hugh and Brad Linaweaver
Based on *Doom* from id Software

© 1995 Id Software

Available from Pocket Star Books

POCKET
STAR
BOOKS